THE
BETRAYED

ALSO BY CASEY KELLEHER

THE
BETRAYED

CASEY KELLEHER

Published by Bookouture
An imprint of StoryFire Ltd.
23 Sussex Road, Ickenham, UB10 8PN
United Kingdom
www.bookouture.com

ISBN: 978-1-78681-123-3
eBook ISBN: 978-1-78681-140-0

This book is a work of fiction. Names, characters, businesses,
organizations, places and events other than those clearly in the
public domain, are either the product of the author's imagination
or are used fictitiously. Any resemblance to actual persons, living or
dead, events or locales is entirely coincidental.

For Mum and Dad
For Everything

x x

PART ONE: 1982

CHAPTER ONE

'Fuck me!' Opening his eyes, Michael Byrne gasped for air, exhausted, as the young girl straddling him peeled herself away from his perspiring body, satisfied that she'd successfully tended to his needs.

Standing next to the bed, completely stark bollock naked – clearly confident with her young firm figure – she lit a fag and smiled down at him with glee.

'Well, I wasn't expecting that!' She'd just given grandad the fuck of his life and had been pleasantly surprised at his stamina. The man was at least fifty, but there was clearly life in the old goat yet, as the bugger had really made her work for her money tonight. 'You're not bad for an old boy!'

Grinning at the compliment, Michael Byrne could see that the girl meant it too. He was glad he still had it in him, if he was honest. Being married to Joanie, he was amazed his dick hadn't completely wilted away and lost all its purpose for the amount of use his frigid wife ever got out of it.

Michael wrinkled his nose in distaste as the stale smell of cigarette smoke began to fill the room. Joanie would go ballistic if she found out someone was smoking in her precious house. Panicking for a second, he almost asked the girl to put it out.

What was he thinking? He chuckled to himself as he watched the girl bend over, leaning down to flick the ash from her fag into one of Joanie's tacky-looking trinket boxes. Cigarette smoke? Fuck me. That would be the least of his worries if Joanie walked in here now. He could just see his stuck-up wife's horrified expression at the thought of her husband and this young tart writhing around in their marital bed.

That only made him smile all the more.

By rights, he should have a guilty conscience. He'd wronged Joanie over the years – a lot – but bringing a tom back here to their home, to their bed that they both slept in, was an all-time low. He didn't feel so much as a pang of remorse for his actions though; in fact, if anything, he felt bloody fantastic. Every thrust, every shudder with Lorna had only been enhanced and heightened by the fact that if his wife Joanie had known what he was up to, she would have done her nut. Just the thought of pissing his wife off had been all he needed to get his todger up and get himself going. In fact, he'd thought about Joanie the entire time.

The stuck-up cow. Parading around in her silk dressing gown, with a face full of fancy creams and potions that clearly didn't bloody work. Joanie was far too precious about herself to ever think about loosening up and having a bit of fun.

Still, she had her uses. Just the thought of her had enabled him to put on the best performance of his life tonight, and he felt amazing for it.

'What are you looking so smug about?' Lorna asked, glad to see such a satisfied customer. She was hoping that she'd get a tip for her services.

'That, my girl, was something else altogether. I could do it all over again.' Grabbing at her waist as he pulled her back on to the bed, Michael tried his luck for an encore performance.

'Bloody hell, Casanova! Slow down,' Lorna said, resisting his pull and wagging her finger at him playfully. 'I need a wee. You be a good boy while I'm gone, okay, then maybe I'll think about it.'

Michael enjoyed the spectacular view of Lorna's tiny pert buttocks as she strutted out of the bedroom in all her naked glory. Listening out as she took a piss in the bathroom, he heard her turn on the shower. At least she was hygienic. It made a change from the usual prostitutes that he picked up. Filthy most of them. Physically and morally. Though that was often what attracted him to them in the first place. He liked women who didn't have any objections with his explicit demands in bed. He could be as rough and as dirty as he liked and the girls not only let him, but they enjoyed it too. Or at least they acted as if they did.

Lorna being one of them. The girl certainly wasn't fussy, but then again, neither was he. He couldn't afford to be anymore. The older he was getting, combined with his lack of funds, meant that these days he took whatever was on offer, and Lorna tonight had been the pick of the bunch.

Still, she was bloody good at her job.

Hearing a loud crash in the bathroom, some toiletries crashing to the floor, Michael imagined the girl rummaging through the bathroom cabinet, helping herself to some of Joanie's expensive perfumes.

Fill your fucking boots, love! he thought jovially.

When his wife finally bothered to grace him with her company again, Michael would just make out that she must have taken her belongings with her, either that or he'd imply that she must be getting on a bit. Losing her memory.

She hated it, did Joanie: being reminded that she was getting on now too. That would teach her for just upping and abandoning him yet again to go and pander to their precious son. Cleaning his flat and cooking his meals as if the lad was some kind of an imbecile and couldn't do it all himself. The woman did his nut in running around for the man, just because he was 'busy working'.

Working. If that's what you called pimping out girls and being a general thug.

The next almighty crash from the bathroom made Michael jump: the bang too loud to be Lorna just rooting around, being nosey. 'You all right in there, Lorna?' he shouted, wondering if he should perhaps muster up the energy to get out of bed and check on her.

Fuck it!

Throwing the blankets back from his naked body, about to go and investigate, he heard Lorna coming back along the corridor towards the bedroom.

Relaxing back down onto the bed, he wondered if he could get another erection. Fully exposed now, he began rubbing his cock vigorously, so that Lorna would be under no illusions about what he wanted from her when she returned.

Only when the bedroom door burst open, it wasn't the lovely Lorna that caught sight of his flaccid penis.

'Oh put it away, for fuck's sake!' Jimmy Byrne spat, his huge frame almost blocking the entire doorway as he looked down at Michael with an expression of pure disgust.

Mortified at being caught red-handed, Michael pulled the cover over him, as he realised Jimmy wasn't alone. His sidekick, Alex Costa, stood behind him in the hallway. He seized Lorna roughly by her arm, before Jimmy caught hold of the naked girl and launched her back into the room, throwing her down into a heap on the bed.

Realising the severity of the situation, Lorna spoke up then.

'I wasn't stealing anything, Jimmy. Honest. I was just looking,' Lorna cried, unaware of what the fuck was going on here. The last thing she'd expected tonight was her boss to burst in on her while she'd been helping herself to some of the expensive-looking perfumes in the bathroom of some punter's house.

Only now it was slowly dawning on her that this wasn't just some punter's house at all.

Jimmy knew Michael.

The old man was her only hope to smooth things over for her.

'Tell him, Michael, I wasn't stealing anything, was I? I was just looking…' Lorna pleaded, looking at Michael for some reassurance.

'Get dressed,' Michael muttered. Sitting upright in the bed, he pushed the naked girl away from him.

Pulling the covers up around him as if they were some form of a shield, concealing his nakedness, as a sickly sensation of dread twisted around inside his stomach, he braced himself for what he knew was coming.

Lorna nodded, confused as she registered the fear that was now spread across the older man's face.

Jimmy wasn't here for her, she realised. He was here for him. The old man. And judging by the tension in the room, Michael was in a world of shit.

Watching as Lorna pulled on her skimpy, cheap lace knickers, Jimmy shook his head impatiently.

'Get your fucking things, and leave, before I launch your scrawny, dirty arse out the fucking window!' he bellowed.

Lorna was lucky she didn't get a clump too after he'd just found her thumbing her way through the things in the bathroom.

Petrified, running around the bedroom gathering up the clothes from where they'd been strewn all across the bedroom floor, Lorna didn't need to be told twice.

Jimmy stood in silence and waited.

Looking at her now, her body on show, he couldn't help turning his nose up in distaste as he eyed the telltale track marks that trailed their way up the insides of her forearms, dotted with scabs and small purple bruises. The insides of her pasty white thighs bruised too.

'I'll be dealing with you later,' he warned, and he meant it too. Lorna was a skag head, and Jimmy couldn't abide that in the girls that worked for him. It was one of his rules. They stayed clean.

Lorna was out now. The girl wouldn't work again anywhere this side of the river, he'd make sure of that.

But first of all he needed to deal with this useless excuse of a man.

About to pull her tights on, to cover some of her modesty, Jimmy roared at the girl.

'Get the fuck out! NOW!'

Naked, she ran. Legging it past Jimmy Byrne as fast as her feet would carry her. Whatever Michael Byrne was in the shit for wasn't her problem and she certainly wasn't sticking around to find out the details. She didn't even care that she hadn't got her money, well aware that she was lucky to be leaving unscathed at all.

'I'll see her out,' Alex Costa said, before following the bird down the stairs, knowing that Jimmy would want to ensure that the light-fingered little mare didn't try and rob anything else on her way out. Not that she'd have the balls to do that now that Jimmy was here.

The two men were alone. The room completely silent as Jimmy stared down at Michael, a deranged look in his eye.

'I was right to have one of my men keep an eye on you. I knew it would only be a matter of time before you were up to your old tricks again. Only, I have to say, I never factored on even you being stupid enough to bring some swanky little whore back here.' Jimmy was seething, trying to contain the anger that was threatening to explode out of him.

That's when the fear really crept in for Michael. He was alone with his psychotic monster of a son.

'To my mother's fucking bed!'

'It's not what it looks like, son,' Michael said, wincing as the barefaced lie shot out of his mouth – feeding his son's temper.

Jimmy's angry expression turned thunderous. 'Bollocks! This is exactly what it looks like. What did you do? Lower your standards to match your morals?' He glared at Michael. 'And to add insult to injury, you brought one of my girls back here? What the fuck do you think you're playing at?'

Jimmy could feel the vein throbbing in the side of his head, the tightness of his jaw as he ground his teeth in pure annoyance. If his mother had come back here, for any reason, and caught that girl, it would have broken her heart. Let alone if she found out that he was making money from his own father getting his nuts in with one of his girls.

His mother didn't suffer fools gladly, but she'd put up with his father's philandering for way too long. The sight of Lorna would have tipped her over the edge. His mother would have had to burn the bed, and fumigate all the carpets to get rid of any contamination from the little skank. This really was the ultimate fucking insult, and one which Jimmy was intent on making his father pay for dearly.

'I'm sorry, Jimmy. I know you won't understand, son,' Michael said, his voice quivering as he spoke, as he tried to justify his actions. 'But me and your mother, well, we don't have sex anymore. We haven't done for years. She doesn't like it, son. Never has.' Michael was almost crying, well aware of how pathetic he sounded as he desperately tried to talk himself out of this awkward situation.

'She's so caught up pandering, I mean, looking out for you, I just get neglected, son. I know it's hard for you to realise that.'

Joanie wouldn't give two shits, not really; the woman was too busy catering to Jimmy's every need to care what her husband was up to. What did she expect him to do? Live like a bleeding monk?

'That girl meant nothing to me, Jimmy. She's a means to an end, that's all. Nothing.'

'She worked for me!' Jimmy shook his head. 'Talk about shitting on your own doorstep.' One of his girls being brought back here and used to humiliate his own mother certainly didn't mean just 'nothing'.

'You're a cunt, Dad! You always have been and you always will be,' Jimmy sneered, staring down at the man as if he was seeing him for the very first time. Old and pathetic. He'd spent a lifetime despising the way he treated his mother while he was growing up. For not being the father that Jimmy had wanted him to be.

All Michael had ever cared about was himself. Every month on payday it had been the same. The man would go missing for days on the trot, spending all his hard-earned cash on booze and loose women. Leaving Jimmy and his mother at home to fend for themselves.

Nothing ever changed. He was still humiliating Joanie, shaming the family name. If anything, the man was only getting worse.

'I'm sorry, son,' Michael said, knowing that his words meant nothing. He'd gone too far this time. 'I had too much to drink, son. I wasn't thinking. I'm sorry.'

Jimmy shook his head slowly.

'I don't know what else you want me to say. What else can I do?'

'What I want you to do is to have a bit of respect for my mother. Your wife,' Jimmy said, his voice surprisingly steady considering that he felt like he was about to implode. 'What I want is for you not to bring toms back here to roll about in the bed that my mother sleeps in.'

'I would have gone somewhere else, a hotel or something, only I'm skint.' Michael gulped down the bile in the back of his throat. He wanted to say that he couldn't afford it. Not now that Jimmy and Joanie were keeping his finances down to a minimum. Only he wasn't a complete imbecile; he knew that right now wasn't the time or the place to start arguing with Jimmy about money. The best thing for him to do was keep his mouth shut and not dig the hole he'd got himself into any deeper.

So he shut up. But his silence wasn't going to help him now either, it appeared.

'Well, *Dad*. This time you've ran shit out of luck,' Jimmy said, as he pulled out the metal baseball bat that he'd brought with him for this very occasion.

There would be no more chances.

'Please, son, don't do this, yeah? Think of your mother.' Michael squirmed as he scampered rapidly to the back of the bed, holding his arms out in front of him as if to shield the blows that were about to rain down upon him.

His eyes flickered to the doorway behind Jimmy, then to the bedroom window as he searched for an escape route.

Jimmy could read the man's mind quicker than Michael could think. His dad wasn't going anywhere. 'That's just the problem, *Dad*. I am thinking of my mother. It's a fucking pity that you didn't, though.'

The last thing Michael Byrne saw was the look of hate pouring from his son's eyes as Jimmy brought the baseball bat down upon his head. The last sound a sickening crack of steel connecting with his skull, a deafening ringing sound in his ears.

Then nothing, only darkness, which, for Michael Byrne's sake, was probably a good thing. He couldn't contend with the wrath of his son, Jimmy.

Not many men could.

CHAPTER TWO

'Is that you, Michael?'

Drying her hands on a tea towel as she heard the front door close, Joanie Byrne rushed over towards the kitchen doorway, suddenly full of hope that her hapless excuse of a husband had finally returned home after almost a week on the missing list.

Her head was pounding because of the man. She'd been worried sick about him and overthinking everything. It was typical really. The man didn't even have to be in a fifty mile radius and yet he could still cause her no end of grief. Knowing Michael, he'd been holed up somewhere with some brash little tart, hungover from his alcohol infused bender. Joanie knew the score by now. She'd been married to the man for long enough. Thirty years. Michael would never change. She'd accepted that a long time ago, and for the sake of her Jimmy she'd chosen to turn a blind eye to their sham of a marriage and just put up with it.

'It's me, Mum,' Jimmy called out as he walked towards his mother, sensing the disappointment on her face that he wasn't his father.

'Oh Jimmy, love, come through to the kitchen, son. I'll do you a bit of dinner if you've got time to stick around for a bit?'

Seeing the look of longing on his mother's face, Jimmy couldn't refuse her. Even though he was already going out for dinner later that night, he could sense that his mother was yearning for company.

'Go on then, Mum. But I can't stay for long,' Jimmy said as he strode towards her, his arm laden with a bouquet of flowers, a huge shopping bag in the other.

'You'd better not have been wasting your money again on me, Jimmy, son. You do a-bloody-nough around here as it is, my boy,' Joanie said sternly; though truth be told, she loved her Jimmy making a fuss of her. For her it wasn't about the money: the real prize was the fact that her son still made time for her. In fact, he doted on her. He was a diamond; especially given what he could have amounted to, with Michael Byrne as his father.

If it wasn't for her Jimmy, she wouldn't even have a roof over her head. Her son had paid for the place for her outright. Buying it solely in her name too, much to his father's dismay.

Joanie was a homeowner. That had set the cat among the pigeons in the neighbourhood with all the curtain twitchers around here. The neighbours had been gossiping about them for months. Wondering where all the money had suddenly come from. The Byrne family were on the up and Joanie wanted to make sure that everyone knew about it.

Jimmy was doing well for himself.

He was a property developer now. An entrepreneur.

She'd heard the rumours about the other stuff: the local gossip about the illegal activities her son was supposed to be involved in; though, of course, Joanie wouldn't even entertain the idea of it. People around here were just jealous. Running their mouths off, trying to put her Jimmy down.

The neighbours could think what they wanted. Joanie knew the truth. Her son was a businessman and he was doing well for himself. She was so proud of how he'd turned out, so handsome and clever, that she could burst.

'I told you before, Mum, if I can't spoil my old dear, who can I spoil, huh?' Jimmy grinned, leaning down to plant a kiss on his mother's cheek as he greeted her.

Joanie thanked the Lord, as she did many times a day, that her one and only child hadn't been cut from the same tainted cloth as his low life father. Jimmy had inherited her good Irish genes. A strapping lad just like her father and brothers had been. He looked nothing like Michael, thank God.

Seeing the wary look on his mother's face as she thought about her husband for the umpteenth time that day, Jimmy guessed what was on her mind.

'Don't tell me you still haven't heard from him?' he said, as Joanie shook her head.

She'd thought she was doing a good job of playing down her fears, of acting normal, but her worry must have been written all over her face. Besides, nothing ever got past her Jimmy.

The creased forehead, the look of concern in his eyes – he could read her like an open book.

'I know he'll show up eventually. He always does in the end.' She shrugged, trying to hide her unease.

'You know what he's like. He's probably just off on another bender of his. Pissed out of his face again in some squalor of a pub somewhere, doing his usual of annoying the arse out of anyone that shares the same airspace as him,' Jimmy added, his tone curt.

Joanie nodded, although this time she didn't look convinced. 'It's been nearly a week now, son.'

Jimmy sighed. He'd thought his mother would have been glad of the respite, but he could see that she was worried out of her mind. It angered him the way that his father could spend a lifetime treating his mother like she was nothing, and yet all his mother did was worry about the man.

'Aren't you glad of the peace and quiet with him gone?' Jimmy said. He watched her gaze flicker towards the doorway as if she was willing his father to walk through it at any minute.

Joanie looked sad. 'Your father is the bane of my existence, Jimmy, but the old bugger is still my husband and, as much as I loathe him at times, he's all I have. He's company for me. Even if his offering of intelligent conversation only seems to stretch to talking about the football results and the price of a pint,' she said, as if she was only just realising this herself. 'He's a bastard, Jimmy, I know that but when I took my vows I meant what I said. Until death do us part.' Joanie was unable to stop the tears that glistened in her eyes.

Jimmy shook his head, bewildered. All his mother ever did was moan about the old man, and since he'd been on the missing list, all she did was mope about, as if she'd lost an arm. Women. He'd never understand them.

'Look, Mum, leave it with me, okay? I'll put the word out. The daft bugger will turn up soon, you'll see!' Jimmy said with conviction; glad when he saw his mother visibly relax at his words.

Bored with talking about his prick of a father, Jimmy changed the subject. 'Something smells bloody delicious, what have you made?'

'Chicken curry.' Joanie beamed. 'I've done it in the new microwave oven you bought me, Jimmy. I tell you what, son, that thing has changed my life. It cooks my dinner for me in just seven minutes. You just shove it in, press a few buttons and hey presto! Sandra from over the road almost went green with envy when I showed her. I'm the only one in the street that has one.'

Jimmy laughed, as Joanie placed the plastic tray of food inside the microwave oven.

'I don't need a demo, Mum. I've got one at my own place! It's dead handy, I'll give you that.' Jimmy was pleased that his mother was enjoying his new-found wealth. He wanted her to have the best of everything. 'Here, before you finish whipping up a three course meal in a matter of minutes, why don't you come and have a look at what I got for you,' he said, showing her the huge bag he was holding.

The start of a smile spread across his mother's face, despite her protests.

'Ahh. You shouldn't have, Jimmy,' Joanie said, with tears in her eyes. 'You have to stop, Jimmy, you spoil me, boy.'

'Just have a look, will ya!' Jimmy grinned, knowing full well that once his mother clocked eyes on the new coat he'd bought her, she'd soon think twice about telling him to stop buying her things.

'Oh Jimmy! You didn't? This cost a bleeding arm and leg!' Pulling out the fancy fur coat that she'd been eyeing up in the window of one of the fancy new boutiques just off Shaftesbury Avenue, Joanie knew that it was an expensive gift. 'And flowers too? You're a thoughtful boy, son. Thank you.'

'You deserve it, Mum! I keep telling you. You did enough for me over the years. It's payback. It's my turn to spoil you now,' Jimmy said raising a brow. 'Besides, I'm celebrating, Mum. Me and Alex signed a big contract today. We've just invested in a huge development off Dean Street. It's a load of run-down flats and shops at the moment, but by the time we've finished, they will be the most sought after flats in London,' he said, still buzzing from the deal that he and his business partner, Alex Costa, had set up together.

He and Alex were proving to be a good team. Jimmy had the kudos and the money to make the investments, and Alex Costa had the brains. The bloke was a clever fucker, and astute with it. They were set to make a killing if they carried on like this. His mother had no idea of the wealth that would soon be coming their way. If she thought that he was doing well at the moment, she hadn't seen anything yet.

'I'm doing good, Mum. Better than good! Besides, you better get used to that and a whole lot more. Now come on, get it on ya and give us a twirl!' Jimmy laughed pulling the expensive coat around his mother's shoulders, knowing full well that she couldn't wait to put it on.

'You're like royalty, Mum!'

'I feel it, son!' Joanie laughed. 'You're a good boy, Jimmy. You know that, don't you?' she said removing the coat and hanging it over the back of the chair. Then hearing the microwave oven ping, she clapped her hands together. 'Take a seat, I'll grab your dinner.'

In her element now, as she dished up a huge portion of food for Jimmy and a small plate for herself, Joanie made her way back over to the kitchen table. Placing the plates down on the mats, she took a seat opposite her son and watched as he took no time in tucking in.

'See! It's good, isn't it?'

Jimmy nodded.

'It's handsome, Mum! Really nice.'

As Jimmy devoured his dinner, Joanie figured there was no time like the present to broach what was on her mind.

'So where are you off to tonight, then? You're not still seeing that young one, are you? What was her name again? Dominatrix or whatever it was?' Joanie asked unable to keep the disapproval from her tone. Jimmy seemed to have a penchant for picking the wrong type of girl, but this last one was something else altogether. He had popped in with her the other night on his way out on a date, and Joanie hadn't thought much of the girl. A proper stuck-up little madam, so she was. Waltzing about Joanie's home as if she owned the place, when she'd only been through the door for less than five minutes.

'It was Dominica, Mum!' Jimmy said, choking back his mouthful of curry, snorting with laughter at his mother's version of the name.

'Dominica? Sounds made up if you ask me,' Joanie said tartly, recalling the girl's appearance in her head. All of five foot nothing, a tiny little frame with the most enormous breasts Joanie had ever seen. She could see what her instant appeal had been.

'As it happens, no I ain't still seeing her. It didn't work out,' Jimmy said, with a nonchalant shrug. To him, women were easy come, easy go. He was never short of offers. As far as he was concerned Dominica was nothing more than a bit of fun. She was a burlesque dancer in one of the little cabaret clubs down on Wardour Street. The girl was as saucy as she was mischievous and Jimmy had enjoyed her company for a while. A few dates here and there wasn't any hardship, especially seeing as she was a real head turner. Everywhere Jimmy and Dominica had gone, he'd seen all eyes on his girl. The men drinking in her doll-like appearance.

Her looks were about the only thing she had going for her though. The girl didn't seem to have much going on between her ears, and Jimmy'd had Dominica's card marked from the get-go. Used to spotting real faces in her line of work, she was a gold-digger. She was only after Jimmy for his money, as were most of the girls he dated. After only a handful of dates, the daft cow had managed to convince herself that Jimmy was 'the one'.

But all she'd ever been to him was a bit of arm candy. Someone to show off at all the important dinners and business events he attended. So Dominica followed the same fate as the rest of them.

'She weren't really my type,' Jimmy concluded.

'And what exactly is your type, son?' Joanie said, her words loaded as Jimmy rolled his eyes, knowing exactly where the conversation was leading.

Catching her son's look of irritation Joanie shook her head.

Jimmy was too strong-minded for his own good. Joanie had learned a long time ago that her son only ever went by his own decisions. Still, as his mother she had to try and help him make the right choices sometimes, even if Jimmy didn't thank her for poking her nose in.

'All I want is for you to settle down, son. With a nice girl. Have a family. You're never going to do that all the time that you are surrounding yourself with nothing but cheap-looking tarts that are only out for your money,' she said, with honesty. 'It's all well and good treating these girls like they are nothing more than conquests, trophies to flaunt in the faces of your peers, but you won't be laughing when one of the little trollops deliberately gets themselves pregnant, will you?' Joanie said, as Jimmy shovelled another large portion of curry into his mouth. 'Her type would bleed you dry. She'd take you for all you have,' she said shrewdly. 'All those loose lips and even looser knicker elastic slappers that you keep going for are no good!' Joanie knew that her breath was wasted. She'd had this conversation so many times with Jimmy yet he never listened. 'You need a good girl, Jimmy. One that will give you a nice home.'

'And a few grandkids too, yeah?' Jimmy said raising his eyes knowingly. His mother was craving grandchildren and she made no bones about the fact. 'Isn't that what this is really about?'

Joanie pursed her lips, unable to argue with him.

'I'm serious, son,' she said, almost brave enough to continue her conversation, but then deciding against it. 'You can still have your fun, Jimmy, if you're clever enough about it, but you need to think about settling down with someone who'll give you a good home. A family. It's what life's all about.' Joanie left the words hanging in the air between them.

'I've got plenty of time for all that, Mum,' Jimmy said as he finished his meal. 'I'm young. I've got loads of time to think about settling down.' While he spoke, he realised the truth was his mother had a point.

Jimmy had been thinking about having a family more and more lately, what with how well the business was doing, how quickly he was building his little empire. It wouldn't be such a bad idea to have someone to hand everything down to one day. An heir to the Byrne throne so to speak. He quite fancied the idea of having a son of his own.

Maybe his mother was right. Only he wouldn't tell her that: he'd never hear the end of it.

'Besides, shouldn't you be warning me off getting married with the amount of aggro that prat of a father seems to dish out to you?' Jimmy said, doing his usual of making no disguise of the dislike he felt towards his old man.

Joanie shrugged once more.

'I guess so, but what can I say? I'm a glutton for punishment and if it wasn't for that old prat, I would never have had you, son. Family is all we have,' she said, feeling her tears threaten once more. 'I know you think I'm being silly, Jimmy, but I just can't shake the feeling that it is different this time. That your father is really in some kind of trouble. He's never gone AWOL for nearly a week before. I think something bad's happened to him.'

Jimmy wrinkled his mouth, unconvinced.

'Nah, that old git is like a bionic cat with one too many lives. I'm sure wherever he is, he's just fine, so stop with your worrying, Mum. He'll turn up,' Jimmy said, then clocking the time on his watch he got up and kissed his mother on the forehead. 'Listen, I hate to eat and run, but I've got to shoot off! I've got a bit of business to sort out tonight.'

Joanie nodded, understanding. 'Off you go, son!'

She walked Jimmy to the front door to see him out. She wasn't one to stand in the way of her son trying to make a good living for himself. She was grateful that he'd popped in for his dinner at all. 'I was going to watch some of my programmes tonight anyway.'

'You do that, and don't you be worrying about Dad either. He'll turn up soon. I'm sure of it.' Jimmy grinned. 'The man's like a bad bleeding smell. Before you know it, he'll be home and annoying the crap out of you again, whilst making the place look untidy.'

'Yeah, you're probably right,' Joanie said, with more conviction than she actually felt. Jimmy was right. Michael could be back any minute and before the man's arse would have hit the settee, he'd have found some way of winding her up.

'I'll see you later, son, thanks for stopping by, and thank you for my lovely coat.'

'Catch you later, Mum!' Jimmy called as he walked up the footpath, pulling his collar up around his neck to keep off the cold chill of the evening air.

Jumping in his motor, Jimmy turned the heating up full whack, before rubbing his hands together to try and generate a bit of heat.

Catching sight of his mum standing at the door waving to him as he pulled away, he couldn't help but notice how vulnerable she looked as she scanned the street in the vain hope that his father would magically appear.

He was annoyed.

He'd genuinely thought that his mother would be better off without his father knocking about. It was a good job he'd only given his father a bloody beating and he hadn't murdered the treacherous cunt like he'd initially wanted to. Still, he'd taught the old bugger a harsh lesson that he wouldn't be forgetting in a hurry. Not only had he beaten the living shit out of him, but he'd left him trussed up in some old abandoned squat in Hackney.

It broke his heart that he'd have to go back and let the man go, it really did.

Jimmy would have gladly left him there to rot, but his mother would be lost if anything happened to the old git and Jimmy Byrne couldn't have anything upsetting his dear old mum.

He just hoped that he hadn't left it too late already, that his old man hadn't gone and fucking snuffed it.

CHAPTER THREE

'Jesus, Edel, what on earth's your Colleen doing up there? For such a slip of a girl, she sounds like a bleeding herd of elephants!' Raising her eyes up to the ceiling as another almighty thud vibrated down through the floor above them, Nellie Erikson had thought at first the noise was Edel Walsh. Her friend had been out the back of the florist, in the little kitchenette, making them both a nice cup of tea. The sounds had been getting louder and louder, and had continued even though Edel was back now, standing in front of her.

Nellie could only assume that the noise must be Edel's daughter, Colleen, upstairs in the flat. Though, how she was making such a noise when Colleen probably weighed less than one of Nellie's thighs, the woman thought enviously, she just couldn't fathom.

'What's all that banging?' Edel said, a frown on her puzzled face. 'I thought that was you.' Convinced her friend was having her on about there being someone upstairs in the flat, Edel placed the two mugs of hot tea down on the counter, just as another almighty thump boomed out from above them.

'What in God's name?' Edel said, perplexed, as she stared suspiciously up at the light fitting as the lampshade started to sway. 'My Colleen's not even home. She's gone to do the weekly shop for me.'

'Well, someone's up there and they certainly ain't light on their feet, whoever it is,' Nellie said, her eyes wide open with exaggerated concern. Though in truth, she loved a bit of a drama did Nellie.

Only, the drama was a bit too much for her today, jumping with fright as the next thud was so loud that it immediately rendered both women speechless; the force of whatever it was, making the whole shop shake.

Suddenly fearful for her life, Nellie let out a high-pitched, deafening screech.

'EARTHQUAKE!' she screamed as panic engulfed her, grabbing at her friend and pulling her down under the counter. 'Jesus Christ, Edel. We need to stay low; get under cover. I've seen it on a documentary, stay low to the floor.'

Crouching down on the cold cement floor of the florists, the two women huddled together in silence, as they waited for another tremor. But the banging and shaking had stopped now.

The next noise they heard was the sound of male voices. Swearing and shouting at each other: loud, jovial banter.

'Here, you old lush, you haven't got a fella up there, have you?' Nellie said, raising her eyes questioningly at her friend. 'Some fancy man tucked away inside your wardrobe? Or a couple of them by the sounds of it?'

''Course I bleeding ain't!' Edel said, crawling back out from the shop counter indignantly, before wiping her dusty hands down the front of her trousers, purposely ignoring Nellie's suspicious gaze as she made her way towards the back room where the staircase was. Unlike her friend here with her wild accusations, Edel wasn't just going to stand around and do nothing.

'Where are you going?' Nellie asked.

'Well, we're not going to find out who's up there by standing around down here playing guessing games with each other, are we? I'm going upstairs to investigate.'

Nellie grabbed at Edel's arm.

'What if it's burglars though, Edel? Or even worse, a poltergeist? You can't go up there on your own.'

The sound of someone shouting orders and the loud shrill of power tools interrupted their conversation, and suddenly the penny dropped.

Workmen. The cheek of them.

'Oh no they bloody don't!' Edel said firmly, as the realisation of what was going on suddenly became apparent. 'Those bloody bastards!' Incensed as she realised what the noise was, Edel grabbed the broom that she had propped up next to the back door. Holding it in front of her like a weapon, her face thunderous, she nodded to her friend.

'You coming or you staying here?' she said.

Nellie shook her head, unsure what the right answer would be. She still didn't have a clue who was upstairs, though apparently Edel had an inkling and by the look on her face she wasn't one bit happy about it. 'What are you planning on doing with that?' Nellie asked, wondering what it was she was missing.

'I tell you what I'm going to do with this: I'm going to go and beat someone over the head with it, that's what I'm going to do,' Edel said, her temper getting the better of her. 'You know what the problem is with the world these days, Nellie? People think they can just bloody take whatever they want from you. That they can just swoop on in and snatch it away from you regardless. Well, they've picked on the wrong bloody gal this time, let me tell you!'

Edel spat, reaching the stairwell. 'You better stay put, this ain't going to be pretty. I'm going to sort these obnoxious bastards out once and for all.'

She stomped up the stairs like a woman possessed.

Nellie had no intention of doing as she was told and staying put. Itching to find out what the hell was going on, and who the 'obnoxious bastards' were, Nellie decided to do the complete opposite of what Edel had told her, quickly following her friend up the stairs. The look on Edel's face was murderous and knowing her friend as well as she did, if Edel Walsh was about to kick off then Nellie didn't intend missing out on the show. Knowing just what a nutcase Edel could be when she lost the plot, Nellie Erikson was looking forward to a ringside seat.

'That's it, lads. We're in!' Reggie Wilkins smiled with satisfaction at the large gaping hole he'd just knocked through into next door's flat. 'That's another job well done, boys! We're ahead of schedule, the boss will be happy.'

Reggie was pleased as punch with the progress that his team of men were making with this project.

'Does that mean we can knock off in a bit then?' one of the workers, Jock, called out, trying his luck. They'd worked their arses off today to make good headway, now that they were in.

Reggie rolled his eyes.

'Sod off, Jock! You only had a tea break half an hour ago.' Shaking his head, Reggie pretended to be disgusted at the suggestion. He was under strict instructions to get moving with this project, but Reggie knew better than anyone that if you looked after your workforce, they'd look after you. His men deserved a few beers after the effort they'd all put in today.

'I tell you what, seeing that it's Friday and I'm feeling generous, I'll make a deal with you. If you clear up this mess and get the rest of this wall down then we'll call it a day. Then the pints will be on me.' Reggie grinned, seeing the genuine smiles plastered across his lads' faces as they all nodded in agreement to his suggestion before getting to work with new-found motivation, clawing back the debris that had fallen around the entrance to the newly formed hole in the brickwork and loading it up into the wheelbarrows.

The job would be done in no time, Reggie thought to himself as he eyed up his workmanship. The large gaping hole enabled him to see right through into the flat next door.

'Here, whoever it was that lived there must have left in a hurry, they left their smalls behind.'

Laughing at the selection of large granny knickers that were displayed in rows on the clothes airer above the bath, Reggie added, 'Smalls being the operative word looking at these under crackers!'

Eyeing the rest of the room, he noted the bathmat and towels still out on display, a pot of toothbrushes still neatly placed on the corner of the sink unit too. Bottles of lotions and potions lining the bathroom shelves – a thick film of brick dust covering everything.

'I thought all the flats had been cleared out?' Reggie said to no one in particular, irritated that this flat had clearly been overlooked. That would mean more work for them, and the last thing Reggie wanted to do today was to get his men to trawl through a flat full of abandoned personal junk that some lazy arsed tenant had left behind them. 'This should have all been cleared before we got on site!' Reggie said, wondering what else had been left in the flat.

Reggie stepped closer to the hole to inspect the interior, a movement beneath the stack of fallen bricks suddenly catching his eye.

'Hold up!' he said, waving his arm frantically for the men to stop what they were doing.

Narrowing his eyes so that he could get a better look, Reggie stepped in closer, his gaze resting on what he'd at first thought was a towel on the floor.

Then he saw movement underneath the rubble.

'What the fuck?'

It was a cat.

Dragging itself out from the pile of debris that had almost buried it, the bewildered cat's fur stood on end, covered in brick dust. Reggie could only guess that the thing had probably been white and fluffy before the wall had gone down on top of the poor bugger.

'That was a close one!' he said, as the cat made a swift exit, racing across the dishevelled bathroom floor, and out onto the landing of the flat. Thankfully unscathed.

Reggie shook his head. His instincts telling him that something wasn't right.

'Fucking hell, lads. I think someone's still living in here?'

Adjusting his hard hat, Reggie was about to climb through so that he could take a better look when he was suddenly stopped in his tracks as a little old lady flew at him, brandishing a wooden broom handle in his direction. A larger lady was standing behind her.

'You bloody bastards, look what you've done to my home. Is this what you're doing now? Using bullying tactics? Forcing me out against my will. You won't get away with this.' The smaller, feistier of the two women launched into her attack, bringing the broom she was holding down on Reggie's head.

Despite the wooden handle bouncing off his hard hat as his safety helmet took the brute force of her fury, Reggie stood there stunned. Surprised at the strength of the woman.

'Jesus Christ, are you mental?' he exclaimed, wondering if the old dear was all there in the head. 'You nearly took my bleeding head off with that thing!'

She was standing in front of him like a raving lunatic as she waved the broom around in front of her, screeching profanities at him. If it had been a bloke attacking him, Reggie would have had no qualms in taking the broom off the fucker and wrapping it around the assailant's head, but as it stood, Reggie would never contemplate hitting a woman. He didn't even like having to raise his voice at one. Especially an old girl like this one. He really didn't know how to handle her. His only option was to try and calm the distraught woman down.

'You shouldn't be here, ma'am, it's not safe,' he tried to reason.

'I could say the same thing to you!' Edel said, about to hit the man with the broom for a second time; only this time Reggie was ready for the woman.

Well prepared for another blow, he managed to catch the broom handle, gripping it with his hand before it had a chance at impacting on his hard hat once again, and snatching it from her grasp, though even that didn't seem to deter the woman's tirade of abuse.

'I'm going to have you lot for this. How bloody dare you. Look at my lovely bathroom, it looks like bleeding Beirut,' Edel screeched, staring in disbelief at her once immaculate bathroom, which was now covered completely in brick dust and debris. The hole in the wall was big enough for Nellie to fit through sideways, and that was saying something as Nellie was a big old girl. 'This is criminal damage. You've destroyed my home.'

Reggie pursed his lips. The woman was indeed a nutjob. Speaking slowly, trying to sound as calm and understanding as he could, he tried to appease her.

'These have all been sold, ma'am. You shouldn't be here. We're just doing our job and clearing the area ready for construction. This is a building site. Technically it's you that's trespassing.' Wondering if the old bat was a sandwich short of a picnic Reggie Wilkins spoke with authority, hoping that the woman would realise that there was some kind of a mix-up. 'I'm afraid I'm going to have to ask you to leave, ma'am! This is a demolition job; the building is being stripped down.'

Edel's eyes flashed with fury then.

'You'll do no such bleeding thing!' she screamed. 'And I'm not "technically trespassing" as you so brazenly put it, this is my home. It's mine, do you hear me. You bloody people! Thinking you can waltz around here flashing your cash and all us little folk just have to comply with your demands. Well, I told you lot months ago, I'm not going anywhere. I was born in this flat and the only way I'll ever leave the place is in a box. Now if you don't all piss off away from my property, I'm going to call the police and have you all removed. Each and every bloody one of you!'

'You'll have to call them then, ma'am, because we have permission to be here and to do the work,' Reggie said, shrugging his shoulders dismissively as the woman and her friend stomped off to make a phone call.

He turned to his men, raising his eyes to Jock and the other workers that were now standing around him.

'You lot might as well knock off early after all,' he said to the men. 'There's no point us all hanging around here like spare parts, while we wait for the cavalry to arrive and sort this nutjob out. Have a pint for me while you're at it.'

He had been well up for an easy day today, knocking off with the lads early to have a few pints and celebrate their first productive day on the project; only, thanks to this crazy old bat in here, Reggie Wilkins had a feeling that his easy day was just about to get a lot bloody harder.

CHAPTER FOUR

'What? So you're telling me that by the time you realised that the old girl was inside, you'd already knocked half her fucking flat down?'

Reggie nodded. He knew how it sounded, but this wasn't his fault and he wasn't going to let Alex Costa pin the blame on him.

'We'd tunnelled a hole into her bathroom wall big enough to get a mini through. How the fuck were we supposed to know she was still living there? You gave us the all-clear, Alex.'

'You're the fucking project manager. The groundsman. Didn't you inspect the site before you and your men started knocking down walls?' Alex Costa was pissed off.

Reggie Wilkins had called an urgent meeting with him, only, as the conversation unravelled, it was becoming more apparent by the minute that it wasn't a meeting at all. It was a circus and his men, it seemed, were nothing but fucking clowns.

'Who the fuck is this Edel Walsh then?' Alex Costa stared down at the paperwork that Reggie Wilkins had just presented him with, scanning the familiar architect's drawings of the new development that he and Jimmy had just invested in. The plot they'd just bought out was set to make them both a fortune. As it stood now, though, it was nothing more than a shamble: a cluster of run-down shops and flats that stood like an eyesore slap bang in the middle of Soho's Dean Street.

Jimmy had come up with the initial idea. Soho was on the up now. Jimmy and Alex had heard it on good authority that Westminster Council was starting to invest some money into the area. The powers that be had decided that Soho would no longer be a place where every schoolboy's dream came true. They were pulling rank. Clamping down on all the sex workers that flooded the area after dusk. The seedy backstreet sex shops and strip clubs were having their licences revoked. The illegal video shops were going too. A new era was coming. 'The birth of the new romantics,' as Jimmy liked to refer to it. Soho would soon be the place to be. A place filled with fancy little coffee shops, and quirky boutiques. There was already an influx in gay bars popping up in the area too. Classy places, not the sleazy jaunts that people had shoved down their throats up until now.

The pink pound was already here and thriving in Soho and that's what Jimmy and Alex were counting on cashing in on. They wanted to build the most exclusive, sought after apartments, right here in the heart of Soho.

The new venture would be the perfect solution for them both to hide away money they had coming in from some of their other lucrative investments. Jimmy's little sideline of running several brothels in the West End was creaming them in a fortune. They needed to stash the cash somewhere and ploughing the money into property was the perfect hiding place.

Jimmy wanted no expense spared. He wanted every fixture and fitting, every item of furniture, to be the absolute best. They'd worked their bollocks off to get as far as they had with the project so quickly and Reggie standing here now telling him that there was a major setback, was not what Alex Costa wanted to hear.

'This is her place, here. She owns unit number seven. The little florist with a flat above it,' Reggie said, pointing to the sheet of paper sprawled out on the desk in front of them, tapping his finger on the only building on the plan with a bright red circle drawn around it.

Typical, Alex thought. The one fucking flat that sat slap bang in the middle of Alex and Jimmy's entire development.

'So what? Some old geriatric's having a senile moment and suddenly at the last minute she doesn't want to leave her flat behind? Tough shit. Everything's been signed. There's no going back. Edel Walsh doesn't have the luxury of changing her mind now. I don't understand why you've called a meeting, Reggie. This is a headache, granted. But it's nothing any half-competent site foreman can't sort out surely?' Alex said, rubbing his temples, frustrated. He had thought Reggie Wilkins would have everything in order, but now he was beginning to question the man's capabilities – coming to him with such minor issues like this was an insult.

'I've got a mega day on, Reggie, I could do without having to babysit you too, mate,' Alex said, glad that Jimmy was currently off out dealing with some personal business right now on the other side of London. While Alex's patience was already wearing thin, Jimmy would have lost his shit listening to this conversation.

'Like I said, boss, the old girl's refusing to leave the site and until we get her to leave we can't carry on with the job. It's a major hold up, boss,' Reggie explained, as the age-old saying of shooting the messenger came to his mind as he recited the bad news to Alex Costa. There was no way that he was taking the flack for this.

Someone had made a major fuck up and it wasn't him.

'It's not rocket science. She shouldn't be there, so get her removed. Physically, if you have to,' Alex said, jabbing the side of his head as he stared at the few members of the workforce that had been brave enough to accompany Reggie to this farce of a meeting. 'You're all big enough and ugly enough to sort one old girl, aren't you?'

'She called the Old Bill out—'

'Well, at least for once they would have been put to good use!' Raising his hands up to the sky, mockingly, he said, 'I bet the plod bloody loved that too. Finally having an excuse to stick their noses in our business. I bet that lot were all sorely disappointed with everything being above board and legit, weren't they? Nosey fuckers.'

Alex rubbed his head.

'I take it they moved her on?' he said, wondering why they were even still having this conversation if the police had been called.

'No, boss.'

'What do you mean "no"? She can't just pull out. All the other tenants have vacated the units. All the builders have moved onto the site. The work has started. Why the fuck didn't the plod move her on?'

Then seeing Reggie's stony expression, Alex raised his brow questioningly.

'Go on… What ain't you telling me?'

'They can't move her on, and neither can we. The police checked her paperwork. She kept everything you sent her. She didn't sign anything, Alex.'

'Bullshit!' Alex spat, rendering the room silent as he stormed across to the filing cabinet and started pulling out a pile of paperwork, sifting through it all until he found the folder with the flat's occupier details and contracts. Thumbing through the documents, until he reached Unit No. 7, Alex scanned the contract.

His eyes lingered on the signature at the bottom.

Only it wasn't a signature at all. The woman's writing barely legible, a mere scribble, she'd simply written:

NOT INTERESTED

Walking back to the desk, Alex slumped down in his chair. Of all the fuck ups, he couldn't believe that this was the one that could cost them the project, and it was his.

He'd fucked up.

Jimmy's job had been to do all the initial groundwork on this project. He'd put down the majority of the money and been working alongside the architects to get all the plans drawn up.

Alex's domain had been to sort out the legalities of the project. He'd been working alongside the solicitors and the council chiefs for months. He'd personally weighed out the Chief Planning Officer of London with a tidy sum of money in order to ensure everything ran as quickly and as smoothly as possible. He'd inspected the site along with the building controls officer, and a structural engineer. They'd granted them planning consent without any question.

He didn't understand how this could have happened; he'd overseen every single document himself.

'I reckon she'll try and sue our arses now too, boss. She's that type,' Reggie said, glad that Alex Costa was finally realising the severity of the predicament they were in. 'I hate being the one that lands this all on you, boss, but as you can see, we had no choice but to down tools.'

Alex nodded. Speechless, with the revelation he knew without a shadow of a doubt that when Jimmy Byrne got wind of this the man would do his nut.

Someone's head would be on the chopping board for this, and right now it looked like it was going to be his.

CHAPTER FIVE

Barely able to lift his head, Michael Byrne was ready to succumb to his imminent fate.

In fact, now, he welcomed it. Anything to end his constant suffering. He still couldn't comprehend that his Jimmy could do this to him. Torment him in this way. Leaving him strapped to a chair in some derelict house, out in the arsehole of nowhere.

Kicking out, instinctively, his movement restricted, his legs tethered together with thick rope; his arms wrenched behind him awkwardly; the plastic cable ties cutting into the flesh of his tightly bound wrists. Michael shuddered as another rat scraped at his boots.

He screwed his eyes shut as if physically pained – he'd had enough now. Jimmy was only fucking with him. He was certain of it. Even Jimmy wasn't mental enough to actually murder him, surely? Jimmy was just keeping him out here so that he would learn his lesson, Michael was sure of it. He had to believe that, otherwise he'd have given up by now.

And he had learned his lesson.

He had no idea how long he'd been here for. Days? A week maybe? All he did know was that he'd had long enough to think about his actions and he was heart sorry. Shagging one of Jimmy's girls hadn't been his smartest idea now that he thought about it, though Michael hadn't thought that Jimmy would have got wind of it. Not now the man was such a high flier. He had more girls on his books than he could keep up with, and Michael had heard a few rumours about a couple of big drug shipments that Jimmy and his business partner, Alex, were currently creaming in.

Businessmen my arse! he thought to himself bitterly. Jimmy was nothing more than a crook. Swanning around London, acting the big I am.

Still, Michael was learning the hard way about crossing his son. If Jimmy didn't come back sometime soon and get him the fuck out of here, Michael was starting to think that he might die here.

The rats were getting braver. Venturing nearer to him each time they scurried across the derelict house's dusty wooden floors. They could smell that he'd soiled himself. The acidic stench of shit that lingered in the air only enticed them to him more.

He just wanted to go home.

Home to Joanie.

A lone, strangled sob escaped his mouth then, as he finally admitted to himself that Jimmy was indeed a mental fucker. Perhaps his boy really would have the nerve to leave him here to die after all. The man was unhinged. Michael had always known that about Jimmy. He had been a fool to underestimate him.

There was no point in calling out for help. Shouting was futile, useless. Michael had tried already for hours. Bellowing and screaming until his throat was coarse and raspy. Until he couldn't physically cry out anymore.

No one could hear him.

No one would come.

Overcome with self-pity for the way in which he was suffering, all he had left were his tears. It wasn't meant to be this way.

His emaciated body shook with fear.

Somewhere behind him, he could feel the icy night air blowing in through a broken windowpane. The cold stabbing his skin now; the bitter chill reaching right down inside his bones.

Earlier, before the pitch-black darkness had settled in all around him he'd been able to concentrate on the small trail of thin white cloud that had spanned out in front of him, at his every breath.

Now he couldn't see a thing, only darkness. Alone with his thoughts and the eerie sounds of the house. The odd creak. A bang. Outside bare branches of trees creaked loudly as they swayed in time with the wind.

He was hungry. His hollow stomach ached as he thought about the dry, stale sandwich he'd eaten the day before. That's all he'd had, that and a few sips of water. He felt weak.

The rats could sense that too.

'Get the fuck off me!' he cried out, feeling the sharp claws of a rodent scratch at one of his legs as the creature tried to scurry up the inside of his trousers.

Crying now openly as he raised both his legs, frantically waving his limbs around with sheer desperation. The chair beneath him rocked, unsteadily. Swaying from side to side, before finally tipping over. Crashing down on the floor with Michael pinned beneath it.

Michael was bawling, sobbing into the damp, threadbare rug he'd landed on. He pressed his face down into it to try and protect himself from the onslaught that would follow.

If death didn't come quickly for him now, the rats soon would.

'Well, there's a fucking sight if ever I saw one!'

Squinting through the darkness as a brilliant white light flashed in his eyes, temporarily blinding him, Michael squeezed them shut. He focused on the noise instead. Recognising the voice. Loud and obnoxious.

Jimmy was back.

Slowly Michael opened his eyes again. Taking his time to adjust them to the bright stream of light that poured in around him from the torch that Jimmy was shining directly into his face, Michael Byrne looked up at the shadowy figure standing over him.

Jimmy peered down at him with a twisted smirk spread across his face.

'This must be your lucky day, eh?' Jimmy said.

He felt Jimmy's strong grip, wrenching him up onto his feet.

'Thank you! Thank you!' Michael said through his tears, his voice sounding pathetic even to his own ears. For the first time this week he was actually happy to see his son.

He wasn't going to die. Not today.

His bawling reduced to sobs, he was overcome with relief and gratitude to the man that had caused him such suffering.

'Get the fuck up.'

It wasn't a request, it was an order. Jimmy was holding onto him, the force of his grip rendering him upright. Michael didn't have the strength to stand on his own.

'Fuck me, you bleeding stink!' Jimmy said then, catching the stench of shit and piss that lingered in the air between them.

Michael bristled, humiliated once more.

Of course he stank. Jimmy had held him here against his will. Leaving him here all day and night on his own, he'd only popped back to give Michael scraps to eat. Or to taunt him some more. He'd had no choice but to soil himself. Then he'd been left to sit there caked in his own excrement for days. His skin sore and blistered. His crotch burning.

Jimmy had brought Michael to his lowest ebb. His son had got a kick out of it, Michael's pain and discomfort too.

But now he was here, and it appeared that he was going to let Michael leave this godforsaken place after all.

'I thought you were going to leave me for dead. If you hadn't come back just now, I'd have been gone by the morning,' Michael snivelled, as he searched the face of his son for a tiny hint of anything that resembled compassion.

There wasn't any. Jimmy stared back at him. His eyes stone cold, void of any feeling at all for his father.

'Well, now. Here's the thing. Despite the fact that you're nothing more than a useless, cheating, lying prick,' Jimmy said, the hatred still evident with his every word as he wrenched the thick rope from his father's feet. 'My mother – your wife, as you clearly need reminding – still seems to give two shits about you. Worried out of her fucking mind she is. Can you believe it? After the way you've treated her all these years? That woman is actually worried about you?'

Jimmy shook his head in disbelief as he slid the scissors in behind the cable ties. Purposely digging the sharp blade into the older man's flesh as he cut. He was in no mood to pander to the old man's whims.

'Just so we're both clear, that's the only reason you're getting out of here alive today, do you get me?' Jimmy said, staring at his old man with disgust.

'From now on, I'm going to be keeping a very close eye on you. You are going to be on your best behaviour, do you get me? You're going to start treating my mother – your wife – like she's the Queen. There'll be no more drinking. No more gambling and no more tarts, do you understand?!'

Michael understood all right.

Nodded obediently, acknowledging his warning as Jimmy led him roughly out of the squalid house, pushing and dragging him when he tripped or fell unsteadily on the uneven, rubbish-strewn floor.

Jimmy held him by the back of his neck. Gripping him tightly, wrenching him upright as he led him outside along the narrow overgrown footpath, to where his motor was parked just outside the front gates.

Michael stood next to the passenger door, expectant, as he waited for Jimmy to open it for him.

Jimmy shook his head.

'Not a fucking chance, mate,' he said as he led his dad to the boot. Opening it up, already lined with plastic sheets. 'You ain't getting in my motor in that state. You're going to have to get in the boot. You're lucky that I'm even letting you in there!' Jimmy spat as Michael did as he was told and awkwardly clambered into the boot.

Degraded once more as he lay down like a stray dog, he shot one last fleeting look back to the derelict house he'd been kept in for the past few days, barely able to comprehend what Jimmy had put him through.

Jimmy read his mind.

'You have got off lightly tonight, now don't you fucking forget it,' Jimmy sneered. 'From now on, not only will you look after my mother but you will go above and beyond to do everything and anything she asks of you. If she says jump, you backflip, you get me?'

Michael Byrne nodded, as Jimmy slammed the boot down on him, plunging him into darkness once again.

Jimmy was wrong.

Michael hadn't got off lightly at all and they both knew it. At least if the rats had got him, his death would have been quick. Instant. Jimmy hadn't given him a chance tonight, he'd only prolonged his suffering even more. Michael was going to have to spend the rest of his days under the watchful eyes of his stuck-up wife and his psychotic son.

Jimmy hadn't allowed him to live, he'd offered him death instead.

One of the slowest and most torturous ways to die of them all.

CHAPTER SIX

Throwing down his cutlery with a loud clang as Alex broke the news, Jimmy Byrne stared at his business partner with disbelief, unable to comprehend what he'd just been told.

It all made sense now – Alex's sudden offer of a dinner tonight at Jimmy's favourite Italian restaurant, Raphael's, in the heart of London's West End – the bloke had just been buttering him up. How Jimmy hadn't worked it out sooner he didn't know. Alex offering to pay for anything should have been suspicious enough. Alex was so tight, he'd even begrudge you the steam off his piss. It had been a standing joke between the two men for years, how Jimmy liked to flash his wealth and buy only top quality, high-end designer clobber, while Alex would sooner wait for something to be on sale before he parted with his precious cash. The man never got his wallet out unless he had to.

'You're a shifty fucker, Alex,' Jimmy said, shaking his head. Finally in the loop about the major fuck up that had gone down on the new site, Jimmy wasn't the slightest bit impressed and Alex knew it. 'That's why you brought me here, isn't it?' Jimmy said, laughing at Alex's cowardly actions. 'What did you think, eh? That because we're in a restaurant full of people I won't lose my head at you?' He was raising his voice now. 'That because you bought me a steak and a few glasses of their finest Scotch, that somehow I'd just fucking let the fact that you fucked up slide?' Alex had underestimated him. Annoyed at Alex for not telling him about this 'Mrs Walsh' sooner, Jimmy didn't give two shits about the people sitting within his immediate proximity.

Let them look, let them stare. He had a business to run, and Alex was acting like a first prize cunt by keeping him out of the loop like this. 'Now, tell me again, what the fuck has been going on?'

'It was an oversight, Jimmy,' Alex said, clearing his throat as if struggling to get his words out. Aware of the other diners watching them, Alex felt foolish for thinking that bringing Jimmy here might soften the blow. 'I thought everything was in order. I thought she'd signed it,' he said, registering the thunderous look on Jimmy's face. If there had been any way that Alex could have sorted this out without involving Jimmy, he would have.

He'd had his solicitors go through everything with a fine toothcomb. The old bird had them all over a barrel. Unlike some of the tenants that were paying the council rent, Edel Walsh owned her flat and the florist outright. The mortgage was all paid off. If she was refusing to sell up then there was fuck all that Alex could do to rectify the matter.

He had no choice now but to come clean to Jimmy about his error.

'THOUGHT?' Jimmy shook his head dismissively. Picking up his Scotch and downing it in one, he nodded to the waiter to bring him another. After the shit Alex had just come out with, he was going to need it. 'What do you mean, "you thought"? She either signed it, or she didn't,' he bellowed, losing his rag. This was not what he wanted to hear. Not at this stage of the work. Not now he'd invested every penny he owned into this project.

This was going to be the job that put him on the map.

This project was going to set him up for life.

'Our men are already on site. They've already started tearing the place apart. Knocking down the walls, ripping everything out in accordance with the plans that my architect drew up, and now you're telling me in the final fucking hour that you THOUGHT that the woman's paperwork had been signed up?'

Nodding to the waiter as he brought over a drink, Jimmy snatched it from the tray and slammed it on the table, staring down at the drawings that Alex had just presented to him.

'This should have been dealt with at the very beginning. It was paramount that everyone signed the paperwork. You knew that.'

'Look, Jimmy, I know you're fucking pissed, mate, I am too,' Alex said shifting uncomfortably in his seat, as more diners looked over at them. He felt mortified at the epic fuck up he'd made as it was, without Jimmy making him look like a cunt on top of it all. 'I thought I checked it all—'

'What? With your eyes fucking closed?'

'Seriously, this woman never let on that there was a problem. She didn't make any fuss. I remember her handing me the signed contract. Not a peep! I had no idea that it wasn't signed. I thought I checked it, but maybe I got distracted.'

'Oh have a laugh, Alex?' Shaking his head, Jimmy sneered. 'The whole fucking project's in jeopardy because you think you "got distracted"? That's the best you can give me?'

Wincing at Jimmy's sarcasm, Alex felt like a right tit.

'All the other tenants were happy with their offers. We paid way above premium to make sure everyone signed. Our solicitors drew up the contracts and sent the monies out to the relevant parties. Only, somehow this flat slipped under the radar. The money never left the account, and no one checked the paperwork. The first any of us heard about a problem was when the old dear tried to rip Reggie a new one.'

Jimmy sat back in his chair, dumbfounded at what he was hearing. He had hundreds of thousands of pounds invested in this development. The money he'd paid out to buy the other properties on the unit alone had cost him a fortune and now they were being held to ransom by some little old lady. It was a complete and utter mess.

'We offered more than a fair price for those flats. Every other fucker bit my right arm off for the money. You think she's pulling a fast one, and trying to hold out for more money?' Jimmy said begrudgingly, his tone clipped as he spoke, convinced that this Edel Walsh must be a shrewd old fucker to have been able to get them all this far along until she kicked up a stink. 'She's got us, hasn't she? The woman can name her price and she probably knows it too.'

Jimmy frowned. He didn't have the time or the inclination to play games with her.

'Tell our legal team to make the woman an offer she can't refuse. We'll double it,' he said simply.

Alex had wanted him to give him the solution to the problem, well Jimmy had just waved his magic fucking wand. 'It's more expense than I was hoping for but at least that will put it to bed a lot quicker and a lot less painfully than trying to battle it out with her. We can't continue with the build until the woman has vacated, and we can't build the thing around her either. So it's our only option. Double it.'

'She told Reggie that she wasn't interested. Said you could offer her a million pounds and she wouldn't budge. He said she was harping on about being born in that flat and the only way she'd be leaving it is in a box. She sounded pretty adamant about not leaving the place. What if it ain't about the money?' Alex shook his head now despairingly.

'Oh come on, Alex. It's always about the money,' Jimmy insisted, his voice determined. 'Everyone's got a price, find out hers.' He had yet to meet anyone who couldn't be swayed by a higher amount of cash.

'And what if she still doesn't budge?' Alex said, not as easily convinced as Jimmy was that the old bird would start playing ball with them.

'If this Edel Walsh is smart, she'll bite off our hands for this generous offer,' Jimmy said, leaning back in his chair, the expression on his face as serious as his tone.

This development of theirs was going ahead no matter what. Jimmy had worked too hard for it to go tits up in the final fucking hour.

'And if she doesn't… we'll just have to find another way of dealing with the problem, won't we?! There's more than one way to kill a cat if it won't be choked with cream. Trust me.'

CHAPTER SEVEN

'It's very quiet in here today, Edel? Is it always this quiet on a Saturday? I thought the weekends were when you did your most trade?' Nellie Erikson said, peering over the edge of her lukewarm mug of tea at the empty florist, knowing full well that her comments were winding her good friend up, exactly as she had intended.

Not a single customer had set foot in the place in the half an hour that Nellie had been here. Whether she wanted to admit it or not, Edel was struggling.

After the dramas of the property developer last week, smashing through the bathroom wall upstairs, Nellie had made her thoughts on Edel selling up perfectly clear.

'You're a fool to stay and try and fight them, Edel,' Nellie had said knowingly. 'You should have accepted their generous offer with glee and got the hell out of here while you could. This place isn't going to make you any real money, Edel. You're the only one left in the block. No one knows your even still trading, most of the street has been cordoned off.'

Nellie had never believed there was money in flowers; she'd told her friend that, too, some years ago when Edel had first inherited the place after both her parents had died.

Would Edel listen though? 'Course not. Even now, when she had been offered well over the odds for the place, her friend still refused to sell up. Determined to stay here and continue the legacy of her parents, running this little florist even if it meant that the place was run into the ground.

Edel always thought she knew better than anyone else.

The woman had been doomed to fail from the start, as far as Nellie was concerned, and Nellie had waited for what had felt like a lifetime in order to be able to say, 'I told you so'. She wasn't going to pass the opportunity up now it was bestowed upon her.

'I just don't understand why you didn't jump at the chance to get out while you still could. Soho's gone to the dogs, Edel. All the seedy little shops around here selling those dirty videos, and the sex shops. I mean, come on. The type of clientele nipping into those places is hardly going to come along here and buy a nice bouquet of freesias with their spare change, are they?' Nellie said, shaking her head in despair, knowing that, regardless what she said on the matter, once Edel's mind was made up there was no convincing the woman.

'It's a sign of the times, isn't it? How can you compete with all these supermarkets popping up all over the place, selling bunches of flowers for a fraction of the price that you are? Smaller shops like this one can't keep up with those kinds of prices. You'll be up to your neck in debt before you know it, Edel.'

Edel bit her lip. Physically bristling at her friend's words, Edel wished Nellie would hurry up and finish her tea and bugger off, so she could continue her day in peace.

Debt. The woman had no idea.

Edel was already struggling financially but Nellie Erikson would be the last person that she'd confess that to. The woman would only use it against her to rub her nose in it.

Nellie didn't have a clue about the history behind this shop and flat. About the struggles her mother and father had both been through in order to live here during a time when London had treated people like her parents as outcasts. When other private landlords had signs in the windows stating 'No Blacks. No Dogs and No Irish' Edel's parents had defied all the odds. A hard-working couple from Dublin, they had not only found this place to both live in and make an honest living from, but they'd also dedicated their lives to buying it outright.

Walsh's Florist had been handed down to her as part of her parents' will and no matter how hard times were getting, Edel couldn't just give that up. It was all she had left of her parents. All she had for herself and one day it would be her daughter's inheritance too. For that reason alone, Edel was determined to make it work. No matter how tough times got, and no matter how much she struggled, Edel had no intention of ever just walking away. To her, this place meant more than just bricks and mortar. More to her than a big fat cheque. Though she didn't expect her friend to understand any of that, nor did she have the inclination to explain it to her.

'It's always quiet this time of day, Nellie, you just missed the lunchtime rush. I was run off my feet earlier.' Edel Walsh lied through her gritted teeth. As much as she was sure Nellie was trying to dress up her never-ending river of advice, which was really just an 'I told you so' in disguise, the woman was slowly but surely doing Edel's head in.

It was typical of Nellie to side with those fancy-pants property tycoons about their offer of buying up this place along with most of the rest of the street. They wanted to build a new development apparently. Tear all these old buildings down and replace them with a huge block of pokey overpriced apartments that seemed to be all the rage these days.

Apartments the likes of her and Nellie would never be able to afford in a month of Sundays mind.

Of course, Edel had dug her heels in and refused to sell up.

There was no way she'd give up her home, her life's work, just to line the pockets of some poncy property investor's pockets, but

Nellie wouldn't let up about it. Especially after she'd just heard how Edel had since had her offer doubled and still had refused it. She thought the woman must be a slice of bread short of a sandwich to refuse the offer and she'd been picking away at her ever since she'd found out.

'The lunchtime rush?' Nellie gawked, unconvinced.

Drinking down her now cold cup of tea in one, Edel tried her best to hide her annoyance at Nellie Erikson's know-it-all-tone. Her friend could be a real cantankerous old goat when the mood took her, and Edel could clearly see that today was one of those days.

'Right, then. I'm going to have to get on, Nellie. We'll have to catch up some other time. I have a delivery coming in any minute.' Having endured enough of the woman's monotonous company, Edel swiped her friend's mug of tea from her hand, ushering her towards the door. 'And it's just as well it is quiet in here at the moment. All your moaning and negativity would only scare the customers off anyway,' Edel said, making a point. Seeing as Nellie was clearly oblivious to the permanent twisted scowl on her face, Edel was about to tell her that she'd scare off any potential customers that braved it through the main door with her miserable face greeting them.

But, before Edel got a chance to finish her sentence, the shop door burst open and in walked her very first customer of the day.

Jimmy Byrne.

Edel couldn't believe her luck.

Beaming at the man as if he was made from twenty-four carat gold, Edel was smug in the knowledge that this little visit would just wind her old friend right up.

'Well, Mr Byrne!' Edel chimed. Not only did she finally have a customer, but of all the people to grace her with their presence it was only one of her newest and most well off customers.

Everyone knew Jimmy Byrne. The man was notorious around these parts. Busy making a name for himself with numerous business deals, Edel had no idea how the man made so much money, but rumour had it he was into all sorts. Each to their own, that's what Edel thought. If the man wasn't hurting anyone, and he was making good money, then good luck to him. Times were hard and all the while that Jimmy Byrne was coming into her shop and buying up huge bouquets of beautiful flowers, Edel was in no position to judge the man.

'Afternoon, lovely ladies,' Jimmy replied, strutting into the shop surrounded by an air of confidence that only a man of his stature possessed, dressed in an expensive-looking suit, which only made him look even more handsome.

'Will you be wanting some lovely purple flowers for your mam again? They're her favourite, aren't they?' Remembering their conversation last time Jimmy came in to buy flowers, Edel smiled at him as she closed the door, allowing Nellie to loiter around for a bit longer.

Besides, it wasn't every day that the notorious Jimmy Byrne popped in to the shop, and spoke to her as if she was an old friend.

The least Edel could do was allow Nellie to witness her good fortune.

'See. That's what I love about this little florist. Attention to detail. Now that's real service for you!' Jimmy grinned. 'Yes, she loved the last lot I bought her. Said they were beautiful. If you could make a bouquet up like that, only bigger this time. I want to spoil her.'

'Lovely!' Edel beamed as she lapped up Jimmy's praise, unable to stop the huge smile spreading across her face.

If it wasn't for the fact that the man would have thought her a raving nutcase, Edel could have kissed him there and then for his kind words. Especially in front of old moany bollocks Nellie, next to her. Her friend had been rendered silent now. Taking it all in, and Edel couldn't have been happier.

To be fair, she was only giving the man the kind of customer care that Jimmy Byrne would expect. People around here went out of their way to ensure Jimmy Byrne was given a first class service. Jimmy was her most valued regular customer at the moment: her only regular customer. Coming in at least once every few days to buy flowers for his mother.

'Will you be wanting something for your girlfriend too?' Edel asked, hoping she wasn't overstepping the line by prying into Jimmy's personal business as she noticed him scanning the shop as if in search of something else.

Jimmy often bought two bouquets. The second was probably for whatever fancy piece the man was taking out that night no doubt. A man like Jimmy would have his pick of the girls around here, that was for sure.

'The usual dozen red roses?'

'I'm not sure. I think I want something a little more… unique,' Jimmy said. He twisted his mouth as he stared around the florist thoughtfully, as Edel made herself busy gathering flowers up for his mother's display. 'I want to make an impression with these ones.'

Excited that Jimmy was putting so much thought into his girlfriend's flowers, Edel couldn't help wondering if the man was smitten with whoever it was. He must be, she thought, to go to so much trouble.

'Give me a minute with these, and I'll help you find something just right,' Edel said, determined to make sure Jimmy got exactly what he'd come in here for.

'Are you on your own today then? Is your daughter not helping you out?'

'Colleen? Oh yes, she's out the back, just putting some Christmas bits together. If you're in a hurry, I can get her to come out and give me a hand.' Figuring that Jimmy probably wasn't in the mood to hang around, especially with old Nellie-the-elephant-ears gawping at him, Edel didn't wait for the man's answer.

'Colleen!' she shouted out towards the back room. 'Can you come and give me a hand, love?'

A few seconds later Colleen came through to the front of the shop, covered in silver glitter spray; she had streaks of the stuff all over her clothes and her face.

Seeing the embarrassment on Colleen's face, as she was faced with the rather handsome Jimmy Byrne, Edel couldn't help but laugh.

'Wow, what happened to you?' she said, taking in the sight of her daughter in her scruffy-looking jeans and T-shirt. The apron that covered her clothing clearly doing nothing to protect her clothes from getting filthy. It was moments like this, when a customer as well-known and respected as Jimmy Byrne came into the shop, that Edel wished her daughter would make more effort with her appearance.

'I was just finishing the last of the Christmas wreaths,' Colleen said, sweeping a long strand of her hair back behind her ears as she spotted Jimmy Byrne staring at her. She suddenly felt self-conscious.

'Finishing off the wreaths? Are you sure they weren't finishing you off?' Edel said laughing, as she discreetly rubbed her own face trying to let Colleen know that she had streaks of silver glitter running across her cheek, before she pointed at her hair, where Colleen had a couple of leaves hanging. 'What are you doing back there? Displaying them, or wrestling with them?'

Colleen blushed. Aware that everyone was staring at her, she felt embarrassed at being the centre of attention.

Edel changed the subject.

'Can you help Mr Byrne here pick some flowers out for his lady friend, while I do the bouquet up for his mother?'

Nodding, Colleen wiped her hands down the front of her apron before she went to serve Jimmy.

'Please, call me Jimmy.' Jimmy smiled. 'Here, you've got something in your hair.'

Leaning in, Jimmy plucked the silver sprayed leaf from where it had caught behind Colleen's ear and grinned as he saw Colleen blush, suddenly shy under his close scrutiny.

'What were you after Mr… I mean, Jimmy?' Colleen said, quickly correcting herself.

Unlike her mother she held no airs and graces for the likes of Jimmy Byrne. Her mother might fall over herself trying to impress the man, but to her, he was just another customer and Colleen treated him as such.

Her mother might be blinded by the man's wealth and notoriety but Colleen had heard about the sort of business that Jimmy Byrne ran. About the girls he had working for him.

Jimmy Byrne was a crook by all accounts. Still, ever professional, Colleen remained polite and helpful as she served him. He was a paying customer after all. Though falling over herself and kissing the man's arse were not things that Colleen would be indulging in.

Catching Colleen's curt tone, Jimmy smiled, amused by the way the young woman acted around him. He wasn't used to females in his company acting indifferently to him. Normally women made a point of going out of their way to impress him. Only Colleen didn't seem to care one bit about who he was. In fact, she didn't seem interested in him at all. The girl's nonplussed attitude only served to intrigue him even more.

'You know, I'm not sure what I want this time. I have no idea what flowers she likes,' Jimmy said, eyeing the vases near to him as he tried to make up his mind. 'Tell you what, I'm going to let you choose. You probably have a better eye for things like this than me.'

Colleen bit her lip, irritated that Jimmy seemed so intent in engaging with her. She'd rather he just picked some red roses like most men did and be done with it. She could have served him in minutes then, and got back to her Christmas project out the back.

'Okay,' she said, trying but not succeeding to hide her irritation at having to appease the man. 'Do you know what colours she likes? What her favourite flower is?' Colleen asked, not bothering to hide her sarcasm as she scanned the rows of flowers in the large metal urns around her, guessing that a man like Jimmy probably didn't take much notice of what the girls he dated liked or disliked. He seemed the type to only look out for himself.

'Hmm, I don't really know. We haven't got that far.' Jimmy grinned his cheekiest smile now. 'I was thinking red roses, but I'm not sure. Maybe I should go with something a bit different this time. What are your favourites?'

Colleen wrinkled her mouth, trying her hardest to keep her expression neutral. Jimmy Byrne really did rate himself.

There was something extremely smug about the man.

He was strikingly handsome, but he had an air about him that he was more than aware of the fact. He acted as if he could charm the birds down from the trees, but he was wasting his time if he thought that he could win Colleen over.

She had no interest in flirting with the man.

'Me? I personally think red roses are lovely, but they are a bit of a cliché,' Colleen said, purposely ignoring the fact that her mother's eyes were now glaring into the back of her – which only made Colleen smirk.

Jimmy Byrne was a walking talking cliché, if ever Colleen had seen one. Flashing his money and his killer smile, as he expected people to fall down at his feet.

'I like something a bit softer. I'd go for cream roses; they look really pretty with some pink chrysanthemums and some euca-lyptus thrown in. They are classy and they'll smell beautiful too.'

'Classy huh?' Jimmy grinned. 'Yeah, I like that. That sounds like exactly what I'm after.'

Staring at Colleen a little too intently for her liking, the girl stepped back. Sensing the flirtation in Jimmy's words, Colleen felt flustered now.

Picking out a selection of the flowers that she'd suggested, in her clumsiness she dropped several of the stems onto the floor. Bending down to pick them up, she could feel Jimmy's eyes still burning into her.

He wasn't the only one staring.

Colleen didn't even have to look over at her mother or Nellie to know that the two women would be standing gawping at them both now too. They'd be lapping up every moment of this, she was sure of it.

'How are these?' she asked as Jimmy eyed the flowers, and nodded.

'I'll wrap them for you then, shall I?' Colleen said, happy to have an excuse to turn her back to the man.

Jimmy waited patiently, grinning to himself that despite the fact Colleen seemed so stand-offish with him, he clearly had some kind of effect on the girl.

That amused him greatly.

Jimmy was enjoying himself now. Getting a rise from Colleen.

'Did you hear that, Edel? Your daughter suggests the cream roses instead of the red ones I've been buying. She says they're classy. Maybe that's where I've been going wrong all these years, eh?'

'Oh, you can't go wrong with cream roses, Jimmy. Red is for romance, but the cream ones are for purity. That's why so many brides opt for them,' Edel said as she placed the display of purple flowers on the counter for Jimmy to inspect. Glad that Nellie had stuck around now after all.

'Maybe this girl will be the lucky one, eh?'

'Maybe, indeed!' Jimmy grinned. 'You never know.'

'There you go,' Colleen said. Turning back to Jimmy, she placed the smaller bunch of flowers on the countertop, next to her mother's bouquet.

'Wow!' Jimmy said as he eyed the flowers. 'You were right, Colleen. They are perfect. Delicate yet beautiful.'

Again Colleen blushed, busying herself with running the two prices through the shop's till. She was annoyed at herself for letting Jimmy have any effect on her. The way he looked at her, like he could see right through her, it was intimidating.

'That's thirty pounds then, please,' Edel said, butting in on the awkward exchange between her daughter and Jimmy Byrne.

'Give my love to your mother, Jimmy,' Edel said as she took Jimmy's money before passing him the large purple bouquet for his mother, purposely making out to Nellie that she was a close friend of Jimmy Byrne and his family, despite the fact that she'd never laid eyes on the woman.

It was just another thing for Nellie to gawp at, Edel thought smugly. The woman had ears like a satellite dish; she was taking every word of this in to repeat to all her old cronies down at the bingo hall later. Edel wanted to make sure that the woman had a good story to tell.

'Thanks, Edel, I will.' Jimmy grinned at the woman, only too happy to play along. He knew the score. Jimmy was more than used to people making out they were best buddies. It was quite funny really, seeing people almost falling over themselves to make him happy, and in return, Jimmy was only too happy to turn on the charm.

'Have a nice afternoon, ladies!' Jimmy said, making his way out of the shop, leaving the smaller bouquet on the counter.

'Wait, Jimmy. You forgot the other bouquet. Your lovely cream roses?' Edel shouted out to him, ready to run over to the counter and scoop them up for him.

Only Jimmy shook his head.

'No. I didn't forget them.'

Turning to Colleen now, he shot her one last smile. 'The beautiful flowers are for the beautiful lady who put them together for me,' Jimmy said, enjoying the look on the three ladies' faces. Edel and Nellie's jaws were on the floor. Colleen had gone a bright flushed red.

'I've left my number there on the card, Colleen. You know, if you fancy going out some time?'

Jimmy didn't wait for an answer. Full of certainty that Colleen would call him, he marched out of the shop.

Leaving all three women staring at the door as it closed behind him. Each one of them speechless, as they watched Jimmy get into his brand new Range Rover that was parked just outside the shop, before quickly driving off.

Edel was the first to speak. 'Well, I never. Talk about hitting the jackpot, Colleen. You couldn't do any better than Jimmy Byrne,' she said, ecstatic at today's turn of events. It was as if she was walking on air.

'I doubt I could do much worse either,' Colleen muttered, not as impressed as her mother clearly was with Jimmy's arrogant attempt at asking her on a date. 'I mean come on, he really just thinks that I'm going to ring him?'

Edel and Nellie nodded in unison.

'Well you are, aren't you?' Edel said, staring at Colleen intently, shocked that the girl would think there was any other option but to call him.

Colleen shook her head despairingly.

'I'm going to finish off those wreaths out the back,' she said, leaving the flowers that Jimmy had left for her untouched on the countertop by the till.

'That's my Colleen for you. Playing hard to get, ain't she? Maybe that's just what the man needs, huh,' Edel said as she looked at Nellie and shrugged her shoulders in dismay at the girl's lack of excitement.

She'd have a word with Colleen later, when Nellie had gone. But for now, Edel was positively beaming.

'You fancy another cuppa before you go?' she asked Nellie, trying her hardest to keep her cool and play down the excitement that bubbled away inside of her.

Her friend nodded, gobsmacked at what she'd just witnessed.

For once Nellie Erikson's loose lips were actually a blessing in disguise. By the time Walsh's Florist closed for business today, the fact that not only Jimmy Byrne had been in here spending a fortune on flowers but also that he'd asked her daughter out on a date would be the talk of the town. She'd soon have customers flocking in through the door.

If this place was good enough for Jimmy Byrne then it was good enough for anyone.

CHAPTER EIGHT

'Have one of my cakes, Jimmy. I made them myself,' Edel said, waving the home-made cakes that she'd baked especially for this very occasion.

If ever there was a special occasion then it was tonight. THE Jimmy Byrne was gracing her home with his presence, not only that but the man was taking her Colleen out on a date.

Who would have thought it?

It had taken a bit of persuasion on Edel's part to get Colleen to go along with it all, but Edel hadn't given up until Colleen had finally agreed to call Jimmy and take him up on his offer of a night out. Edel was convinced that once Colleen let down her guard, and spent a bit of time in Jimmy's company, she'd soon show a bit more enthusiasm.

She couldn't make sense of the girl. A funny one was her Colleen. Any other young woman would squeal with excitement if Jimmy Byrne even so much as looked at them sideways. Colleen, on the other hand, was treating tonight as if it was some kind of chore. She'd only gone along with the date to shut her mother up, Edel knew that.

One date. That was all she'd agreed to.

Though one date was all the girl needed, Edel thought to herself smugly.

Now, wafting the tray of cakes under Jimmy Byrne's nose, Edel could barely contain herself.

'Oh, no thank you, Edel, I'm saving myself for my dinner,' Jimmy said with a smile, as he sat waiting patiently for Colleen to join them. Then seeing the look of disappointment flicker across the woman's face, he had a change of heart. 'Oh go on then, seeing as they look so delicious. One won't hurt, will it?'

Edel handed Jimmy the biggest one. Watching him intently as he took his first bite of the cake, she took a seat opposite him.

'She won't be long. She's just finishing getting ready. She's been looking forward to this date all day,' Edel lied. She was pleased that Jimmy was clearly enjoying her cake, when she saw him pop the entire thing in his mouth and practically swallow it down whole.

'Have another one if you want? Made them all today. There's plenty more,' she said, picking up the tray and thrusting them in Jimmy's direction once more, always glad of a man who appreciated good old-fashioned home cooking.

Jimmy shook his head. Unable to talk with the dry slab of cake lodged in his throat, he gulped hard, before coughing loudly and giving Edel the thumbs up to let her know he was all right when he saw the look of concern on her face at him choking.

'Eyes bigger than my belly!' he laughed before adding as convincingly as he could possibly muster, 'That was bloody delicious, Edel, but, honestly, I can't have anymore, I won't be able to eat my dinner.'

Edel winked at him.

'I'll tell you what, Jimmy, I'll wrap you up a plate of them to take home with you. I'll have them ready for when you drop Colleen home later tonight,' she said, puffing her chest out, pleased by Jimmy's flattery.

Tonight was just getting better and better.

She felt like pinching herself. THE Jimmy Byrne. Sitting on her settee, eating her special recipe rock cakes, waiting to take her daughter out on their first date.

'So, Edel? That's a good old-fashioned Irish name, isn't it?' Jimmy said, taking in the woman's proud smile at his compliment.

'That it is, Jimmy. My family are from Dublin. My parents named me after Edel Quinn, a Catholic missionary who worked in Africa. What about your family? Byrne is a good old Irish name too?'

'My mother was born in Cork. She met my dad on her holidays one summer when my dad was over here working,' Jimmy said, not bothering to add that back before he was born was probably how long it had been since his father had actually held down a job. 'They settled here. I guess there was more opportunity for them both to find work and make a life together,' he said with a smile. 'We often went back though, to visit family and spend our summers out there. Ireland is a beautiful place.'

Nodding, Edel couldn't agree more with Jimmy. Despite living here in London for most of her life, she still classed Ireland as her home really. Her accent had faded greatly over the years, but she still had a Celtic tilt to it. Beaming, now that she knew that Jimmy's family were clearly from good stock, Edel liked the man even more.

Jimmy was perfect for her Colleen. Just perfect.

'So are you off anywhere nice tonight?' she said, prodding for information. Edel guessed, rightly, that a man like Jimmy didn't do 'nice': he did the very best. That was the type of life the man lived. The man was like a local celebrity.

He had the aura of a Hollywood movie star.

Even sitting here in her lounge, his huge frame taking up half the settee, Jimmy had a real presence about him. Edel had always known that her Colleen was destined for big things, and if Jimmy Byrne became part of the family then life around here was only going to change for the better for her and Colleen, she was certain of it. She just hoped her daughter realised what a lucky so-and-so she was to have snared a man of Jimmy's calibre. This was Colleen's one and only shot; Edel just wanted to make sure she took it.

'I thought we'd just go out for a nice little dinner. There's a lovely Italian place up the West End that I think Colleen will love.'

'Oh, Italian. *Ciao Bella*!' Edel said, reciting the only bit of Italian she knew as she nodded approvingly; she had no doubt that Colleen would love it too. The restaurants around the flat charged a fortune and she could only imagine the type of service that Jimmy received when he was out. He probably had the best seats in the house reserved for him, the best champagne money could buy. Everyone running around and looking after him and Colleen. Catering to their every whim.

'Colleen loves a bit of pasta! And pizza. She loves food in general actually,' Edel said, missing the amusement on Jimmy's face as she babbled on in her excitement. 'I had to stop her from gorging on the contents of the biscuit barrel before you got here. Wouldn't touch my cakes mind. Said that she could break a window with them, let alone her teeth. Cheeky madam,' Edel said, rolling her eyes at Colleen's tart little comment about her cakes.

Jimmy laughed.

'Your daughter is a tonic, Edel. It's nice that she's got her own mind. She's a lovely girl; you must be so proud,' Jimmy said again. He was in his element as he seemed to have Edel Walsh eating out of his hand; he knew exactly how to sweet talk the lady.

Colleen was clearly cherished.

'I got lucky with her, Jimmy. She's got a heart of gold that one,' Edel said proudly. She meant it too. 'She's a lovely girl inside and out. She's a bit shy sometimes, that's all. She just needs someone to help her out of her shell.'

Jimmy nodded, glad of the titbits of information that Edel was so generously throwing at him; they would stand him in good stead later. He had a feeling that he was going to need all the help he could get.

Edel was thinking exactly the same thing.

Peering towards the door, there was still no sign of Colleen; while she was out of earshot there was no real harm in giving Jimmy a little shove in the right direction. 'And you've certainly had an effect on her already, Jimmy. The girl's done nothing but stare into space since she got off the phone from you the other day, and she's never been that way before over a man.'

'Don't you worry, Edel. I'm a gentleman. Your Colleen will be in very safe hands tonight with me, I give you my word.'

Colleen was exactly the type of girl that his mum had been harping on at him to date.

A good, old-fashioned type of girl. All he had to do now, was impress her.

'Between you and me, Jimmy, she hasn't ever gone out on a date before. Not a proper date like this one. She's not really had a boyfriend of any kind either. Prefers her own company I guess.' Edel nodded knowingly, her eyes wide as saucers. If Colleen could hear her now her daughter would kill her for butting her nose in, but mothers always knew best, and Edel was doing her a favour. 'Or, maybe she just hasn't met the right man until now,' she said, laying it on thick. Sod the old saying of treat them mean and keep them keen; if you wanted something bad enough you grabbed it with both hands.

And Jimmy Byrne was more than worth grabbing hold of. Edel was sure of that.

In fact, if she was thirty years younger herself, Edel would have taken a shot at the man, and back in her younger days, Jimmy Byrne wouldn't have known what to do with her.

'Let's hope so, eh!' Jimmy grinned. It pleased him no end that he seemed to have won the delightful Colleen over already, and that she wasn't the type to have a lot of boyfriends.

'Oh here she is,' Edel said quickly, as Colleen walked into the room, and almost caught the tail end of the conversation. 'You look beautiful, darling,' she said; Edel was pleased that Colleen had gone to such an effort tonight, and judging by the stunned look on Jimmy Byrne's face, it was an effort clearly worth making.

Jimmy stared at Colleen, speechless, for a few seconds. Finally he spoke.

'You look stunning!' he said as he looked Colleen up and down approvingly. He meant it too. The girl was almost unrecognisable. Her red hair teased into loose simple curls; a slick of make-up on her lips and eyes. The dress she wore was basic, simple. A little black number that sat just above the knee, the neckline high. Revealing barely any flesh, yet making her look even more alluring because of that.

It was classy and elegant.

Just like Colleen.

'Really lovely!' Jimmy said, smiling at Colleen as he greeted her with a kiss on her cheek.

'Now you behave yourselves tonight, do you hear me,' Edel said, wagging her finger playfully at Jimmy as she caught the lustful look on the man's face.

'Mum!' Colleen said, feeling her cheeks go bright red, but also loving the effect she was clearly having on Jimmy. She'd spent ages getting ready this evening, but the way he was looking at her now had made every minute worth it.

'Right, when you've both stopped gawping at each other like a pair of love-struck teenagers, maybe you could hurry up and bugger off out to whatever fancy place you're off to,' Edel said, clapping her hands as if to make a point. 'I've got my own hot date tonight myself, with a very handsome Les Dawson. *Blankety Blank* is just about to start; I love that programme, so if you don't mind,' Edel said as she shooed the pair of them out towards the front door, eager for them both to go off and have a fabulous time together.

'We'll get out of your way then, Edel, leave you and Les Dawson to it.' Jimmy winked, held his hands up good-naturedly, smiling at the old lady before kissing her on the cheek.

It was Edel's turn to blush then. The sheer size of Jimmy, his presence in the room. There was just something about the man that was so captivating. If he stayed here any longer he was going to make her go giddy at the knees.

'Go on, off with you both.' Giving her daughter a swift peck on the cheek, Edel had barely waited for them to step out the door before she closed it behind them, unable to contain herself any longer before she screeched with excitement. Clapping her hands together wildly, she practically skipped to the kitchen to pour herself a cheeky celebratory gin and tonic.

Now that was a couple in the making if ever she saw one. Colleen looked smitten tonight, and if she wasn't much mistaken, Jimmy Byrne did too. Sod her Colleen and all her sensible comments about Jimmy not being her type. The girl never left the flat enough to know what her type was. Besides, as the old saying went, mother always knew best, and if her hunch was right about Jimmy and Colleen, then she would be buying herself a fancy hat in no time.

Those two were destined for each other. Edel just knew it.

'You look gorgeous, Colleen!' Running around to the passenger side of his Range Rover, Jimmy Byrne opened the car door and offered Colleen a seat. He was determined to make a good impression tonight, to make sure Colleen had a night to remember. Seeing as she had good-old fashioned values as Edel had also warned him, he intended on being nothing more than a gentleman this evening.

Especially now he'd laid eyes on Colleen. She'd clearly made an effort for him, which could only be a good sign he figured. Colleen looked classy. Sophisticated even.

'You look stunning!' he said again as if he'd forgotten he'd already told her, giving Colleen one last approving glance as he jumped in his motor and started up the engine. He wasn't just saying it either. He was unable to take his eyes off the girl.

He was certain that his mother would most definitely approve, and the best thing was that Colleen didn't even appear to be trying to impress him. She was just being herself.

A little shy and nervous, but he could tell that underneath it all, she actually had a calm, self-assured confidence about her. As if she was happy in her own skin. Not needy like some of the other girls he'd dated.

Colleen didn't seem to care what Jimmy thought of her. That was a new one on him. A woman who was a bit aloof. Jimmy had to admit that he rather liked it. It was a refreshing change to his usual bad choice of gold-diggers that he seemed to attract. In fact, Colleen was the polar opposite of anyone Jimmy had ever gone out with: the obvious girls who wore too much make-up and not enough clothes. The girls that always seemed to have something to prove.

Colleen was a breath of fresh air.

'Thanks. I didn't know what to wear, really. I've been working in the shop with my mum since I finished college. I don't really get many excuses to dress up,' Colleen said blushing. Instantly annoyed with herself that part of her felt pleased with the reception she'd got from Jimmy tonight, flattered almost. Her faithful little black dress had been a good choice; Jimmy hadn't taken his eyes off her since they'd both said hello. Which was just as well, seeing as this was just about the only half decent thing she had in her wardrobe. She didn't really own anything fashionable or designer. She'd always preferred to wear clothes for their comfort rather than their look.

The way Jimmy was acting though, was having an odd effect on her. She felt suddenly attractive. It was a weird feeling. A nice feeling, and that's what caught Colleen off guard.

Glancing up at the flat, she spotted a glimpse of her mother peering out through the lounge window. Waving them both off enthusiastically.

'Oh God, how embarrassing,' Colleen said, offering Jimmy a small smile by way of apology as she nodded back to the house. 'I'm so sorry about her, she gets a bit carried away.'

Turning to see what Colleen was looking at, Jimmy laughed, as he clocked the old woman peeping out at them from behind the net curtains and waving at them both frantically, like a demented lunatic. He politely waved back.

'Ah, bless her. She's just looking out for you. She seems lovely, a real character!' Jimmy said with a small chuckle as he pulled away.

'She's a real something, all right,' Colleen replied, not wanting to add that her mother had been a nightmare this evening. Flapping about in a constant state of both panic and excitement, unable to contain herself at the fact that THE Jimmy Byrne was coming to their house.

She'd spent the day cleaning the flat like a demon, so much so that Colleen was convinced that even now in the car she could smell the overpowering stench of furniture polish and bleach as if they were ingrained in her clothes.

'I can't believe that she made you bloody cakes! Honestly, if I hadn't hurried getting ready tonight, and rescued you from her company, the woman would have probably had a good go at force-feeding you the entire plate before we left. I think she was more excited about this date than me.' Laughing along with

Jimmy now, relieved that he could see the funny side in her mother's quirky nature, Colleen relaxed a little.

'Ah, well it's a shame that she was looking forward to seeing me more than you were,' Jimmy said, mocking a face of a wounded man. 'Though I have to say I do like the sound of you "rescuing" me.'

Feeling herself blush again, this time at her choice of words and with the obvious lack of enthusiasm about their date evident in her voice, Colleen quickly backtracked.

'Oh, I didn't mean that I wasn't excited about seeing you. Well, I wasn't excited,' Colleen corrected herself, not wanting Jimmy to get the wrong idea and think that she was actually interested in him. 'I mean, it's lovely that you're taking me out and all that. It's just, well… if I hadn't called you my mother would have never let me hear the end of it. I mean, that's not the only reason I called you… Oh God, I'll shut up, shall I?' Biting her lip, Colleen realised that she was digging a hole for herself with every word she spoke.

The truth was she'd actually been dreading tonight. Her mother had gone on and on, nagging her into picking up the phone and thanking Jimmy for his flowers, and accepting his offer of a date. Colleen knew that her mother wouldn't let up about it until she'd phoned Jimmy. So, reluctantly, she'd called him, though she'd regretted it ever since. Still, she'd promised her mother one date, to get the woman off her back. One date, and she'd never have to see Jimmy again.

Now she was here, sitting next to him in his fancy car, she knew she'd been right to have doubts. Jimmy Byrne wasn't for her. The man just wasn't her type.

Her mother might think that Jimmy Byrne was a successful businessman but Colleen knew better. Jimmy had a reputation. Colleen had heard all the stories about the man. How he was ruthless when it came to business. How he was involved in all sorts of shady business dealings. Drugs and brothels. Colleen wasn't sure if the rumours were entirely true as she knew better than anyone how much people liked to exaggerate with gossip, but she was also a firm believer that there was no smoke without fire.

Jimmy was clearly doing well for himself, so he was earning his money from somewhere. That was one of the reasons Colleen had been so reluctant to go on this date tonight. She wasn't the type of girl that wanted to be part of Jimmy's 'colourful' life. The money, the power, it meant nothing to her. Material things didn't impress Colleen. She and Jimmy were opposites. Two people from completely different worlds.

He was a gangster. A charmer. She was bland and boring. He was totally out of her league and it wouldn't take him long to realise it either. She was shy, quiet, preferring to spend her time helping her mum out at the florist, and her evenings spent with her head inside a good book.

So she was convinced that Jimmy had made a mistake in asking her out. That any minute now, he'd realise how dull and boring she was and take her straight home.

'Look, if you don't want to come out with me, you really don't have to,' Jimmy said with a friendly smile as he realised the score here. He knew that this date had been more of Edel's idea than Colleen's and decided to just bite the bullet and say so.

'People around these parts talk, and I'm sure you've heard all sorts about me. Christ, even I've heard things about myself that I didn't even know I'd said or done.' He laughed. Then he looked at Colleen seriously. 'You're not silly, Colleen. You seem like the type of girl that is more than capable of making your own opinions,' Jimmy said, hoping that him being so honest would put the girl's mind at ease. He knew that he'd hit the proverbial nail directly on the head. 'You don't seem the type that would believe idle gossip from nosey bitter people who are jealous of my success.'

'I'm not, honest,' Colleen said, suddenly feeling very guilty for doing exactly that. It wasn't fair of her to prejudge him. She'd been dreading tonight for all the wrong reasons.

Jimmy was right. She hadn't even given him a chance and, so far, he'd been nothing but polite. A true gentleman. Buying her flowers, picking her up, charming her mother. Feeling consumed with guilt now at how rude she'd been, Colleen felt awful.

'I think it was just my mum pushing me into this, you know? I think she's taken a real shine to you, that's all,' Colleen said eventually, hoping that she hadn't offended Jimmy as they continued to drive in silence. She felt bad for assuming everything she'd heard about the man was fact. She was better than that. Of course he deserved a chance.

Deciding to make more of an effort, to be polite at least, Colleen persevered. 'She'll have us married off before we've even finished our starters tonight.'

'Well, I can't blame her. Your mum has good taste,' Jimmy joked, glad to see that Colleen was lightening up a little. He wasn't offended in the slightest; he'd already guessed that the reason Colleen had even contemplated going on a date with him was massively due to Edel playing her part and persuading her. In fact, that's exactly what he'd been depending on during the weeks he'd been going in there buttering up the old dear, for that very reason.

Only it appeared that the old lady was a lot easier to win over than her daughter was. He had to hand it to the mother, she'd even had him fooled. All that stuff that Edel had fed him about Colleen being keen to go on a date had just filled him with false hope. Colleen wasn't acting aloof or playing hard to get, she was only here because her mother had made her.

'Look, we don't have to think of tonight as a date if you're not comfortable with it. Let's just call it "friends," yeah? I get to spend an evening in your lovely company, and you get to keep your mum off your back. No strings, no funny business. We'll just enjoy some nice grub and conversation, and I'll have you home straight after dessert. How does that sound?' Jimmy said, shooting Colleen one of his killer smiles. 'Give me a chance, yeah? One date, that's it?'

'Okay.' Colleen smiled approvingly, her smile genuine now, as she visibly relaxed for the first time that evening. 'So where are we off to then?'

'I thought we could try out that new Italian place in Covent Garden. They do a mean bit of grub,' Jimmy said as he put his foot down once more, eager to get to the restaurant now that he knew Colleen was happy to be out on a date with him. 'Oh, and they do the best cannoli you've ever tasted.'

'What's a cannoli?' Colleen giggled, picking up on Jimmy's enthusiasm.

'Are you kidding me? You've never had a cannoli?' he laughed, shaking his head. 'Where have you been? They're only the best Italian desserts in the world. Oh, Colleen you my girl are in for a treat.'

He meant it too.

Tonight he was going to do everything in his power to make this the best night that Colleen had ever had. He felt slightly on edge, excited even at the thought of having to win over a girl's approval. He wasn't used to having to try so hard. The type of girls that he went for had always been so easily impressed, desperate to be the candy on Jimmy Byrne's arm; as long as Jimmy was throwing his money about they were happy to go along with whatever Jimmy did or said.

Colleen wasn't like that though. The girl didn't seem to care about his money or his kudos. Nor did she seem the type to play any games, which again only seemed to go in her favour.

This was new to him.

One thing Jimmy Byrne always enjoyed was a challenge, and this one he fully accepted. By the time he was done with Colleen Walsh the girl would be smitten with him. He was sure of it.

After all, he was Jimmy Byrne and everyone loved Jimmy.

CHAPTER NINE

Hearing a loud crash downstairs, Edel Walsh put her book down on her bedside table and looked over at the clock. It was almost midnight. She'd been waiting up for Colleen to get home so that she could find out all about her daughter's date.

They were being awfully loud downstairs though, now that they were back, considering how late it was.

Deciding that she would go down there and check that the two of them weren't up to anything untoward, Edel got out of bed and slipped into her dressing gown and slippers. But hearing another loud crash downstairs as she opened her bedroom door she bristled.

'Colleen? Is that you?' she shouted down the stairs, her instincts telling her that something was up.

She was met only by silence.

Until a few seconds later when she heard another almighty crash. This time the sound of glass shattering. Like an explosion. It must have been the main shop window?

Wrapping her robe tightly around her, Edel stood at the top of the stairwell unsure what she should do. Thinking that perhaps a car had crashed into the window, a second later her body tensed as she heard footsteps inside the shop.

'Colleen?' she shouted again. Knowing full well it wasn't her daughter down there, but hoping her voice was enough to deter whoever the intruder may be.

It didn't.

The footsteps continued. Along with the sound of her plants being kicked over and smashed.

Whoever it was down there was wrecking the place. There were several people by the sounds of it. Speaking in hushed whispers, and laughing amongst themselves.

About to go for the phone, Edel heard the sound of Mr Tiddles, her beloved cat, as a loud, guttural meowing drifted up the stairs. Hearing her little cat sounding so distressed, Edel didn't even stop to think twice about going down there.

Rushing down the stairs she switched the light on, her heart pounding inside her chest as she was faced with the group of masked intruders, with scarves wrapped around their faces and their hoods pulled up to conceal their features.

They'd destroyed the shop.

There was glass everywhere.

The floor was covered in shards of glass where the thugs had completely obliterated the large window. The bricks they'd used to break it were also strewn on the floor, along with the beautiful contents of her window display. The intruders had sprayed the place with graffiti too. Red and blue streaks of writing that was too illegible to read had been sprayed across the wall behind the till.

'The police are on their way,' Edel lied. Speaking with more bravado than she felt, she tried to stop her legs from trembling beneath her, hoping that if she stood her ground, the gang would leave her be.

The masked men didn't move.

Caught red-handed, they stood staring at her, as if challenging her on what she was going to do next.

It was them against her.

Five strapping lads and a little old lady.

She realised how stupid she'd been to come down the stairs.

As the tallest of the men stepped towards her, a crowbar gripped in his hand, his eyes firmly on her, Edel felt the fear creep in. Involuntarily flinching, she closed her eyes as she waited for the man to do his worst.

To strike her. To hurt her.

Only when she opened her eyes a few seconds later, she realised that he'd walked right past her.

He was at the till. Turning the key, he nodded, satisfied with himself as the drawer popped open. Then helping himself to the takings, he waved the small bunch of notes at Edel and laughed.

'It ain't fucking much,' he said, enjoying the fact that he was taunting her before turning his attention back to his boys. 'But it will do for a night's earn. Let's get the fuck out of here lads!' he shouted, as he shoved the money into his pockets and kicked over a large urn of flowers in Edel's direction.

They were gone. As quickly as they'd come, they fled through the large gaping hole in the main shop window. The same way they'd come in, Edel realised.

Shaking now, she went for the phone, about to call the police when she heard Mr Tiddles meowing once more. The sound muffled, as if he was somewhere far away.

Stumbling her way through the disarray, Edel searched amongst the damage, looking for the poor thing.

'Where are you Mr Tiddles?' she called, guessing that her poor baby was obviously terrified, and was hiding from all the noise and commotion.

Then seeing the upturned crate, she realised that the gang must have put her cat inside a box on purpose. Lifting the crate up, Edel gasped at the state of her precious little cat. The bastards had completely covered his lovely white fur in a bright blue spray paint.

Pulling the cat up to her chest, Edel stared around the shop in shock. Fragments of glass and broken flowers were scattered around her feet. The place was completely destroyed.

The bright yellow headlights of Jimmy Byrne's Range Rover pulled up outside, and the sound of Colleen's concerned voice sounded as her daughter jumped out of the car.

'Mum?' she shouted as she ran towards Edel.

'They've just taken off. There was five of them. Look at the state of the place, Colleen. They've wrecked the shop.' Relieved that Jimmy and Colleen had come back when they had, Edel broke down crying now as Colleen ran to her mother's side.

Jimmy had stayed in his car.

'I'm going after them,' he shouted, before speeding off down the road.

'Oh Colleen. Thank God, you're home. I was petrified. Look what they've done to my poor Mr Tiddles,' Edel said, holding the cat up for her daughter to see.

'Never mind poor Mr Tiddles. What about you?' Colleen said, seeing the look of fear on her mother's face.

It was the first time in Colleen's life she'd seen her mother look so helpless. It broke her heart to see her mother so genuinely scared.

'It's okay, Mum. Jimmy will find them, I know he will. He won't let them get away with this.'

CHAPTER TEN

'Man, that was wicked! Did you see the woman's face? She looked like she was going to fucking wet her knickers.' Ryan Denman laughed as he held out his hand for his cut of the money that his mate, Stuart Matthews, was currently dishing out.

'We didn't get much though. Still, that isn't the main payout.' Stuart shrugged as he counted out the measly takings that he'd robbed from the shop's till and handed each of the boys a five pound note. 'And what the fuck did you do to that fucking cat, mate? The thing looked like a smurf by the time you'd finished giving it a makeover. The woman will do her nut when she sees the state of it.'

'Good. I hate cats.' Ryan shrugged, glad that he'd given the boys a laugh, as he pulled out his cigarettes and passed them around to the group.

Huddled in the doorway together, lighting up cigarettes, they all went over the break-in, oblivious that just a few yards up the road, a motor was pulling up and they were about to have company.

The first thing Stuart Matthews knew about Jimmy Byrne being hot on their tail was when he felt the strong grip of hands around the back of his neck and the force of being dragged out of the doorway, away from his boys, who on seeing Jimmy's furious face, had all been rendered completely silent.

'Jimmy?' Stuart said, as he was swung around. 'Fuck man, you scared the life out of me. I thought you were Old Bill then for a second,' he said, trying to save face in front of his mates.

'Well it's just as well I well ain't. Isn't it?!' Jimmy sneered at the boy. Then shook his head at the others. 'Or you stupid little cunts would have all been nicked, wouldn't you?'

He was scanning the shop and the immediate vicinity for security cameras.

'Get your fucking arses around here now,' he ordered, still clutching Stuart by his neck as he dragged the older kid into the darkened alleyway next to the arcade.

'Fuck man, you're hurting me!' Stuart said, as Jimmy practically lifted him off his feet.

The man was pissed off. Stuart could see that. Though he wasn't sure why. He was taller than all his peers, but he was no match for Jimmy. The man was a brick shithouse.

'Not exactly fucking clever, is it? Vandalising the old girl's shop then hiding out in the next street. If I had no trouble finding you then the Old Bill won't either,' Jimmy warned.

'Sorry, Jimmy,' Stuart said, shaking his head in agreement as he sensed Jimmy Byrne's annoyance at him for not being cleverer about their getaway. 'I didn't think, Jimmy.' He was aware of how lame and pathetic he sounded, but right now his street cred was the least of his worries. Pissing off Jimmy Byrne was not something that Stuart Matthews had set out to do. Trying to justify his actions, he hadn't factored on Jimmy turning up personally to see that the job had been done to his standards. Tonight had been about impressing the man. Showing Jimmy that he was good for the job. The last thing he wanted to do was royally piss the man off.

'Well start fucking thinking then! 'Cos if you cause any shit for me, you really will be sorry. Do you hear me?' Jimmy said, finally loosening his grip on the older boy, and giving him a shove for good measure.

Stuart nodded obediently. Then hoping to impress the man, he added, 'We did exactly as you asked us, Jimmy. We made a nuisance of ourselves, smashed the place up a bit. The old girl was shitting herself.'

Jimmy couldn't argue with that. He'd seen the state of the shop, the state of Edel when he'd pulled up a few minutes ago. The boys had done a right number on the place. Stuart still had a lot to learn though, but he'd proved himself as more than willing tonight, and that stood for a lot in Jimmy's book.

'Yeah, you did good. Dish this out and then get the fuck out of here,' Jimmy said as he took out the wad of money he'd promised the boys. He handed Stuart the pile of notes.

'But the next time I pay you to do a job for me, make sure you lay low afterwards okay? The last thing I need is you lot getting a tug, and the Old Bill asking questions that might lead you back to me. If I can't even trust you to do that, you'll be out! Do you understand?'

CHAPTER ELEVEN

'I didn't realise this place would be so posh!' Colleen whispered, tucking her hair behind her ears self-consciously, as Jimmy signalled to the waiter to bring over his usual. The finest bottle of champagne the restaurant served.

Looking around the Mayfair restaurant nervously, Colleen couldn't help but feel out of place as she eyed the couple in the booth closest to them. She'd thought the last place that Jimmy had taken her to had been fancy, but this place was something else altogether. Here, people were dressed to the nines. The couple next to them no exception. Both wearing their fanciest clothes. The man was dressed in a black tuxedo and bow tie, the woman dressed head-to-toe in sequins, her floor-length gown shimmering under the crystal chandeliers that hung just above them.

Colleen, in contrast, was dressed in a white-and-red floral sundress, despite the fact that it was the beginning of December. Like the little black dress that she'd already worn, it was half decent. Fashion had never really been Colleen's priority, only now, tugging down her dress, feeling slightly frumpy, she wished that she had made it one.

'This restaurant is probably the fanciest place I've ever been to,' Colleen whispered across the table to Jimmy as she stared around in awe. 'In fact, there's no probably about it. It is.'

'We could learn a thing or two from the French. They seem to ooze class and sophistication, especially when it comes to fine dining,' Jimmy said, glad that the venue he'd picked tonight seemed to impress Colleen.

'They certainly do,' she agreed as she glanced at the à la carte menu that she couldn't understand. Then casting her eye back across the room, she took in every last detail. The tables all dressed with crisp white tablecloths and a whole array of sparkling cutlery and wine glasses. Even the waiters were dressed like extras from a James Bond movie: immaculate suits and fancy white gloves. All these people sipping fancy-looking cocktails, and glasses of champagne, whilst the pianist owned the huge centre stage in the middle of the restaurant, the hypnotic sound of the classical music he played setting the tone for the vibrant, civilised atmosphere.

'I must stick out like a sore thumb.'

'Don't be daft. You fit right in,' Jimmy said, unable to stop himself from smiling. Sensing the girl's apprehension, Jimmy squeezed Colleen's hand as if giving her his reassurance, while the waiter attended their table, popping the champagne cork loudly as he opened the bottle that Jimmy had requested, before filling both of their glasses.

Colleen took her glass, thanking the waiter politely.

Jimmy smiled at that too. Manners as well as gratitude. The girl looked thrilled to be here. Excited even.

That in itself was a novelty.

Most of the girls Jimmy had brought to places like this lapped it up, as if it was expected: part and parcel of being 'Jimmy's girl'.

'If anyone should feel out of place tonight, it's all these other women. You knock spots off them all, Colleen. You really have no idea, do you?'

Colleen smiled gratefully at Jimmy's kind words, despite the fact that she didn't believe them for a moment. He was just being nice, trying to set her mind at rest. They both knew that the women in here tonight were different: wealthy, upper class.

Adorned in the fanciest of clothes and more jewellery than Colleen had ever seen before in her life. It was the perfect little place to people watch and she couldn't help staring, star-struck every time she spotted a celebrity she recognised from the TV. This place was just unreal, like another world.

To Jimmy though, this was just the norm. This was his world, and he didn't seem at all fazed by the fact that people were constantly staring over at them both. At the notorious Jimmy Byrne.

'How's your mum doing now?' Jimmy asked, knowing full well that the events at the florist had left the woman shaken.

Tonight was the first night that he'd taken Colleen out on a date since the break-in, and they were making a proper night of it, so he figured that Edel was just getting on with it now. The woman was a tough old bird, he'd give her that.

'She's not easily scared my mum,' Colleen said with honesty. 'But I think it really shook her up.' She sipped her champagne, before adding, 'She really appreciates all your help, Jimmy. We both do. I don't think I could have left her if you hadn't sorted the shop out and given her that pager. She doesn't let the thing out of her sight. I guess it makes a difference to her knowing that you're at the other end if she gets any more trouble.'

'I'm just glad to be of service,' Jimmy said, and nodded. 'I don't blame her for being shaken up. The lads that wrecked the place were probably just some local scrotes. Knocking about causing trouble 'cos they were bored or something. It's a shame I didn't catch up with them. I would love to have taught the cocky little shits a lesson or two,' he said, his temper getting the better of him.

Colleen shook her head.

'You did more than enough, Jimmy. Seriously. Me and my mum are so grateful.' She meant it too. Jimmy had scoured the streets for the gang of lads that had ransacked the shop; despite not being able to find them, he'd still come back to the shop and spent hours clearing the place up and boarding up the window as best as he could, determined to make sure that Edel and Colleen didn't have any more unwelcome visitors during the night.

The next morning he'd turned up at the crack of dawn, together with a glazier who replaced the window for Edel with a special toughened glass at Jimmy's request. Jimmy had insisted on footing the bill for it all too.

'It's been well over a week now and they haven't come back. Maybe you're right? Maybe it was just a bunch of kids causing trouble.' Colleen shrugged. 'Maybe now they've damaged the shop they've moved on to bother someone else?'

'Yeah, let's hope so.' Jimmy nodded, though he could see that Colleen wasn't completely convinced. 'Are you sure you're okay being out tonight? Going to the club and everything. If you don't want to stay out that late, we can give it a miss. I can drop you home a bit earlier? It's no bother,' Jimmy said, seeing the look of concern etched on Colleen's face. The girl was clearly worried sick about her mother, and Jimmy could relate.

'No honestly it's fine. My mum insisted that I go out and enjoy myself tonight. She wanted me to come out,' Colleen reasoned.

'And more importantly, did you want to come out?' Jimmy said with a grin, seeing Colleen blush as he deliberately toyed with her.

'Well, I'm here, aren't I?' Colleen smiled, playing down the fact that actually she did want to see Jimmy again. Despite all the things that Colleen had heard about Jimmy, he had surprised her. He'd come round to the flat every day since the break-in, but with her mother there, they'd had no time alone. Colleen had been looking forward to her date with Jimmy tonight.

She'd been wrong to judge him without getting to know him first. Jimmy was nothing but the perfect gentleman. Taking her out to only the best places. Insisting on paying for everything, and after how he had helped her and her mother, Colleen couldn't help but feel herself really starting to like him.

'Yeah, your mother mentioned that you were looking forward to tonight,' Jimmy laughed then, hinting at the conversation he'd had with Edel when he'd gone to pick Colleen up.

'Oh Christ, what else did she say?' Colleen rolled her eyes playfully, as she realised that Jimmy was teasing her. Her mother had probably told Jimmy all sorts while she was upstairs getting ready. Unable to help herself the woman had no filter at all when it came to speaking her mind.

'Oh, nothing much, she just said that you had been getting ready for ages. That you were really excited about coming out tonight.' Jimmy pursed his lips.

'Well, what can I say? I have a thing about French cuisine.' Colleen giggled.

'Oh you only came for the food, eh? And here I was thinking that I must be doing something right, seeing as this is our second date. Unless, of course, you're only here to please your mother again?' Jimmy teased. Feeling smug. Safe with the knowledge that he already seemed to have won the girl over. Colleen wasn't going to be such the challenge that Jimmy had first anticipated.

Colleen raised her brows at that comment. She deserved it. It was, after all, the only reason that she'd gone out with Jimmy in the first place.

'Look, I'm just going to be honest with you, Jimmy. I'm not sure what I expected at first. I mean, I've heard all these stories about you.' Colleen shrugged. 'People around these parts talk and whenever your name comes up, it's always been linked with something shady that's gone on. Maybe they're just stories, I don't know.' Saying it out loud, she knew that she sounded ridiculous even to herself and Jimmy's nonplussed reaction was making her doubt everything she'd ever heard about the man.

'Stories? About me?' Feigning innocence, Jimmy raised his brow pretending that he had no idea what Colleen was talking about. Which only made her laugh.

Jimmy wasn't a silly man. He knew what she was getting at.

'People can be very jealous, Colleen. If they see someone doing well for themselves, of course they talk. It's human nature. Most people can't seem to help themselves but drag another man down, especially if it makes them feel better about their own dreary, sad lives,' Jimmy said, his cool, calm reaction speaking volumes about his attitude towards local gossip. Jimmy didn't care.

That alone was enough to make Colleen realise that was all it was, rumours.

'Trust me, though, not one of those backstabbers would have the balls to say any of their lies to my face. It's all just chat! Mindless bullshit,' Jimmy said, before taking a mouthful of his drink. 'When it comes to work, I take my business very seriously. Yes, I can be ruthless. Yes, I piss a lot of people off. But that's work. It's how I earn my living. It's not who I am.'

Colleen nodded in agreement. She could see that about Jimmy. He was the complete opposite of what she'd expected. What she'd been led to believe. Jimmy was funny and charismatic, not only that but he had a certain charm about him too. He made Colleen feel safe.

It was a weird feeling.

'I guess, you're not who I expected,' she said, trying to play down the fact that Jimmy Byrne had actually really surprised her.

'So I've exceeded your expectations then?' Jimmy said, teasing Colleen as he placed his hands on hers.

The warmth between them made Colleen's stomach flutter. Enjoying their date immensely now, she was about to answer when a loud voice behind them interrupted them mid-conversation.

'Well isn't this looking very cosy.'

An attractive-looking couple were approaching their table; Colleen felt certain that she recognised the stocky man, with his tanned olive skin and handsome chiselled looks. She couldn't place him though. Familiar as he was, Colleen figured she must have seen him around somewhere. Eyeing the young girl at his side, she thought how stunning the pair were. Like two models from a magazine.

'Fancy bumping into you here, eh.' The man, slightly younger than Jimmy, beamed, opening his arms and hugging his friend, as he stood up to greet him.

'A coincidence indeed,' Jimmy replied to the shorter man.

Despite returning his friend's hug, he looked unimpressed by the unexpected interruption.

'Colleen. This is Alex Costa. My business partner,' Jimmy said, making the polite introductions that he knew were expected. 'And this is his…' Unsure what Tiffany was to Alex, despite the fact that Alex had been 'dating' the girl on and off for a good six months, he said, 'The delightful Tiffany. Smith.'

'Careful there, Jimmy, you almost said girlfriend then! You know how funny he gets when you stick a label on anything. Especially our relationship.' Tiffany cackled loudly, the thick mask of make-up she'd painted on her face almost cracking as she smiled. Not waiting to be asked if she would like to join them, she pulled out a chair at their table.

Taking in the girl's heavily painted face, and the hot pink minidress, with a fluffy white ostrich feather jacket wrapped around her shoulders, Colleen could see that Tiffany was no wallflower.

Other diners hadn't been able to help notice the girl either as she sat down at the table, sticking her chest out, proudly displaying the ample cleavage that spilled out the top of her dress.

Even Colleen didn't know where to look.

'Please, join us,' Jimmy said, his sarcasm completely lost on Tiffany as she smiled back at him, already sitting down.

'You don't mind do you, Colleen?' Jimmy asked, his mood changed now that they had company. Exchanging a look, he raised his eyes at Colleen as if to apologise for the unannounced guests.

''Course she don't mind!' Alex spoke up before Colleen had a chance. Then turning to the waiter behind him, he clicked his fingers arrogantly. 'You got another couple of glasses there, mate?'

Colleen looked at Jimmy.

'Honestly. The more the merrier,' she mouthed, picking up on the vibe that Jimmy wasn't best pleased about Alex and Tiffany joining them. She didn't want to cause any problems by letting him know that secretly she'd been looking forward to spending time with him. Alone. Besides, if these were Jimmy's friends then she wanted to make a good impression.

'It's very nice to meet you both,' she said, holding out her hand to greet Alex, though he didn't reciprocate. Instead he busied himself pouring out two glasses of champagne for himself and Tiffany.

'We should make a toast,' Alex said, holding his glass up and staring at Jimmy, a mischievous glint in his eye that said he was well aware that he was winding his mate up.

'What should we drink to, eh? New friendships?'

Jimmy nodded. He could see that Alex was in one of his volatile moods again. Coked up to his fucking eyeballs he and Tiffany had no doubt spent the early part of the evening shoving gear up their noses.

Alex knew exactly what he was doing turning up here tonight. This was no coincidence. Jimmy had purposely not told Alex that he was coming here, for this very reason. The last thing he needed was Alex hanging around like a bad smell and fucking everything up for him now he'd got this far with Colleen.

'What is this then? Must be your seventh date, isn't it?' Alex asked, the sincerity of his smile not reaching his eyes as he spoke.

'Second actually.' Colleen smiled, squeezing Jimmy's hand. Though suddenly Jimmy didn't seem as forthcoming in talking about their dates.

'Only the second?' Alex said. Staring a little too intently at the girl, he decided on the spot that he didn't like her.

'I feel like I haven't seen you all week, mate?" Alex eyed Jimmy then.

'Me and Colleen have been enjoying each other's company,' Jimmy reasoned, smiling at Colleen to lighten the mood before adding: 'And last time I checked I didn't have to run my every movement through you, Alex.' Jimmy's eyes flashed a warning. He was determined not to retaliate to Alex's bullshit, but Alex was purposely trying to push his luck. Even coming here tonight was a massive piss-take.

The bloke had almost jeopardised everything. If Colleen had recognised Alex from his dealings with the councillors and builders at the developments, the bloke could have completely blown their cover. Alex should have stayed the fuck away, and let Jimmy deal with his business any way he saw fit.

But, of course, Alex wouldn't have thought about that, would he? That was the man's problem. High on gear, Alex wasn't capable of thinking much about anything at all. All that shit did to him was make him even more paranoid and aggy and Jimmy wasn't in the mood for his dramatics tonight.

'How about you two? Have you been together long?' Colleen said. Sensing the atmosphere at the table, and desperate to defuse the situation, she turned her attention to Tiffany, who, unlike her, seemed oblivious to the ever-growing tension. Tiffany seemed more interested in her drink by all accounts. Downing the last of her champagne she tapped her nails impatiently against the empty glass, indicating to Alex that she wanted a refill.

Alex however just snubbed her.

'Together? Oh we're not together, are we, Alex?' Tiffany laughed. Then seeing the confused expression on Colleen's face she continued, 'There's three words that you can't use when it comes to me and Alex: "Together," "Relationship," and "Girlfriend".' Tiffany rolled her eyes in Alex's direction and continued to talk as if he wasn't even sitting in the room let alone sitting right next to her. 'He's what you could call a commitment-phobe,' Tiffany said in a pouty voice as she stuck her tongue out at Alex playfully. 'What are we? I guess you could call us friends with benefits, though the benefits lately have been few and far between,' she said, deliberately trying to get a rise from her boyfriend. All they'd done lately was argue and tonight looked like it would be no exception.

'Oh wind it in, Tiffany. I'm sure the last thing these two want to listen to is you harping on about how bloody miserable you always are.' The undercurrent of her words instantly irritating Alex.

'And why am I always so bloody miserable?' Tiffany rolled her eyes once more then holding the empty bottle of champagne up, undeterred by Alex's snide comment, she turned her attention to Colleen.

'Shall we get another bottle or what? You'll have a few more drinks, won't you, Colleen?' Tiffany said to Colleen for backup.

Looking at Jimmy, not sure what to say as an answer, Colleen could see that the girl was already wasted. Slurring her words, and intent on causing a row with Alex, she thought that Tiffany had probably had more than enough, but she was too shy to say. So as Jimmy shrugged, resigned to the fact that Tiffany and Alex were going to order more drinks no matter what, Colleen simply nodded.

'Good. It's nice having a drinking partner and I fancy getting wasted,' Tiffany said, shooting another stare in Alex's direction. 'Especially seeing as there's nothing else to do tonight.'

'Great. You keep drinking, love,' Alex sneered at the girl. 'Hopefully you'll drink enough to pass out, and then we won't have to listen to your whiney fucking voice no more.'

Jimmy, remaining silent while he watched the awkward exchange, glared at Alex now. He was pissed off at how tonight was panning out; if Tiffany and Alex were both on one and drinking, it only meant one thing: Tonight was only going to get a lot worse.

Alex not only had the hump, but seemed intent on ruining Jimmy and Colleen's evening too. And Alex Costa never did anything by halves. If he was intent on ruining Jimmy and Colleen's evening he would do so, as only the man could.

In spectacular Alex Costa style.

Staring ahead at the long queue of girls all waiting to use the loo in the fancy toilets of Mayfair's Tranquillity Nightclub, Tiffany Smith grabbed Colleen's hand and led her to the disabled toilet at the end.

''Scuse us. She's not very well,' Tiffany lied, marching ahead of the row of girls as she and Colleen jumped the queue. 'I'd mind out of the way unless you want to get covered in puke.'

Triumphant, as the two girls bundled inside the cubicle and locked the door behind them, Tiffany pouted.

'See! That's how you do it, babe!' she said as she hitched up her minuscule dress and sat down on the toilet, clearly not fussed about Colleen seeing everything that she had.

Colleen was already of the understanding that Tiffany was anything but shy.

'We'd be out there queuing up for ages, and that's valuable drinking time lost.' Tiffany grinned as she finished having a wee, before getting up and letting Colleen have her turn.

Tiffany was hammered. The girl had drunk more than her body weight in champagne tonight, and since they'd arrived at the club, she'd had her fill of cocktails too. Still, at least the alcohol seemed to lighten up her mood.

Colleen was actually really enjoying Tiffany's company, now that she had got to know the girl. Sure, she was a bit brash and outspoken, but Colleen admired her confidence.

Tiffany didn't hold back; Colleen liked that about her.

Sitting down on the toilet herself, Colleen giggled as she almost slipped and fell off the seat. Holding on to the cubicle wall so that she could try and keep her balance, Colleen realised that she was drunk. It wasn't just her head that was spinning, the small cubicle was too. She needed some water.

'So? You and Jimmy seem pretty smitten with each other?' Tiffany said, too busy reapplying her make-up and examining herself in the mirror to notice how drunk Colleen was.

'Yeah, he's nice. He's different to how I first thought.'

'Oh yeah, Jimmy's different all right,' Tiffany said raising her eyes knowingly. 'He can be a real charmer, but I wouldn't wanna cross the man. If you think Alex has a temper on him, you should see Jimmy in action.'

'Really?' Colleen said, finding Tiffany's words a little hard to believe. She might have only been on a couple of dates with the man, but after seeing him every day back at her flat this week, already Colleen was starting to feel as if she really knew Jimmy. Tiffany was probably just exaggerating. 'Well, he's been nothing but the perfect gentleman to me,' she said, a little more curtly than she intended.

'He's trying to impress you!' Tiffany grinned, pouting into the mirror as she smudged her lipstick. She turned to her new friend. 'I've never seen him look so smitten if I'm honest. He's like a different man when he's around you. I think he really likes you.'

'Do you think?' Pleased at Tiffany's words, Colleen tried to play down her happiness that even Tiffany had noticed the effort that Jimmy was making with her tonight.

Colleen wasn't sure if it was the amount of alcohol that she'd consumed, but she was really starting to fall for Jimmy. She had a sneaky suspicion that her feelings were reciprocated but it felt nice to hear that Tiffany thought so too.

'So, how long have you and Alex been friends?' she asked, wondering how Alex and Tiffany would even class themselves as mates seeing as the pair of them had done nothing but spend the entire night constantly making snide remarks to each other.

'It's complicated,' Tiffany said, absentmindedly as she searched around inside her handbag. 'It's a love-hate relationship, only there isn't much love. In fact there isn't any love.' Tiffany shrugged, not sounding overly bothered. Smiling as she found what she'd been looking for, she pulled out a small vial of white powder.

'Alex is a bit of a commodity. Half the time I don't even know why he bothers to invite me out. I think he just wants company, though fuck knows why when he can't even be bothered to speak to me. Most of the time we go out he makes me feel like I'm fucking invisible.'

Tiffany was speaking honestly now. The drink had loosened her tongue, and the paranoia from snorting so much gear had started to kick in. Though she wasn't just paranoid. Alex was being really off with her, much worse than usual.

'I don't know what it is that's pissed the man off tonight, but he seems intent on taking whatever it is out on me and I'm not having it,' Tiffany said, her nose firmly put out of joint at the way she'd been treated this evening.

'Maybe you should talk to him?' Colleen offered, unsure about getting involved in the girl's relationship problems. She'd only met Tiffany and Alex a few hours ago, and to say their relationship looked volatile would have been an understatement to say the least.

'Talk?' Tiffany squawked loudly as if Colleen had just said something completely ridiculous. 'Alex doesn't do talking. In fact the man doesn't do fucking much. Do you know what, we ain't even sleeping with each other. How fucked up is that?' Tiffany made eyes at Colleen as if it was the craziest thing she'd ever said out loud. 'I mean, I'm not blowing my own trumpet but fucking hell, he's lucky to have a girl like me. Especially after the way he treats me. No one else would put up with his shit. I dunno why I do half the time.'

Concentrating on tipping the contents of the vial onto the edge of her closed fist, Tiffany brought her wrist up to her nose, pressing her finger against one of her nostrils, before snorting back the line of cocaine expertly in one swift movement. 'All he wants is a sidekick, you know. Just some dolly bird on his arm, so he looks the part. The truth is, the bloke's so miserable, if it wasn't for the fact that he showered me in gifts, and this shit, then even I wouldn't stick around.' Rubbing the remnants of residue from the corner of her nose before reapplying her lipstick, Tiffany shook the little vial of gear in Colleen's direction.

'Do you want some?' she asked, pleased when Colleen shook her head, refusing her offer.

'Good. I've only got a tiny bit left, and with the mood Alex is in tonight, I've got a feeling that he won't be giving me anymore,' Tiffany said, placing the small vial back inside her handbag before watching as Colleen rinsed her hands under the tap.

'Men huh? They make out we're the difficult ones.' Tiffany was getting more animated as she spoke, her tone changing as the cocaine started to take immediate effect.

Colleen could hear the angst building with every word. Drunk, and now high on cocaine, Colleen had a feeling this wasn't going to end well for the girl if she started to work herself up.

Ever the peacemaker, Colleen shrugged. 'I think you're reading too much into it all,' she said lightly, hoping that her little white lie would be all it took to help Tiffany calm down a bit. 'You might not have noticed but Alex hasn't been able to keep his eyes off you all night. I've been watching him, the way he looks at you when you're not looking. Do you know what I think? I think he's playing hard to get. Some men are like that. They like playing games. Keeping you on your toes. Especially as he probably knows how much attention you get from other men.'

'Do you reckon?' Tiffany asked, hanging on to Colleen's words as if they were a lifeline. 'I never really thought about it like that, but now you've said it, it makes sense, doesn't it? I mean, if he didn't like me, he wouldn't keep inviting me out with him, would he? And I do get a lot of attention from other men.'

Colleen nodded, glad to see that her words of reassurance seemed to be doing the trick. The truth was that Colleen didn't think Tiffany was the problem tonight at all. Something was going on between Alex and Jimmy. Colleen didn't know what was going on, but she'd picked up on the veiled undercurrent between the men, and she could tell that Jimmy was properly pissed off about something. It was as if Alex was purposely trying to goad the man into an argument.

But then he had been pretty mean to Tiffany, and Colleen could tell that Alex had taken a disliking to her too. He'd spoken to her a few times, mainly asking her questions about herself, but Colleen couldn't shake the feeling that Alex was interrogating her. That he didn't actually want to know, nor care about anything about her.

Maybe Tiffany was right. Maybe Alex was just a horrible, miserable person?

'Do you know what, Colleen? You're actually all right, you know,' Tiffany said, giving her new friend the royal seal of approval as she hooked her arm inside Colleen's and guided them both back through the throng of girls still queuing the length of the nightclub's toilets.

'Jimmy normally goes for pretentious bimbo types. Girls that look a bit like me, only they ain't as clever as me, you know,' Tiffany said, not realising that a bimbo was exactly how Alex and Jimmy both classed her. 'You got something about you. I reckon you're a lot tougher than you look too.'

And Tiffany really hoped Colleen was. She'd need to be if she was seriously thinking about getting involved with the likes of Jimmy Byrne. Tiffany was hoping that the girl would be sticking around.

'You're right about Alex too I reckon. I ain't going to let the bastard get me down. If he wants to sit around looking miserable then that's up to him, but I'm going to get out there tonight and have some fun!' Feeling much better now that Colleen had helped her put everything into perspective, Tiffany smiled wickedly. 'If Alex Costa wants to play games, then let me tell you, darling, he has well and truly met his match.'

CHAPTER TWELVE

Alex Costa was drunk.

Barely able to stand now, he'd moved on from the copious amounts of expensive champagne and was downing Scotch like it was going out of fashion. Though the alcohol was doing nothing to soothe the thunderous mood he was in; if anything it only seemed to magnify it.

'So what happened to our little plan then, Jimmy?' Alex spat, as he drained the dregs of his drink and signalled for the waitress to bring him another. 'I thought we were going to drive the old cow out? I thought you'd paid those kids to go round there and fuck her place up? Only instead of shitting the old girl up and making her want to fucking leave her flat, now you're dating her daughter? What the fuck's going on, Jimmy?'

'I know what I'm doing, Alex,' Jimmy said rubbing his temples; he'd been doing his best to avoid getting drawn into an argument with Alex tonight, but now that the girls had gone off to the ladies, and they'd been left alone, Jimmy knew that Alex wouldn't just leave it.

'Two dates? You've been around there every night this week? Fuck me, Jimmy. Who are you kidding? We could have had it all dealt with by now. What's the matter, eh? Are you going soft or what?'

'You're drunk,' Jimmy said, tapping his fingers on the hard cold leather of the seat beneath him. He was trying to do everything in his power not to jump up out of his seat and bury his fist inside Alex's throat for cunting him off the way he was tonight.

Jimmy held his temper though. Not wanting to lose his shit in public, with everyone watching. That wasn't how he worked. Patience was Jimmy's virtue, especially when there were witnesses present. Tomorrow, he'd deal with Alex properly, when the man was sober enough to comprehend the extent of his anger. Alex would be fucking sorry for his actions here tonight, Jimmy would make sure of that.

'And as it happens the plan's changed. I'm doing things my way. Edel and Colleen just need a nudge in the right direction. Maybe driving them out isn't the right way to go about it.'

'Are you serious?' Alex sneered, unable to believe what he was hearing. 'We need them out and pronto. That's the only way. What are you thinking of doing? Fucking playing happy families with the pair of them? What next, you gunna pop the fucking question, Jimmy? Have a laugh, Jimmy.'

Knowing it was pointless trying to reason with Alex when he was in one of his moods, Jimmy didn't bother to answer, which only ignited Alex's temper further.

'You actually like her, don't you?' Alex said, the realisation only hitting him as he spoke the words. 'Fucking hell! I've seen and heard it all now. Is this your new grand plan? You want to settle down with that? Mrs fucking goody two shoes. Fuck me, Jimmy, the girl's duller than a three watt lightbulb,' Alex said raising his voice. 'You must be desperate.'

Then, recalling the conversation he'd had with Jimmy about his mother harping on at him to settle down, find himself a decent wife, have a few kids, Alex realised that this was exactly what this was about.

Jimmy's little plan to get Edel and Colleen Walsh out of their flat had somehow been sidetracked. Now the man seemed to be playing the long game. He was going to butter them up somehow first, and then move them both on, bagging himself a new wife and mother of his kids in the process.

'Maybe I should take a leaf from your book, eh?' Jimmy said, unable to hold his tongue any longer. 'Land myself someone like Tiffany, huh? Another wannabe gold-digger that's only out for my fucking money.' The vein in the side of his temple was twitching. Taking a deep breath, the tension palpable between them now, Jimmy'd had enough.

Alex could be a nasty fucker with a drink inside him, and judging by the snippy remarks he'd been making towards Colleen all evening, he'd clearly taken an instant dislike to the girl. He'd be even worse when she came back with Tiffany, and Jimmy wasn't prepared to put up with it.

'Why don't you put your claws away, Alex? You're acting like a first prize cunt. This is my business, so let me deal with it!' Jimmy said, his tone sharp as he let Alex know that in no uncertain terms would he entertain his bullshit. 'She's a nice girl. A decent girl. I've done a lot worse.'

'Ain't we both,' Alex sneered.

His mood worsening now that he and Jimmy had just rowed, he stared over to where Tiffany and Colleen had just emerged through the crowd. As if right on cue.

Just the sight of Tiffany lapping up all the attention that she was receiving as she strutted towards the VIP booth in her six inch hooker heels made Alex cringe. She looked like she'd styled herself on a cheap, tacky Barbie doll, in her hot pink minidress.

Jimmy was right about her too. They both knew it. The girl was only here for the money and the gear that Alex plied her with. No self-respecting girl would put up with Alex's temperament. Yet as long as he kept throwing his money at her, and supplying her with enough shit to shove up her nostrils, the girl seemed to be happy to just keep coming back for more.

'And while we're on the subject of Tiffany, you need to rein in how much shit you're giving her. She's off her fucking face.'

Tiffany could be a liability at the best of times. The girl was opinionated and with a gob on her to rival the size of the Dartford Tunnel she didn't often hold back.

Staring over at Colleen he was relieved to see her smiling. Her going off on her own with Tiffany, out of earshot, had made Jimmy feel on edge. Alex always swore that he didn't ever discuss their private affairs with the girl, but Jimmy wasn't entirely convinced. Alex could be just as bad as Tiffany when he was on one, a right nasty bastard, especially with a drink in him. Who knows what the man had said when he'd been caught up in the moment?

Still, Colleen looked happy enough. In fact, judging by the way the two girls were talking and laughing so animatedly with each other, it looked as if they were genuinely getting on.

Unaware of the argument the two men had just had, and with Colleen's words of advice still circling around her head, Tiffany decided that she was going to take the bull by the horns and try and make amends with Alex. They'd already wasted enough of the evening as it was.

'Ah, did you miss me, baby?' Tiffany purred, strutting in between the two men, and draping herself seductively across Alex Costa's lap.

If he wanted to play games, then so be it. Tiffany was a pro at them. She was going to kill the man with kindness. She had no choice. She was low on gear and if she wanted more coke then she knew she had to tolerate Alex's sulky moods. She'd done a lot worse to get what she wanted.

'Leave it out, Tiffany.' Alex shrugged the girl away from him, irritated as she started slipping her fingers under the fabric of his shirt.

'Oh come on, Alex, lighten up a little bit yeah!' Tiffany said tartly, realising that Alex wasn't going to make this easy for her.

Grabbing her hand harder than he meant to, Alex removed it himself.

'Ouch! That hurt,' Tiffany exclaimed. Then seeing his stony face, she gave up. Who was she kidding? Alex wasn't playing hard to get. He was a bona fide arsehole and no matter how nice she was to him, the man was still going to treat her like she was nothing.

'You know what, you can be a right moody prick sometimes,' she said, deciding to stand up for herself. Though one insult was as far as she got.

Alex was up off his seat. Incensed that Tiffany thought she could cunt him off so publicly, talking to him like that, he launched the girl off him.

Screaming loudly as she hit the club floor with a thump, Tiffany half expected Alex to apologise to her. To say that he didn't mean to push her. Sprawled out on the floor, she looked up and saw the steely glint in his eyes. He didn't give a shit about her. Other people were looking over now too. Clubgoers standing nearby were all watching with fascination as the scene unfolded in front of them, pointing over to where Tiffany was lying in a heap on the floor. She felt her cheeks redden. Alex was making a holy show out of her. Humiliating her in front of everyone.

She tried to save face. 'What the fuck did you do that for?' Rubbing her knees, the skin grazed and bleeding where she'd scuffed them across the coarse black carpet, she was grateful that Colleen was immediately at her side.

'Are you okay, Tiff?' Colleen asked, looking up at Jimmy as if he should do something. She was horrified at Alex's actions.

Though Tiffany wasn't done yet.

'What the fuck is your problem, Alex?' Trying to get back on to her feet, the girl was beyond mortified, her embarrassment quickly turning to anger. Alex had gone too far this time. 'I don't even know why you invite me out to these places. You don't even like me.' Tiffany was close to tears. 'You're a fucking bully, do you know that?' Tiffany said now, no longer caring if she pissed the man off for good this time. No amount of money was worth being treated like this. She was done, and apparently so was Alex.

'And you're a fucking mess! Look at you! I bet you've hoovered all that shit up your hooter already, haven't you?' Alex shook his head with disgust, as he took in the sight of the girl still sprawled across the floor. Everything he despised about women. Desperate and needy. Alex was simply surprised that he'd put up with the slapper for as long as he had, if he was honest.

She was right, he couldn't stand her and he was bored of pretending otherwise.

'Why don't you do yourself a favour, Tiffany, and fuck off home!' he said, shooting the humiliated girl one final look of contempt, stomping off, leaving her in floods of tears.

Jimmy stepped in then. Giving Tiffany a helping hand up.

'He's had too much to drink. Ignore him. He didn't mean any of that,' he said, feeling sorry for the girl.

Tiffany knew better.

'Do you know what? Fuck him! Even if he came crawling back to me tomorrow on his hands and knees, begging me for forgiveness, I ain't interested no more,' she said, trying to control the tremor in her voice that almost gave away the hurt she was trying to conceal. 'The man's got issues, and I'm done with trying to work out what the fuck they are.'

Fighting back her tears as she tried to regain her composure, she felt mortified that she had let Alex Costa get the better of her in front of all these people. She just wanted to go home now. Get out of this ridiculous outfit she was wearing and snuggle up with her cat.

'I'll have a word with him. He was bang out of order tonight,' Jimmy said, seeing the look on Colleen's face too. She did not look one bit impressed.

'I think we should put her in a cab, Jimmy. It's the least we could do,' Colleen said, linking arms with Tiffany. 'I think I'm going to go home too.'

Jimmy nodded. He could clump Alex for the drama the man had caused tonight. In fact, if he stayed here for a minute longer he probably would.

'Yeah, I think it's safe to say that the night is over,' he agreed.

Throwing one final look at Alex, Jimmy shook his head wearily as he led Colleen from the club, while Alex stood at the bar downing more shots, no doubt celebrating the fact that he'd achieved his mission and ruined the evening for them all.

CHAPTER THIRTEEN

Tossing and turning in her sleep, Colleen felt panic engulfing her.

She was trapped somewhere. In her nightmares. In her dreams. Trapped. Lost inside a deep forest, her eyes searching for an escape route. Only there wasn't one. It was dark and murky and Colleen was running. Desperately trying to get away from something or someone.

Who was she running from? A person? A monster?

Looking down at her feet, the skin torn and scratched by the broken twigs that cracked beneath her; her pale skin turning red, as she felt the heat.

The forest was on fire. The flames were drawing in. Cackling loudly as black smoke filled her lungs.

Her chest felt tight, constricted. She could barely breathe. She could smell burning. Mild at first, then suddenly all-consuming. Heavy on her chest. Making her cough and splutter as she fought to get her breath.

She was awake. Back in her bedroom.

Wondering if she was still drunk from her night at the club with Jimmy, disorientated, she sat bolt upright in her bed. Trying to focus on something, to see through the darkness of the room, her eyes searched through the grey haze of smoke that swept in under the gap in her bedroom door.

The fire wasn't a nightmare. It was real, she realised, gripped with fear, her gaze resting on the crackling and spitting of bright yellow fire that she could see through the crack in the doorway.

'Fire,' she said, as if the word needed to be said aloud so that what she was seeing could engage with her brain.

'FIRE!'

Paralysed with fear and panic, Colleen could barely think straight. She didn't know what to do first. All she did know was that she had to move and quickly. The flat was on fire.

This was bad. Really bad.

'MUM?' Shouting at the top of her voice, the large influx of toxic smoke-filled air made her instantly splutter. Coughing manically, her chest wheezed.

Keep low.

That's what they said to do in all those fire safety adverts she'd seen when she'd been at school.

Heat and smoke rises. She needed to stay low to the floor.

Crawling on her hands and knees, the smoke was getting thicker. She could barely see her own hand stretched out in front of her now. Rubbing her hand on the carpet, feeling her way to the end of the bed, her fingers made contact with her small wooden chair in the corner of the room. Reaching up, Colleen grabbed at a T-shirt that she knew was draped over the chair's arm. Wrapping it around her face, covering her nose and mouth, she hoped that it would act as some kind of a filter.

The room was getting darker, foggier. Filling up with thick clouds of smoke. Her eyes were stinging now too. Watering, she could feel the blistering heat coming up through the floor beneath her.

Then she heard the loud sound of glass shattering downstairs in the shop. The sudden explosion making her jump with fright.

The window that Jimmy fixed.

The rapid force of the heat breaking the glass panes.

Colleen needed to get to her mother. She needed to make sure that she was okay.

Focus, she told herself sternly, as she continued crawling along the floor towards the bedroom door.

Maybe that's what the noise was, she thought, hopeful.

Her mother trying to get out. Or the Fire Service trying to get in.

Reaching up to the handle, Colleen wrenched the door open, the blast of heat that hit her making her recoil for a few seconds, shrinking back into her room once more before she took a deep breath and peered back out along the hallway.

The flames were far worse on the stairs. The fire was spreading rapidly throughout the building, the blaze licking its way up the wooden banisters towards them.

Colleen eyed her mother's bedroom door through the thick black smoke. It was closed. Fuelled by adrenaline and the fact that if they didn't get out of here soon they would both perish, Colleen pressed the T-shirt tightly to her face before making a run for it.

Running, she felt light-headed, dizzy as she pushed the bedroom door open, immediately closing it once she was inside. The smoke was even denser in her mother's room. It felt as if there was no oxygen in here at all.

She could hardly breathe.

'Mum?' Colleen called as she made her way to her mother's bed, feeling her way through the thick flumes of billowing smoke. Crouching back down, crawling towards the bed, the heat beneath the floor made the carpet beneath Colleen's knees feel hot.

'Mum, can you hear me?' Choking as she frantically patted down the mattress, her hands lifting the duvet up and sweeping the empty sheets in search of her mother, she realised the bed was empty.

'Mum are you in here?'

Looking over towards the window. It was still shut. The opening at the top of the glass far too small for a person to climb out. The only other way out was down the stairs.

Had her mother already got out?

Panicking that she'd been left alone in the flat, that she was trapped here all by herself, Colleen started for the bedroom door again. Stopping suddenly before she got there as she felt a niggling inside her.

Her instincts were kicking in. Her mother wouldn't have left without her. She knew that with a certainty. About to leave the room, Colleen's intuition told her not to be so hasty.

Crawling back around to the other side of the bed this time, to the narrow gap down beside the bed and the wall, Colleen reached out her hand, pressing on the carpet, until her fingers touched against something soft. Fine. Her mother's hair, splayed out around her head; her mother was lying on the bedroom floor.

'Mum, we need to get out of here. Mum, wake up.' She was crying now. Hysterical at finding her mother sprawled out on the floor, the reality of the situation was finally dawning on her.

They might die here tonight.

Colleen needed to get them out of here and fast.

'Mum, please. Wake up.' Wildly shaking her mother's unresponsive body, Colleen fought desperately to try and wake her up.

Edel didn't move.

Colleen had no choice but to try and hoist her up. Dragging her forcefully by her arms, using all her strength, she could barely move her. Her mother was a dead weight. Colleen wasn't even sure if her mother was still breathing.

Colleen was struggling too. Her own body getting weaker now as the T-shirt she'd wrapped around her head lay discarded on the bedroom floor where it had fallen in her struggle. She was breathing in too much toxic smoke. Choking frantically.

Turning on the floor, Colleen groped her way back through the darkness of the black, poisonous smoke.

Alert to a strange noise just outside the bedroom door as she neared it: a scraping sound. Scratching. Followed by a long strangled meowing.

Mr Tiddles. Her mother's precious cat. The poor thing was trapped out there on the hallway landing, petrified of the heat and the flames as it tried to claw its way inside the room to safety.

Opening the door, Mr Tiddles ran inside.

Only there wasn't safety here either.

It was a sanctuary of false pretence. A trap.

Now they were in here, there was no way out.

Colleen stared at the stairwell, the inferno too intense for her to even consider going down there. Her mother's room had no way out either. Their only hope would be to get back to Colleen's bedroom. She could open her window. Climb out onto the windowsill.

At least then she would be able to breathe.

Only she couldn't leave her mother. Crawling back to her mother's side once more, Colleen couldn't go any further.

She was too weak now. Her eyes blurry, she was losing her vision. She collapsed in a heap on the carpet. Unable to even lift her head up, she fought to stop her eyes from closing.

Reaching out behind her, she grabbed hold of her mother's hand, clutching it tightly as her chest wheezed, making her gasp loudly. Her lungs screamed for air.

They were both going to die, here, in this flat tonight.

Though Colleen wasn't fighting that fact anymore. Instead, finally closing her eyes, she was resigned to it.

CHAPTER FOURTEEN

Rushing down the corridor of University College London Hospital to the ward where one of the nurses had just told Jimmy Byrne he could find Edel and Colleen Walsh, Jimmy wasn't sure what to expect.

Colleen had sounded distraught when she had phoned him, crying hysterically as she relayed the night's events. Jimmy hadn't been able to believe what he was hearing. The shop and the flat had gone up in flames. Colleen and Edel had almost died.

Jimmy had driven down Euston Road like a demon to get here. Abandoning his Range Rover in the hospital car park, he'd hurried in towards the cubicle in the far corner, his eyes fixed on the lady perched at the end of the bed, not recognising the blackened, soot-covered face looking back at him, the whites of the lady's eyes so bright in comparison they looked as if they were glowing.

'Jesus, Edel?' Jimmy gasped, realising who it was. He rushed to her side, instinctively taking Edel's hand as she stared back at him seemingly unfazed. 'You look awful!'

Edel had aged suddenly. She was frailer somehow.

Until she opened her mouth that was. Wrenching the oxygen mask from her face, after a few seconds of coughing and spluttering, she found her voice.

'Oh that's just fecking charming, isn't it, Jimmy? I mean, I know my hair's a bit of a state but you don't need to be so rude.' Cackling with laughter, Edel shot Jimmy one of her crooked smiles.

Jimmy couldn't help smiling too, glad that Edel was in such good spirits after the horrific ordeal she'd endured.

'Thanks for coming, Jimmy,' Edel said sincerely, pleased that he had come. Colleen had not long gone off to find a payphone. Jimmy must have raced across London in record time to get here. The man was a diamond. Sensing the concern on his face, Edel pointed at the chair for him to sit down.

'Colleen's just gone off to get me a cup of tea. Not that I'm holding out much hope of it being half decent in this place. I'll probably leave sicker than I came in but beggars can't be choosers. I'm parched, and all they've given me is a poxy jug of water. What I'd really like is a stiff G&T, but there's no chance of getting one of them around here!'

'Colleen told me what happened, Edel. Are you okay? You're not hurt, are you?' Jimmy asked, worried, though he could see that Edel Walsh was still as feisty as ever. 'Colleen said that you were unconscious. That you'd been dragged out of the flat by firefighters?'

'I'm grand now, Jimmy. The lovely fireman who rescued us said we were lucky to get out unscathed. I don't remember too much about the fire to be honest. One minute I was in my bed having trouble breathing and then next thing I knew I must have passed out.' Edel shook her head, still unable to believe how much of a close brush with death she'd had. 'The firefighters found me and Colleen and got us out in time, Jimmy. We both lost consciousness. The doctors have checked me over and they're just treating me for a bit of smoke inhalation.'

'Well you certainly seem a lot better than I was expecting,' Jimmy said, in awe of the woman's strength.

'I'm just counting my blessings, Jimmy. The fireman told me that the flat and the shop are completely destroyed. Everything's gone, Jimmy, but it could have been a lot worse. Colleen's alive. I'm alive. That's all that matters.'

Jimmy nodded. She was right, of course, but the way she was just taking everything in her stride so calmly made him anxious. She had to still be in shock surely.

'Things are things. Everything's replaceable. I'm just glad that my Colleen's okay.' Reading the man's thoughts, Edel looked sad then. 'The firefighters couldn't find Mr Tiddles though. You don't think that you could have a look could you, Jimmy? I know he's just a cat, and a wild little thing at that, but I've had him since he was a kitten. He's my baby. He'll be scared on his own.'

'Don't you worry, Edel. You leave it with me. I'll have a look for him,' Jimmy said, not holding out much hope on finding the cat alive from what he'd heard about the fire damage.

He changed the subject. 'I can't believe it, Edel. I mean, I only dropped Colleen home in the cab about two, before going back to my place. I must have only been asleep a couple of hours when she called to tell me you were both here. Do you know how the fire started?'

Edel shook her head.

'I can't be sure, but I think I must have left an oil burner on in the shop. I was burning some lovely orange and bergamot oils today. I mustn't have put the candle out. The thing must have caught light. Unless it was some kind of electrical fault?' Since she'd regained consciousness, Edel had been racking her brains to try and work out what could have started the fire.

'Well, whatever it was that started it, don't you fret, Edel. The fire officers will do a thorough investigation and will find out what happened. In the meantime, I'll get a couple of my guys to go around and see if we can salvage anything, and have a look for Mr Tiddles for you. How does that sound?' Jimmy said, not wanting the woman to get stressed out any more than she already was after her ordeal.

'Thanks, Jimmy, love. You're a good man, you know that.'

'Don't even mention it, Edel. I'm just glad that your Colleen thought enough of me to call me,' Jimmy said truthfully, glad that he had been the first person that Colleen had thought to call. Jimmy wanted to do all he could to help. Remembering what Colleen had told him about being an only child, and her mother being one too, Jimmy realised that maybe Colleen didn't have an awful lot of options. She'd said that since both her grandparents had passed away, herself and Edel didn't really have any family to speak of. Edel had brought her up as a single parent. Colleen had never clapped eyes on her biological father. The man had upped and scarpered before she was born.

'What are yours and Colleen's plans when you leave here? Have you got somewhere you can go? Some family you can stay with?'

'I guess we'll have to check into a hotel for now.' Edel shook her head. She hadn't even thought that far ahead. It hadn't really sunk in that she was actually homeless now. She and Colleen had nowhere to go. She had no idea what they were going to do next.

'There's just so much to think about, so much to try and sort out. I don't even know where to start.'

Jimmy was decided then.

'A hotel? No chance. You and Colleen can come and stay with me, and before you say anything else on the matter, I'm insisting. I won't take no for an answer.'

'Ahh, we couldn't put you out like that, Jimmy!' Edel said, not wanting to put him to any trouble.

'You're not putting me out, Edel. But you will be if you don't accept my offer. I've got loads of room at my place, and it's the very least I can do to help you both.'

'Thank you, Jimmy. I really appreciate that,' Edel said, unable to disguise the tears in her eyes at the generous offer. The reality was that they wouldn't have been able to afford to stay in a hotel.

They would have had to look for a cheap B&B or a hostel. Edel was too proud to admit that to Jimmy.

Seeing the worry written across the woman's face, Jimmy squeezed her hand gently.

'It's okay, Edel. We'll have you sorted out before you know it. Once the fire officers have done their investigation and you get your insurance payout, you can get back on your feet again. Like you said, it's all replaceable.'

'You're right, Jimmy. Thank you!' Edel nodded resolutely, which only made Jimmy smile. The woman was old school. As tough as old boots. Edel Walsh was one of life's survivors and Jimmy really admired that.

Then getting up off the bed, Jimmy decided to go in search of Colleen, so that he could break the news to her that she would be coming to stay with him. "Right, now let me go and see where your lovely daughter's got to with this tea. I won't be long, and if I find any gin and tonics on my travels I'll smuggle one back for you!'

'Blimey, Jimmy. This is a lovely place you've got here,' Edel Walsh said, as she nosed around the interior of Jimmy's apartment, nestled in a bustling street off Mayfair, overlooking Hyde Park. 'This must have cost you a fortune.'

'Mum!' Colleen said, nudging her mother, who, ever since they'd arrived, had done nothing but try to add up the cost of everything.

'It's okay.' Jimmy laughed, placing his keys down on the large oak dining table that sat directly in front of the huge floor to ceiling window. 'It did cost a fair few bob, but it's an investment. I got it for a good price and then did a complete renovation. I've probably doubled my money on it already. This place is my pension.'

'It's very fancy, isn't it?' Edel said, casting her eye across the impeccably decorated room, admiring the tasteful neutral colours and statement pieces of furniture.

'It's like a palace compared to our place, isn't it, Colleen, with all our clutter and junk we've collected—' Edel stopped then. Catching herself for a moment, as Colleen looked down at the floor. 'God! Listen to me. "Our place". It still doesn't feel real, does it?' Then not wanting to upset Colleen any further by getting emotional herself, Edel added: 'I can't see this place being very child-friendly, Jimmy; you know, if you were eventually going to settle down and have a family of your own.' She raised her eyebrow questioningly.

She'd taken a real liking to Jimmy Byrne. Not only was he from back home in the Emerald Isle, but he had proved himself to be worth his weight in gold and now that Edel had seen where the man lived, she'd decided she liked him even more.

Jimmy Byrne was clearly a good, respectable man who worked hard for his money.

'This is more of a bachelor pad; follow me and I'll give you the grand tour,' Jimmy said, knowing full well that Edel Walsh couldn't wait to have a nose around the place.

Leading the two women into the kitchen, Jimmy watched as Edel's eyes lit up at the size of it. 'It's more than enough for me, but when I do eventually settle down and have kids I'll probably look for somewhere a bit more spacious. A house with a bit of land attached, you know, a nice big old garden. I'd like a few more bedrooms too. I quite fancy myself as a family man one day.'

'Well, it sounds like you've already put a lot of thought into it,' Edel said, winking at Colleen as she followed Jimmy through to the master bedroom.

'Wow! Your bed's huge. You must get lost lying in that thing on your own.' Edel winked at Colleen again; only this time

Jimmy saw her and couldn't help but laugh loudly at the woman's brazenness.

Which in turn made Colleen blush wildly.

'Mum!' she said, knowing that her pleas were falling on deaf ears. The woman wasn't going to let up trying to matchmake.

'What? I'm just making an observation!' Edel said, feigning innocence.

Colleen was far too cool. Taking things slowly was one thing. Only if Colleen went any slower she'd grind to a complete stop. Jimmy Byrne didn't seem like he was the type to play games. If Colleen played it too suave, the man might lose interest completely, and there was no way that Edel was having that.

If anything, Colleen should be grateful for Edel's encouragement; she was only doing the pair of them a favour. They'd thank her for being so pushy one day, she was sure.

'I just think that you must get ever so lonely. A lovely man like yourself, here on your own.'

'Well, I won't be here on my own for a while now, will I? Not with you two lovely ladies staying here with me,' Jimmy quipped, lightening the mood as he saw the look of embarrassment on Colleen's face at Edel laying it on so thick. 'Let me show you to your room, ladies.'

Walking through into the second bedroom, Jimmy pointed out the large double bed and the sofa bed that sat under the window.

'You can share the main bed, or pull out the sofa bed, it's up to you, ladies,' he said, hoping that his gesture of putting the two women in together was okay with Colleen. They hadn't spent the night together yet, and Jimmy didn't want to cause her any embarrassment by making her wonder where she would be sleeping. Colleen seemed like a decent, traditional girl, who wouldn't want to rush into anything.

'There's an en suite there too for you both to use, and I'll get you both some keys so you can come and go as you please.'

'Thank you so much, Jimmy! We really can't thank you enough,' Colleen said, grateful to him for being so generous and helping them out like this. Welcoming them both into his home. Colleen didn't know what else they would have done if it wasn't for him. 'It will only be for a few days, hopefully. Just until we get ourselves sorted out!' Colleen quickly reminded him, conscious that Jimmy was going out of his way to let them both stay here. The last thing she wanted to do was take advantage of his generous offer.

'Of course.' Jimmy nodded knowing how adamant Colleen had been not to be a burden to him. 'And I'll do whatever I can to help you both but until then, please, my home is your home.'

'Oh! Don't go saying things like that, Jimmy! I've always fancied living somewhere flash like this. Once I've got my feet under your table, you might never get rid of me.' Edel chuckled and Jimmy joined in. Edel's humour was infectious.

'Right, now how about I make you both a decent cuppa?' Jimmy offered leading them back into the kitchen.

'Oh that would be lovely,' Edel exclaimed as they followed him through to the kitchen and took a seat at the stools around the centre island. 'Then I'm going to have another shower and a lie down if that's okay. Last night's really taken it out of me.'

'I bet it has, Edel. You've had an awful shock the pair of you. You both must be exhausted,' Jimmy said as he busied himself filling up the kettle. He'd stayed at the hospital all morning with the women and insisted on bringing them back here when the doctors finally gave Edel the all-clear and discharged the lady. None of them had had much sleep at all last night.

'We are, aren't we, missy? It was a night from hell. I can't even begin to think about how we're going to rebuild our lives after this. We'll be starting again from scratch.'

'We'll be all right, Mum,' Colleen said, placing her hand on her mother's. 'Like Jimmy was saying, once the fire officer does the investigation, we can contact the insurers. We'll start again. I know it will be hard, but I'll help you, Mum.' Colleen smiled warmly. 'We'll be just fine.'

Edel patted her daughter's hand. Unlike Colleen, she wasn't able to be quite so optimistic.

Jimmy smiled warmly at Colleen. He could see the love she had for her mother. He couldn't imagine how the girl was feeling seeing her mum so upset. Especially as Jimmy himself was so close to his own mum. It would break his heart to see her so broken.

Then, interrupted by the apartment's intercom, Jimmy excused himself from the room.

'Sorry, ladies. I won't be a minute.'

'I might as well make the tea,' Edel said, busying herself, starting off where Jimmy had left it. 'The very least we can do while we're here is help out. I'll make Jimmy some nice Irish stew later. A big lad like him will appreciate a bit of home cooking I'm sure,' she said taking a nose inside Jimmy's fridge and cupboards to see what ingredients she had to play around with.

'I tell you what, Colleen, this place is bleeding immaculate. You could eat your food off the inside of these cupboards.'

'Mum!' Colleen shook her head in dismay. 'He's probably got a cleaner!'

'Of course he has. A thriving businessman like Jimmy wouldn't have time to clean this place as immaculately as it is. The man's far too busy.' Edel nodded in agreement. 'What a life though, eh, Colleen?' Then whispering playfully, she added: 'If you don't snatch this man up with both bleeding hands, I might see if I'm in with a chance.'

Colleen giggled, glad that her mum was still finding the funny side of things.

'Sounds like he's got some company,' Edel said as she heard Jimmy talking to someone out in the hallway. Not quite being able to catch the conversation, she could hear the hushed tones of a male voice.

Making her way closer so that she could have a listen, Edel nearly jumped out of her skin when Jimmy walked through the door, almost hitting her with it.

'Ladies!' Jimmy announced as he entered the room. 'This is a friend of mine. Jack Taylor. He works on the force. He's got something that might be of interest to you, Edel.'

The policeman stepped into the room, holding Mr Tiddles tightly to his chest.

'Oh, my baby! You found him.' Edel was up out of her seat then, crying as she took her beloved soot-covered cat from the man's arms and hugged it to her.

PC Jack Taylor smiled at Edel, before his expression turned sombre.

'I'm afraid I'm the bearer of some bad news, too, Mrs Walsh,' the police officer said. 'Do you want to take a seat?'

Colleen and Edel could see that the policeman wasn't just here on a personal call.

'Is everything okay?' Edel said, glad that she had her precious cat back, but the feeling was bittersweet as she sat and waited for PC Taylor to break whatever bad news he had for her. 'Have you had news about the fire?'

Seeing the look that the two men exchanged Edel waited with baited breath for the answer.

'I'm afraid I do, Mrs Walsh. I've just spoken to the Chief Fire Officer leading the investigation. I haven't got good news.'

Jack Taylor shifted on his feet uncomfortably. He'd been working for Jimmy for almost a year now, and when Jimmy had called to ask him to find out what had happened at the flat, and to look for Edel Walsh's cat, Jack had been happy to oblige. Normally Jack was asked to do something more risky like accessing police records or getting Jimmy some private information about a case or a person. A cat for an old lady was one of Jimmy's more pleasant requests.

Only what he'd uncovered hadn't been the best news for the old lady. There was no easy way to break it to the old dear, other than just to simply say it.

'I'm afraid that the Chief Fire Officer found the cause of the fire,' he said. Taking a seat across from Edel and Colleen Walsh, he knew this conversation wasn't going to be easy for either of the women.

'Was it my aromatherapy oil burner?' Edel asked, still racking her brain to work out how the fire had started. She'd convinced herself that somehow this had all been her fault, wracked with guilt that her home and livelihood had all gone up in flames all because she'd carelessly forgotten to extinguish one of her stupid scented candles. 'I'm normally so good at locking up at night and checking all my candles are out, but I can't remember putting that one out. I'd had it burning in the shop all day.'

Seeing the doubtful look on the officer's face, Edel continued: 'Or maybe it was some kind of electrical fault? Did something overheat? I always switch my plugs off at night, but it's a very old building; the electrics are probably older than I am!'

Jack shook his head. Then looking to Jimmy as if for reassurance, and seeing the man nod, giving him permission to break the bad news to Edel, Jack had no choice but to tell her straight what the officers had found.

'I'm really sorry to tell you this, Mrs Walsh, but the fire officers suspect that the fire was started on purpose.'

'On purpose?' Edel said, the confusion written all over her face. 'But I don't understand. Why would anyone do that? How do you know that it wasn't just an accident? How can you be sure?'

Shaking his head, Jack persevered. 'They found traces of petrol, Mrs Walsh. The fire officer tested some of the materials that we removed from the property as part of the investigation and it appears that the shop had been doused in the stuff prior to the fire starting,' he said, as he let the news sink in.

'Do you think it was that gang of lads that were hanging about, Mum? The ones that broke in?' Colleen said, piecing everything together. 'It must have been. They must have come back?'

'A break-in?' Jack said, raising his brow. 'Did you report it?'

Edel shook her head.

'Mum!' Colleen said, glaring at her. 'Why not? You said you would?'

'I only said I would so that you'd stop nagging me,' Edel said truthfully. 'They were just kids, Colleen. Boys being boys. I thought that it was just a one off.'

'Oh really? A one off? Our home's been destroyed! They've cost us bloody everything, Mum! It must have been them; who else could it have been?'

Sensing the growing tensions, Jack continued: 'Do you know who these boys are, Mrs Walsh? Would you recognise them?'

Edel shook her head.

'There were a few of them. It was dark and they had their hoods up. The ringleader had a scarf tied around his face too. I didn't get a look at any of them, and as soon as they got the money out of the till, they all scarpered,' she said, feeling foolish that she hadn't taken the time to report the crime after it had happened. 'I've never had any trouble before. I've lived in Dean Street all my life. I thought it was a one off. I thought that if I got the police involved it would only cause more trouble for us.'

Jack Taylor nodded understandingly. 'I'm going to have to ask you to report the break-in and I'll need you both to make statements. I'll need a full description of the group of boys,' he continued, though he knew the chance of catching the scrotes that did this were slim to none.

'Are you sure that the fire officer hasn't made some kind of mistake? Are you sure it wasn't just an accident?' Edel asked, refusing to believe that someone would deliberately cause her to lose her home and her business, along with all her worldly possessions.

And to think that she and Colleen were lucky to be alive.

'No one would be that cruel surely?'

'There's no mistake, Mrs Walsh,' Jack said sincerely. 'I'm really sorry but the fire was started deliberately. We are treating it as arson.'

CHAPTER FIFTEEN

Staring at the security camera, Alex watched as Jimmy got out of his Range Rover and steamed towards the office. Going by the thunderous look on his face, he was clearly still reeling from last night at the club.

Alex knew he'd gone too far, and he'd been waiting for Jimmy to show up so that he could apologise for his actions. Deliberately ruining Jimmy's date last night had seemed such a good idea at the time, when he'd been off his face on gear and Scotch that is. Now though, in the cold light of day, when he was sober and faced with the wrath of Jimmy Byrne, Alex knew that he'd majorly fucked up. And going on the way the man was marching across the gravel driveway, visibly enraged, it was going to take a lot more than an apology to make this right with Jimmy.

Holding up his hands as if to call a truce as he burst through the office door, Alex started talking. 'Before you say anything, Jimmy. I'm sorry, all right,' he said, trying to be the bigger man and own up to his actions. 'You were right. I had too much to drink, and too much gear. I shouldn't have slagged off Tiffany the way I did but the girl was doing my brain in. You know how trappy she can be. I acted like a complete twat last night, Jimmy, and I apologise profusely.'

Jimmy had forgiven him for his unruly behaviour many times before, and Alex was certain the man would forgive him once more.

Only Jimmy wasn't having it this time, it seemed.

'A twat? Is that what you fucking call it?' Enraged, Jimmy launched at him. Grabbing Alex firmly by his throat and wrenching him out of the chair, he pinned him up against the wall.

'What else are you sorry for, Alex, huh? What else did you do last night?' he spat, incensed that, as per usual, Alex thought he could just do and say as he pleased and that there would be no repercussions.

Alex saw red.

'I only turned up at the restaurant in the first place as I thought you might appreciate some decent company. I thought I was doing you a favour. That I'd be helping to relieve the boredom of you having to endure sitting with some straight-laced fucking bore like Colleen,' he said, annoyed that Jimmy had taken things so out of context. 'How was I supposed to know that the plan's all changed now that you've gone all soft on the girl? I thought we had a fucking plan, Jimmy. I thought the whole point in you getting involved with the girl and her mother was to get them out of the flat?'

'And what? I wasn't doing it quick enough for you, is that it? You couldn't just let me do things my way, could you?' Jimmy said; his face was so close to Alex's that their foreheads almost touched. 'So what? You thought you'd take things into your own hands and burn their flat down? Are you some sort of moron?'

'What are you talking about, Jimmy?' Alex shook his head. He'd never seen Jimmy so angry. Glaring at him with rage, Alex could see the vein on the side of Jimmy's head throbbing as his adrenaline surged through his body. His anger consuming him. 'I was off my fucking tree last night, Jimmy, and I behaved like a complete cunt. I admit that. But burning down their flat? Come on, Jimmy.'

'Oh bullshit. You did nothing but snipe at Colleen all evening. You took an instant dislike to her on sight and after our conversation last night, I know you set out to deliberately muck everything up for me. You're pathetic, Alex,' Jimmy bellowed.

'Seriously, Jimmy. I left the club straight after you did last night. I was home in my bed by half two. I was fucking wrecked, Jimmy. Wankered. The taxi driver had to help me to my front door. I could barely put one foot in front of the other let alone go and start a bleeding fire. I'll get the cab firm's number if you don't believe me. You can check!'

Alex flinched. Off his face on way too much cocaine and enough drink to put most men in a coma, he had a vague memory of a phone call he'd made on the way to get the cab.

Jimmy let go. Seeing the solemn look on his friend's face, he stepped back, as if he'd been physically winded.

'You did it, didn't you?'

'Shit,' Alex said, shaking his head as if trying to shake the memory from his mind. 'I made a call, Jimmy. Fuck! I was so out of it, I wasn't thinking straight.'

Speechless, Jimmy bit his lip.

'Fuck!' Alex thumped the side of his head with his fist. He'd majorly messed up, he knew that now and he had no choice but to confess. Jimmy would only find out otherwise.

'I asked that kid that we paid to do the break-in to go round and stir things up a bit. I said I'd had a fucking nuff of pussyfooting around the old woman. I told him to make sure that this time she knew we weren't messing about.'

Alex was pacing the office now. This was his fault. He'd had enough of Jimmy hovering around Colleen and her mother. So consumed in his drink and drug-fuelled rage, Alex had wanted the woman dealt with quickly. He'd wanted her out of the flat.

'I wasn't thinking, Jimmy,' he said, running his fingers through his thick black hair as he remembered the phone call that he'd made to Stuart Matthews when he'd ordered him to go around to Edel Walsh's flat the night before.

Jimmy didn't speak. Slumping down in the chair, he was beyond pissed off with Alex.

'They're investigating the fire for arson,' he said, glaring at Alex, unable to comprehend the length he'd gone to behind his back. 'If anything comes back to us, I'm holding you personally responsible, do you understand?

'Fuck me, Alex. What were you thinking? I told you that I would sort it. I said that I had it all in hand. What the fuck is your problem?' Jimmy knew what the problem was though. Alex had made that blatantly clear last night.

Colleen.

'They could have fucking died, Alex. They were both in there. Both in their beds. The firefighters had to carry them out. Unconscious they were. You and that moron Stuart Matthews could have been responsible for killing them both.' Jimmy wasn't even raising his voice now. Never in his life had he felt so angry, so irate. Yet the enormity of Alex's actions, of his betrayal, only left him numb.

'I feel like I don't even know you these days, Alex.'

'I'm sorry, Jimmy. I wasn't thinking straight. Fuck, I wasn't thinking at all. I didn't think that the fire would rip through the place. I thought it would just cause a bit of damage downstairs. That it would shake Mrs Walsh up a bit. Make her want to reconsider moving out,' Alex said, rubbing his neck from where Jimmy had grabbed him, knowing how pathetic he sounded right now. 'We needed to get her out so that we could get moving with the development. She's costing us money.'

'It ain't just about the money though, is it?' Jimmy said, his eyes cold, devoid of emotion as he stared at Alex, as if he was looking straight through him. They both knew what this was really about, only Alex was too gutless to admit it.

Alex didn't trust Jimmy's judgement, so he'd taken it upon himself to sort the Walshes out. Only, his actions could have cost them everything in the process.

'I can't do this anymore, Alex. I can't work with you when you're like this. The drink. The drugs. It's too much!' Jimmy said, his voice quiet, almost eerily subdued.

'I'm sorry, Jimmy. I'll sort it, okay. Leave it with me,' Alex said, realising that he'd pushed Jimmy too far this time. 'I'll pay Stuart off and get him to lay low for a while. I'll make sure nothing comes back on us.'

Jimmy nodded. Alex would certainly do that much all right. That was a given. There was nothing else he could say on the matter. Alex's stupidity, his rash decision had been made without his knowledge and the damage was done now. Colleen and Edel were out of the flat for good. The place was beyond repair. All Jimmy could do was try and salvage the situation as best he could. His head was spinning. Sitting in the chair, in silence, the thunderous expression on his face unwavering.

'I'll sort the girls out for the party tonight. You look like shit. Why don't you go and get your head down and leave me to sort out the job tonight, yeah?'

Desperate to make up to Jimmy for his epic fuck up, Alex knew he was going to have to work his bollocks off to get back into his good books.

'What job?' Jimmy said, his head still spinning from Alex's revelation. Having been at the hospital most of the day, and hardly having any sleep last night, he'd lost track of what day of the week it was let alone what job they'd sorted for tonight.

'Mr Donoghue. You know: our client with the penchant for getting a bit handy with the girls. Likes it a bit rough, shall we say. He's asked for two girls tonight. I'll do the drop and the pickup. At least that way, the girls will still be in one piece when he's done if he knows that I'm personally couriering them about. The man's a fucking lunatic.'

Jimmy nodded. The best thing for them both right now was for Jimmy to be as far away from Alex as possible. He couldn't deal with anymore dramas. He was done in.

Let Alex sort out tonight's shit.

Jimmy couldn't stand Mr Donoghue. The man was a first grade bastard to the girls. With a fetish for inflicting a bit of pain on them, he'd pushed his luck with the last girl that Alex and Jimmy had sent around there for one of his special 'parties'.

Jenny Rowe had come back covered in bite marks and cigarette burns, and traumatised from being tied up all night while Mr Donoghue and his friends had their fun with the girl. Raping and sodomising her with all kinds of objects. The only reason Jimmy and Alex hadn't strung the man up by his bollocks when they'd later paid him a visit was because the man was worth a fucking fortune and had made an agreement with the two that he'd pay an absolute premium for girls in the future.

Thousands of pounds a night for Jimmy and Alex to send him a girl that doesn't mind being roughed up. Alex had agreed to it without a second's thought, though Jimmy hadn't felt entirely happy with the arrangement. Still he'd gone along with it once the men had agreed on a couple of ground rules.

The girls could be tied up and roughed up, but Mr Donoghue and his friends were forbidden to leave any marks on them, and after Alex had stipulated that it would be he or Jimmy that would be collecting the girls personally at the end of the night, Mr Donoghue had been happy to make sure that he stuck to the agreement.

Getting to his feet, Jimmy needed to get the fuck out of there. Away from Alex before he said or did something he'd regret. He didn't even want to be in the same room as the man.

'From now on, Alex, what I say goes. You don't question me and you don't fucking go behind my back. And make no bones about it, Alex, if anything comes back on us about the fire, if there's even so much as a whisper that somehow we were involved, me and you will be done for good. Do you get me?!'

Not waiting for a reply, Jimmy stormed out of the office.

Alex Costa had crossed the line and if he wasn't careful Jimmy would bury the man himself.

CHAPTER SIXTEEN

'I can't believe that you found me this place, Jimmy. I never thought I'd say this after losing my home, but it's perfect,' Edel said as she stared out of the window, down onto the bustling Piccadilly Circus: hordes of tourists filled the square, along with shoppers and theatregoers, stopping to sit at the foot of the Eros statue on a bronze water fountain in the centre of all the commotion. Down the road Edel could see a stream of people pouring in and out of the tube station. Wandering beneath the twinkling illumination of all the Christmas lights, glittering above them.

'I'm only a five minute walk from Dean Street so once the shop downstairs is all up and running, I'll still be able to keep the small clientele that have been coming to me for years,' she said optimistically. 'And just look at all these people out here now. The area is packed.'

'It's prime location, Edel,' Jimmy said. 'Not only that, but at least now you're away from that gang of kids that were hanging around the old place.'

'I honestly can't thank you enough for all you've done for me,' Edel said, her voice thick with emotion. Without Jimmy's offer of help, God knows where she and Colleen would have ended up. Probably slumming it in some hostel somewhere. Edel would be eternally grateful for everything the man had done for them both.

'Don't be silly, Edel. Besides it's like you said: it's a business arrangement. You'll see me right once your insurance pays out. In the meantime, I'm more than glad to help out.'

Edel beamed as she stepped aside as two of Jimmy's men carried in a brand new sofa that Jimmy had insisted on buying her as a moving in present.

It had been almost a month since the fire and Edel had to admit that it felt good to be starting afresh. As lovely as it had been staying at Jimmy's the past few weeks, she couldn't wait to have her own space again, and as kind as it was of Jimmy to give up his spare room, she knew that he was probably looking forward to having his lovely apartment all to himself again after the month that she and Colleen had been there now, and Edel didn't blame him.

'The place is lovely, Edel. I'm sure you're going to be very happy here,' Jimmy said as he followed her into one of the bedrooms so that they could measure up for a bed.

'This is going to be Colleen's room. It's big enough for a double bed, isn't it? If we put it there under the window. It might be a bit of a squeeze, do you think? Maybe I should order a single bed? What do you think?'

Jimmy put the measuring tape down then.

'I was going to talk to you about that. I think I can help.'

'Not a chance, Jimmy, you've done enough. I'm perfectly able to buy the furniture on my catalogue. I've always kept up with the payments. A couple of beds won't bankrupt me. I can probably even stretch to a wardrobe. I won't even hear you suggest that you'll pay for them.'

Jimmy laughed.

'Jesus, Edel. You don't make things easy, do you?' he said, as he straightened his collar, the room feeling a little hot.

Edel looked puzzled, convinced that she'd missed something. Jimmy had a strange look on his face. Like he wanted to tell her something but he didn't know how to say it.

'What is it, Jimmy?'

'I don't want to buy Colleen bloody bedroom furniture.' He grinned. Then slipping the small navy box out of his pocket, Jimmy opened it and showed the contents to Edel. 'I want to buy her this. A ring. I want to marry her, Edel, and I'm asking your permission.'

Staring at the beautiful cluster of diamonds on the simple platinum band, Edel Walsh was left momentarily speechless. Only momentarily though, of course.

'Oh dear God! Jimmy, it's beautiful!' Edel cried as she flung her arms around the tall strapping man, hugging him to her. 'I couldn't be happier for the pair of you. Of course you have my blessing, Jimmy,' Edel said as happy tears cascaded down her cheeks.

In the few months that Jimmy had been in their lives so much had happened, but one thing Edel was sure of: Jimmy Byrne was the best thing that had ever happened to her Colleen.

She couldn't wait for her daughter to become a Byrne.

CHAPTER SEVENTEEN

'Edel! What a unique choice of dress,' Joanie Byrne said, her eyes roaming the questionable outfit. She was unable to hide the smirk from her face as she took in the sight of Edel Walsh dressed up to what could only be described as the proverbial dog's dinner. Not only was the dress at least two sizes too small for the woman, but the cheap, shimmery material did nothing for her figure, in fact, from the back Edel's arse resembled a bag of spanners.

As a woman, you either had class or you didn't, and poor old Edel didn't have a clue – accessorising her gaudy outfit with a psychedelic-looking floral clutch bag, black clumpy shoes that wouldn't have looked out of place on a donkey and jewellery that resembled something Joanie could have pulled from a Christmas cracker. The woman looked like she'd run through a jumble sale and been hit by every rack on her way back out again. Which, knowing how much her son had spent on the woman and her daughter ever since they'd lost their home and business in the fire, Joanie knew certainly wasn't true.

Jimmy had spent an absolute fortune on the pair of them. Though class, it seemed, was something that couldn't be bought.

Unlike Edel, Joanie didn't even have to try when it came to making an effort with her appearance. She oozed sophistication, naturally, prided herself on it in fact. Blessed with a naturally slim, tall figure, she could have worn a bin bag and made it look good.

The plum-coloured jumpsuit that she wore today was designer, of course, a Vivian Westwood classic. Everything from the luxurious silk material to the statement padded shoulders screamed the very height of eighties chic. Accessorised with a pair of the very finest Italian pumps and a classic silver clutch bag, not only did Joanie look like a million dollars, but she'd almost spent that amount too.

Still it was her only child's wedding, she had reasoned and her efforts had been worth every penny if she said so herself. The only consolation about Edel looking so awful was that at least Joanie would look even better in all the photographs.

'Neon pink is so on-trend right now, but it's such a hard colour to pull off I find. Very daring of you to give it a go, though!' Joanie smirked. She needn't have worried about the mother-of-the-bride outdoing the mother-of-the-groom after all. There was clearly no chance of that happening.

'It's coral actually!' Edel corrected the woman, not biting to Joanie's obvious dig.

'Well, you look very, what's the word I'm looking for? Vibrant.'

'Cheers! You don't scrub up too bad either. Though I have to say, if anyone's "daring" it's you, love. You're the first person I've ever seen wear pyjamas to a wedding.'

Suppressing a snort as he tried not to laugh, Michael Byrne, who up until that point had been standing quietly minding his own business, couldn't help but laugh at Edel's little comeback.

'It's a jumpsuit,' Joanie said, tight-lipped, unable to keep the clearly taken offence from her tone, as she shot her husband a berating glare.

'Jumpsuit, pyjamas, they all look the same to me, Joanie, but then what do I know about fashion huh?' Edel waved her hand dismissively, winking at Michael then on the sly, knowing full well her sarcasm would be wasted on Joanie. The woman was so highly strung, Edel could have probably flipped her over and played a tune on her.

Biting the inside of his cheek, Michael was trying his damnedest not to fall about laughing at Joanie getting a taste of her own medicine for once. He liked Colleen's mother. Edel Walsh was a woman that didn't stand for any shit from Joanie; the woman was giving back as good as she got and Michael admired that. Anyone that took on his Joanie deserved to be championed.

'Yes, well, that statement speaks for itself, doesn't it?' Joanie pouted.

'Can we get you a drink, Edel?' Michael butted in; recognising the familiar patronising tone to his wife's voice, he knew that this wouldn't end well for Edel if she got the better of Joanie. The woman liked to hold a grudge.

All joking aside, today was a big day for them all. A day that their two families became one. Only Edel and Colleen didn't have a clue what they were up against when it came to Joanie making sure that she forever ruled the Byrne family roost. The woman was insatiable, stopping at nothing to make sure everything always went her way. 'What would you like, Edel? Champagne? A glass of wine?'

'Ohh, thanks, Michael, I'll have a large Baileys with ice, ta darling. Make it a big one.'

Leaning up against the bar, Edel slipped her aching foot out from her chunky black shoes, rubbing the throbbing arch, oblivious to the look of horror on Joanie's face as she looked down at her neglected feet, taking in the disturbing sight of the long, jagged toenails, void of any polish. Though as bad as they looked, they had nothing on the hard skin on the back of Edel's heels that broke off in small flakes as she brushed her hand over it, before sprinkling itself all over the floor.

Joanie twisted her face in disgust.

'My bleeding bunions are playing up again,' Edel offered without any form of apology. 'I don't know how you totter about in those fancy-looking shoes, Joanie, really I don't. These haven't even got a heel on them and they kill my feet. I'll take them off later for the dancing. Hopefully, by then, everyone will be half-cut and they won't notice the whiff!'

Cackling loudly, Edel slipped her shoe back on, before running her fingers through her hair.

Which only caused Joanie to feel physically sick. Edel's apparent lack of etiquette too much for Joanie, the woman was glad when the barman interrupted them.

'Would Madam be wanting a double measure?' he asked, holding up a tall glass tumbler.

'Oh Madam! Get him!' Edel chuckled, rolling her eyes at Joanie and Michael playfully. 'Madam would not like a double measure, no! Madam would like you to fill it up to the brim!' Edel insisted, then seeing the doubt on the barman's face at her request she added seriously, 'Go on, fill it up. Saves me having to keep getting up and coming to the bar every five minutes. Besides it's not every day that I'm the mother-of-the-bride, is it? I'm celebrating.'

The barman nodded obediently and poured half a pint of Baileys into the glass for the older woman. Then turning back to Michael and Joanie she added, 'It is a free bar after all. It would be rude not to, wouldn't it?' Edel grinned, taking the glass from the barman and swallowing a huge gulp of her drink. A thin, milky residue lined her top lip when she'd finished.

'Well not exactly free, is it, seeing as Jimmy's footing the bill for it all.' Joanie mumbled another dig about Edel and Colleen rinsing her son, unable to hide the clip to her tone as she stared at Edel's milky moustache. Then again, the woman seemed good at fleecing Jimmy. What was another few drinks on top?

'Ahh, well, the boy knows only too well. It's not just happy wife, happy life. He needs to keep his old mother-in-law happy too. I told him that's the key to a healthy marriage. Healthy as in allowing the man to stay alive. I warned him the other day, I said: "Jimmy, I have a real soft spot for you, lad".' Edel winked at Michael. '"It's at my little allotment, behind my shed – and that's where you'll end up if you upset my Colleen".' She roared with laughter once more, snorting loudly at her own wit. Which only made Michael join in. Though the icy glare that Joanie threw at him quickly warned him to shut up as the disapproval radiated from his wife in waves.

'It must be a sad day for you, Joanie?' Edel said. 'A boy's best friend is his mother and there's no tie stronger than her apron string. Until they get married that is. That's why I was always glad I had a daughter. They always need their mum no matter what; boys tend to leave their mums behind, don't you think?'

Joanie bit her lip. Edel had just hit her where it hurt: picking up on her weakness as an overprotective interfering mother.

The woman hadn't had a single nice thing to say about Edel or Colleen since she'd met them, and yes, the wedding had been arranged rather quickly, but Edel could see that Jimmy and Colleen were genuinely happy. It was a shame that Joanie was too bitter and selfish to be pleased for them both.

'I'm sure Jimmy won't be forgetting me anytime soon,' Joanie finally spoke up. 'We're very close. Married or not, nothing will change that.'

Michael tried to hide the grin he was suppressing. He was actually enjoying himself for once. He was still trying to suss out if Edel was completely oblivious to Joanie's obvious dislike of her, or she just didn't give two shits, and judging by the gleam in the older lady's eyes, Michael had an inkling that it was the latter. He reckoned that Edel was smarter than Joanie and gave the woman credit for it. More than that, Edel was real. Unlike Joanie who was as fake as they came, Edel made no airs and graces, pretending to be something that she wasn't.

It was only a shame that he was on such a tight leash these days, otherwise, given half the chance he would have joined the woman in drinking half pints of Baileys himself if he thought for a second he could get away with it. At least that would be fun. Only there was no such thing as fun these days: under both Joanie's and Jimmy's watchful eyes, he was on a final warning to remain on his best behaviour at all times.

'This place is bloody gorgeous, isn't it?' Edel said, looking around in awe at the fancy venue. 'I never in my wildest dreams thought that my Colleen would land on her feet like she has. This place must have cost an absolute bomb.'

'You could say that!' Joanie smiled smugly.

Of course her son had gone all out. Why shouldn't he? Jimmy was doing well for himself. He was a self-made businessman who had a lot to live up to. His guests here today weren't just family and friends. There were business colleagues too. Associates, co-workers.

The venue was exquisite. An old Edwardian manor house, filled with character and charm, from the glistening teardrop crystal chandeliers to the ornate spiral staircase that led down into the Orangery where the ceremony was soon to take place.

'The flowers look a bit anaemic looking though,' Edel said as she eyed the silver urns and vases full of beautiful cream roses, woven intricately between pillars of candles, still peeved that Joanie had refused to let her do the arrangements. She wanted Edel to 'enjoy the day' apparently: 'not have to work'. Though Edel had a sneaky suspicion that Joanie just didn't want her to have any part in the arrangements. Ever the control freak, the woman clearly wanted to do everything herself.

Even poor Colleen had been sidelined in favour of some of Joanie's inputs on the wedding.

'Oh, who's that ghastly looking woman?' Joanie asked, staring down into the Orangery as a woman in one of the rows waved over at them. 'I don't recognise her, do you, Michael?'

'I'm not sure who it is?' Michael said, narrowing his eyes. 'I can't really see her from here.'

'Can't really see her? You can't bloody miss her, Michael, that one there in the middle of the row. Dressed like a banana,' Joanie quipped, staring back at the woman, dressed from head-to-toe in yellow, frantically waving her arms about in their direction.

'That's my Nellie,' Edel said protectively, catching Joanie's stuck-up jibe at the woman's choice of outfit as she spotted her friend. 'She's colour-blind as it happens,' Edel lied waving back, her face beaming with pride as Nellie held her arms up, in awe of the place, clearly thinking how well Edel and Colleen had done for themselves.

Her friend had plonked herself in a row full of men. Most of them well-known faces. Friends of Jimmy's no doubt. Nellie looked as if she was in her element, grinning widely as if she was at a celebrity wedding. Which, by all accounts, was exactly what it felt like, Edel had to admit. Everyone who was anyone was here today.

In fact, the only person that Edel and Colleen had invited had been Nellie. Colleen didn't really have any good friends that she ever spoke of, and they had no family on their side.

'She's a good girl is Nellie. She might not look all fancy as some, but Nellie has a heart of gold and you won't find her making snippy remarks like some people here either,' Edel lied again, knowing full well that Nellie Erikson was one of the biggest gossips she knew. Nellie could teach old hoity-toity bollocks here a thing or two when it came to bitching but she kept that comment to herself.

Edel was just glad that Nellie had made it. She wasn't sure she had the strength or the patience to endure the company of Joanie and her likes today. The woman drove her around the bend sometimes. The rest of the congregation were here to support the Byrne family. Besides, she wanted Nellie to see how well her Colleen had done for herself.

How well Edel had done too.

Their lives had changed so drastically in the past few months and it was all down to Jimmy Byrne. The man was a saint. Edel really couldn't have asked for better for her daughter.

Today was the start of new beginnings for them all. A new fruitful, happy life and there was no way that she could let her best and only friend miss it for anything.

'Right, you'll have to excuse me. I'm going to go and say hello to Nellie before I go and fetch Colleen.' Downing her drink in record time, Edel wiped the milky residue from her top lip before plonking her glass down on the bar. 'Oh, I needed that to calm my bleeding nerves. Not long now, eh and we'll all be one big happy family.'

Tipsy now and glad of it if she had to spend the day with the stuck-up old cow, Edel shot Joanie and Michael a parting smile before bidding them both goodbye and marching off to greet her friend.

'What a vile woman,' Joanie sneered, sipping her drink delicately as she watched Edel walk off, wobbling in her clumpy black shoes as she went; the drink had clearly already gone to the woman's head.

'Oh, I don't know,' said Michael, trying his hardest not to chuckle to himself, glad that he'd been proved right all along. Edel didn't care what anyone thought of her, least of all not someone like his stuffy-nosed Joanie. The two women's exchange had been a pleasure to endure. 'I thought she was rather nice actually. Quite refreshing.'

'Refreshing?' Joanie said, with a look of complete disbelief. She shook her head. Typical bloody Michael. The man couldn't see the wood for the trees when it came to women. It was always the same. 'They'd rinse Jimmy for all he was worth I reckon. What with Jimmy buying her that tacky little shop in Piccadilly Circus. Only he's not stupid my boy. She might be living in it, but he's kept it all in his name. He's just letting her think that he's done her a favour. I'd love to tell her; that would soon wipe the smug grin off the old cow's face,' she said spitefully, ignoring Michael's comment. She knew her husband was only disagreeing with her to wind her up, and today of all days she wasn't in the mood for his petty comments.

As much as she hated to admit it, she was struggling, because ultimately this was her doing. She had been the one to push Jimmy into the idea of getting married. Encouraging him to find a nice girl and settle down. With all her son's philandering over the years, the numerous tasteless girls that never lasted longer than a few dates, Joanie had honestly never thought this day would come. Though now that it had, she wasn't so sure she was happy about it anymore.

She'd seen a change in her son lately that she didn't like.

Getting close to that hideous Edel, and as for Colleen, the girl was wetter than a dishcloth. She had nothing about her. Joanie had hoped that her son would have had better taste than that. She had expected Jimmy to be attracted to someone more like her. Someone with opinions and something worthwhile to say for herself.

It didn't help that Edel and Colleen were somehow rinsing Jimmy dry. So far that awful woman had got a new flat and a florist by courtesy of her son's generosity. Jimmy had sworn to her that it was nothing more than a loan, but Joanie wasn't convinced. She was keeping a firm eye on the pair of them from now on. Married or not, no one was going to make a fool out of her son. Her only consolation was that she knew no matter how well her son pretended otherwise, Jimmy didn't love the girl. He couldn't. Colleen wasn't his type.

Not anything near.

Joanie knew Jimmy better than anyone. Better than himself it seemed. This was all just a massive mistake that somewhere along the line would all go terribly wrong. Until then Joanie was just going to have to bide her time. At least one or two good things might come from this farce of a wedding, she thought to herself.

Grandkids.

That's what Joanie had to keep thinking about every time she felt that her son was being snatched away from her today. That was what this was really about. And Joanie couldn't wait. After today, when all the fuss died down, she'd have her Jimmy back again, she knew that. No one would drive a wedge between her and her son, she'd make sure of that.

Watching Edel walk unsteadily in her clumpy shoes, the half pint of Baileys clearly gone to her head already, Joanie screwed her nose up to show her distaste.

'There's clearly no accounting for taste with some people,' she said, walking away from the bar, determined not to allow her husband to piss her off today of all days.

'Clearly,' Michael said to himself, his voice full of regret.

He was guilty of having bad taste himself as it happened. Especially when it came to meeting Joanie. He'd been so blinded by his wife's beauty, so captivated by the act that she put on that he'd been sucked right in; only discovering what an ugly person Joanie could really be when it was already too late. It had been a small oversight at the time, but a mistake that Michael had spent the rest of his life paying dearly for, he thought begrudgingly as he downed his glass of champagne.

He hated weddings with a vengeance. All this money. All this fuss just for one 'so-called' special day. It made him laugh how people always referred to it as the happiest day of their lives. Why did so many grooms get so pissed at their weddings? Because after this they knew that it would all go downhill.

Michael knew that personally from experience.

The day he'd married Joanie had been a celebration indeed; he hadn't known it at the time but he'd unwittingly celebrated his own funeral, with his delightful wife Joanie doing her damnedest to bury him ever since.

If only he'd known back then what he knew now.

Instead he'd spent the past thirty years tied miserably to the woman. Michael couldn't even fart these days without Joanie breathing down his neck, lecturing him on his manners and hygiene. The woman was like a tyrant. Her only purpose in life seemed to be to make Michael as miserable as possible, and she was exceedingly good at it.

Picking up his wife's unfinished champagne that she'd discarded on the bar, Michael downed that too for good measure. Though the way the day had gone so far, he had a feeling he was going to need a lot more than a couple of drinks to get through today.

CHAPTER EIGHTEEN

'Knock, knock.' Tapping on the bridal suite door with anticipation, Edel was glad that she'd had that large glass of Baileys now.

She suddenly felt nervous. *Nervous of seeing my own child: who'd have thought it*, she thought to herself with a grin. She was though. She was bubbling. The excitement and suspense building in the pit of her stomach. This was the moment that Edel had been both dreaming about and dreading all of her life: the day that her little girl got married.

'Are you ready for me?' Edel called through the door, desperate to get a glimpse of her daughter in her wedding dress.

'Just a minute,' Colleen called back.

Edel smiled. Things would change after today, she knew that. She'd been winding Joanie up earlier, but the truth was, things were going to change for them both.

Marriage always did that.

Colleen would be starting her new life with her husband. *Kids one day too, please God,* Edel thought. Her little girl would be a woman, with her own family to take care of. It was bittersweet. Edel just hoped that she'd done well in bringing Colleen up so that she'd know never to forget about her dear old mum along the way.

'Ok, you can come in now!' Colleen called, interrupting her mother's thoughts. Glancing at herself in the mirror once more, she straightened up her veil, before picking up the bouquet of purple lilies that Joanie had picked out for her. She stood in the centre of the room, awaiting her mother's entrance and, more importantly, her reaction to how she looked.

No one had seen her dress yet. Not a single soul.

Throughout all the wedding planning, all the decisions that had been made by Joanie without her, Colleen hadn't made a single demand. She didn't care about the seating plan or the table decorations. Joanie had already had enough involvement in Colleen and Jimmy's big day. The woman had firmly planted herself in the middle of the wedding plans, submerging herself with all the details of the venue, flowers and invites: at one point Colleen had actually questioned Jimmy on who he was actually marrying. Jimmy had laughed, explaining that was just how his mother was. She took over, liked everything done just so. She didn't mean any harm by it, she just wanted the day to be perfect for them. Never one to cause a fuss, Colleen had let her get on with it.

She barely knew anyone that was here today as it was; there was no one she wanted or needed to impress. Only Jimmy.

And this had been her one and only stipulation: no one, but no one was to see her dress before her mother.

Colleen had never known her father. Her mother had brought her up as both mum and dad since birth, and Colleen had never wanted for anything. It felt right that it was her mother giving her away. Doing her the honour of walking her down the aisle. Colleen wanted this final moment before she said her vows to be just for them.

Even Joanie hadn't dared to argue with that.

Stepping into the room, Edel was ready to say the thousand things that she'd rehearsed in her head, but seeing her daughter standing there in the middle of the room, like a vision dressed in white, a beautiful angel, Edel couldn't find her voice. For the first time in her entire life, she was rendered completely speechless.

Opening her mouth to speak the only noise that escaped was a small strangled gasp.

Colleen laughed.

'Oh Colleen!' Edel finally managed. 'My darling…' Overcome with emotion, Edel started to cry. Not gentle little tears of joy either. Big racking sobs.

'What is it? Don't you like it?' Colleen said, suddenly feeling panicked at her mother's reaction. This level of emotion was completely out of character. Her mother rarely cried. She always prided herself on her strength, on staying in control.

'Oh God. You think it's awful, don't you? Do you think it looks a bit old-fashioned? Does it make me look fat?' Colleen said, kicking herself for not letting anyone else see her dress until now as she examined her reflection in the mirror, wondering how she'd got it so wrong.

'Don't be so silly!' Edel laughed, holding out her hands, as she clasped Colleen's tightly, smiling at her daughter through her tears. 'Colleen. My girl.' Edel shook her head, clearing her throat, still visibly choked. 'You look absolutely beautiful,' she said, admiring her daughter with such love and affection she thought she would burst. 'In fact I've never seen a bride look so perfect!'

Colleen smiled. That was all she'd wanted to hear.

'You look like an angel,' Edel said, her eyes drinking Colleen in.

As biased as Edel might be, being the girl's mother, she meant every word she said. Colleen looked sensational. Her figure-hugging dress swept down to the floor, embellished with thousands of tiny pearls that shimmered in the light with Colleen's every movement.

'There is one small thing that I'd change though,' Edel said pursing her lips.

'What?' Colleen asked wide-eyed. She thought she had everything covered. She was wearing simple silver sandals so that her feet wouldn't ache, her jewellery minimal and understated so that it didn't look too much against the intricate detailing of the dress. Her hair and make-up natural-looking but expertly applied. She hadn't forgotten anything, she was sure of it.

'It's only a suggestion. I won't be offended if you don't want it. Hang on.' Stepping out of the room, Edel returned seconds later holding up a small bouquet of flowers she'd made for Colleen: a delicate spray of cream roses, each displaying a crystal centre, entwined with eucalyptus leaves, all tied together with a string of pearls – the same flowers that Jimmy had first bought her.

'Oh, Mum! They are breathtaking!'

It was Edel's turn to smile then.

'I know Joanie told me to enjoy my day today and not to worry about getting involved with the flowers, but I couldn't help myself with this one. I know that they are your favourites.' Then looking down at the purple lilies that Joanie had chosen, Edel couldn't help herself.

'As much as that Joanie one rates herself, she hasn't got a clue when it comes to flowers. Money can't buy you class indeed! Lilies are a funeral flower, they're not for weddings.'

Taking the bouquet, Colleen stepped back and observed her reflection in the mirror once more, overcome with emotion now too at her mother's thoughtfulness.

Her bouquet was perfect.

Flinging Joanie's flowers down on the bed, Colleen let out a small laugh.

'These ones are awful, aren't they? I don't even like purple!' she said, choosing her words carefully. The truth was Joanie was really overbearing.

'Well don't tell Joanie that, will you. She's wearing her best purple pyjamas today.'

'Pyjamas?' Colleen laughed.

Edel batted her hands at her flyaway comment. 'Sorry, it's a "jumpsuit". You should see her swanning about downstairs in front of all the guests. She looks like Anneka bleeding Rice.'

'Mum!' Colleen said, trying her hardest not to laugh at her future mother-in-law's expense. She couldn't help herself, her mother never being one to hold back on her thoughts or opinions and, to be fair, she seemed to have got Joanie sussed out.

'Me and Nellie were just sat there taking the piss out of her, watching her walking around chatting to people as if she's bleeding royalty. Making eyes at them, while sticking the knife in as soon as they walked off. Two faces that woman's got, yet still she chooses to wear the ugly one!' Edel shook her head at the bouquet of lilies once more. 'Anyway that's enough about Joanie Byrne. Today is your day, my lovely. How are you feeling?'

Colleen shook her head, unsure at this precise minute of how she felt.

'Nervous. Excited. A bit sick!' she said truthfully. 'You don't think I'm rushing into it all do you, Mum? I mean it's all been a bit quick, hasn't it? We've only known each other a few months.'

Edel placed her hand over her daughter's. In usual circumstance, maybe so, but Colleen and Jimmy hadn't had a usual start to their romance. Colleen's life, along with Edel's, had been turned upside down, and the only one that had been there for them both was Jimmy Byrne.

She couldn't be happier for the two of them to get wed; the sooner the better she decided, too, seeing as the alternative would be them both living together out of wedlock.

'When you know, you know, Colleen. Jimmy is a good man.' Looking into her daughter's eyes, Edel said wisely: 'I know that he's not as straight as he could be, what with his business dealings and so forth,' she said honestly. Nellie Erikson had been telling her a few stories of Jimmy's line of work lately and as much as

Edel didn't agree with some of the things she'd heard, she knew that Jimmy's business was exactly that. His business.

He was a good man to her daughter and he'd make her happy. As far as Edel was concerned that was all that mattered.

'You'd be pushed to find anyone else like him. He'll take good care of you, Colleen. I just know it.'

Edel spoke softly, knowing full well why Colleen was having her doubts. Her and Jimmy's relationship had been a whirlwind romance. Jimmy had picked Colleen up off her feet and whisked her off into a world that Colleen hadn't even dared to imagine existed. Wealth, and kudos. It was almost like living a celebrity life and Colleen was more than aware of exactly what Jimmy really was.

He was a face. Notorious. It was no wonder the girl was having last-minute jitters. Colleen was soft. She was sensitive too. She wasn't hardened like Jimmy when it came to the ways of the world, but then that's why it probably worked, thought Edel. They were like chalk and cheese the pair of them.

'Look at all he's done for us already, huh. Helping me with the florist. Sorting out the flat. That's the sort of man that he is, Colleen. Forget about the stories you've heard, and the rumours. That's all just chat. The man has a reputation to protect. So he's shrewd when it comes to his work. Good for him. As long as he treats you well, that's all that matters.'

Colleen nodded. Her mother was right. The only thing that mattered was her and Jimmy, and so far, all he'd done was treat her well. Taking her out to lovely restaurants, buying her fancy gifts. But the way he'd helped out with the florist after the fire had been the thing that had made Colleen love him the most. He mother had been devastated by the damage the fire had caused. If it wasn't for Jimmy's help, they'd have lost everything. As it was, he had helped Edel find a new location, in Piccadilly Circus and he was doing all he could to help get her mother's little business up and running again. He really had gone out of his way to help her mother in any way that he could.

'Do you think I'm just being silly? I feel like a nervous wreck,' Colleen said with a small smile, hoping that was true and that it wasn't her intuition coming into play.

'You're not being silly, love. Every bride has last-minute doubts, Colleen, it's normal. But that's all they are, the jitters. You're doing the right thing. Trust me.' Then holding out her arm to lead Colleen down to the ceremony, Edel smiled warmly, overflowing with love for her daughter.

Colleen took a deep breath, and returned the warmth, smiling at her mother in the mirror.

'You're right. Marrying Jimmy is the best thing I'll probably ever do.'

Edel nodded in full agreement.

'Right, are you ready to go and knock the socks off your future husband and show him and everyone else down there what a bloody beautiful bride you make or what!'

CHAPTER NINETEEN

The sight of Colleen walking slowly down the aisle towards Jimmy Byrne affected him more than he'd anticipated.

This was a big step today for them both, and he'd be lying to himself if he didn't admit that, up until a few moments ago, he'd been wondering if he was doing the right thing.

It had all happened so quickly.

But as he watched Colleen glide down the aisle, so natural-looking yet so breathtakingly beautiful, he knew that he'd made the right decision. Smiling at Colleen, Jimmy realised that he was holding his breath.

He wasn't the only one to notice.

'Not bad if you like that sort of thing,' Alex quipped, unable to hide his distaste for Colleen.

Jimmy shot him a warning look. Even now, on one of the most important days of his life, Alex couldn't help himself. Jimmy held his tongue. His and Alex's friendship had been hanging by a thread these past few months. Somehow Jimmy meeting Colleen had driven a wedge between them, and Alex was clearly bitter. Still, he was here, standing next to him, playing the dutiful role of his best man, so that counted for something he guessed. He just wished Alex would accept his decision; he wished he would respect his need to have a family. Children.

As the harpist's music came to a stop, Jimmy took Colleen's hand as she stood next to him, and smiled at her.

'You look beautiful,' he whispered.

And she did.

A sea of adoring faces told him so. All eyes were on Colleen. The beautiful, blushing bride. This was the dream. This was what everyone in this room strived for: a relationship like this; Jimmy and Colleen looking so in love. So happy.

Jimmy was a good actor.

He knew deep down in his heart that Alex was right. He wasn't capable of loving Colleen. Not really, not the way that she wanted him to. He wasn't capable of loving anyone if he was honest. It just wasn't in him.

He did care about the girl, which had surprised him at first.

Colleen and Edel: Jimmy had taken a liking to them both.

Besides, this was the closest he'd ever get to being 'normal'. A loving wife. Two point four children and the obligatory picket fence. Maybe a dog thrown into the mix too just to complete the perfect picture that Jimmy intended on painting.

The rest would somehow fall into place. It had to.

As the registrar started the ceremony, and Colleen vowed to love Jimmy for all eternity, Jimmy Byrne did what he always did and went along with it all. Full of charm, a perfectly poised smile plastered to his face.

Colleen was his now, and Jimmy would take his vows very seriously.

Until death do us part.

CHAPTER TWENTY

Taking a deep pull of his cigarette as the loud music floated out from the grand hall's main doors, Alex Costa strolled among the hundreds of twinkling white lights that danced across the beautiful courtyard.

It was peaceful out here.

Pressing himself up against the wall, under a blanket of shadows, he was glad to get away from all the fucking madness of Jimmy Byrne's wedding reception. Joanie Byrne was doing her usual, swanning around like lady muck as she lapped up being centre of attention, trying her hardest to outshine the bride, while Michael Byrne had somehow managed to get himself as pissed as a fart. Goading for a row, the man had stood perched at the bar, glaring at his wife with pure hate. It didn't take a clairvoyant to tell Alex that tonight wouldn't end well for Jimmy's parents. That was marriage for you, nothing more than a noose around your neck, and Jimmy had just set himself up for a life sentence.

He still couldn't get his head around what Jimmy was playing at, marrying a girl like Colleen. She wasn't enough for him. Jimmy must know that. He was right about her being different to all the other girls that Jimmy dated, Alex could blatantly see that. Colleen wasn't the usual bimbo that Jimmy normally attracted, that generally only wanted Jimmy for his money.

That's what probably bothered him most about the girl.

Colleen genuinely thought that she loved Jimmy, but she didn't have a clue. She had no idea what she'd married into, but Alex knew it would only be a matter of time before the girl found out. Until then, he'd just have to put up and shut up.

He knew that he'd been treading a fine line the past few weeks. Jimmy was still being off with him and the last thing Alex wanted to do was piss the man off any further by saying his piece, by having his opinion about Colleen. He knew it had riled Jimmy. He just couldn't help himself. What sort of mate would he be if he didn't speak up and tell Jimmy what he really thought? Still, he'd said his bit, and Jimmy hadn't fucking listened. So what else could he do?

Alex just hoped that all this would be worth it for the man. Though he wasn't going to hold his breath. Drinking back the last of his whisky, Alex thought he'd spent the day on his best behaviour. As weddings went, the day hadn't actually been too bad. None of this was done to Alex's taste though. The venue, a fancy Edwardian manor house, in the arseholes of nowhere, was a bit too poncy for his liking. It wasn't even Jimmy's taste either come to think of it. The place was too stiff and formal for Jimmy: Jimmy liked everything brand new and modern. This place was all for his mother's benefit. Good old Joanie. Never missing a trick to impress everyone around her, even on her son's big day.

And boy had they impressed everyone, in true Byrne style.

Jimmy must have forked out an absolute fortune for exclusivity for the weekend, with its twenty bedrooms and thirty-five acres of beautiful woodlands. He'd hired some of London's finest chefs to cover all the catering too, not satisfied with the more than adequate chefs that worked here.

It was genius really.

Today had set the precedent for what lay ahead for Jimmy. Everyone that Alex and Jimmy knew was here tonight. Every business associate, every contact. All of them here to wish Jimmy well. Though it was Jimmy who was playing the real blinder. Today wasn't just about a wedding for Colleen: today was Jimmy's way of letting everyone know that he'd made it.

The flats had all gone through now. Edel's unit had caused them a major setback, and the insurance claims adjuster had picked every detail of the insurance claim apart. Still, they had paid out eventually, and Jimmy had somehow persuaded Edel to take the deal that was originally offered to her and sign what was left of her flat over to the property developer while she still had the chance.

Mint Property Developments.

Little did the woman know that was Jimmy and Alex. Jimmy had joked that the development was going to leave them minted when he'd come up with the name, and never in their wildest dreams had they realised the truth behind the words. They'd both already made a complete fortune from the units that they had found tenants for.

On top of that, business with the girls had really taken off. Now that Westminster Council was clamping down on all the sex shops and shows in Soho, the massage parlours were becoming increasingly popular. Business was booming in every sense of the word, and now that Jimmy Byrne was part of London's elite, he wanted everyone to know about it.

A man stumbled towards him in the darkness, staggering down the pathway, clearly another drunken wedding guest worse for wear after indulging in Jimmy's free bar. Alex shook his head in amusement as he took another deep lug of his cigarette.

But the hilarity of the man's sobriety vanished as rapidly as it had first appeared, as the man neared and Alex got a better look at him.

It wasn't a man at all.

It was a bloody kid. Stuart fucking Matthews to be precise.

'What the fuck are you doing here?' Alex said. Dragging the kid into the doorway of the old barn he was standing outside, Alex was incensed. 'I told you to lay low. Coming here to Jimmy's wedding isn't the smartest of moves, is it?'

'Come on, man! I couldn't miss out on all of this, could I? The wedding of the century.' Stuart Matthews opened his arms widely in exaggeration. 'Fuck me, the man's doing well for himself these days, isn't he?' Slurring as he spoke, Stuart propped himself up against the wall behind him for support and lit up his own cigarette before taking a deep puff and blowing out the cloud of white smoke. Watching it disintegrate into the black night sky.

If he was purposely trying to piss Alex off, it was working.

'What are you doing here?' Alex said, sternly. The boy was so drunk that he could barely stand up straight. He wondered what Stuart thought he was doing. Even turning up here tonight had been forbidden, let alone turning up here and allowing himself to get into such a state. 'I told you to stay away,' Alex warned, thinking that Stuart must have a death wish for going against his orders. The mood Alex was in now, he had a good mind to swing for the kid. But the last thing Alex wanted to do was draw any attention to the fact that he was even here. Though he had a feeling that Stuart knew that too. In fact that's what Stuart was probably depending on. Safety in numbers and all that. At a venue so full of people he knew that Alex couldn't and wouldn't do anything to him. That's why the jumped up little shit was looking so cocky.

'What? The rest of the firm are here but I'm not welcome?' Stuart said, his tone full of sarcasm as he feigned his surprise. 'I only came for the evening do. The piss-up. Couldn't turn down all this free drink, could I? Besides, Jimmy probably wouldn't even fucking notice that I'm here. He's too busy with his new bird,' Stuart said, slyly looking over at Alex. He took no time in getting down to business. His intentions suddenly made clear.

'I know who she is!'

Alex bristled. Stuart might be drunk, but he clearly wasn't completely without his faculties. The lad had a fucking axe to grind, that was obvious. Why else would he have turned up here, spouting his shit? He must be either extremely brave, or extremely stupid to come here to Jimmy Byrne's wedding.

Alex figured on it being the latter.

Fuelled by the skinful of alcohol he'd clearly consumed, Stuart was deluded into thinking that he was being clever. Only he'd already got Alex's back up, and with the mood Alex was in, he was treading a thin line.

'I recognised her old dear too. See, last time I saw her I got a real good look at her.'

Hearing the slur to the kid's voice, Alex decided to try and keep his cool. Not biting to Stuart's words he carried on toking his cigarette. He could feel his temper getting the better of him, but for now, he was trying to wait the conversation out. See where Stuart was going with the shite he was spewing before he decided what he was going to do about it.

'I saw them both standing at the bar. The blushing bride and her eccentric mother. It took me ages to try and place where I'd seen her before, then it hit me!' Stuart grinned triumphantly, as if he'd just lifted his personal best at the gym. 'That was their flat you sent me to, wasn't it? Her and that little old lady of hers. They are the ones from the florist in Dean Street. You and Jimmy were paying me to cause aggro for them both.'

Stuart was glaring at Alex now, his eyes boring in to the man. He had the upper hand. For once in his life, he actually had something big on someone. Someone like Alex Costa and it felt fucking good. Like suddenly, Stuart was holding the man by the balls. He felt powerful.

'But, I get it. You and Jimmy wanted me and the boys to go around and cause a bit of aggro. Wind the old bird up a bit because you wanted her out of the flat,' he said, taking another long drag of his cigarette. 'Paying me to set fire to the bastard thing is seriously fucked up even going by Jimmy's standards.'

Stuart raised his eyes at Alex, letting the man know that he was on to him.

'Jimmy must be one serious ruthless bastard to actually want to burn the old lady's flat to the ground. Especially knowing that his future bride and mother-in-law were inside. Man, that is bad. Only, then I got thinking about you telling me to lay low. What am I laying low for? The fire was weeks ago?'

Stuart flicked his fag onto the ground and stamped it out with his shoe.

'So now I'm thinking two things. One – you don't want me around the old bird and her daughter in case they recognise me? 'Cos let's face it, that wouldn't look good, would it? And two – it ain't just the old girl and her daughter you want me to keep away from. You don't want me around Jimmy either, do you?' Stuart said with certitude, as he waited for Alex to react.

Only Alex wasn't giving him jack shit.

'He doesn't know, does he? The fire was all down to you.'

This was his moment of glory. The reason he'd come here tonight to Jimmy's wedding. Knowing full well that they were surrounded by every face in London. No one could do jack to him somewhere so public.

'You paid me £2k to do your dirty work, which as it goes was good money for a night's earn. Only I've been paying the price ever since. It's been six weeks since the fire and I'm all out of pocket now. So the way I see it, £2k don't cut it. I want more.'

The very least the man could do was see him right financially. If Jimmy had this kind of wealth to literally piss up the wall, Alex wouldn't be too far behind.

'See, I like to think I'm a fair bloke, Alex. You ask me to do a job for you, and I do it, no questions. But making out that I need to lay low for my own protection? When really you want me to lay low for YOUR protection. You don't want Jimmy to find out that you were the one that told me to torch the place.' A couple of grand shoved inside an envelope for the job he'd done, which in all fairness for five minutes' work had been a right touch. Stuart had doused the shop in petrol and lit a match. It was hardly fucking slave labour. Only Stuart realised now that he'd missed a trick.

If Alex didn't want Jimmy to find out that it was him that had ordered the fire then that meant there was more money to be made here. Much more.

'I might go back in there you know, and make a little speech. Welcome the new bride and her mother into Jimmy's family properly, before I let Jimmy in on a few home truths. How's that sound? Bet he'd love to hear what his right-hand man's been up to behind his back.'

Alex had heard enough.

Throwing his cigarette to the floor before grabbing Stuart by the lapels of his jacket, he slammed the kid into the brickwork behind him, winding the snide fucker with the force of his strength.

Stuart Matthews was a liability of the worst kind; drunk, he was dangerous, at best, but factor in the fact the kid must be brain-dead when it came to his level of intelligence and Alex wondered what the fuck the kid was thinking. Waltzing in to Jimmy's wedding and threatening him.

Him. Alex Costa. Who did the muggy little prick think he was? It was all he could do not to shove his fist down the kid's mouth and bust every one of his yellowed, nicotine-stained teeth.

Scanning the empty courtyard to make sure no one was listening in to their conversation, Alex leaned in close to the boy, digging his closed fist hard against Stuart's windpipe.

'You need to watch your fucking mouth!' Alex spat. 'Don't even think about trying anything funny, Stuart. I'm warning you. I told you to lay low, and I told you that for a reason. So don't come around here trying to blackmail me, 'cos you, son, are going to cause fucking murders for yourself.'

Giving the lad one last dig, Alex let go.

Stuart doubled over, struggling for breath as the last bit of air escaped from his lungs. For a second he thought he might lose his bottle. He'd forgotten how brutal Alex could be. Jimmy was ruthless, but Alex was a hard fucker too. He was no match for the man. Only, catching a glimpse of Jimmy Byrne walking up the path towards them, Stuart suddenly realised that he once again had the upper hand.

'Jimmy!' Stuart said, his arms outstretched, his tone overfamiliar, which only indicated to Jimmy that the lad was half-cut.

'Congratulations, man! What a place huh? It's like a fucking palace.'

Turning his attention to Alex, Jimmy kept his voice down.

'What the fuck is he doing here?'

Glancing around anxiously to make sure that Colleen and Edel weren't around, the last thing Jimmy needed was anyone recognising Stuart from the break-in at the shop. He couldn't risk his wife and mother-in-law spotting the kid here, it was far too risky.

'Ah come on, Jimmy man! I fucking grafted for you. You're not going to begrudge me being here tonight to wish you and your lovely Mrs well, are you?' Stuart said with a sneer. 'Me and Alex were just saying what a lovely couple you both make. Weren't we, Alex?'

Knowing that was a blatant lie and seeing the irate expression on Alex's face, Jimmy knew that there was something else going on here: his instinct telling him that he'd clearly interrupted what seemed to be a heated conversation.

'What's going on?' he said agitatedly. He'd been on his way up to the honeymoon suite. Colleen had called it a night. Wanting to sneak out of the wedding without anyone realising that they'd gone so as not to cause a fuss, Colleen had gone up to the room to wait for her new husband to join her.

The day, so far, had been perfect and the last thing Jimmy wanted right now was any aggro.

Stuart looked at Alex and shrugged.

'Alex was just saying that he needs to sort me out some money that he owes me, weren't you, Alex?' Stuart said, knowing this was his one and only chance to completely mug Alex Costa off. The man would be desperately wanting to save his own arse right now, to ensure that Jimmy didn't find out what Alex had paid him to do.

'Oh yeah? What money's that then?' Sensing Stuart's undertone, Jimmy stared at the kid questioningly. He wasn't buying Stuart's bullshit story.

'It's nothing, Jimmy. Forget it,' Alex intervened.

Then turning back to Stuart, Alex flashed the lad a warning. 'Tonight isn't the time and place to sort out business. So let's do this another day, yeah? You were just going to get off, weren't you? You only popped in to wish Jimmy and Colleen all the best, didn't you?' Alex glared at the kid, his eyes boring into him, willing him to just shut the fuck up, and go along with what he said.

His warning wasn't enough to deter the stupid fucker though.

'Don't treat me like a cunt, Alex,' Stuart spat back. Alex would love that, wouldn't he? Stuart to just skulk off back to where he'd been 'laying low'. Out of sight, out of mind. Well, Stuart was resolute; he wasn't going anywhere until Alex agreed to pay up. 'Why don't you tell Jimmy why I'm really here?'

This would teach Alex for thinking that he could get him to do his dirty work, and then mug him off as if he was nothing. If the man wasn't prepared to pay the premium to keep his mouth shut, then he was only too happy to let the treacherous fucker be on the receiving end of Jimmy's temper, even if that did make Stuart a grass. At least he'd be showing his loyalty to Jimmy.

Alex didn't speak.

It spurred Stuart on to thinking that he had the man where he wanted him.

'That fire on Dean Street. Your wife and mother-in-law's place. It was Alex told me to go round there and torch it. Rang me up pissed out of his nut. Told me you'd okayed it all.' Stuart blurted everything out. 'Only now I've done it, the bloke wants to banish me from the face of the earth. Why's that, eh? 'Cos he doesn't want you to find out what I did; 'cos it will drop him right in the shit. Well I ain't no one's mug.'

'You stupid cunt,' Alex said, screwing his mouth up in distaste as he shook his head at Stuart's confession.

'I thought you said you sorted this?' Jimmy said to Alex, not so much as faltering at Stuart's confession.

The man was acting as if he hadn't even heard the words that had come out of Stuart's mouth.

'Hang on a minute.' Stuart stared at the two men, dumbfounded – the sudden realisation that he'd read the situation completely wrong. 'You knew?' he stuttered. 'You knew about the fire?'

'I told you it was too much of a risk letting this cunt run his mouth off. You were supposed to deal with him.' Jimmy was talking now as if Stuart wasn't even there. Looking only at Alex as he spoke.

Unable to believe what he was hearing, Stuart was starting to feel on edge. This was why Alex had been making him lay low. Alex had been trying to save his arse only Stuart had been too stupid to realise it.

'You shouldn't have come here tonight!' Alex said, the initial sympathy he'd felt for Stuart replaced with irritation. He'd tried to do the kid a favour. He'd thrown him a lifeline, and Stuart, being the gormless prick that he was, had chucked it all back in his face.

Jimmy had wanted Stuart dealt with properly. He hadn't wanted any loose ends that could lead anyone back to them regarding the fire. But Alex hadn't the heart to see the order through.

Stuart wasn't even eighteen. Just a kid.

As it turned out, Jimmy was right. Stuart was a liability. Clearly not capable of keeping his mouth shut after all. If the kid had even half a brain he'd be dangerous. Still, there was nothing that Alex could do to save his arse. Not now he'd come here tonight and tried to pull a stunt like this.

Realising that he'd fucked himself, Stuart didn't know what to say to redeem himself. His only hope was to beg.

'I get it now,' Stuart said, backtracking. 'I misread the situation. I thought Alex was mugging me off, mugging us both off, Jimmy. I won't say a thing, you have my word.'

But Jimmy and Alex both knew that Stuart Matthews's word was worth shit. He'd already proved that he couldn't keep his mouth shut. There was no way that Jimmy Byrne would let the man fuck everything up for him. Not when he'd worked this hard to get where he was.

The lad barely had time to register what was happening as the two men dragged him behind the old barn at the back of the courtyard.

He'd come here tonight to try and cause murders for the men. Unbeknown to Stuart Matthews, the only murder he had managed to instigate was his own.

CHAPTER TWENTY-ONE

Colleen Byrne sat on the edge of the bed sipping her glass of champagne, as if she was still in some sort of dream world.

Her head was spinning. The magic and excitement of today had been everything that she'd wished for and more. Every minute of her and Jimmy's wedding had been every bit as wonderful as she'd hoped it would be. The venue, the food, the atmosphere. It was like something straight out of a movie.

Now she was married, she couldn't really believe it. She was a Byrne: Jimmy Byrne's wife, and as she waited for her husband to return to the honeymoon suite she couldn't help but feel a mixture of both apprehension and excitement at the thought that they were going to consummate their marriage.

Colleen had been both dreading and anticipating this moment for weeks. Still a virgin, Colleen just hoped that she was going to be good enough for Jimmy. He'd made no secret of the fact that he'd had a lot of girlfriends before her. The man had years of experience ahead of her.

Downing some more champagne as she stared at the clock, the longer she waited for him, the more her nerves were starting to get the better of her. Jimmy had been ages. He'd told her that he'd sneak out and follow her up; but she'd been up here waiting for ages now, and currently on her second glass. She was in danger of drinking too much champagne and passing out drunk if he didn't get here soon.

Suspecting that someone was keeping him talking, Colleen smiled to herself. If anyone would have cornered him as he tried to make his getaway, she could bet her life it would be her mother.

Her mum just adored Jimmy.

She'd be talking the hind legs off the man right about now, and Jimmy would be too polite to interrupt her.

Finishing off her drink, tipsy, Colleen decided to go back downstairs and look for Jimmy. She was his wife now and it was her duty to rescue him, she thought to herself with a giggle.

'Leave it, Jimmy. For fuck's sake, he's had enough, Jimmy!' Using every bit of strength he had, Alex Costa dragged Jimmy Byrne away from the mess that was now Stuart Matthews.

'What the fuck's got into you, Jimmy? He's just a kid. He fucked up!' Alex spat, rubbing his head in dismay.

He'd never seen Jimmy like this before. Not at this level of lunacy. The past few minutes Jimmy had been like a man possessed. Incoherent. Like the lights were on, but no one was home as he viciously attacked Stuart Matthew. The kid didn't stand a fucking chance.

Vexed that Stuart Matthews had the audacity to come here on his wedding day, that he could have cost him everything, Jimmy hadn't held back his fury.

What scared Alex the most was that even he hadn't been able to stop Jimmy. Unhinged, Jimmy had carried out his incisive attack until it had gone way too far for Alex's liking.

Now it was too late.

'Look at the state of him, Jimmy. There's nothing left,' Alex said as he stared down at the sickening mush of red pulp that had once been Stuart's face. His head had caved in, his nose and eye sockets sunk under the force of Jimmy's punches and kicks, leaving him unrecognisable.

Not even human anymore.

He was dead.

Unable to stomach the sight of the kid's lifeless body sprawled out in a pool of his own blood on the concrete at the back of the old barn house, Alex leaned against the wall, spewing out the contents of his stomach, dry heaving until there was nothing left to come up. Alex normally had a strong constitution for shit like this; it was all part and parcel of the business they were in. Dealing with people as and when they had to.

Only Stuart Matthews had been one of them. He'd been part of Jimmy and Alex's workforce and that's exactly why Alex had thrown the kid a lifeline.

'Fuck, Jimmy! Look what you did!' Alex said, spitting out the last of the bile that had risen at the back of his throat. This was exactly the reason that Alex had told Stuart to lay low in the first place.

Jimmy had been gunning for him.

If Stuart had just done what he'd told him, and kept his fucking head down, then he'd have been all right. It would have all died down after a couple of more months. Stuart would still be alive.

But no, the stupid bastard had other ideas.

Coming here to Jimmy's wedding and trying to cause shit for him. *Fuck me.* All Alex had tried to do was help the kid out, and for his troubles, Stuart had swiftly stabbed the man in the back. Still, that didn't mean that Alex wished the stupid fucker dead.

Stuart was still technically a kid. His life had barely started and now Jimmy had ruthlessly snubbed it out.

'Fuck!' It was Jimmy's turn to swear. Snapping out of the red mist of rage that had consumed him, it was as if he'd just woken up from a trance, seeing suddenly what Alex could see.

'Christ! I didn't fucking mean to kill him. Not here. Not tonight.' Staring down at his once crisp white shirt, his eyes registered sprays of claret before his brain did.

Blood. Stuart's blood.

He was covered in it.

The brute force of his every punch had relieved the hot rage that he'd felt towards Stuart. Coming here tonight, and trying to publicly humiliate him at his own wedding.

'Fuck,' Jimmy said again. His hand over his mouth. Shocked. Sickened by his actions. It was as if he'd just blacked out.

'We need to get him the fuck out of here,' Alex said, the panic evident in his voice at the predicament Jimmy had just put them in. It was almost one o'clock in the morning. Once the music stopped and people came off the dance floor, they'd never be able to get rid of Stuart's body. The place would be crawling with people and by the time they'd all fucked off to bed, it would be starting to get light. If they got caught for this, the police would throw away the key.

Alex was panicking. Pacing the floor, shaking his head in dismay, he could see that Jimmy clearly wasn't thinking straight right now. It would be down to him to get this shit sorted out and quickly.

'Jimmy?'

Turning around the two men stared in horror as Colleen stepped out from the shadows of the doorway.

The girl looked at the two men, then down at the ground, a strangled scream leaving her throat as her eyes rested on the bloodied man.

'What's happened?' she cried. Her eyes searching Jimmy's for an answer. Willing him to say something that would make this all right.

She eyed his blood-splattered shirt. His swollen red fits. Then looking back down at what was left of the battered body on the ground, she knew without a doubt that whoever he was, he was dead.

'What have you done, Jimmy?' Colleen was shaking. Her hand trembled violently as she held it over her mouth, trying to stop another scream from escaping. To stop herself from throwing up.

'Colleen, baby!' Jimmy said, stepping towards his new wife, as if to shield her from the horrors of what was already ingrained into her brain. 'It's not what you think.'

'Don't touch me,' Colleen spat; seeing the blood on Jimmy's outstretched hands, the look of shock and disgust on Alex's face, she knew that Jimmy was lying.

'You murdered him?' she said, erratically shaking her head from side to side, as if the words she spoke couldn't be the truth. She was crying now, her face streaming with tears and black steaks of mascara.

'He's dead? You did this? You murdered him, Jimmy?' she asked, her voice almost a whisper, as if she was speaking only to herself, trying to make sense of it all.

She was going into shock, her voice loud, high-pitched as she realised what she'd just witnessed.

A loud, deranged wail escaped from her mouth.

'HE'S DEAD. YOU KILLED HIM. YOU'RE A MURDERER, JIMMY, A MURDERER. WHAT HAVE YOU DONE?'

Jimmy was there, wrapping his arms around Colleen, hugging her, muffling her cries as he led her back, away from the sickening sight of the boy he'd just brutally killed.

'It's okay, Colleen. It's not what you think.'

'Jimmy?'

Joanie was there then too.

She'd heard the loud commotion from the far end of the courtyard. Thinking that Jimmy and Colleen were having some kind of spat, she'd decided to investigate. Only now, staring at her son covered in blood, the dead body on the ground, she realised that the newlyweds having a lover's tiff was the least of her worries.

'What the hell's going on, Jimmy?' Joanie said as she took in the harrowing sight.

'Mum, you need to go back inside,' Jimmy warned, the situation suddenly getting well out of control.

Colleen was wailing like a banshee, beside herself, crying. Jimmy wouldn't be able to let the girl out of his sight.

'You need to send Reggie Wilkins out here. He'll help Alex sort out all of this.'

Joanie went to open her mouth, but no sound came.

'Mum?' Jimmy said, his voice stern as he tried to get his mother to snap out of her shocked trance. 'We need to get this sorted. We can't let anyone come out here. You need to keep them all inside while we fix things.' Jimmy eyed his mother, making sure that she was well aware of the severity of the situation. Whatever her thoughts were about Jimmy's actions tonight, this wasn't the time and place to voice them.

They needed to act fast.

'Do you think you can do that, Mum? Keep everyone inside?'

Joanie Byrne nodded obediently.

'I'm going to take Colleen back upstairs. Alex, you and Reggie need to get him moved and get this place cleaned up—'

Interrupted while giving out his orders, Jimmy bristled as he recognised a voice calling out to them.

'Jimmy? Colleen? Are you out here?' the woman called.

Jimmy and Joanie locked eyes as they heard Edel Walsh's voice booming out from the venue doors.

'Is that you, Jimmy?'

'Mum?'

Joanie Byrne didn't speak. Nodding, she did as her son had instructed. Turning on her heel, she did the one and only thing that she could do: she was saving Jimmy's arse, plastering the biggest smile onto her face as she marched back towards the venue to see to Edel Walsh.

'Oh, Joanie. I was just going looking for my Colleen. Have you seen her?' Edel said, searching through the darkness from where Joanie had just come. Edel could have sworn she'd just heard raised voices. 'I just wanted to check that she was all right.'

'I have indeed seen her.' Joanie Byrne grinned, taking Edel Walsh by her arm and leading her back inside the hall. 'And she's more than fine. The two love birds have called it a night; they've both gone up to their honeymoon suite.'

'Ah!' Edel said, sad that Colleen hadn't said good night to her old mum before she'd called it a night. 'I wonder if I should just pop up and say good night to them both.'

Joanie shook her head. Friendly, she led the woman back into the hall and closed the doors behind her. Bolting the locks.

Joanie Byrne smiled.

'You'll do no such thing, Edel. Those two looked more than preoccupied when I left them. I'm sure they have better things to do on their wedding night than chat to you, if you know what I mean.'

Seeing the slight disappointment on Edel's face, Joanie winked.

'Don't look so down, Edel. It's been a beautiful day, and you know what happens after weddings?' She raised her eyes playfully. 'Babies!'

Edel grinned then too. Happily letting Joanie lead her to the bar.

*

Clinking a champagne glass loudly to quieten down the room, Joanie shouted above the throng of noise and people; her voice commanding everyone's attention as she made her speech.

'Ladies and Gentlemen! Jimmy asked me to inform you all that he and his beautiful bride have now retired to the honeymoon suite for the night.'

A loud crowd of cheers and claps ensued and Joanie smiled before she continued: 'But Jimmy told me to tell you all that he wants you to carry on without him. He said to make sure that you drink this bar dry!'

Picking up the champagne glasses that the barmen were topping up at the bar, on Joanie's instruction, she lifted one of the glasses nearest to her into the air.

'To Jimmy and Colleen Byrne – To the Happy Couple!'

Everyone raised their glasses high in the air to match their spirits.

Edel followed suit, realising that it was selfish of her to be upset at not saying good night to Colleen. It was only natural that she wouldn't be her daughter's first thought tonight. Edel would have to get used to that now. Of course Jimmy and Colleen had other things on their minds. It was their wedding night after all.

'Kinky buggers,' Edel said good-naturedly as she winked at Joanie, a huge smile appearing on her face. 'Here, Joanie, this means that we could be expectant grandmas before the night's out.'

Clinking her glass against Edel's, Joanie downed her champagne in one, her nerves shot to pieces at tonight's events.

It might be Jimmy and Colleen's wedding night, but the last thing on their minds tonight would be making her and Edel grandmothers.

CHAPTER TWENTY-TWO

Staring down at her naked body as she lay in the roll top bath, Colleen couldn't remember stepping into the water. Scanning the bathroom, in search of her wedding dress, she couldn't even remember taking it off, but there it was, lying in a heap just inside the doorway. The gown once beautiful, embellished with tiny shimmering pearls, a delicate layer of tulle, was now abandoned on the floor. Tainted for ever more.

A vague memory flashed in her mind of Jimmy undressing her. He'd been speaking to her, his words soft and gentle as he'd guided her carefully into the bath.

She'd watched him. Her eyes fixed on Jimmy, as he stood at the opposite end of the bathroom. As he stood in the shower beside her. Watched him in silence as he undid the buttons on his once crisp white shirt, now ruined by the jagged sprays of red, and let it fall to the floor. Watched him standing under the warm water, running red, cascading down his body, and forming a pool of pink at his feet before finally dispersing down the plughole.

He was gone now.

She could see him through the small crack in the bathroom door. Pacing the bedroom suite.

Alex was there too.

Colleen strained to listen to their hushed voices, their words filled with panic.

'We put him in the back of Reggie's motor. He's going to make sure that the body's disposed of. We'll burn it. Make sure there's nothing left of it. Mikey and Jay-Jay are doing a clean-up op at the barn as we speak. The guests have all fucked off home now, and the ones that are staying here at the hotel have called it a night. I told the night staff to shut the bars so that no one can pull an all-nighter. The place will be like new again by the morning. No one will be any the wiser.'

Alex.

The man sounded like a robot. His tone cold. Devoid of any feeling.

Colleen could see Jimmy. Nodding, as he made his way over to the minibar.

'Fuck's sake!' he said, as he peered into the fridge that had been stocked with only champagne and fancy chocolates for the newlyweds. 'I need a fucking proper drink, not this shit.'

Grabbing hold of the bottle, Jimmy popped the champagne cork.

Colleen jumped at the sudden noise, the water she was sitting in sloshing over the top of the bath.

She felt cold. Freezing in fact.

The haze of steam that drifted up from the surface of the water told her that the water was warm. Colleen couldn't feel its heat.

Lifting her hand up in front of her face, she stared for a few moments at the water dripping from her newly manicured nails, her wedding rings glistening under the bright bathroom lights, wondering if this was all real.

It was.

She was really here.

She was numb.

She realised she was crying, sobbing uncontrollably, a stream of tears running down her face, dripping down into the bright red hue of bloodied water, as it swished all around her. The watery, red liquid lapping up over her pale white stomach.

Blood?

She felt herself begin to panic as a sudden flashback filled her mind. This time she could see it all so clearly.

Jimmy and Alex standing over the body. The vicious look on Jimmy's face. His fury. Remembering how she'd tried to call out for help but no noise had escaped her mouth. How Jimmy had taken her in his arms, desperate to console her, and to try and stop the strangled screams escaping from her mouth.

Blood all over Jimmy. All over her. All over her beautiful dress.

The young man, his life snatched away from him so brutally, and now Jimmy was sitting in the next room drinking champagne.

'What about her?'

Hearing Alex's question, Colleen almost stopped breathing. She hadn't even considered that she could be in danger. But she was, wasn't she?

Holding the edge of the tub tightly, so that she could stay deadly still, she wondered if they had forgotten about her in here, if they didn't realise she could hear their conversation. She could feel her heart beating erratically in her chest, beating loudly. Her pulse quickening to match it.

'What if she talks; might she talk, Jimmy? What are you going to do about her?'

Colleen felt sick, panic engulfing her as she waited for Jimmy to answer.

He finally spoke. His voice sharp, adamant.

'I'm not going to do anything to her.' Jimmy was incredulous. 'She's my wife!'

Colleen stood up, suddenly claustrophobic. Desperate to get out of the bath, out of this room. Away from Jimmy and Alex and their sickening ways.

A strangled cry escaped from her mouth as she sent the water cascading from the tub, splashing out all over the floor in her urge to get out of the water, away from the blood. From Jimmy. The urge so strong, she slipped in her haste.

Jimmy was there then. Standing at her side, holding her up. Taking a bathrobe from the heated rail behind him, he wrapped it around her, as he held her tight to him once more.

She could smell that familiar musky scent of his. The smell that used to make her feel so safe. Now it was suffocating her. His lingering scent overpowering her; she felt dizzy and sick.

'Come and lie down, Colleen. You've had a nasty shock.'

Scared for her life, Colleen didn't know what else to do but play along. Knowing what Alex had just said and what Jimmy was more than capable of, Colleen could only nod obediently as she allowed Jimmy to lead her into the bedroom.

Sitting down on the bed, she saw the look that Jimmy exchanged with Alex, before Alex quickly left the room.

Then Jimmy handed her a glass of champagne.

Colleen stared at the drink, horrified. Jimmy, seeing the look on his new wife's face explained: 'It's all there is. Drink it, it's for the shock. It will take the edge off.'

Holding the champagne flute to her lips, Colleen sipped the liquid, choking as she tried to swallow it down, her throat constricted by the heavy lump of emotion there. Hot bile threatened to push it back out.

Jimmy tipped the glass, making sure that Colleen drank it all.

She was crying again. Big racking sobs making her whole body shake. She wanted to leave. She wanted to go and find her mum, tell her everything.

Jimmy wouldn't allow that.

'Lie down, Colleen. Rest. You've had a fright,' he said. His voice softly spoken, soothing almost, as he lifted the covers and helped Colleen slip inside, wrapping the blankets around her tightly so that they engulfed her trembling body.

She obediently complied. Doing as she was told, she lay her head on the pillow, the thick towelling robe still wrapped tightly around her too. She hadn't realised how exhausted she was. Her body suddenly so weak and tired, her eyes heavy, unaware that Jimmy had laced her drink with the sleeping tablets that Alex had brought for him to use.

Closing her eyes, she could feel Jimmy sitting beside her, the warmth of his hand on her head as he stroked her wet hair. Soothing, rhythmic movements, giving Colleen a fleeting feeling that everything would be all right again. That somehow this had all been one big, awful mistake.

Jimmy wasn't a monster?

Not her Jimmy?

She was gone then. Her confused thoughts replaced with the oblivion of nothingness as she was plunged into complete darkness. Her sleep, because of the drugs Jimmy had given her, would be void of nightmares.

The same couldn't be said for the reality she faced when she finally woke up.

PART TWO: 1985

CHAPTER TWENTY-THREE

'Well that's me done for the day.' Shaking off his work boots so that he didn't get mud all over Joanie's pristinely clean floors and give the woman something else to moan about, Michael Byrne made his way into the kitchen.

'I swept up all the leaves out there, and gave the shed a good tidying too,' he lied, convinced that he'd managed to get away with the fact he'd been hiding out in his shed for the past two hours catching up on the *Match of the Day* highlights on his miniature television set. The little portable analogue TV that he'd bought himself from Woolworths had been a lifesaver these past few years. His only escape from Joanie. Of course, he couldn't let on that he actually enjoyed himself out there in the shed. He had to make out that he'd been busy doing his chores. Otherwise the woman would put a stop to that too. Anything to make his life hell. That was all Joanie seemed to live for.

'I'm exhausted. Any chance of a nice cup of coffee?' Michael asked, hoping that his wife might be in a good mood and oblige.

'Kettle's there,' Joanie said tartly. Not bothering to look up from where she was standing, rooting around inside the kitchen drawer for her reading glasses, Joanie found them and slipped them on. Scrutinising her husband, she shook her head.

'And don't think I don't know what you've been up to, Michael. Tidying the shed? Is that what you call hiding away out there? I wasn't born yesterday. I bet you were out there pawing over those cheap newspapers with all those tarts that call themselves Page Three girls, and watching the football, weren't you?'

About to deny that that indeed was exactly what he had been doing, Michael decided not to bother arguing with the woman. Joanie had a penchant for being able to spot his bullshit from a mile off. His best bet was to come clean. Apologise profusely to keep the old nag happy. Anything for an easy life. Though life was never ever easy being married to Joanie Byrne.

'You got me, Joanie.' Michael held his hands up, shooting her a wry smile as he tried instead to make a joke out of his little fib. What he really wanted to do was scream. This is what Joanie and her incessant nagging had driven him too. He was a grown man having to hide out in his tiny four foot by six foot little wooden sanctuary, just so he could get away from the old bag, and even that place was no longer sacred anymore it seemed.

'Nothing gets passed you, my love.' Gritting his teeth, Michael made his way over to the kettle to make his own coffee.

'And don't you forget it, my love,' Joanie retorted, rolling her eyes, aware that the backhanded compliment was actually a dig. 'And while you're at it, you're going to have to fetch your own tea tonight too,' she added, sounding bored, as if she had other things on her mind. Important things that didn't involve Michael no doubt. 'I'm going over to Jimmy's. He's having troubles with Colleen again. I said I'd go round there and give him a hand with young Nancy.'

'Oh that will be nice for you.' Michael bristled as he only just noticed that Joanie was already wearing her coat, her face made-up with a hint of make-up, an overnight bag down by the kitchen doorway. He was annoyed that he'd have to make his own dinner whilst Joanie rushed to Jimmy's aid. That once again Jimmy was the woman's priority and Michael was being left to fend for himself. Treated like some kind of an afterthought. He also hated that Joanie was so involved with their granddaughter's upbringing, while he was always excluded.

He and Jimmy gave each other a wide berth these days. They were only ever in each other's company if they really had to be. But Michael adored his firstborn granddaughter, Nancy. The child was the apple of his eye.

He knew what would happen eventually though: Joanie and Jimmy would turn the little thing against him.

It was only a matter of time.

As it was he barely got to see her. Still. If Joanie was going out, at least he'd have a bit of peace and quiet tonight. For once he could eat his dinner on his lap, whilst watching shit on the TV, instead of being forced to sit at the dining table and endure Joanie's monotonous conversations.

'Colleen's had another one of her funny turns, and Jimmy's got some business to attend to. He wants me to look after Nancy for him.'

Michael raised his eyes at Joanie's terminology. A 'funny turn?' Fucking hell! That was an understatement. The girl'd had a full on mental breakdown shortly after she and Jimmy had wed. Jimmy had to have her admitted to a psychiatric ward. Colleen was riddled with anxiety and panic attacks, and it was no wonder, Michael thought to himself, being married to Jimmy would be enough to make anyone lose their mind.

'She's been getting bad again,' Joanie said. 'Jimmy said that the doctors are saying that it's postnatal, but Nancy's almost two. If you ask me the girl's just not the full picnic. I told Jimmy that she needs to pull herself together, but you know how he won't hear a bad word about the girl. He's always tiptoeing around her like she's made of glass.'

Michael held his tongue.

Typical Joanie, as sympathetic as always. Then nodding down at the bag, Michael added, 'Well how long are you going to be this time?' Part of him now relishing the thought of having the house to himself. He'd obviously done a good job at convincing Joanie that he didn't want her to leave, as the woman pursed her lips at her husband's neediness.

'I know exactly what's going through your mind, Michael. You're worried about who's going to cook your dinners while I'm gone, aren't you?' Joanie said, rolling her eyes once again, this time despairingly as she continued to make her way into the lounge and collect some of her belongings that she might need: her comfy slippers from under the armchair, and her Mills and Boon book that she'd been thoroughly enjoying despite it being ever so racy. 'Well, Michael. This is going to be a shock to your system but you see those long dangly things hanging out from your shoulders? They are called your arms. On the end of them you'll find a pair of hands. I'm sure even you can manage to use them to press a few buttons on the microwave oven. You're more than capable of cooking your own dinner for a couple of weeks.'

'A couple of weeks?' Michael gasped, as he heard the loud beep of Jimmy's Range Rover outside.

'That will be Jimmy,' Joanie said, leaning down to get her bag.

'Let me get it for you,' Michael said, grabbing it before Joanie could. 'It's the least I can do before you leave.'

Joanie felt bad then. As much as Michael had driven her to pure distraction over the years, he really seemed to be trying lately. The dynamics of their relationship had changed drastically over the past few years, ever since Jimmy had found Michael wandering the streets that time he'd gone missing. Her husband had been set upon by a group of thugs. Beaten and tied up in some squalor of a house somewhere, her Jimmy had told her.

The man had been a mere shadow of himself after that. He never really ventured out of the house anymore, and mostly these days he agreed with everything that Joanie ever said. To the point that it was almost annoying. Still, it was better than him going off every five minutes and getting himself drunk and into all sorts, she figured. The man had at least been trying.

She felt bad for abandoning him.

'I can't leave little Nancy in Colleen's care. The woman can barely look after herself. I'll be back before you even know it. You'll manage without me just fine.'

'I'll manage, but I won't do such a good job without you.' Michael nodded before planting a small kiss on her cheek.

Joanie nearly fell over with shock. She couldn't remember how long it had been since the two of them had shared any form of affection.

Patting Michael on the arm, awkwardly, she took her bag from him, and made her way out the front door, to where Jimmy was waiting.

Michael shut the door behind her, not bothering to stand and wave them both off, just so Jimmy could sit in his motor glaring at him like he was some kind of an arsehole. Instead, Michael leaned up against the front door, and listened to Jimmy's Range Rover pull away from the house.

A couple of weeks without Joanie. No more nagging and moaning; no more getting a lecture if he so much as farted. It was like he was suddenly given time off for good behaviour.

'Ding dong the witch is fucking dead!' he sang to himself, jumping up and down with happiness that his miserable cunt of a wife had finally fucked off for a few weeks.

Michael Byrne couldn't believe his luck.

CHAPTER TWENTY-FOUR

'Have you cleaned all the toilets properly this time, Sasha? Last time you left, I had to give them all a going over again, myself. I wasn't best pleased. I'd only had my manicure that morning too. Chipped all my lovely polish off, I did, in the process.' Joanie Byrne berated the younger plump girl with disdain. 'I told Jimmy that I'd be having a word with you about it today. We can't be paying someone to come out and do the cleaning, if I have to do it all again myself after you've gone.'

'Yes, Joanie. I've done all the jobs that Mr and Mrs Byrne have asked me to do. And seeing as you've already mentioned the toilets to me twice now, I gave them an extra special scrub just for you,' Sasha Layton said through gritted teeth, ignoring the older woman's permanently sour scowling expression. Sasha never let the likes of Joanie Byrne try and get the better of her the way she thought she could with everyone else around here.

Ignoring the woman's glare, and bored with having to humour her, Sasha turned her attention to little Nancy, sitting in her highchair, waving at Sasha excitedly. The sight of the girl made Sasha's heart melt.

With those piercing green eyes, the child was the spit of her father, Jimmy.

'Hello, beautiful,' Sasha said, stepping forward and touching the little girl's fingers, as Nancy Byrne shot her one of her hypnotic smiles.

'I hope you've washed your hands,' Joanie said tartly, scooping the child up into her arms, letting Sasha know that she wasn't welcome to touch her precious grandchild.

'Well, I'm done for the day now, Mrs Byrne. I'm just going to go out and say goodbye to Colleen then I'll be off.'

Joanie waved her hand at Sasha as if to dismiss her. She was far too wrapped up in playing with Nancy to be bothered with what Sasha was doing.

Making her way out through the huge kitchen, Sasha wondered what it would be like to live in a house like this. Right on the doorstep of Richmond Park, with its six bedrooms and enormous driveway, the place must have cost an absolute fortune; but then Jimmy Byrne was clearly good for it.

Sasha had been cleaning for the family since they'd moved in two and half years ago, and in that time, the wealth had just poured in.

Making her way out to the garden, to where Colleen was sitting waiting for her with a fresh pot of tea, Sasha saw Colleen glance up at her, grateful that Sasha was joining her once again for a cuppa and a chat.

'This is turning into a regular little thing now, isn't it?' Sasha said with a smile, pointing at the teapot. 'I ain't being funny, Colleen, but shouldn't it be me making tea for you? I mean, I am the staff you know,' she said with a wink and a smile as she sat down with Colleen.

Then catching the disappointment on the woman's face, realising that she sounded like she was only taking the time to sit with Colleen just because she was getting paid, Sasha added: 'Cheers, mate. I'm gasping for a cuppa.'

'Is the old battleaxe still in there slinging her weight around?' Colleen asked as she poured Sasha a cup of tea, before glancing inside the patio windows, glad that Joanie seemed to be leaving her alone. Colleen wasn't in the right frame of mind to tolerate her mother-in-law this morning.

'She's just giving Nancy her breakfast,' Sasha said, knowing how Joanie liked to try and rule the roost when she was here. Sasha had seen how the woman took over when it came to minding little Nancy. She could see it upset Colleen too, but Colleen wasn't mentally strong enough to stand up to the woman and say anything. 'God, she's adorable, Colleen. She's getting so big now too. And those eyes. I've never seen eyes so green. She's very like Jimmy, isn't she?'

'Oh, yeah, she's a true Byrne all right.' Colleen nodded, not bothering to disguise the bitterness in her voice.

'You all right, Colleen?' Sensing that Colleen wasn't herself today, Sasha watched as she picked up her mug, her hand visibly shaking as she brought it to her mouth. Colleen was struggling.

'You not having a top up?' Sasha asked, pointing at her and then to the teapot.

Colleen shook her head, looking away too quickly, which only confirmed Sasha's suspicions.

She was drinking again.

Doing her old trick of hiding vodka in her cup and making out like she was drinking tea. Jimmy and Joanie probably didn't take much notice: too busy caught up in the business and Nancy to care what Colleen was secretly doing; but Sasha wasn't stupid.

'Are you sure you're okay?' she asked again, knowing that it wasn't her place to say anything that might upset her. Sasha liked Colleen.

She wasn't like a lot of Sasha's other customers: the trophy wives with more money than sense that acted as if they were well above their stations, talking down to Sasha as if she was beneath them, or even worse, treating her as if she was stupid.

Colleen was a nice girl. The only customer who ever sat with her after her work was done and made her a fresh pot of tea; but Sasha knew Colleen was just desperately lonely.

'Yeah, I'm fine.' Colleen shrugged. 'She just sets my nerves on edge.'

'She is a bit of a snotty cow,' Sasha whispered, feeling brave at letting on what she really thought of Joanie Byrne, then seeing Colleen laugh at her words, Sasha shot her a knowing grin. 'So, are you doing anything nice today?' she asked Colleen. She wondered how Colleen spent her day when Joanie was here, making a nuisance of herself. 'You should take Nancy down to the park, I bet she'd love to feed the ducks,' Sasha said, trying to encourage Colleen to get out of the house, to spend some time with her daughter away from her vile mother-in-law. The fresh air would probably do the woman some good.

'Yeah. Maybe,' Colleen said with a vacant nod, knowing full well that wouldn't be happening. She could barely leave the house these days without having major panic attacks. Riddled with anxiety, Colleen preferred the solitude of her bedroom. Besides, Joanie would think of some excuse to stop Colleen from spending time with her daughter.

Her mother-in-law always did.

Sensing that this was the case, Sasha wasn't prepared to give up. Colleen looked a bit lost today; she looked like she needed a gentle shove in the right direction.

'How about inviting some friends over then?'

'What friends?' Colleen said, in a rare moment of opening up to Sasha, speaking honestly.

'I ain't got no friends. I don't see anyone. I never go out. The only people that ever come to the house other than Joanie are you and my mum. The only people I could class as some form of friends are you and my mum: my cleaning lady and the woman who gave birth to me. How sad is that?'

Staring out across the beautifully manicured gardens, Colleen took another mouthful of her drink.

Even her mum was busy these days, working hard in her new shop. Enjoying her new flat. It was as if everyone's life had moved on and Colleen was still stuck here. Trapped.

'Well, I don't think it's sad at all. I mean come on, you'd be hard pushed to find a better mate than me. I'm quite a laugh you know, plus I love a good old chat. I could talk for ever if the mood took me,' Sasha said hoping to lighten the mood. 'You know if you ever wanted to talk to me, Colleen, you could.'

Colleen liked Sasha. She was confident and feisty. Unlike her, Sasha didn't take any shit from anyone. Colleen had even heard her put Joanie in her place once or twice, clearly not intimidated by the woman.

Colleen couldn't remember what it felt like to have someone to confide in, and the way she was feeling lately she could certainly do with a friend.

About to speak, Sasha continued: 'I know about your postnatal depression. Jimmy told me. It's okay you know. Loads of new mothers suffer with it. My mum had it for years. At the time it made her feel as if she was going mad, but by the time I was three she was back to her old self again. You will get through it you know.'

Sasha spoke gently, hoping that Colleen could see that she understood what she was going through.

'Jimmy told you that I've got postnatal depression?' Colleen said, staring, trying to read her thoughts. Wondering now if this was the reason why Sasha always made time for her. She only hung about for a cup of tea because she felt sorry for Colleen.

Sad, pathetic, Colleen. With her postnatal depression and her mother-in-law coming in to look after her child as she clearly couldn't even look after herself.

That's what Sasha must see when she looked at her. That's what everyone else saw too.

'Well yeah. I mean he didn't say much to be honest. Just that you'd suffered a little bit with it,' Sasha said, shifting uncomfortably in her chair now as she realised that she'd said something she shouldn't. The last thing she wanted to do was upset Colleen. Sasha was trying to be nice. To get through to the girl. For a brief second, she'd thought that she had.

The truth was Sasha knew more than she was letting on. Jimmy had told her a lot more than just that. With Sasha working in their home so often the man had thought it only fair he filled Sasha in on Colleen's unruly behaviour. He'd told her about the chronic depression she suffered with, and Sasha knew that Colleen had been admitted into a psychiatric ward for a few weeks shortly after her and Jimmy had been married.

After Nancy had been born, she'd been sent to rehab too, to deal with her addiction to painkillers and sleeping tablets. Alcohol too.

'Jimmy only told me because he was worried about you,' Sasha said, trying to convince Colleen that they hadn't been maliciously talking behind her back, but she could tell the damage was already done.

Colleen didn't look happy to find out that Jimmy was confiding in Sasha about her personal business.

Colleen's moods had been spiralling downhill again lately, Sasha thought and today Colleen seemed to be on one of her major downers again.

Paranoid and edgy.

Sasha knew that she'd said the wrong thing as Colleen drained the rest of her mug. Shutting herself off from her, she looked suddenly guarded once more.

Of course Jimmy had sounded concerned about her, Colleen thought to herself. That was the role the man played. The dutiful husband and his poor fucked up wife. Postnatal depression? That was the story that Jimmy had been using and, so far, everyone seemed to have fallen for it. Even her own mother had believed it.

Good old Jimmy.

The man was such a hero. Doing more than well for himself these days. The money was rolling in. He'd bought and sold so many developments that Colleen had lost count of how much property he owned.

But Jimmy's fortunes didn't stop there. He had other money-making schemes going on too. Not one to miss out when there was a killing to be made, Jimmy dealt in other shady things, like pimping out girls and running seedy brothels. He and Alex had recently taken on some shipments of drugs. Or as Jimmy liked to refer to it, his 'new import and export' business.

Jimmy, the successful businessman. Her husband was a criminal. A murderer and con artist.

He had everyone fooled.

Everyone, except Colleen.

She cursed herself for almost slipping. For a few minutes, Colleen had almost forgotten the power her husband had over everyone around them. The girl was on Jimmy's payroll.

'I'm fine,' Colleen lied, unable to remember what it felt like to really feel okay it had been so long. She abruptly stood up, letting Sasha know that their little 'chat' was now over. 'And If I wanted to talk to someone, it wouldn't be one of my staff.'

Walking off then, close to tears, Colleen needed another drink. She'd been stupid to believe that she could have a friend in Sasha. An ally. That maybe one day she could trust the girl to open up to her.

Colleen Byrne couldn't trust anyone.

'Open wide!' Joanie Byrne smiled down at her precious grand-daughter Nancy, as she spooned the last of her dinner into her mouth before kissing her gently on her head. 'There's a good girl for your nana. You love your nanny's mash, don't you, darling!'

'She's almost two, Joanie. She doesn't need to still be spoon-fed. She needs to learn to do it herself.'

Startled as she heard Colleen's voice from the doorway behind her, Joanie Byrne hadn't realised that she was skulking around the place, watching her. She'd thought that her daughter-in-law would be been doing her usual today and moping around in her bedroom.

'Well if it was left down to you, she'd be doing everything herself, wouldn't she, poor little mite. Besides, it didn't do my Jimmy any harm and I spoon-fed him until he was almost three!' Joanie said tartly, her eyes scanning Colleen with disdain. It had gone six o'clock in the evening and the woman was still walking about in her dressing gown. She looked a state, as if she hadn't even bothered to drag a hairbrush through her hair today, let alone have a wash or brush her teeth.

'Well, that's a matter of opinion, isn't it?' Colleen muttered to herself, raising her eyes at Joanie's idea of perfect parenting.

Her little angel, Jimmy.

What a joke.

The truth was, Joanie had created a monster. It wouldn't have surprised Colleen to hear that the woman had breastfed Jimmy until he was fifteen, knowing what a control freak she could be. In fact, if Joanie was capable of lactating now, Colleen wouldn't put it past her to try and breastfeed Nancy too while she was at it. That's what she wanted: to make herself indispensable, so that Jimmy and Nancy couldn't live without her.

'Besides. It saves time this way. I've got enough to do. Looking after Nancy is a full-time job, and seeing as you're barely capable of looking after yourself, you're hardly one to talk, madam.' Losing her temper now: Colleen always seemed to know how to push her buttons. 'Speaking of which, are you even going to bother getting dressed today?'

'I don't feel well.'

'You don't feel well? Oh come on, Colleen, you never bloody feel well. You need to pull yourself together. Do you think Jimmy wants to come home to this every night?' Joanie extended her arm in Colleen's direction. 'Look at the state of you. It's no wonder he's out working every hour. You want to be careful you know. A handsome man like Jimmy could get any girl he wanted.'

'I bet he could.' Colleen's eyes flashed with fury at another one of Joanie's twisted jibes, playing on Colleen's insecurities. Beating her down with her words, making her feel crap about herself. As she did every day. Telling her how she wasn't good enough for Jimmy or Nancy. Trying her hardest to make Colleen feel shit about herself, when the truth was Colleen couldn't feel anymore awful about herself if she tried.

Joanie was right. Jimmy probably had found someone else.

He worked around the clock these days, barely coming home. When he did, the only person he seemed to have any time for was Nancy. Jimmy doted on his daughter.

Since they got married they'd only made love a couple of times. Though love it certainly hadn't been. Both times they'd had sex it had been Jimmy that initiated it; both times he was drunk. Rough with her. Cold. It had merely been an act carried out between them because Jimmy so desperately wanted a family.

Colleen hadn't enjoyed the sex at all.

Lying back, numb of feeling. Every time Jimmy had thrust himself inside her, all she'd thought about was that boy he'd murdered on their wedding night: the same boy that Joanie had completely banished from her mind, as if he'd never even existed. The woman was as bad as Jimmy. They were both as sick and twisted as each other.

Bored arguing with Joanie, Colleen decided to ignore her, focusing on her daughter now instead.

'Hey, baby!' she said, waving her hand awkwardly, as she tried to catch Nancy's eye. But Nancy showed her the same level of interest as her nan. The child seemed totally uninterested in her, not even bothering to glance over in her direction at the sound of her voice.

Joanie had trained her well.

'Hey, Nancy, baby, do you wanna hug from Mummy?'

As she stepped towards her daughter, Joanie quickly got up from her seat, and scooped the child up into her arms. She held Nancy close to her, raising her eyes up at Colleen.

'I was just taking her up for her bath.'

'That's okay, I'll take her,' Colleen said, but Joanie wouldn't even hear of it.

Making her way to the door, she was stopped dead in her tracks as she felt her daughter-in-law reach out and grab at her arm.

'Please, Joanie. I'm her mum.'

'Get your hand off me,' Joanie said indignantly before shaking Colleen's hand away from her.

Sensing an argument, she placed Nancy down on the floor and watched as the little girl made a run towards the stairs.

'Wait there for Nana, Nancy. Be a good girl.' Then she turned to Colleen, narrowing her eyes as she looked her up and down. 'You've been drinking again, haven't you?' she said, recognising the glazed look in Colleen's eyes. Her face flushed, the slight slur to her speech.

'Nana!' Nancy squealed as she waited impatiently at the bottom of the stairs for her nana to take her hand so that they could carry out the usual bedtime ritual.

The child's little voice ripped right through Colleen, her heart aching for her daughter to call out to her. Joanie had made sure it wasn't to be. She'd turned Nancy against her. Gradually, without Colleen even realising, until the child didn't even acknowledge her any longer.

Attempting to move, Colleen stepped in front of Joanie.

'I'm taking my daughter tonight,' she said firmly, the resolve in her voice surprising even her.

Joanie shook her head.

'You can't. Not if you've been drinking. Jimmy won't be happy about that!'

'Well, like you said, Jimmy's not here, is he?' Colleen replied.

'You're going to upset her, Colleen. Let me put her to bed,' Joanie argued. Colleen was just being stupid. Trying to make a point, at poor little Nancy's expense. 'Can't you see she doesn't want you, Colleen? She wants me.'

The slap that came next surprised them both.

Grasping her flaming hot cheek, where Colleen had swiped her, Joanie looked momentarily shocked at her daughter-in-law's sudden attack.

'Why don't you just fuck off,' Colleen shouted, feeling suddenly empowered at standing up for herself. At finally putting her mother-in-law firmly in her place.

Joanie was speechless.

Behind them, picking up on the tension, Nancy began bawling. She was inconsolable.

'You did this. You've turned her against me. Nancy is my child, Joanie. Mine.' Determined more than ever not to let the woman get the better of her again, Colleen was defiant. Marching out to the stairs, she picked up her daughter, ignoring the child's cries as Nancy held out her arms for her nana. 'I'm taking her tonight and if you try and stop me, I'll rip your fucking head off your shoulders. Then I'll tell Jimmy that it was my medication. You know all the pills you and him keep feeding me. I'll tell him that the meds messed my head up, that I had a bad reaction. How about that?' She'd finally lost her patience. She glared at Joanie, challenging her to say another word.

Joanie didn't dare.

She'd never seen Colleen like this. So angry, so unhinged.

'Go ahead. Like you say, you're her mother,' Joanie spoke quietly, still dazed from where Colleen had struck her. She wasn't going to row with the girl anymore. She'd let Jimmy deal with her once he was home. Joanie would get to him first and make sure that he knew exactly what had gone on tonight, and after he learned that Colleen had attacked her, he most certainly would sort the girl out.

Stomping off to the kitchen, to get away from Colleen, Joanie's only consolation as she put the kettle on to make herself a cup of tea was the sound of Nancy still wailing from the bathroom upstairs.

She shook her head despite herself. That little girl up there loved the bones of Joanie. Just like her Jimmy. Colleen might be Nancy's mother by birthright, but the girl didn't care for Colleen one bit.

Joanie had well and truly seen to that.

Her daughter-in-law may have won the battle this time, but when it came to her Jimmy and Nancy, Joanie would fight tooth and nail to get what she wanted, and Colleen Walsh would never win the war.

CHAPTER TWENTY-FIVE

Slumping down on her bed, Colleen leaned back against the headboard and squeezed her eyes shut. She was exhausted. Just a few hours with her daughter tonight had left her completely drained.

It was gone ten o'clock now and she'd only just managed to get Nancy off to sleep. Her daughter had been a nightmare. Talk about 'terrible twos' and Nancy wasn't even there yet. Screaming and crying for almost an hour, she had point-blank refused to get into the bath, and when she had finally got in, she'd cried that the water was too cold, and she wouldn't let Colleen dry her hair.

Colleen had eventually given up trying. Wrapping Nancy in a huge towel she'd carried her into Colleen's bedroom and placed her in her big double bed. When she'd lain beside her and tried to read Nancy a storybook, Nancy had kicked up a right fuss asking for her nana once more. Hitting the book from Colleen's hands in a rage, and kicking the covers off herself until finally, what felt like hours later, Nancy had knackered herself out and fallen asleep.

Sasha was right: Nancy was just like Jimmy. Not only in looks, with her emerald green eyes, but in temperament too. For a child still so young, Nancy was stubborn. Nothing deterred her from what she wanted and the child had wanted Joanie.

Her daughter felt nothing for her. The realisation broke Colleen's heart. She hadn't been well, this past year and a half, even throughout the pregnancy. Battling with her conscience, with her nightmares as her mind replayed that fateful night. The night that Jimmy had murdered that poor kid.

Colleen couldn't get the images out of her head.

She'd been part of it. She'd been there. She'd seen it with her own eyes, and hadn't told a soul. That made her just as bad as Jimmy surely?

It was fair to say she wasn't coping. The depression started to eat her up inside, consuming her so that by the time the panic attacks came, Colleen had all but lost her mind.

Joanie had taken advantage, Colleen realised that now. She'd so graciously stepped in offering to look after Nancy, all the while doing her very best to poison Colleen's daughter against her, and the worst thing of all was that Colleen had allowed her to do so.

She hadn't been strong enough, or well enough to fight her.

Three years she'd been married to Jimmy; trapped in this loveless marriage like a prisoner, with Joanie always lurking about. Inside their home, inside their lives, manipulating and controlling them all.

The woman ran the household. She mothered Colleen's child.

Colleen had been made redundant. Neither wanted nor needed. Even Jimmy had no use for her anymore; tolerating her, tiptoeing around her. He said all the right things, pretending that he cared, but Colleen knew. She knew the real Jimmy Byrne: the way he could pretend to be so charming, so genuine.

Colleen barely left the house anymore unless Jimmy insisted on dragging her along to some client dinner, so that she could help him play the role of happy couple. He'd said it was good for business. Having his wife on his arm made him appear more genuine, more authentic. Apparently, people trusted a family man.

The irony.

Colleen didn't trust Jimmy one bit.

Crying now, she opened the drawer of her bedside table. Grabbing the small bottle of vodka that she'd hidden away especially, she unscrewed the lid. Glugging down the liquid. Relishing its burn at the back of her throat.

She stared down at the plastic pot of tablets. Shaking the bottle, she knew that if she took them all now, there'd be no coming back.

It would be final.

These had been Joanie's answer to everything. She'd told Colleen that they would help. Painkillers, sleeping pills, antidepressants. She'd said that they'd make her feel better in time, but they hadn't. They'd made her feel worse.

Staring down at Nancy, Colleen felt an overwhelming sense of sadness as she watched her daughter blissfully sleeping. Her perfect soft skin; the long dark eyelashes that rested gently on the tops of her cheeks. Nancy was every bit a Byrne and as time went on Jimmy and Joanie would only turn her more and more against Colleen. Already the child wanted nothing to do with her and it hurt – more than anything Colleen had ever experienced before.

Unscrewing the bottle, Colleen cupped the pills in her hand before swallowing them all down at once. Glugging down the vodka until every last one had been forced into her stomach. Until she choked.

Crying now, Colleen lay down next to her daughter. Stroking the child's head. Inhaling her soft, delicate smell.

'I love you, Nancy,' she whispered before closing her eyes.

She waited for the numbness that she knew would come.

CHAPTER TWENTY-SIX

'Let me fucking go. I haven't done anything. Get off me!'

Incredulous, as Jack Taylor threw the man down onto the wet pavement with far more force than was necessary, he cried out at the brutal thump as his head bounced off the cold, hard concrete. Though he knew he was wasting his breath. This filth clearly didn't give a shit about his protests and the fact that he was hurting him. He was probably doing it on purpose. Getting his job satisfaction any way he could.

'You're under arrest, mate! You have the right to remain silent…' Straddling the assailant as the man swung his arms and legs out wildly – kicking and hitting out in a desperate bid to break loose from the officer's grip – Jack was struggling to detain the man as he writhed beneath him. Losing his patience, Jack had had enough. Gritting his teeth, he wrenched the man's arms up roughly behind him using all his strength, ignoring the screams of pain from the assailant as he slapped the metal rings tightly over the man's wrists, restraining him. He wasn't in the mood for this bullshit tonight.

'Oh, have a laugh, will you! It was just an argument. A lover's tiff,' the man spat, kicking out with his legs in protest. 'Ain't you pigs got nothing better to do?'

'As it happens, yeah, we bloody do.' Jack Taylor shook his head in disgust at the pure gall of the man, visibly annoyed that they'd been called out to this pair of drunken morons yet again.

The husband and wife duo were well known to the police.

They were harmless really. Just a pair of old drunks. But Jack was getting fed up wasting his time and energy on scum like this who had nothing better to do than hang around on the streets, brawling with each other. The two of them. Rolling around on the pavement outside one of the pubs, beating the living shit out of each other.

'It's a shame there's always idiots like you two wasting our time.'

The man's wife was on him then too. The scrawny woman bent down, grabbing the officer with her bony hands as she tried to pull PC Taylor off her husband.

'You're hurting him. There's no need to sit on him, you fat bastard. You'll flatten him.'

She was pulling at Jack's jacket. But the gobfull of phlegm that hit him in the face a second later caught him off guard.

'For fuck's sake!' Jack shouted, as he wiped the string of saliva and blood off his cheek with disgust. The woman had been clumped by her husband just as the officers had arrived. She'd been assaulted, but suddenly they had somehow become her target.

'Can someone grab this one? Knowing my luck she'll be riddled with fucking AIDS or rabies.'

'You can't talk about me like that! I want your badge number!'

Dragging himself up off the floor, clearly not in the least bit threatened by the woman, Jack Taylor pulled the man up onto his feet along with him, before leading him over to the awaiting police van as PC Adams ran over and intervened with the woman.

'Oh, two against one now, is it?' the woman squeaked as she continued her tirade of abuse, and lashing out with her fists and legs.

'Why don't you calm down? There's no need for all this,' the younger officer said diplomatically, as he held the woman by her arms in order to detain her. But his interference only seemed to infuriate her even more. Lashing out even more in blind fury, she was much stronger than her five foot nothing frame had led him to believe.

'Fucking pigs. Go on, what you gunna do, huh? Beat me up en all?' she spat, pounding the officer repeatedly with her closed fists, as PC Adams exchanged a look with his fellow officer.

It was clear that they were both thinking exactly the same thing: chance would be a fine thing!

'How do you like it, eh?!' The woman cackled as she caught PC Adams with a sharp blow, causing his nose to explode on impact.

'Right that's it. You're nicked too!'

Wrenching the handcuffs around her wrists, he ignored her cries of them being too tight as he felt the trickle of blood running down his face and into his mouth. Grimacing at the horrible metallic tang, he knew that, despite his injury, the woman was still in no mind to relent.

Christ knew how much she'd had to drink tonight, but the woman didn't seem to have any understanding of the shitstorm she'd just caused herself by assaulting him and, judging by the potent stench of alcohol radiating from her breath, PC Adams was convinced that the woman was far too wasted to give a shit.

'Get the fuck off me, and get the fuck off my husband!' The woman was acting deranged now.

'Your husband knocked your front teeth out, love. So we've arrested him. It's called assault.' PC Adams spoke through gritted teeth. 'And now you're being arrested too, for assaulting a police officer and resisting arrest. So you carry on, love, and we can always add some more charges while we're at it. No skin off my nose,' he snarled as backup arrived in the form of another police van.

Leading the woman over towards it, he couldn't wait to get back to the station. Just like his colleague, he wasn't in the mood for this shit tonight. He'd only started his shift a couple of hours earlier, and already they'd been called out four times tonight for similar offences.

This was what was known as a typical Saturday night in Richmond High Street. The end of the month, payday. Tonight, the world and his wife were out on the lash and didn't he know about it.

The other bars hadn't started kicking out yet, so it was only going to get worse from here. This was the calm before the storm.

'Get your fucking hands off me.' The woman snapped her head to the side then, trying to bite the officer; only PC Adams was two steps ahead of her, pushing her into the back of the police van.

'What are you gawping at?' he said, as the woman stopped resisting, looking down next to the officer, her eyes trying to focus on something else.

He followed her gaze, almost doing a double take when he saw the small child standing next to him.

A head of red hair. The little girl's face streaked with tears. Wearing only her pink pyjamas, the kid's feet were bare and, judging by the shade of blue that they had turned, the poor kid must be freezing cold.

'What the fuck?' PC Adams signalled over to where PC Taylor stood behind him. 'Where's this kid come from?' Then turning back to the woman he glared at her in disgust. He wouldn't put it past this pair to have dragged a kid out with them. Selfish fuckers.

'Is she yours?'

'Behave,' the woman squawked, as if the police officer was trying to set her up for something else. 'I don't even like kids.'

PC Adams closed the van door on the woman, ignoring her loud angry protests, before crouching down to the little girl's level.

'Hey, darling, where have you come from, huh?' he asked, his voice softened as he took in the sight of the child. 'Where's your mummy and your daddy, eh?' he persisted as the little girl continued to sob loudly. Seemingly too young to be able to talk, the child was near hysterical.

Scanning the street behind the child, PC Adams checked to see if any front doors were left open on the High Street, or if there was anyone frantically searching for the girl.

No one seemed to be looking for the poor mite.

'Here, Taylor. Grab us the blanket out of the boot, will you? The poor kid's freezing.'

Jack Taylor did as he was asked. Grabbing the blanket he marched over to his colleague. And then, taking a good look at the child, his reaction mirrored PC Adams's: he did a double take.

'Nancy?'

He was eyeing the little girl more closely, recognising her from the many occasions that he'd been up at Jimmy Byrne's house. She was like a little doll, he remembered. Jack Taylor couldn't believe his eyes.

'It can't be? Jesus. There's no way Jimmy Byrne would let his kid out of his sight.'

'Hang on. This is Jimmy Byrne's kid? As in THE Jimmy Byrne?'

Jack nodded. Then crouching down to Nancy's level as he wrapped the blanket around the little girl's shoulders, he spoke softly to her.

'It's okay, Nancy. My name's Jack. I'm a friend of your daddy's. I'm going to take you home.'

'Ain't we supposed to call this in?' PC Adams asked warily. He was still fairly new to the job, but he knew the protocol for dealing with a missing child.

'No. I'll sort it,' Jack said, placing Nancy in the back of the police car and fastening the seat belt around her. Nancy had stopped crying now. Recognising Jack, and knowing that she was being taken home, she'd sunk down into the blanket. Glad of the warmth. 'Trust me, you call this in and Jimmy Byrne won't thank you for it, mate. You might have heard a few stories about the man, and let me tell you, every one of them is true. See this little thing here, the man is besotted with her. I don't know why the fuck she's roaming the streets on her own, but I do know this: you call this in and Children's Services will probably end up taking the child into care. Do you really want to be the man that takes Jimmy's kid away from him?'

PC Adams shook his head, indicating to his colleague that his imminent threat had been heard loud and clear. He had quickly cottoned on to the way things worked around this part of London. Certain people were above the law it seemed and Jimmy Byrne was one of them. He had heard the rumours about Byrne having a few police officers in his pocket, and judging by the way that Taylor was acting, his colleague was clearly one of them.

There was no way that Adams was leaving himself in the firing line of either man. It would stand him in better stead to turn a blind eye, he decided.

'Yeah, you're right. Besides, we'll only be lumbered with a week's worth of fucking paperwork to fill out,' he said, showing willing that he was playing along.

'You go and sign in those two numpties and I'll meet you back down at the station,' Jack said before jumping in the police car and pulling away.

Jack had saved Jimmy a whole world of dramas tonight by dealing with the situation. He'd be set to make a nice little earner from it too, he reckoned.

Jimmy would owe him for this. Big time.

Joanie Byrne padded down the stairs, wrapping her dressing gown around her body tightly. If the loud banging on the door wasn't enough to make her feel suddenly wide awake, the shrill coolness of the marble tiles beneath her feet had done the job. The great big marble staircase was her son's pride and joy; if it had been down to her, Joanie would have opted for a nice thick carpet.

'Hold your horses,' she shouted, as she reached the middle landing. Then staring down at the open front door, at the police officer standing in the hallway with little Nancy wrapped in a blanket asleep in his arms, Joanie never moved so fast.

'Sorry to disturb you, Mrs Byrne,' the officer said, seeing the horrified expression on the older woman's face as she clearly wondered what the hell was going on. 'The front door was wide open. I'm guessing that's how this little one got out. She must have moved that chair so she could reach the latch.' Jack Taylor pointed to where the chair sat in the middle of the doorway.

'Nancy? What in God's name is going on?' Joanie asked, reaching the officer. She stared down at her granddaughter lying in the officer's arms, wrapped in a blanket, sound asleep, blissfully unaware of all the drama.

'We found her wandering down the High Street,' Jack explained. 'She's okay. Just a bit cold. Poor kid didn't have any shoes on her feet. Must have just decided to go for a wander. Who knows what goes on in the little one's head, eh?'

Joanie nodded, knowing full well that the policeman was trying to play down the seriousness of tonight's events.

'I don't understand. She was in bed with her mother tonight,' she said, staring at the clock as she wondered what time it was. And then bristling as she saw that it was almost midnight.

Jimmy still wasn't home. He stayed out most nights, and Joanie wasn't convinced that the business he was tending to at this time of night was strictly professional. She wouldn't be surprised if her son had some fancy piece somewhere. With Colleen as a wife, Joanie couldn't blame him.

That girl.

Joanie would murder Colleen for this. The one and only night her useless excuse of a daughter-in-law had insisted on looking after her own child, and Joanie's precious little granddaughter had been roaming the streets in the middle of the night.

'COLLEEN!' Joanie Byrne bellowed up the stairs, her voice booming out louder than PC Taylor would have ever given the slight woman's tiny frame credit for. 'COLLEEN. Get your arse down here! The police are here!'

Shuffling awkwardly on his feet, still holding the child, PC Taylor could feel the anger radiating from Joanie Byrne. If she wasn't careful she'd wake up Nancy with all her shouting. The last thing he wanted was to be stuck here tonight with two feuding women and a screaming baby.

'Shall I carry Nancy upstairs for you, Mrs Byrne?' he asked, trying to be helpful. 'I'm still on shift and we're a bit understaffed tonight. I just wanted to make sure that Nancy got home safe and sound. And that Jimmy didn't get any repercussions from anyone else tonight,' he added, making sure that he got that nugget of information in before he left.

'Thank you, officer. Jimmy will appreciate that.' Joanie hadn't even thought about repercussions. Colleen could have caused a world of shit for them all tonight. 'And yes, if you don't mind carrying Nancy up. You can put the child in my bed. It's the second room on the left. I'm going to go and see to my daughter-in-law.'

Marching towards the younger woman's bedroom, Joanie threw open the door that she now realised was already ajar and snapped on the bedroom light, hoping to drag the woman from her slumber with a short, sharp shock.

Colleen was lucky that Joanie didn't drag her out of the bed by her hair.

The smell hit Joanie as she entered the room, the acrid stench of vomit so strong that it caused her to recoil. Her eyes were watering as she stared over at her daughter-in-law lying in the bed.

The bedroom was immaculate. A giant double bed in the middle of the room. The decor, simple, understated. The dressing table pristine: everything sitting in neat little rows, immaculately tidy. It was almost clinical. Void of the personality of the woman lying there.

She wasn't moving, splayed out on the bed, the covers tossed to the side, wearing only a nightshirt, her bare legs and knickers exposed. Her body twisted awkwardly. Her head turned to the side, as if she was half hanging off the bed.

'Colleen?' Joanie said, her voice faltering as she realised something wasn't right. Had the girl been sick? Stepping around the bed, Joanie let out a scream.

Her gaze was focused on the awkward angle of Colleen's head as she spotted the spray of vomit that was dripping down the side of the duvet, forming a puddle on the floor. The girl's skin was deathly white; her eyes had rolled to the back of her head.

Next to her lay a discarded bottle of vodka. Empty. Along with what looked like a number of plastic bottles of prescription medication.

'Oh, my God. Colleen! Call an ambulance,' Joanie shrieked as the police officer came running into the room. 'We need to call an ambulance.'

Joanie ran downstairs to the telephone, as Jack Taylor tried his best to find out if Colleen Byrne was responsive. Feeling for a pulse, he stared down at Colleen's glassy expression.

Then, relief when he felt the faint throb under his fingertips. She was still with them. Just barely.

'It's all right, Colleen. You're going to be all right,' he said, the calmness in his voice surprising even him. Tonight was turning out to be a major fucking fuck up of epic proportions, and judging by the state of Colleen Byrne it didn't look like it was going to get better anytime soon.

CHAPTER TWENTY-SEVEN

'Oh Jimmy! Thank God, you're here. I take it Jack Taylor got hold of you, son,' Joanie Byrne said, as her son marched down the hospital corridor towards her. His thunderous expression melted the instant that he saw Nancy, sleeping peacefully, wrapped up in a thick hospital blanket, on the seat next to his mother.

'Thank Christ Nancy's okay!' Jimmy said, immense relief washing over him as he looked down at his daughter. That was a small mercy, at least, he figured, which was more than could be said for Colleen. Jimmy could kill Colleen for what she'd put them all through. Having already got the general gist of tonight's events from Jack Taylor, to say he was not impressed was a massive understatement. Jimmy Byrne was bloody fuming.

'She's fine, son, just exhausted. The poor little mite has been around the bleeding houses tonight, quite literally,' Joanie said, seeing the concern in her son's eyes.

'Where's Colleen?' Jimmy asked, his tone vexed, and Joanie could understand why. Summoned to the hospital in the middle of the night, he'd better things to do with his time than have to come and deal with another of his hapless wife's dramatics. But that was Colleen for you, though: a selfish little mare through and through; that girl only ever thought of herself.

She'd proved it tonight. By putting their Nancy at risk, Colleen Walsh had crossed the line.

'The doctors are in with her, Jimmy. Edel's in there too. They said they'd let us know when we can see her. Stay here for a bit, yeah? Let her mum have some time alone with her. You can't go in there in the mood you're in. You need to calm down, son. Get your head straight.' Praying that Jimmy wouldn't storm into the room where Colleen was with all guns blazing, Joanie got up and slipped some money into the vending machine next to them, hoping that a nice hot cup of tea would entice him to stay by her side.

Joanie couldn't face anymore drama. Jimmy was stressed out enough as it was, without her having to mention that the tension between her and Edel Walsh was at an all-time high.

Edel had been wailing like a banshee when she'd arrived at the hospital earlier, distraught at hearing Colleen had been brought in for attempted suicide; she'd flown at Joanie when she'd heard the lack of empathy as she'd recited the night's events, still enraged at the trial Colleen had put young Nancy through.

Heartless. That's what Edel had called her before the doctors had quickly ushered Edel into the private room, so that she could stay by her daughter's side.

'Take a seat, Jimmy. Drink this. They don't have any alcohol in them things; shame, as they'd probably make a fortune if they did,' Joanie quipped, disappointed when her son turned down her offer, shooing the hot drink away. She placed it down on the table beside them instead.

'I don't want to take a fucking seat and I don't want any poxy tea. I want to know what the fuck's been going on! Taylor said it was attempted suicide? He said Nancy had been in the bed beside her?' Jimmy said. The initial fleeting concern for his wife had dissolved completely by the time he'd got off the phone to Jack Taylor, once he'd had time to process everything.

'I don't know what she was thinking, Jimmy, I really don't. The main thing now, though, is Nancy is fine and the doctors said Colleen is stable,' Joanie said, trying to placate her son.

'"Colleen's stable"?' Jimmy spat. 'Fuck me, now there's two words I'd never thought I'd hear in the same sentence,' he sneered. 'I tell you what, she may not have succeeded in topping herself, but I'd be happy to have a fucking good go at it when I get my hands on her!' he said, his temper getting the better of him.

'The state of her, Jimmy. You should have seen her. Covered in vomit, her skin tinged blue. She was completely lifeless. It was no wonder Nancy went out bloody wandering. She must have been petrified waking up and seeing her mother in that state. Thank God Jack Taylor found her and knew to bring her back up to the house. Anything could have happened to her, Jimmy. All those nutters out there these days. The perverts. It just doesn't bear thinking about,' Joanie continued, hoping her words would sink in. She was sick of Jimmy trying to pretend that Colleen was okay. Sick of the man trying to play down Colleen's 'problems'. The girl was sick. Jimmy needed to realise that he couldn't just sugar-coat this anymore.

Colleen needed real help.

'Jack Taylor is the only reason we haven't had any of the Old Bill and Children's Services snooping around. Can you imagine the bloody field day that lot would have had with tonight's drama?'

Jimmy nodded in agreement. Taylor had done well tonight. Jimmy Byrne wasn't going to forget that in a hurry. The man had not only made sure that his Nancy got home safely, but he'd also made sure that tonight's events had been kept away from the knowledge of anyone in authority. On top of that, he'd personally dealt with the staff here at the hospital too, so that they didn't inform anyone else down at Richmond nick. The last thing Jimmy needed was the local plod or the do-gooder social workers poking their noses in.

His mother was right, the authorities would have bloody loved that, wouldn't they? They were always trying to get the notorious Jimmy Byrne on something. Though the fuckers hadn't succeeded thus far.

He certainly owed Jack Taylor big time for his help tonight.

'The only reason I agreed to Nancy sleeping with her is because Colleen was so insistent on taking her for the night. She slapped me, Jimmy. In front of Nancy. The poor child was so distressed, I didn't know what else to do.'

'It's not your fault, Mum.' Seeing the genuine upset on his mother's face at what she'd been left to deal with, Jimmy could barely contain his anger from rising once more. 'How were you supposed to know that Colleen would do something so fucking stupid, huh? It's not your fault, Mum. You can't watch Nancy twenty-four-seven: Colleen is her mother. She should have been able to look after her child without pulling stupid stunts like this.'

'She'd drunk a litre of vodka and thrown back enough painkillers to put a horse out of its misery. She isn't right in the head, son,' Joanie said, choosing her words carefully; she was only saying out loud what they both knew to be the truth.

'The doctors said it's postnatal depression, she'll be fine,' Jimmy said unconvincingly, repeating the little mantra that he'd used to excuse Colleen time and time again.

'Depression?' Joanie rolled her eyes at that. 'And what in God's name has that one got to be depressed about? She has it good, Jimmy. She has everything a woman could wish for. A loving husband, a beautiful child, that grand old house. Everything handed to her on a plate.' She shook her head in disgust. 'Is it any wonder the girl is feeling depressed? She's so far up her own arse, all she can see is darkness. You can't keep making excuses for her. She hasn't been right for a long time,' Joanie said, leaving her words to hang in the air between them. They both knew what she was referring to.

Neither of them had mentioned it since.

'You can't keep turning a blind eye to the woman's antics and making excuses for her, Jimmy. You need to deal with her. She's getting worse.' Keeping her voice down, Joanie was speaking with only brutal honestly now, as only she could. As Jimmy's mother, she was perhaps the only person in the world that could say her bit, and Jimmy had no choice but to listen to it.

'I know, Mum.' Jimmy sighed, the raw emotion evident in his voice as he spoke, finally admitting what he'd refused to accept as the truth even to himself.

He didn't love Colleen. He never had, but that didn't mean that he didn't give a shit about the girl. Colleen was his wife, the mother of his child.

And he knew: he did this to her.

He made her this way.

That's why he had chosen to turn a blind eye to the woman's behaviour. The drinking and the pills. He'd ignored it, hoping that somehow Colleen would be able to dispel whatever angst she still seemed to have inside her. But the truth of the matter was that Colleen Walsh wasn't cut out for this world. For Jimmy's world.

For all his wealth and success, Colleen didn't want any part of it, especially once she realised how Jimmy had come by his fortunes. She hated it all. Everything that Jimmy stood for. Everything that he did.

She hated him.

'I can't reach her anymore, Mum. It's like she's just not here.' Even as he said the words out loud, he finally felt like a weight had been lifted from him.

It wasn't often that Jimmy Byrne suffered with his conscience, but with Colleen he did. He knew he'd broken her. Beyond repair. And now he knew the lengths she would go to escape her life with him, it cut him to the bone.

He tried for so long to pretend that everything was okay, but Colleen had slowly got worse. Moping around the place, as if Jimmy physically kept her in the house against her will. Disengaging from everyone and everything.

She didn't even bother to conceal her drinking from him anymore. In fact, it was as if she was purposely rubbing it in his face. As if she got some kind of a kick from goading a reaction from him. As if she was testing how far she could go.

Tonight though, Colleen had pushed him way too far. He knew he couldn't turn a blind eye to her actions anymore. He was her husband, and he needed to get this sorted out once and for all.

'I've had enough of sitting around and waiting. I'm going to see her. She's my wife. I should be in there,' Jimmy said, the conversation with his mother clearly over. 'Take Nancy home, Mum. Get a cab, yeah? You both look shattered. Try and get some sleep.'

Agreeing with Jimmy, Joanie got up and scooped up her granddaughter. They could both do with some rest.

Kissing him on the head, Joanie spoke seriously. 'You need to get this sorted out, son. We can't have her putting Nancy at risk again.'

That was her final parting shot, pleased that finally she'd been able to get through to her son and that Jimmy had finally realised that he needed to do something about the girl.

Once her son's mind was made up about something there was very little anyone could do to change it.

'Jimmy, son!' Edel said, allowing her tears to fall as her son-in-law walked in to the room, looking every bit like a man defeated. 'Colleen look who's here. It's Jimmy, love.'

Staring blankly at the wall ahead of her, as if she hadn't heard her mother, Colleen didn't respond.

Edel shook her head apologetically, shrugging to Jimmy. She was at a complete loss as to what to do.

'She looks a lot worse than she is, Jimmy. She's on a drip to help raise her blood pressure and they've administered Activated Charcoal to stop the poison from doing its worst. Apparently, it pushes the drugs out through the gut, stopping the body from absorbing it.' Edel spoke softly, repeating all the information that the doctors had given her, hoping that she was putting Jimmy's mind at ease. It was probably an awful shock for the man to see Colleen in such a way. Edel knew exactly how the poor man must be feeling.

'She won't talk to me, Jimmy,' she said sadly as Jimmy hovered awkwardly over by the doorway, neither of them really knowing what to say to each other. 'Maybe you might have more luck?'

Seeing the hope in Edel's eyes, Jimmy nodded, though he very much doubted that Colleen would speak to him either.

'I know she's been bad before. With her depression and all that,' Edel said, still trying to make sense of the night's events, of finding out her daughter had tried to kill herself. Edel just couldn't understand any of it. It was as if Colleen was unreachable; she just didn't talk to her anymore. 'But I thought she'd turned a corner? I thought she was seeming much better?'

Again Jimmy didn't speak.

He'd always acted on the understanding that what Edel Walsh didn't know, wouldn't hurt her, he'd downplayed Colleen's addictions, hiding whatever he could from the girl's mother, in the hope that somehow, eventually, Colleen would snap out of whatever it was she was going through.

Sensing that Jimmy would want some time on his own with Colleen, Edel wiped away her silent tears, before reluctantly tearing herself away from Colleen's bedside and getting up from her seat.

'I'll go and get a cuppa and leave you both to it,' she said, squeezing Jimmy's arm as she passed him.

* * *

The room suddenly silent now that the woman had gone, Jimmy stood staring at Colleen. Lying in the bed staring vacantly at the ceiling. An intravenous drip being fed into her arm.

Colleen didn't bother to acknowledge his presence, pretending as if she didn't even know Jimmy had entered the room.

He'd been fuming with her up until this point, but now seeing her lying in the bed – so fragile and broken – he felt heart sorry for his wife. Taking a seat next to the bed, he decided it was time for them both to start talking.

'I'm sorry, Colleen,' Jimmy said and for once in his life he really meant it. 'I know what you did tonight was because of me, because of how much you hate me.' He spoke softly now. The anger he'd felt earlier had completely disappeared, replaced only by sadness as he finally accepted the truth. 'I don't know what to do to make this better, Colleen. I don't know how to fix this.' He shook his head, the words hitting a nerve suddenly, now that he was finally voicing them out loud. 'Please, Colleen, we can't go on like this. Forget about me. Think about your daughter. Think about Nancy. She was lying in the bed with you when you tried to kill yourself, Colleen. She went wandering when she couldn't wake you. Taylor found her down at Richmond High Street. She's traumatised,' Jimmy said, speaking about their daughter in the vain hope that maybe then he might get through to his wife.

It worked.

Finally Colleen acknowledged him. Turning her head to face her husband. Dark circles around her sunken eyes, her lips all cracked and dry. Dehydrated from where she'd been violently sick.

Jimmy waited for Colleen to say something.

Anything.

To call him names. To shout. To cry. To say she was sorry. Anything.

The last thing he expected was for her to laugh at him.

A manic strangled noise escaped from the back of her throat as she finally looked Jimmy dead in the eyes.

'I didn't try to kill myself, Jimmy,' Colleen said, her voice cold, hardened; but her tears betrayed her as they fell. 'I'm pregnant.'

Then reaching down to her stomach, Colleen pressed her hand to where the life she'd tried to flush out somehow, despite all the odds, was clinging on to her, despite Colleen's wishes.

'I don't want to give birth to another baby of yours, Jimmy. Another one of the Byrne spawn. I was trying to kill it.'

PART THREE: 2003

CHAPTER TWENTY-EIGHT

Colleen closed her eyes as she fought back the sudden urge to scream. Consumed with grief, she wanted to throw herself down on top of her mother's coffin and shout to everyone around her how much she wished more than anything that she was dead too.

A heart attack of all things. It was so unexpected that Colleen still couldn't even comprehend that her mother was really gone. It just didn't seem real. Her beautiful mother taken from her like that.

As the priest started reciting the final committal, and the other mourners started throwing down the clumps of earth on top of the coffin, to say their final goodbyes, Colleen opened her eyes and allowed her tears to come.

Unable to look as her mother's coffin sat down inside the grave now.

Unable to bear the thought of the woman that she loved the most in the world being placed down there deep in the ground, soon to be covered with six feet of dirt. Left to rot.

This couldn't just be it!

This couldn't be all that was left for her. This sad, shitty existence of a life with only death ahead of them all.

Blinking back her tears she glanced at the other mourners around the grave, focusing on them instead as she tried to regain her composure. She was left with all of them.

With them.

Looking over at her so-called family, her gaze rested on her two grown children: Nancy and Daniel. The pair of them were so like Jimmy that just the sight of them literally broke Colleen's heart. Daniel, the baby. Ironically, he stood taller than his father now. At eighteen years old, he'd grown into a big strapping young man. Broader than Jimmy, his features sharper, more chiselled. Though he was more like Colleen in personality. Softer in some way. Not quite as brutal or direct as Jimmy.

Staring over at Nancy: the enigma that was her daughter, Colleen eyed her, fascinated, as she always did. She carried a lethal combination of both Jimmy and Joanie – a Byrne to her very core. Blessed with beauty beyond measure, and she knew it too. Even at just twenty years old, she'd already mastered the art of manipulating all those around her into doing things her way, the way Jimmy had always managed to do. Only Nancy had the added bonus of an angelic disguise to hide behind.

Even Jimmy had fallen under his daughter's spell: mesmerising and heartbreaking to watch. The girl so full of false charm and promise, when deep down she was just as calculating and conniving as her father.

Colleen watched Nancy staring down at her nan Edel's coffin; she was holding it together as Colleen knew the girl would. Edel had loved Nancy just as fiercely as Joanie, but Nancy was all about Joanie. Edel's sudden death didn't seem to affect her in the slightest, Colleen thought. Taking in Nancy's expression, not so much as a flicker of feeling or emotion registered on her daughter's face. Those same emerald green eyes as Jimmy, casting out an icy cold stare, void of any real emotion. The only trait of Colleen's Nancy seemed to have was her vibrant red hair. Other than that Nancy was all Jimmy. It was because of this, Colleen assumed, that Nancy was so favoured by Jimmy. Joanie too. She had been from the day she was born. Seeing themselves in her, they'd doted on the child.

Poor Daniel never stood a chance. Her son never got a look in. Standing back from them all and looking in from a distance, Daniel had always been shunned in favour of Nancy. Living his life in his sister's shadow, always vying for Jimmy's attention, striving to be good enough – but he wasn't. He never could be. He was too like her. Too like his hapless mother, and no one matched up to Jimmy's daughter.

Nancy caught her eye then, staring over, offering Colleen a rare small smile. Colleen didn't smile back. The gesture was empty. To anyone else watching it would have appeared affectionate, but then that was exactly the point. Her dear children knew how to play the game. 'Course they did, they'd learned from the very best. Jimmy and Joanie had taught them well. The Byrne family were all about keeping up appearances. Why should today be any different?

They were all here together, united in both their grief and as a family. Showing their support for Edel as she was laid to rest. Their support for Colleen.

What a joke.

The truth was none of them ever had the time of day for Colleen. Her children included. They never had and they never would. She'd accepted that long ago. Her two precious children. Born from her, yet they'd been raised by their evil witch of a grandmother, Joanie Byrne.

Staring at her mother-in-law, Colleen felt the familiar feeling of hate bubbling in the pit of her stomach. Joanie was looking old now. In her seventies, her mouth pinched, giving her a permanent soured expression. Standing between Daniel and Nancy, Colleen thought she looked like she'd shrunk suddenly too. Small and frail-looking.

An illusion.

There was nothing frail about Joanie Byrne. She was as fierce as she was mighty. She'd won in the end. Managing to turn the children against Colleen, just as she'd set out to from the moment Nancy was born.

Sensing Coleen's eyes boring into her, Joanie looked back at her. Deliberately twisting her hands around her grandchildren's arms and pulling them both in closer to her, she kept her eyes locked with Colleen's. Another small gesture of affection, only there was no sentiment behind the small movement at all. Joanie was just staking her claim. Smug in the knowledge that she'd won the war; purposely goading Colleen, knowing that she was too weak and pathetic to even try to fight back.

Well Colleen wasn't going to be weak and pathetic today. Not on the day that she was burying her mother. Determined to be strong, Colleen held Joanie's stare, refusing to look away first. Forcing herself to hold the woman's eye, she glared at Joanie with the full ferocity that burned inside her.

Forcing Joanie to divert her gaze.

Colleen looked at Jimmy then. Her husband every bit as handsome as the first day she'd met him. Time had been so cruel to Colleen. She could no longer bear to look at her haggard reflection in the mirror, the bleak lines etched firmly across her face. The dark bags under her eyes. Yet for Jimmy, time had stood still it seemed. It was like the past twenty years hadn't happened. He'd gained weight but it looked good on him, his greying hair only making him look distinguished.

Her poor long-suffering husband. Isn't that what everyone thought of him secretly? Jimmy Byrne, the man with the heart of gold. Putting up with his mental patient of a wife that he'd been lumbered with. What a good man he was. He could have anyone, and yet he'd stayed true to her.

Colleen bit the inside of her cheek, her hands twitching at her side as she felt the overwhelming familiar pull inside her:

needing a drink. Today more than ever, the hate bubbled away inside her, so rapidly today, so uncontrollably strong that Colleen really wasn't sure she could contain it.

He did this to her. Jimmy. And for that she hated the man with every cell in her body. For everything he'd done, and everything he was. Colleen's only small mercy throughout it all was that her mother had been spared the truth. Colleen had made sure that Edel never found out about the murder she'd witnessed all those years ago. She'd made sure that her mother never knew what a wicked and cruel man Jimmy really was.

It consumed Colleen. Her hate for her husband had eaten her up inside, so much that there had been days that Colleen had been unable to look at herself. It had driven a wedge between her and her mother over the years too. She'd allowed her mother to think that she was sick, rather than confess the truth. Her mother hadn't questioned any of it, believing that her daughter just couldn't cope after the birth of Nancy. That she'd suffered with acute postnatal depression. She did what everyone else did: she went along with Jimmy's story, accepting it wholly. She believed it because Colleen let her.

Zoning back in on the service, Colleen realised that the priest had stopped talking. It was all over. Jimmy had even ruined today. Too busy thinking about him, her hatred for him, she hadn't been fully present for her mother's funeral. Her own mother. Another important occasion that had just passed her by.

People were surrounding her now. Too close. Touching her. Pulling her in towards them. Wrapping her tightly, their arms around her as they whispered their words of condolences. Only there were no words that would ever console Colleen for her loss. And these peoples' words to her meant nothing. The people meant nothing to her. They were all here for Jimmy.

'Get off me,' she screamed.

Staring over at the grave now, knowing that she'd have to leave her mother here, alone, cold in the ground, Colleen felt the overwhelming feeling engulf her once again. Her breathing erratic so that her lungs could barely keep up. Her heart was pounding inside her chest. Echoing inside her ears. Gasping for air now, lost in another crippling panic attack, Colleen felt as if she would die. Her chest rising and falling rapidly, as she tried to suck in some air. Her lungs grabbing at the little oxygen they could find. Light-headed, she could feel her legs collapsing beneath her.

Then Jimmy was there at her side once more. The good, dutiful husband that he was. Pulling Colleen up on her feet, holding her upright, as he wrapped his arm around her waist and led his fragile wife back to the awaiting funeral car.

And Colleen did as she always did. Without a murmur, she let him play the role that he so desperately wanted the world to see. She let him be the hero of the hour. Because that was all it was about for Jimmy. Reputation, appearances. Colleen had learned that a long time ago.

They'd go back to a house full of people now. So that people could eat the wonderful spread of food that Joanie Byrne had prepared especially for them all. And drink the expensive Scotch and wine that Jimmy would no doubt be serving. Only the best would do. Even for her mother's wake. A house full of people. Strangers.

Yet, once again Colleen would be all alone.

CHAPTER TWENTY-NINE

Joanie Byrne couldn't have been prouder of the way her grand-children had behaved today.

The pair of them had really held themselves together following Edel Walsh's death. Of course, they'd never been as close to her as they were to Joanie. Joanie had always made sure of that. Even back when Jimmy had bought Edel her new shop after she'd lost her home in the fire, Joanie had made sure that it was the other side of London, so that the woman would be kept busy and out of her way.

Still, a part of her would miss Edel now. While they'd never really been close, Joanie and Edel had put their differences aside over the years and got along, for the sake of the children. She hadn't been much older than Joanie either. That was the thing that had affected Joanie the most. The woman's sudden passing was a reminder to her that, while life sometimes led you to believe you were immortal, when your time was up, it was up. In reality that's how short and shocking it could be.

'You all right, Nan?' Nancy Byrne said as she placed her arm around her dear nan, hugging her tightly. She'd clearly been thinking the very same. Always worrying about her poor old nan. The girl was a diamond, she really was.

'I'm grand, girl.' Joanie smiled, a genuine smile, blinking back the tears in her eyes at how blessed she was. She'd never thought she'd love anyone as much as she loved her Jimmy, but her granddaughter had stolen her heart.

'Look at those two!' Joanie said, glancing over to where Colleen and Michael were sitting at the kitchen table. The pair of them like the two black sheep of the family, segregating themselves from everyone else, as they proceeded to drink themselves stupid. Though, Michael had already done that many moons ago. The chance of him having any brain cells left in his hollow head was probably few and far between.

'She's an embarrassment,' Nancy said, staring at her mother with irritation as the woman continued talking animatedly to her grandad – who was another one that Nancy didn't have any time for.

Her grandad had always had a soft spot for Colleen. Sitting with her now, letting her mother vent as Colleen's voice got louder and more high-pitched the more that she drank.

Nancy smarted. Looking around the room, she could see by the faces that she wasn't the only one to think that her mother was a state. Her puffy eyes, black with mascara that she'd smudged across her cheeks and down her face; a trail of snot streaming from her nose, which she wiped away with the sleeve of her black dress. Bawling now. Sobbing hysterically, as she talked shit to Nancy's grandad, stopping only to glug back some more of her precious wine.

'We've not even been back here an hour, and she's pissed already.' Nancy's tone, like herself, was so detached from her mother that she didn't feel an ounce of sympathy that she might be struggling today. Instead she felt only annoyance.

'She's making the rest of the guests here uncomfortable,' Joanie added, purposely fuelling Nancy's disgust. 'I'd say something to her, but you know how she gets if I try and offer her any advice. She'll only throw it back in my face, accuse me of having a dig or something equally ridiculous. You know how she likes to convince herself that she can't do any wrong.'

Nancy nodded. Oh she knew all right. Her mother was ever the victim.

'I'll go and have a word. She'll listen to me,' Nancy said, knowing how her mother and nan only grated on each other.

'Don't you think you've had enough, Mother,' Nancy said, her tone clipped as she didn't bother to wait for a response. Swiping her mother's wine glass from her hand, she knew too well that she would only argue the toss with her, and Nancy wasn't in the mood. Not here and now, in front of everyone they knew.

'Er excuse me,' Colleen shrieked, instantly rendering everyone else in the room silent at her sudden outburst; but clearly not giving two shits as she snatched the glass back from her daughter's grasp. 'I'll say when I've had enough.'

Nancy leaned in close. Keeping her voice low, controlled, as she spoke through gritted teeth. 'You're making a holy show of yourself! People are looking at you!'

It was a warning. Colleen knew that. This wasn't the Byrne way, was it? Being real. Showing any form of emotion. Well fuck Jimmy and his pathetic rules. Colleen wasn't prepared to play nicely. Not today.

'So what if they're watching me. Who cares! Let them fucking well look,' she shouted, sloshing her wine out of the glass as she flung it around exaggeratedly, letting everyone in the room know that she wanted them to hear what she had to say about them all. 'Look at them! Dressing their nosey bastard ways up as sympathy and concern. None of these people are here for me. Most of them aren't even here for my mother. They're all here for Jimmy and Joanie. Stuffing their faces full of all our food and wine. Like it's some kind of free for all. Treating my mother's funeral like it's some kind of social occasion.' Colleen was shouting now.

Aware that everyone was looking at her. And of Jimmy standing across the room with his sidekick, Alex, and that bent copper,

Taylor. All staring back at her, horrified, as she did what they'd been expecting her to do. To kick off.

'Colleen love, don't do this,' Michael whispered softly beside her, placing his hand on hers, to try and get her to sit down.

Colleen knew that her father-in-law only ever meant her well. He was the only one in the family that genuinely had her back; the pair of them were the same. The man was just as controlled and browbeaten as she was by the rest of the Byrne crew. They were both outcasts in their own family. Well Colleen wasn't going to allow her daughter to speak to her this way. Not here, and not today of all days. Shrugging Michael's hand away, Colleen had had enough.

'I don't care if they're all listening. Let them. This is what they are all waiting for anyway, isn't it? Colleen Byrne to make a show out of herself yet again. Well you can all fuck off! Do you hear me? This is my mother's wake and I don't want you here.'

'That's enough,' Nancy said shortly. Berating her mother, her voice sounded like a bad imitation of her grandma Joanie's. The girl was just like her.

'You know what, you're right.' Colleen laughed. Nodding, she couldn't agree more. 'I've had ENOUGH of all this bullshit.' Standing up, wobbly on her feet, Colleen swept the wine glass from the table; happy when it hit the floor and shattered into hundreds of pieces, causing the people standing closest to her to step back. Out of her way.

Apologising profusely to the guests around her, Nancy grabbed her mother's arm roughly, guiding her around the glass shards at her feet, making sure that she didn't cut herself. The last thing she needed was her mother having to be taken to A&E to have her foot stitched up.

'You are a fucking disgrace,' she spat. Her fingers digging into her mother's fleshy arm she leaned in close but her voice was loud now, and everyone in the room could hear her. Though Nancy no longer cared about trying not to create a scene; as always, thanks to her mother, the damage was done.

'Oh, I get it!' Ignoring her daughter's rant, Colleen caught the smug look of defiance on her mother-in-law's face as Joanie stared back at her with glee.

The master puppeteer. She'd orchestrated all of this and Colleen, drunk, had played right in to her hands. Watching the event unfold just as she had known it would. Colleen was as predictable as ever.

'That old witch sent you over, didn't she? That's just her style. Getting her granddaughter to do her dirty work and try and show me up. I bet you're loving this, aren't you? Fanning the flames and then you just stand back and watch the destruction. All you've ever done is turn my kids against me. Well, do you know what Joanie Byrne? Today, of all days, you can go and fuck yourself.'

Colleen didn't know what hit her; the stinging blow that Nancy administered came from nowhere.

Nancy had been down on the floor, on her knees, brushing the glass into a pile. Cleaning up her mother's mess yet again. Hearing her mother attacking her nan was too much for the girl. Springing to her feet she backhanded her mother in the face.

'Don't you dare talk to my nan like that ever again, do you hear me?!'

Colleen fell back against the chair. The slap, though brutal, wasn't the hurt that she felt. The real wound was from the way Nancy was looking at her, the way the girl always looked at her: with pure venomous hate in her eyes.

Colleen had always hoped that, one day, she would somehow redeem herself to her daughter, that she could perhaps explain how her life had come to this, how she was broken inside. But she knew now, in this very moment, it would never be. Her daughter was lost to her for ever.

'My nan has done nothing but help you, you ungrateful cow. That's all she's ever done. If it wasn't for her, me and Daniel wouldn't have had a mother. She stepped in and did your job for you. You should be kissing her arse,' Nancy continued, seething. Her mother had pushed her too far this time. Making a holy show of their family in front of everyone they knew. Well her mother wasn't the only one that had had enough. They'd all been making excuses for far too long: allowing her to continue to drink herself into oblivion on a daily basis. Letting her stagger around the house, slurring her speech as she spoke.

She'd been worse lately. Her father had made allowances for her declining behaviour because of her mother's passing, but there was more to all of this than just that.

'Well, I'm not having it anymore, Mother! You need to treat our nan with respect.'

Holding her face, humiliated beyond measure, Colleen's voice was barely audible.

'You don't understand, Nancy. None of you understand,' Colleen said, though the words sounded so pathetic as they tumbled out of her mouth.

'Course we don't understand! Unlike you, we're not mental!' Nancy said through gritted teeth. 'All my life I've put up with you walking around in a drunken haze, so self-medicated that you can barely function. Even now, look at you. At Nan Edel's funeral. Your mother will be turning in her grave.'

Nancy's words hit Colleen in the heart because she knew them to be true. Her mother would be disgusted at her behaviour. At seeing her in this state. Consumed with guilt, she started to cry. This was all such a big mess.

'You haven't even bothered to ask how Daniel and I are? Do you know that? Our nan has passed away. We miss her too! But then you never once thought about us, did you? So busy in your own little world, there's only ever been you.'

'That's enough now, Nancy. Your mother's not well. She's grieving. Let her be.'

She felt her dad step in behind her, his hand on her shoulder pulling her back, trying to stop her from continuing her attack on her mother. But his words only ignited Colleen's anger once more.

'What's the matter, Jimmy?' Colleen said, glad that she was showing the man up in front of all these people – Jimmy's so-called friends and business associates. 'This not quite the impression that you wanted to give people. The perfect little family? Only we're far from that, aren't we?'

Locking eyes with her husband, Colleen was tempted to blurt it all out: the reasons why she hated this man so much; the things that he'd done over the years. Trampling on people, murdering people, all for this. This big house, his so-called reputation. All of it had come at the very highest price.

It was Daniel's turn to step in. Unable to watch anymore of his mother's outburst, he knew that he could calm the situation. His mother would listen to him. He was certain of it. He knew how much she so desperately wanted to bond with her son; he'd use it to his advantage.

'Come on, Mum,' Daniel said softly. 'Let's get you out of here, yeah? It's been a long day. Let's get you off to bed, yeah?'

Overcome with emotion that her Daniel was sticking up for her, helping her, Colleen nodded, allowing her son to lead her from the room.

Colleen continued to hold her face, the heat of the slap still stinging. She needed to get out of here. Away from these people. Away from Jimmy, Nancy, and Joanie.

She could feel Daniel's arm around her now. Holding her tightly as he led her up the stairs and into her room. The warmth of him holding her. She'd never experienced that before. Her boy. Her precious boy. Her mind filled with so much regret. How different everything could have been.

Lifting up the blankets, Daniel guided his mother, fully clothed, into her bed. The fumes of the alcohol on her breath potent, as she turned to face him.

'Sit with me for a while?' Colleen asked, her eyes pleading with her son not to leave her alone just yet.

Daniel agreed. More for himself than anything. He couldn't face going back down into that room, to where all those people would be whispering about them. Picking holes in what their father had always made out was such a perfect life. Only it was far from perfect. All this wealth and notoriety and they were just as fucked up as everyone else.

Sitting with his mother, Daniel listened as Colleen mumbled away to herself. The alcohol had taken its toll now. Half the shit she was coming out with didn't even make sense.

Colleen finally drifted off to sleep. Daniel tucked the blanket around his mother. Staring down at her as she slept.

He felt sad then.

All his life she'd been almost a stranger to him. Nancy was right. It had been their nan who had been more like a mother to them both. Daniel didn't have one memory of his mother kissing him, or holding him. Not one memory of his mother ever laughing or playing any games with him. All her life, she'd been a shell of a person. There, but not really there at all.

Remembering the story that his nan had told him about when Nancy was just two years old – how his mother had tried to kill herself as she'd slept beside his sister in the bed; how she'd tried to kill him: the tiny defenceless baby inside her – Daniel now knew why.

In her drunken state, his mother had just told him everything: about her wedding night, about the young man his father had murdered, about the life of guilt and fear that his mother had been forced to live. She was so out of it, Daniel suspected, tomorrow she wouldn't even remember telling him. So for now, he decided, he'd keep what she'd told him close to his chest.

Daniel shook his head sadly before leaving the room and closing the door behind him. Maybe Nancy was wrong about their mother after all.

All this talk about loyalty. By the sounds of it, his mother had been the most loyal of them all, and so far, it had cost her everything.

CHAPTER THIRTY

Living above a greasy fish and chip shop in King's Cross hadn't exactly been Gavin Hurst's idea of living the dream when he'd finally plucked up the courage to run away from the children's home in Essex just before his sixteenth birthday, but the irony was that that was exactly what this dingy cockroach-infested shithole of a flat had turned out to be.

It was his very own little sanctuary. He was king of his own castle now. Away from his childhood abusers who had tormented him throughout his entire time in the care system, it was Gavin who called all the shots these days. If men wanted to use him to satisfy their sexual needs, then so be it; but this time it came at a cost.

Gavin had learned to put the years of abuse that he'd suffered to good use. Practice makes perfect and all that. Gavin knew exactly what men wanted and he took great delight in charging the fuckers a premium to get it. Long gone was the vulnerable victim, the poor helpless little child that men had wanted to take advantage of. Gavin was the one who did all the advantage taking nowadays. The damage that had been done to him had properly fucked him up in the head. As it would do. The things that he had done and seen, from such a young age, ensured that his mind and morals were royally corrupted.

Still, he'd learned from the very best. Putting the river of knowledge from every rape, every sexual encounter, every time he'd felt scared or vulnerable into doing what he knew he did best.

Satisfying men.

And why not? He knew he was good at it.

As a child he'd been the vulnerable boy that men had desired, but now he was all man. Strong, muscular, a model type. Only models didn't earn the sort of money that Gavin earned doing this job.

As his mobile phone rang and he saw the caller's ID, Gavin smiled to himself: he had been looking forward to seeing this little liaison all day. For more reasons than one.

Glancing around the flat as he buzzed the man in, Gavin rolled his eyes. Chiding himself. What the fuck was he doing? This punter wasn't here to inspect his decor. Who cared if the place was a bit untidy? Gavin had put fresh sheets on the bed, and sprayed a bit of his expensive aftershave around the room. That was about as domesticated as he stretched to.

Giving himself one final once-over in the mirror in the hallway, Gavin liked what he saw. Tanned and good-looking, he prided himself on his appearance. And he worked hard for it. Treating his vocation as if it was his profession of choice, he invested all his time and money on staying ahead of his game. Going to the gym every morning to ensure his body was toned to perfection, rock-hard and muscular, just as most of his clients liked him to be. A real man, like them. Dressed in designer clothing, Gavin could fit right in with the best of them. That only added to his appeal. He could be seen out in public with these men, be it under the pretence of a new work colleague, or friend. He'd even pretended to be a nephew on a few occasions. Whatever role needed to be played Gavin was good for it. So good, in fact, that sometimes he even fooled himself. That's why he was the best in the business.

This was all part of his job – what put him ahead of the rest of the opposition in King's Cross. His adversaries around London came in their hordes, mainly in the form of scrawny-looking rent boys. A lot of them much younger than him, marketing themselves to the men with paedophiliac tendencies, men that liked to fuck vulnerable boys. Vulnerable and desperate, they were often the ones that set themselves up for abuse. Risking their lives getting into strange men's cars or taken down the back of some dirty alleyway. Competition might be rife around here but it certainly wasn't fierce. That's why Gavin had set himself apart. Intent on making some real money for himself so that he could make a proper life away from all of this one day. A life where he could be normal, without having to comply to some perverted man's every whim.

Gavin had set himself up as more of a male escort, homing in on attracting some of London's elite. He'd managed to find himself a job at one of the West End's most prestigious restaurants. Working most evenings just so that he could meet the extortionate rent on this place, his evening job opened him up to finding his pick of customers too. Real men. Men with power and money and, more importantly, reputation.

Gavin could tell a gay man from a mile off, his 'Gaydar' homing in on even the ones that had convinced themselves that they were straight. Married with children, hiding so far back inside the closet that they were almost in fucking Narnia. They were Gavin's most generous customers too. The ones that always paid a premium for Gavin's professionalism and discretion. Men that after a weekend of traipsing around clothes shops and watching soaps on the TV in the boring monotonous company of their wives always paid out a premium for Gavin, good money to flip them over onto their knees and give them what their wives never could. A good hard fuck. Some release.

It was ingenious really. Gavin had made a fortune over the years. Not that you'd think it from looking around at this dive that he lived in. All his money was hidden under the floorboards of the flat.

Today he was set to make even more. In fact, Gavin knew for certain that his next client was going to pay him an absolute fortune.

Hearing the knock at his front door, Gavin went to let the punter in, aware that he was looking forward to today for reasons that he shouldn't. He had started to let himself get emotionally involved with this one. Letting his guard down, he'd actually enjoyed the sex with this man. He knew his punter had too. A wealthy businessman, older than him. Old enough to be his father, in fact. He hated to admit it, but this one was much more personal. The man had been so cold and aloof with Gavin for months, but he also got so much pleasure out of fucking Gavin. Maybe that's what had appealed to Gavin: he'd taken this man to the very edge. He was like a drug to him.

For six months they'd carried on their illicit relations. No talking, no emotions, just fucking. Like animals. Passionate, raw. Just the way Gavin liked it. The punter too apparently. Somehow Gavin had fallen for the man, and he had a feeling that the man felt the same. That had been the magic of it all but also the danger. And that's why Gavin knew that it was time to get out. It was a shame really, the way that things had turned out. If Gavin hadn't been such a cold, calculating bastard himself, who knew, this might have worked out for them both. Though, he highly doubted it. Men like this punter only ever wanted young men like Gavin for their own gain. He was nothing more than a dirty little secret. A sordid, repulsive urge that they didn't have the willpower or the self-control to suppress.

Gavin would be cast aside eventually. He knew that. That was all part and parcel of his job. No matter how much he liked to think that he was the one calling all the shots, ultimately the men were still using him really. Taking what they wanted, what they craved, and then throwing some cash at him to keep him sweet and ease their conscience before they skulked back to their perfect lives in suburbia. Repeating the same pattern over and over again, until eventually the novelty of him wore off and then they moved on to the next. Gavin knew the score.

This man was no different. The outcome was always inevitable. That's why he had a backup plan. He switched on the cameras that he'd rigged up around the apartment before opening the front door and stepping aside to let the notorious Jimmy Byrne in.

Gavin felt the flutter of excitement in his groin as he greeted the man. Tonight, for the very last time he was going to let Jimmy Byrne do what he always did best, and own him.

One last time.

Then Gavin Hurst was going to show Jimmy Byrne what it was really like to get royally fucked by a pro.

CHAPTER THIRTY-ONE

Staring up at the ceiling, Jimmy Byrne took a deep pull of the cigarette in Gavin's hand and breathed out the large white plume of smoke. He was relaxed now, after the hellish week he'd had. Edel Walsh's funeral had taken place six days ago now and still the tension in his house was unbearable.

Gavin was just the sort of light relief he needed, though their physical encounter hadn't erased the guilt that he felt when he'd arrived here earlier this evening. Colleen was starting to become a liability. Jimmy had seen something change in her lately. Just as he had on the day of her mother's funeral. There had been a sudden defiance in her eyes as she'd stood in front of the room full of people at her mother's wake, challenging him. Knowing full well that she held all of his secrets on the tip of her tongue. Jimmy couldn't trust her. Not anymore. She'd changed. It was like something inside her had just snapped, and she'd given him the impression that at any second she would call him out.

With Edel gone now and the children making it blatantly clear that they wanted nothing to do with her anymore, Colleen had nothing left to lose, he guessed, and in Jimmy's eyes that made her a very dangerous woman. A woman who could cost him everything, who could ruin him and everything that he'd worked so hard to build for himself, for his family. It saddened him to realise that he was going to have to do something about her now.

'What are you daydreaming about?' Gavin leapt off the bed to extinguish his cigarette that had almost burned down to his fingers. 'My big gorgeous shlong of a cock?'

Raising his eyes playfully at Jimmy as he spun around, he exposed his instantly erect penis, despite the lengthy sex session they'd just enjoyed.

The magic of youth.

Smiling at Jimmy as he saw the lust for him once more in the man's eyes, Gavin was enjoying the fact that Jimmy couldn't take his eyes away from his lean muscular body. Taking a seat by the window, his body lit up by the dull light of the table lamp, he would let Jimmy enjoy the view of his body for just a few minutes longer.

Why not?

The man would soon be paying a small fortune for the privilege. That thought alone had been all Gavin had been able to think about as Jimmy pounded him so violently from behind tonight. The power that he had over the man, that Jimmy didn't even know about yet. The thrill of what Gavin had come to mean to him only heightening the intensity of their sex, which, in turn, meant that Gavin had just experienced the most intense climax of his life.

Still, all good things had to come to an end.

Jimmy had got what he came for. He'd used Gavin's body to fulfil his every pleasure and soon it would be Gavin's turn to let Jimmy know that that privilege was going to cost the man dearly. Jimmy was a ruthless, violent man. This was the most dangerous job that Gavin had ever pulled off and for now he was going to have to play it smart.

'Am I the best fuck you've ever had?' he asked Jimmy, almost teasing. He knew he was. He just wanted Jimmy to say it.

Smile for the cameras, Mr Byrne. This is all being taken down and used against you.

'You know you are!' Jimmy Byrne said seriously, irritated by the train of conversation. Gavin knew that Jimmy never talked about his feelings or emotions.

'Better than your wife?'

'You what?' The question caught Jimmy off guard. Frowning, as he turned onto his side, he stared over at Gavin questioningly. The boy was crossing the line, and judging by the slight tilt to his voice, Gavin was more than aware of it.

Gavin grinned, amused at Jimmy's expression but slightly scared by the edge to Jimmy's voice. He'd got carried away with himself. He'd only been testing the water, seeing how much Jimmy would say without realising he was being filmed. He'd forgotten how volatile Jimmy could be.

'Sorry. That's none of my business,' he said holding his hands up, seeing the fury spread across Jimmy's face at his brazen audacity of mentioning the precious, oblivious Mrs Byrne.

'Damn right it isn't.' Jimmy was up off the bed. Gavin's mention of Colleen, after what the two men had done, was an instant reminder of Jimmy's life as a lie. His shame at who he really was. His head was fucked already, he didn't need to have all this shit to deal with too.

'Don't go!' Gavin said, seeing Jimmy pulling his trousers on, his face thunderous now. Instantly in a bad mood. It almost made Gavin feel jealous that the mention of Jimmy's wife could have such an effect on him. Another sign that he'd let this 'relationship' drag on too long.

That had been his only error. Six months of Jimmy coming here to the flat whenever he took the fancy, and both men had become attached. There it was. That was the truth of the matter. Jimmy's reaction was a stark reminder of the reality they were both facing though. He and Jimmy were just fucking. That was it. There was nothing more.

Pure, animalistic, raw sex. No magical love story, no happy-ever-after. He was just Jimmy's little fuck-boy and once the novelty wore off, which it always did eventually, Jimmy would move on and find someone else for his needs.

Lighting up another cigarette, Gavin sat in the chair under the window. The stream of light shining in on him, illuminating his naked form in all its glory.

'Jimmy, I'm sorry.'

Jimmy shook his head.

'Forget it. I've got to go anyway. I'll see you another time.' Grabbing his jacket from the side, he winced as he knocked Gavin's photos down from the side unit.

'Leave it! It's okay. I'll sort them,' Gavin said, jumping to his feet so quickly that Jimmy couldn't help thinking the lad was acting suspicious.

Jimmy ignored him and picked up the frame. A younger looking Gavin, smiling back at the camera with his mum sitting at his side. Gavin had told him it was the only picture he had of his mother, when he was four, before the woman had taken a heroin overdose and Gavin had been whisked off into care. Placing the frame back on the shelf, as Gavin hovered anxiously next to him, Jimmy sensed there was something the boy didn't want him to see.

He almost missed it. Tucked away so discreetly, cut into the back panel of the wooden unit.

Jimmy pulled out the small black camera. Turning to confirm that the lens had been pointing directly at the bed.

'What the fuck is this?' he said as he saw the look of fear spread across Gavin's face. 'Are you for real?' He slammed the camera at the wall, watching the chunk of metal smash against it and smash into several pieces.

Gavin didn't speak. Unable to find his voice, he wasn't sure what to say to redeem himself. There was nothing he could say. He'd been caught out, red-handed.

'You were going to blackmail me?' Jimmy laughed, as he realised that was exactly what this opportunistic little prick intended to do. He was going to try his luck at blackmailing Jimmy. Though how the hapless moron thought that he could actually get away with it, he had no idea.

Jimmy pounced then. Completely losing the plot he barely gave Gavin time to register that, for him, he'd made his last and ultimate mistake. The boy wouldn't be getting out of this one alive.

The first slam of Gavin's head to the chunky wooden side table he was sitting in front of split his left eyebrow completely open, the heat of the slam radiating through his skull. The second violent slam knocked Gavin out cold. Unconscious now, which was just as well, as Jimmy pounded Gavin's face into an unrecognisable bloody pulp, punching and kicking the boy with all of his fury.

He didn't stop.

Not until he was covered in blood, his body spent. Exhausted from his violent outburst, he collapsed on the floor beside the now mangled boy.

FUCK!

He'd done it again: lost himself in his rage. Now Gavin was dead.

Leaning against the bed, he closed his eyes. Opening them a few minutes later when he'd gained some much needed clarity. The flash of a tiny green light from the bottom of the unit caught his eyes. Chasing the black cable that led inside the cupboard door, Jimmy opened it and found where the light was coming from. He swore again as he held the computer up, checking the disk drive for a CD. It was empty. No memory stick either.

Staring at the little green light at the top of the camera as it flashed sporadically, Jimmy stared into the camera.

A webcam.

Linked up to somewhere. To someone. Someone was recording him? Watching him right now?

Then the light went out.

Shit.

Snapping the laptop shut, Jimmy got up, stepping over the naked body of Gavin Hurst. Someone else had seen everything. They probably had a copy of everything that had happened in the room tonight burnt onto a disk. Hurrying to get the fuck out of the boy's squalid shithole of a room, Jimmy Byrne was shitting himself. The cocky little fucker had driven him to this. Gavin was dead because he thought that he could fuck with Jimmy and because of that he'd paid the ultimate price.

Only now Jimmy was royally fucked too.

CHAPTER THIRTY-TWO

'Jimmy?' Opening the front door, Alex Costa stepped back as Jimmy Byrne pushed past him into his apartment. He hadn't been expecting to see Jimmy tonight. In fact, lately, he hadn't seen Jimmy at all. It was clear the man wasn't here on a social call.

'Jesus! What the fuck has happened?' Dishevelled, standing there with blood dripping down his shirt, Jimmy looked as if he'd been crying. In all the time that Alex had known him, Jimmy had never cried.

'What the fuck's going on? Is it Colleen?' Alex wouldn't put it past the crazy bitch to do something stupid, especially after the way the deranged cow had acted last week at her own mother's wake.

Jimmy shook his head. Unable to speak, he stomped across Alex's apartment, back and forth, pacing the length of the floor. Erratic with his movements, running his shaking hand through his hair, he finally broke.

'I'm fucked, Alex. Big time. I've done something fucking bad.'

Alex raised his eyes questioningly. 'Like what?' He'd seen Jimmy do all kinds of shit over the years, most of it bad. He couldn't help wonder what made whatever this was so different.

'This is really, really fucking bad.'

Staring at Jimmy, realising he wasn't exaggerating, Alex shook his head, bewildered.

'Fuck!' Jimmy shouted, unsure if he should have even come here, if he had the bollocks to open up and admit what he'd done to his best friend. He had no one else he could turn to though, no one else who would help him. Things had been rocky between him and Alex for a while, but Alex had always stood by him.

'For fuck's sake, you're making me dizzy walking about the place in circles. Sit down and I'll pour you a drink, you look like you could do with one.' Unsure what was going on, Alex did the only thing that he thought might help, he poured his friend a large Scotch.

Handing the glass to Jimmy, Alex watched him knock it back in one.

'Are you going to tell me what the fuck is going on?' he said, downing his own drink; he had a feeling he might need it.

Jimmy sat down, still rubbing his head frantically. He didn't know where to start.

'There was this lad. A waiter, down at one of the clubs. Only he did other stuff on the side, you know.'

'Other stuff? Like what, washing-up?' Alex said sarcastically, suddenly realising where Jimmy was going with this.

'I was fucking him,' Jimmy declared, knowing there was no gentle way to break it to Alex. His confession rendered his friend silent. 'I know that's difficult for you to hear, Alex, but there you have it. He meant nothing to me. It was just sex. No emotion, no ties, just a service.'

Jimmy was lying. It was part of the reason he'd totally lost his shit tonight. Jimmy had fallen for Gavin. He knew it would never work: the bloke was far too young for Jimmy for it ever to be anything serious. Still, he'd let his guard down. He'd been seeing Gavin for months and the sex had been the best Jimmy had ever experienced. Exciting, passionate. You couldn't have that kind of sex without some kind of feeling behind it. Jimmy had physically wanted Gavin. He'd craved him like a drug. Only Gavin had been using him all along. He'd set him up for his own gain.

Alex sat down. Breathless. The shock of Jimmy's confession left him physically winded.

'This is why you've been avoiding me?'

Jimmy shook his head. Lying again.

'Bullshit,' Alex spat. Jimmy had been acting strange for months. Busy with the ever-expanding business; Alex had thought it was down to work. Then when Edel had passed away, he figured the man had been busy with his nutjob of a wife. When really all this time Jimmy had been avoiding him because he'd been secretly getting his end away with some fucking gigolo.

'It gets worse,' Jimmy said, looking down at his swollen knuckles, the blood splattered all over his clothes. 'I've killed him.'

Alex almost dropped his glass. 'You've killed him?'

Jimmy winced at Alex's disgusted tone. The hurt and disbelief in his best friend's eyes. He needed to make Alex understand. This wasn't his fault. He'd been driven to it.

'The conniving fucker tried to blackmail me. He filmed me, Alex. He had cameras rigged up in the apartment. I think it was rigged up to a laptop. Someone else was watching me too? Fuck, Alex. He wasn't much older than my Daniel. He was just a kid really.'

'You're a stupid fucker you know that, Jimmy! What the fuck were you playing at? That bloke didn't set you up, you set yourself fucking up! You should have been smarter.' Alex didn't even bother to hide his anger at what Jimmy had got himself involved in.

Slamming down the glass on the kitchen table, he couldn't contain his anger anymore.

'I didn't think, Alex—'

''Course you fucking didn't. You're a man. When your dick gets hard, your brain gets soft, ain't that right?' Alex spat, the resentment and hurt clear in his voice.

Jimmy was almost crying now and it was no wonder. This was an epic fuck up on his part. His head was all over the fucking place. He'd been stupid to keep going back to the same fucking bloke. Anonymity was key if he didn't want to put himself through shit like this. Shit that could blow Jimmy Byrne's world wide open.

'I'm sorry, Alex,' Jimmy said, knowing Alex was right to be upset. Jimmy had hurt him badly. He knew how Alex felt about him. The man loved him. He had done for years. It had always been Alex and Jimmy.

'Sorry for what?' Alex said, tapping the edge of the glass irritably with his fingertips. 'For leaving me dangling? For never committing to me? Come on, Jimmy.' Alex had never felt so angry with Jimmy in all his life. 'I put up with a lot from you over the years, Jimmy, you and I both know that. All those tarts you used to surround yourself with. The bimbos that you used to parade around, too embarrassed to confess who you really are. Too weak to admit you are gay. Fuck, you even had me doing it too. The pair of us both acting out a lie in public in case anyone guessed our dirty little secret.'

Alex stood up, unable to bear Jimmy sitting in such close proximity to him.

'You know how I feel about you, how I've always felt about you. Even when you insisted on marrying that fucking fruit loop, Colleen. How did that turn out for you, huh, Jimmy? Your good little wife at home.'

Pouring himself another drink, Alex drank it down in one.

'That bitch got the ultimate prize, and the irony is since the day she married you, she hasn't wanted you. How fucked up is that? As soon as she realised what you are, she didn't want to know.' He stared at Jimmy. 'I know you, Jimmy. The good, the bad and the ugly. Why was that never enough for you?'

'You know why,' Jimmy argued.

'Oh fuck off will you, Jimmy!' Alex said, as they both stumbled back onto the same argument that their relationship had always boiled down to.

Jimmy was embarrassed to admit to the world, to himself, that he was gay because somehow he'd convinced himself that being gay was something to be ashamed of. That it meant that people wouldn't respect him, that people wouldn't take him seriously.

'This isn't the dark ages, Jimmy. No one gives a shit if you're gay, straight or you bend both fucking ways. You hid behind Colleen like she was some kind of shield. As if having a wife and kids would somehow stop the world from seeing the real you.'

Alex slammed his glass down on the side.

'But I saw you, Jimmy. I saw you and I fucking loved you.' Alex loved him still. Jimmy was all Alex had ever wanted. He knew Jimmy's demons and he didn't care. But Alex would never, ever be enough for Jimmy Byrne. He was finally admitting to himself now, after years of going it alone, of stealing whatever small scraps that Jimmy would offer him.

What a waste of time. The man was a walking, talking fucking cliché. This conversation wasn't going anywhere other than round in circles. Alex needed to get a grip. He needed to think of a way to sort this shit out. He couldn't even look at him right now. Couldn't bear the sight of him.

'Take off your clothes,' Alex said.

Startled, Jimmy narrowed his eyes, which only caused Alex to really cop the hump with him.

'You're covered in blood, Jimmy. You need a shower. Take off your clothes. I'm going to have to get rid of them.' As if he'd touch Jimmy now, after he knew where he'd just come from. What he'd just done.

Jimmy did as he was told. Stepping out of his clothes, he threw them down in a pile on the cold tiles of Alex's kitchen floor, standing in his friend's apartment completely stark bollock naked.

Taking them, Alex placed the lot in a bin bag, before leaving the room to turn on the shower for Jimmy.

'What's his address?' Alex said, returning just a few minutes later and throwing him a towel. 'I'll get some of the men around there to do the clean-up. We'll get the laptop too. We'll get it sorted.'

Reciting the address, Jimmy nodded gratefully.

'Get yourself cleaned up,' Alex said, about to walk out of the room, knowing that tonight he would end up doing what he always did: cleaning up Jimmy Byrne's fucking mess.

Only the drama wasn't over yet.

He heard a message come through on Jimmy's pager.

Jimmy read the text, then holding out the pager to Alex, he waited for the words to sink in before adding, 'I'm being blackmailed. This is just the start. Whoever Gavin was working with wants half a million pounds.'

CHAPTER THIRTY-THREE

'Dad?' Nancy Byrne asked, walking into her office at the back of the warehouse, only to find her dad sitting at the desk, rummaging through the desk drawers, just where she and Daniel had been told they would find him by one of the other 'concerned' workers. There were files and folders everywhere.

Spotting the bottle of whisky on the desk, Daniel picked it up and stared at the small amount of liquid.

'Fucking hell, Dad, you on a mission or something tonight?' he asked playfully, sensing that something was up with his father, as the man had barely bothered to acknowledge their presence.

'We've already got one drunk in the family we don't need another.'

'What did you just say?' Jimmy said. Stopping what he was doing, he glared at Daniel as the boy stood in front of him, a twisted smirk on his face. 'Have some fucking respect for your mother.'

'Who said I was talking about my mother?' Daniel bit back, not letting his father get the better of him.

'What are you doing here, Dad?' Nancy asked, as her dad went back to the files, pulling out bits of paper from all the company's accounts folders and throwing them on the floor when he saw that they weren't what he'd been looking for.

Nancy had always prided herself on keeping every bit of paperwork in order: clearly marked and organised in folders exactly where she knew everything should be. It would take her ages to clear up all this mess.

'I need to sort out some finances, Nancy. You're going to have to help me.' Jimmy had been searching through the figures unable to make head nor tail of the system that Nancy had going. Not that he doubted everything was in perfect order. Nancy might have a pretty head on her shoulders, but the girl had a sharp mind for numbers too.

'I need to move some money about, but I don't want Alex getting wind of it.' Getting up, Jimmy indicated to Nancy to come and sit down at her computer.

'What do you need it for?' she asked, wondering what the hell was going on here, why her father seemed so on edge and why he was trying to take money from his own company but yet he didn't want Alex to know anything about it.

'It's personal,' Jimmy said, pacing the office, working himself up into a frenzy. His head was all over the place. 'Can you do it or not?' he asked, raising his voice as he stared up at the clock. 'I haven't got all fucking night, Nancy.'

'Okay! Okay,' Nancy said quickly not used to hearing her father swear when he spoke to her. 'How much do you want?' she asked, as she logged on to the accountancy system.

'A lot,' he said rubbing his head. 'Too fucking much.'

'How much is a lot?'

Jimmy stopped walking up and down the room and stood tapping his fingers on the desk; he didn't want to even speak the words out loud, but he knew that he needed his daughter's help. He'd be screwed otherwise. He couldn't access funds like that without making sure the money they'd tucked away was all accounted for. Alex was as shrewd as fuck when it came to their money.

'I need half a million pounds.'

Nancy laughed. Then seeing the seriousness on her father's face she shook her head.

'I can't cover up for a sum of money that big?'

'Well, Nancy, you are going to have to try. I'm not messing. I need that money, and I need it now.'

Nancy not only handled the legitimate side of the accountancy she also sorted out all the other money that Jimmy and Alex had hidden away. A lot of it was tied up in other ventures, but the men had a good bit stashed away too. If her father wanted half a million pounds then Nancy could get it for him, but it would take a bit of juggling about if he didn't want Alex to notice.

Alex Costa rarely missed a trick.

'Okay, well. Let me see what I can do,' she said, looking at her brother for help, hoping that he would step in and talk some sense into their father. Seeing that he was more edgy than usual and drunk too, she knew that there would be no arguing with him.

'Do you need it right now, Dad?' Daniel asked. 'Why don't we go home and get some dinner, yeah? You look like you could do with a decent meal inside you. How much have you had to drink, eh?' While trying to placate Jimmy, Daniel was attempting to guide him out of the office, mistakenly thinking that his father was so pissed, Daniel could easily manipulate him in to going home.

Only Jimmy wasn't playing.

'Why don't you fuck off home yourself, Daniel?' Jimmy said, swiping his son's hand away from him. 'This is serious. It's not a fucking game. Why do you always treat everything like a game?'

'Dad!' Nancy said, hearing her father's complete overreaction. He was taking Daniel's actions completely out of context.

'Daniel was only trying to help.'

'Help? Daniel? Do me a favour. The boy ain't got the clout to know how to fucking well help, let me tell you. Go on, go home,

Daniel. Nancy can help me here. Your sister knows what she's doing. You are about as useful as a chocolate bleeding teapot.'

Even as he said the words Jimmy knew he was acting like a first prize prick, but he just couldn't help himself. He and Daniel had always had a volatile relationship. The boy had a way of winding him up just by breathing.

Only now, Jimmy had the added bonus of seeing Gavin Hurst staring back at him whenever he looked at his son. The two young men had been so similar in age. Just the sight of Daniel made Jimmy feel physically sick, he was so consumed by guilt at what he'd done. Who he was. He just wanted this all to be over. He wanted to get the money and get all of this shit sorted out once and for all.

'Well in that case, I'll leave you in Nancy's more than capable hands, shall I?' Daniel said with a sneer, his nose firmly put out that once again his father seemed to do nothing but put him down.

'Daniel, don't go!' Nancy called out, as her brother ignored her pleas and stormed out of the office.

His sister was annoying him just as much as his father. Daniel'd had enough of pretending that his father's words didn't hurt him. Nothing he ever said or did would ever be anywhere as good as Jimmy's precious Nancy.

And as of tonight, he'd given up trying.

CHAPTER THIRTY-FOUR

Placing the freshly made lasagne on the table, Joanie Byrne sat down beside her husband as Michael did the honours and dished up for everyone.

'Well this is looking lovely,' Michael said as he spooned the food onto the plates, not drawing any attention to the fact that dinner time in the Byrne household had turned into a very strange affair indeed. Colleen was sitting at the table with them once again, for the second time that week, at Michael's insistence and the strangest thing of all was that Joanie hadn't protested.

Ever since Edel's funeral, where Colleen had got herself worked up into such a state, Michael had insisted on the two women calling it a truce. Michael felt sorry for the woman: Colleen had lost her mother after all. Edel Walsh was a hard act to follow, Michael thought sadly to himself. The woman's death had affected them all. Joanie must have felt that too, not to have kicked up a fuss.

'Well, I can't have you all going hungry now, can I?' Joanie smiled tightly. Still not keen at having to put up with Colleen's company, but for now she would keep her peace with the woman. Not wanting Nancy and Daniel to think she was a complete heartless cow.

'Are we dishing up for your father then or not?' Joanie said, quizzing Nancy once more. She'd convinced herself that Nancy knew more than she was letting on.

'He didn't say, Nan. I told you. He didn't say much,' Nancy said tartly, knowing that her grandmother was like a dog with a bone once she got a notion in her head.

'I just think it's strange that he didn't mention where he was going tonight?' Joanie knew that she was acting irrationally, but staring at Nancy, she knew she had every right to be. The girl was so like her father in so many ways, even down to the way she lied. Just like Jimmy – badly. Joanie could always tell.

'It's not like him to get drunk in the middle of the day, is it? And why was he hanging around the office?'

Nancy shook her head, wishing she'd never started the conversation now. She should have just said that she hadn't seen her father.

Her nan just wouldn't drop it.

'Are you sure there's not anything that you're not telling me, missy?' Joanie said, not believing that Jimmy was just slightly 'worse for wear' this evening, as Nancy had so diplomatically put it. She had a feeling her son was in some kind of trouble and was unable to shake the awful feeling that lingered in the pit of her stomach.

'She's told you all she knows, Joanie. Leave her be. You do know he's a grown man, Joanie? I don't think Jimmy's answered to anyone about his whereabouts since he was thirteen,' Michael quipped, trying to make light of his wife's strange behaviour as she picked at Nancy about her beloved son.

'I'm worried about him, that's all,' Joanie said. 'Unlike yourself.'

Michael might not give two hoots about Jimmy, but Joanie knew her own boy better than anyone else here at the table. She was his mother after all. It was as if she had a sixth sense for these types of things. Lately he'd been acting so strange. He just hadn't been himself. He'd been short-tempered and snappy, even with her.

'He seems to have a lot on his mind. It's not work, is it? You'd tell us if you knew anything, wouldn't you?' Joanie said, her question more of a statement.

She knew that Nancy wouldn't tell them jack shit. Nancy and Jimmy were thicker than thieves. Her granddaughter worked for Jimmy full-time now. A sharp brain for figures, Jimmy trusted the girl implicitly to do his accounts, and Nancy wanted to be accepted into her father's business so badly, to help her father run his empire, she was only too happy to take on whatever role he offered. Nancy probably knew all sorts of things about her father's business dealings, and Joanie would never be any the wiser.

'Jesus, Joanie. Will you drop it? She's just said that she doesn't know anything else. Will you leave her be, so she can eat her dinner instead of making her endure the Spanish bleeding Inquisition.'

'Oh be quiet, Michael. No one was asking you to pipe up,' Joanie said, her voice full of irritation as she continued to stare at Nancy, knowing full well she knew more than she was letting on.

'Another delightful family dinner I see!' Daniel smirked as he walked into the kitchen and got himself a beer from the fridge; then taking the bottle of orange juice, he filled his mother's glass, not bothering to offer a drink to anyone else.

Everyone stared at him, no one more surprised than Colleen at her son's rare token gesture. Her son had softened to her of late too. Ever since her mother's funeral. She suspected that, like Joanie and the rest of them, he just felt sorry for her. The novelty would soon wear off, she thought, but for now she was happy to take whatever the boy gave her, which was more than could be said for her daughter. Nancy was pretending like she wasn't even in the room.

'What?' Daniel said, his eyes wide as he took in the puzzled faces of his family. 'Can't I even pour my own mother a drink?'

Though he knew the response his gesture would get him. They were as predictable as ever. Besides, he enjoyed winding the rest of his family up, the quizzical look in their eyes as they tried to work out what his motives were.

'Dad not back yet?' he asked, downing his beer. Having caught the tail end of the conversation they'd all been having, Daniel wasn't done with his vexatious routine just yet.

'Did you see him as well then, Daniel? I know there's something going on. Your sister said he'd had a bit to drink. Did he say anything to you?'

'He didn't say much, did he, Nance? Too busy slurring his speech; he'd had way more than a bit to drink. He was half-cut. Rude as fuck to me. How the tables have turned, eh?' he quipped, nodding at his sober mother.

'Oh piss off, Daniel,' Nancy said, recognising that her brother was on one of his wind-ups. She moved her food around her plate, her appetite gone. The truth be told, she was worrying about her father too. She'd never seen him like he was this evening. Her nan was right to feel worried. Something wasn't right. It hadn't been for days.

'Here, Grandad, do you remember when we were small and you used to refer to my dad as "Saint Jimmy" whenever you copped the hump with him and you thought that no one could hear you?'

Joanie bristled, staring at her husband, immediately annoyed that the man had disrespected Jimmy in front of his children. Even if it was way back when the kids were small.

'Did I?' Michael coughed down his food, not sure how to react as he felt Joanie glaring at him. 'I don't really recall—'

'Yeah, you used to always say it whenever he pissed you off and Nan flapped around him making a fuss of him. Don't you remember? "Oh here we go again, everyone fall over themselves for Saint-fucking-Jimmy",' Daniel mocked his voice, not caring that he seemed to be the only one in the room that found his impression in any way funny.

'Watch your mouth, Daniel,' Joanie retorted, much to her grandson's amusement, before he continued as if she'd said nothing.

'Well, this is Saint Nancy. Butter don't melt, does it, sis? Little Nancy can't do any wrong, can she?'

'Oh fuck off, Daniel,' Nancy said, scraping her chair back. She'd had enough. She wasn't in the mood to sit here listening to her brother spouting crap. Sometimes Daniel really did make it hard for himself. She'd actually felt sorry for him earlier, hearing the way that her father spoke to him, and seeing the visible hurt on his face. Now though she realised that Daniel probably deserved it. Her father was right, he never took anything seriously. Everything was just a joke to her brother.

'I take it you haven't told Nan about the money?'

About to walk out of the room, Nancy stopped as she heard Daniel's voice.

'What money?' Sensing the tension between her two grand-children, Joanie knew she was right to have her suspicions. Something was going on and she wasn't going to let it lie until she got to the bottom of it.

'Oh it's probably nothing but he was asking Nancy to pull half a mill from the company bank accounts. He asked her to do her best to cover it up that the money was gone; he was pretty adamant that he didn't want anyone to find out about it.'

Nancy shook her head. Her father would murder Daniel for talking about his private business dealings. He'd told them both specifically not to say a word to anyone.

'There you go again, Daniel. Proving Dad's point about you. You're a snake.'

'Ahh it's a shame you're Saint Nancy, and not Saint Patrick then. Wasn't he the one that drove away all the snakes, Nanc?' Daniel said, sarcastically. Bored with the conversation that he'd stirred up, he shot them all a parting smile. 'I'm going out. Have fun y'all.' Scooping up a slice of garlic bread from his grandad's plate, Daniel strutted out of the room, making a hissing sound in his sister's direction as he passed her.

He hoped their nan did nothing but give her earache for the rest of the night, trying to dig more information from her. That would teach Nancy to always think that she was so much better than him.

CHAPTER THIRTY-FIVE

Leaning his head back against the cool leather headrest as he waited for the call to come in, Marlon Jackson was buzzing for tonight's job. He'd parked up exactly where he'd been told: down the quiet end of Tilbury Docks, in Essex, tucked away behind some old derelict warehouse.

He stared out across the dockyard, taking in the bleak view that consisted of nothing more than a few abandoned cars scattered amongst the row of huge steel containers. To his right there were a couple of old fishing boats, bobbing about aimlessly in the water at the dock's edge. The place looked spooky as fuck. It didn't help that a wonky street light above him swayed in the wind, causing the bulb to flicker in keeping with the lamp's swift movement, casting eerie shadows out across the ground. It felt like there was no other fucker around for miles, which was exactly why, he guessed, they'd chosen this location in the first place.

Further down, Marlon could see the main working dock, the largest container port in the UK. Even at this ungodly hour of the morning the north bank of the River Thames was bedlam. The dockyard workers never seemed to stop. Marlon eyed the glistening lights far off in the distance, watching as the cargo ships were unloaded by the huge industrial cranes. The headlights of cars and lorries were dancing across the horizon. The flashing lights of the security and police patrolling the area as everyone went about their business.

They were further back on the South Bank, up near the old Tilbury Fort: just a couple of miles away from all the chaos, yet this place was like a graveyard in comparison.

Marlon wasn't alone, though. Staring ahead to the white Beamer that was parked up in front of him, he tried to see if there was any sign of movement. Not only was it dark now, but the tinted blackout windows meant he couldn't see shit. But he knew that his comrade was in there, waiting. Just as he was. Both of them sitting pretty, as they waited to strike. As soon as he got the signal, they were off. Marlon was wired tonight. They weren't even off yet and already the adrenaline was surging through his body like electricity.

Tapping his fingers on the steering wheel of the van he'd stolen especially for tonight, Marlon tried to focus on something else, thinking about the new little bird he was seeing and all the fun they'd had when he'd paid her a visit at her flat this evening.

Gina Jones. The girl had knackered him out. The fact that the girl was friends with his Mrs wasn't exactly the brightest idea Marlon had ever had. He didn't believe in shitting on his own doorstep, no matter how many rewards he was set to reap. He'd made an exception for this bird though. But if Jordanna found out he was playing away again she'd do her nut.

Last time had been bad enough: she'd threatened to stick his balls in a blender whilst they were still attached, and Marlon wouldn't have put it past Jordanna to do it either. She was a full on psycho when the mood took her, nuttier than a squirrel's turd, and Marlon knew that he was playing a dangerous game doing the dirty on her with one of her so-called mates.

His phone beeped for the second time in just as many minutes and Marlon fixed his eyes on the name that flashed up on the screen.

'Gina Jones.'

The girl must be gagging for it, sending him messages, asking him to come back. Flashing another look at the white Beamer, Marlon felt like a naughty little school boy. He'd get a right bollocking for giving the girl this number, but the way he saw it, he could kill two birds with one stone. First and foremost for the job in hand tonight, but also Jordanna didn't even know he had another phone. Marlon's opportunities with women had just opened up tenfold now he had a way of contacting birds without Jordanna ever needing to find out about it. It was a right fucking touch.

But tonight, no matter how much he fancied getting his nuts in again, the job had to come first. Marlon had put in far too much groundwork on this job to fuck it all up now at the last minute on account of some bit of skirt.

Hearing his phone beep again, Marlon looked down at the screen expectantly. This time the message wasn't from Gina. It was from an unknown number; the number from the passenger of the car in front, saying simply:

'Show time!'

Seeing the red glare of the rear lights coming to life as the Beamer's engine started, Marlon followed suit. Chucking his phone down in the passenger seat beside him, Gina Jones was going to have to wait.

Starting the van up, Marlon cast his gaze along this strip of Tilbury Dock, till he spotted the vague twinkling of lights reflecting into the water from an incoming boat docked a few hundred yards further down.

This was it. He just hoped he didn't lose his bottle at the last minute.

Tugging down his balaclava to cover his face, he felt the sweet combination of excitement and trepidation bubbling inside him all at once. Tonight was a complete game changer for him. There would be no going back after this, which was fine by Marlon because he had no intentions of going back. His goal was to keep moving forward, to better his life, and this job was going to change everything. Tonight it was finally payday.

Everything was hanging on the next ten minutes.

Putting his foot down, Marlon accelerated his van down the narrow dirt track, making his way towards their target who would be waiting for their arrival at the next unit much further along. Speeding through the high mesh gates that led to the derelict warehouse, Marlon eyed the lone figure standing in the distance next to his car.

Jimmy Byrne.

He was raising his hands in the air as the car and the van came hurtling towards him, to show the men that he wasn't armed. He looked like a rabbit caught in the headlights, and that's exactly what Marlon knew they were counting on. Jimmy had done just as they'd told him to do. He'd come alone and wanted no trouble.

The man was smart.

All he had to do was hand over the money and this would all be over in minutes.

The BMW skid to a halt, the driver jumping out, dressed head-to-toe in black, a balaclava over his face; his identity hidden as he stretched out his arm and pointed the gun that he was clutching directly at Jimmy Byrne.

Marlon followed suit. Jumping out of his van then too.

He shouted: 'Keep your hands up. Don't fucking move.'

Lifting up the double-barrel shotgun, Marlon fired it into the night sky before aiming it back towards Jimmy, letting the man know that they meant fucking business; so that he wouldn't be tempted to do anything stupid.

Tonight wasn't personal. Tonight was only about the money.

With that in mind, Marlon concentrated on the job in hand. Aiming the gun at Jimmy Byrne, he prayed that he wasn't going to have to use it. Marlon didn't want to have to shoot him, but he would if he had to.

Jimmy Byrne was all about loyalty, and Marlon had always been loyal to his boss, but tonight, for once, he was going to be loyal to the one person that mattered. The one person that, for ever a lackey, could do with a fucking break: Marlon was going to be loyal only to himself.

The genius part about their little plan, with their heavy balaclavas hiding their identities, was that Jimmy would never have a clue who they were, which in turn meant there would never be any reprisals.

They were going take his money, and then swiftly get their arses out of here.

And no one would ever be the wiser that it had been them.

Looking over at his accomplice, Marlon nodded. His mate had been right. This was going to be too easy.

Who knew that taking money from the notorious Jimmy Byrne would be as easy as taking candy from a fucking baby?

CHAPTER THIRTY-SIX

'What the fuck?'

Seeing the car and the van screech to a halt, Jimmy Byrne's first thought was *what if this was all some sort of elaborate set-up by the Old Bill?* Maybe they had found out what he'd done and had come to capture him. Swooping in to make the arrest of the decade.

But as the two masked men jumped out of their vehicles, dressed in black and donning balaclavas, Jimmy registered that these men were not amateurs. They knew exactly what they were doing.

Throwing a fleeting glance at the clapped-out old banger that he'd parked up along the warehouse's entrance, the opposite side of the dockyard, Jimmy hoped that Jack Taylor was keeping well out of sight. He was counting on his friend to help him get out of this tonight. There was no way that Jimmy was going to let two cunts just rob him of half a million pounds.

He could feel his gun digging into the back of his waistband, but now that he was faced with the gunman he decided to not even think about trying to go for it; especially when one of these robbing fuckers was aiming a double-barrel shooter right at his head.

'I said, don't fucking move. Keep your hands in the fucking air!' the man standing next to the van shouted as he fired a single shot into the air, eager to show him that he meant business, and Jimmy didn't for a second doubt it.

'All right! All right!' Sensing the immediate danger, Jimmy Byrne did as he was told.

Praying that he had made the right decision in going ahead with this tonight, he felt guilty for not telling Alex that he'd agreed to his blackmailer's demands. The bloke would have only talked him out of it anyway. Besides, Jimmy wasn't in a position to ask the man for advice and favours. Alex was barely talking to him as it was. Despite saying that he'd help by doing some digging and finding out who these fuckers were, Jimmy had yet to hear fuck all from the man. Alex was clearly still furious at Jimmy's blatant betrayal.

So Jimmy had decided to sort his shit out himself, once and for all.

This was his mess.

He'd been given a week to get the money together, and in that time, he'd been told in no uncertain terms that if he didn't pay up then these two cowboys in front of him were going to make public the recording that they had of him.

They'd sent Jimmy a full list of addresses that they intended to send the recording out to which contained every contact that Jimmy had ever worked with. Every police officer with a grudge to bear; every judge that had been forced to let Jimmy off over the years. The evidence they had on him would crucify him, and Jimmy wasn't about to take that risk.

Only now, standing across from these fuckers, staring down the barrel of the gun, Jimmy couldn't shake the feeling that the worst was still to come. He was anxious. Call it intuition, or some sort of a sixth sense, Jimmy felt deep in his gut that there was going to be some sort of a major fuck up.

'You got the money?' the man standing beside the van, wielding the shotgun, shouted.

'I've got it.' Jimmy nodded.

The first gunman by the Beamer stepped forward. The silent assassin. Still not speaking, the man held out his hand, his instructions blatantly clear: nodding towards the boot of Jimmy's car. He wanted the bag of cash.

Clenching his fists, consumed by anger at the liberties these two numpties were taking, Jimmy knew that for now he had to play along. Nodding in reply as he eyed the two gunmen disdainfully, he quickly debated what his options were. They were fuck all, that's what they were. What else could he do?

It would take two seconds to reach for his gun, but it was two seconds that he didn't have with these men watching his every move. Jimmy had no idea if the gun-toting madmen in front of him had the bollocks to actually shoot him, but it wasn't a risk that he was prepared to take.

The fact that they had planned all of this meticulously, that they'd come here tooled up, concealing their identities from him was more than enough to let Jimmy know that whoever these two pricks were, they meant business.

That and the fact that they knew what Jimmy had done to Gavin Hurst. That was the most shameful thing about this whole ordeal. These fuckers knew things about him that he had spent a lifetime trying to hide from the rest of the world and this was the price he had to pay to keep it that way. Half a million pounds of his hard-earned cash and these fuckers just thought they could take it.

As the vein in the side of his temple throbbed, anger bubbling away inside him, Jimmy did the only thing that he could. He complied. He had no choice but to cooperate.

Reaching in and grabbing the holdall, he reached down into the concealed floor of his Range Rover's boot and slid the metal tyre jack up inside his jacket sleeve.

'Get a fucking move on!' the man standing further back by the van shouted, the atmosphere rife with tension as he jabbed the shotgun in the air towards Jimmy.

The first gunman standing nearest to Jimmy, the one that still hadn't spoken a word, nodded to the ground, not chancing any funny business from Jimmy.

Doing as he was told, Jimmy placed the bag down on the floor in front of him, before kicking it out with his leg towards him. All the while Jimmy's eyes never left the masked man's. Scrutinising him, Jimmy wondered if perhaps that's why this one wasn't talking. He wondered if he knew the fucker. He wondered if this was an inside job. Someone from the firm; how else would they know about this place? This dock was Jimmy's little gem. It was where he did all his drops. Import and export business, but only of a very sought after, illegal variety.

This place was where Jimmy made all his real money these days.

Unless this really was the Old Bill? A couple of bent coppers that Jimmy had on his books. That wouldn't surprise him at all. That lot were so corrupt it was unreal. Working all their lives for a minimum wage, they'd kill to earn the sort of money that Jimmy regularly brought in. He wouldn't put it past those fuckers to get greedy and pull a stunt like this, somehow getting wind of the drop tonight and fancying their chances at having a go at taking on Jimmy and his men. He had half the local plod on his payroll as it was. A pig in your pocket, as Jimmy liked to call them.

The only copper he really trusted was Jack Taylor and that was because the man had stuck by his side since day one. Digging him out of all kinds of shit. Even now, crouching down in the car over by the back wall. Waiting for his signal.

The man always had his back.

Or maybe Jimmy didn't know these men at all. Maybe he was just being fucking paranoid and they were just a couple of greedy little cunts that Gavin had used to set Jimmy up, and now they were seeking revenge for their friend.

Whoever these fuckers were, there was one small detail that they'd clearly overlooked when they'd planned this attack: Jimmy Byrne was never ever going to allow them to get away with this.

It was a good thing that they seemed to know the value of money, but there was one thing much more valuable that they stood to lose and Jimmy intended on making these two fuckers pay him back with that ultimate price: their lives.

Keeping his eyes locked on the first gunman as he picked up the holdall and walked backwards towards the Beamer, Jimmy waited for the man to open the boot to place the bag inside.

His eyes flickered away for just a fraction of a second.

But it was only a split second that Jimmy needed.

He shouted. Alerting his men that this was their cue.

A motorboat shot up along the side of the dock, the white light beaming from it startling the two masked men, just as Jimmy had planned it would. Not one to give up without at least trying to fight, he had no intention of letting these fuckers get the best of him tonight.

He had it all planned out. One of his main men, Kieran Dobbs, had been waiting on the motorboat that had been moored up just out of sight, watching from the sidelines until he got an opportunity.

Firing his gun at the two masked gunmen, all havoc broke out, the gunshot echoing loudly around the dockyard as the bullet flew past the first, silent assailant.

'FUCK!'

Kieran Dobbs had missed his opening shot. The sudden rush of the waves as the boat jerked to a stop in the water caused him to throw his aim.

Alerted now of the impending attack, the masked men were forced to fire back. Kieran Dobbs fired again. This time his aim was on point, but his target moved, ready for the next shot, throwing himself down on the ground behind the Beamer.

Kieran aimed at the other target: the man by the van, rigid with fear, as he held the double-barrel shotgun out in front of him, too fucking frightened to use it. Pulling back the trigger of his gun, Kieran didn't get to fire it. He hadn't spotted the first gunman getting back up on his feet again. Firing one single perfect shot.

The bullet tore straight into Kieran's chest with such precision and velocity that he could only scream out in pain, before he dropped into the murky waters of the Thames.

Eyeing the car at the back of the docks, Jimmy didn't have time to wait for Taylor to make his presence known. It was every man for himself right now and Jimmy Byrne needed to look after himself. He ran at the first gunman – the taller man nearest to him by the Beamer – raising the wheel jack above his head ready to strike out, his other hand going behind him to the waistband of his jeans for his gun. He had one chance.

But the masked gunman got there first.

Aiming the gun at Jimmy's head, he shot him at point-blank range. The loud gunshot echoed out across Tilbury Docks as, this time, the bullet couldn't fail to hit its target.

The searing pain that ripped through Jimmy's skull felt like an explosion. A flash of white light, temporarily blinding him as a ringing sound screamed loudly inside his ears, replaced as quickly as it had come by numbness.

Then, nothing at all.

Jimmy Byrne was dead, lying in a pool of his own blood on the cold concrete of Tilbury dockyard.

CHAPTER THIRTY-SEVEN

'Fuck!' Marlon shouted as he pressed the buttons of his phone, driving at full speed back down the dirt road. The white Beamer hot on his heels.

Marlon waited for his accomplice to pick up before screaming down the phone.

'You fucking killed him, man! That wasn't the fucking plan!'

Desperate to get the fuck out of there, Marlon was on autopilot now as he floored the accelerator and drove like a maniac through the tall metal gates. He didn't even know how the fuck he was managing to drive the van and talk at the same time. He couldn't even think straight right now.

Jimmy Byrne was fucking dead.

That had not been the plan at all. They were supposed to just get in there and get the money. In and out. No one was supposed to get hurt. The guns were only being used as decoration, that's what Marlon had been told. They'd only brought them along because they'd guessed, rightly, that Jimmy wouldn't do as he'd been told and turn up alone. They wanted to make sure that no one caused them any trouble.

'He's fucking dead,' Marlon said again, repeating the words over and over, as if somehow the information would sink in. Only, Marlon was in shock now. The sheer panic evident in his voice. Shaking violently, his body flooded with so much adrenaline that he felt like his heart was going to burst out through his chest.

This was bad. Really bad.

From where Marlon had been standing, further back in the yard, facing the bright lights of the motor boat, he hadn't been able to see fuck all. Certainly not the men's faces.

He had a vague idea that the man on the boat had been Kieran Dobbs. His fucking mate. He was dead too. As the gunshots had fired out around him, Marlon had simply frozen. He'd watched as Jimmy had tried to make a run for it, holding the double-barrel shotgun in the man's direction, only there was no way that Marlon could shoot him.

Not Jimmy.

The man had helped Marlon. All those years ago, when Marlon had first rocked up at Jimmy's warehouse looking for work, Jimmy had given him a chance when no one else would. Aware that Marlon had no experience, the man had taken him under his wing. He'd given Marlon a chance to prove himself, letting him start out at the bottom, but slowly Marlon had worked his way up.

That was the most head fucked thing about all this.

Robbing the man, Marlon could just about justify. Jimmy had money coming out of his ears. Half a million was nothing to the man. For Marlon, though, it would change his life.

Killing Jimmy had never, ever been part of that plan.

What the fuck had they done? They'd both be royally fucked now. Stealing a load of cash from Jimmy would have initially pissed a few people off, but murdering the man in cold blood, this was the start of a fucking war. There would be repercussions.

'What the fuck are we going to do now?' Marlon said, trying to hold the phone to his ear steadily, as his hand shook violently. He tried not to cry.

'You need to lay low for a bit. Go home. I'll give you a call tomorrow and tell you what we're going to do,' the voice at the other end of the phone said calmly, as if nothing remotely untoward had just happened. As if Jimmy Byrne hadn't just been murdered.

That was the scariest fucking thing of all.

Then the phone went dead.

Marlon watched as the Beamer sped up, before overtaking him.

'FUCK!' he bellowed, thumping his hand hard on the steering wheel; scanning the roads around him to make sure that he wasn't being followed, he felt paranoid as fuck now, convinced that someone would see him, or that his motor would be picked up by CCTV.

Marlon may not have pulled the trigger but he was part of this. He was there. That made him an accomplice.

Screeching the van to a halt, he pulled over at the side of the road. Scrambling out of the driver's door, almost falling out on his arse in his haste, Marlon doubled over as he threw up violently all over the gravel.

He was crying now; he hadn't even realised until he felt the tears streaming down his face. The harrowing image of Jimmy lying on the floor, his blood pooling around him; the gunshot wound to his head; the sickening gaping hole in the man's skull.

Spitting out the last mouthful of bile that burned inside his mouth, Marlon wiped his mouth with his sleeve before getting back inside the van.

As the sudden flash of headlights reflected in his rear-view mirror startled him, Marlon almost did a double take. Turning around to check that he wasn't just hallucinating, that his eyes weren't playing tricks on him, his mind went into panic mode as he spotted the car, just off in the distance behind him, coming out from the dockyard that Marlon and his assailant in the white Beamer had just come from.

Hurtling towards him at speed, it was gaining on him.

Shit!

Marlon put his foot down, desperate to get out of there before the cavalry arrived. He swerved his motor onto the opposite side of the uneven dirt track. Staring in the mirror he could see the lights hurtling towards him now. Getting closer. Following him.

'FUCK!' he shouted again.

Someone else had been at the dockyard tonight? Someone who had slipped underneath the radar.

Someone knew.

Almost losing control of the van, Marlon skidded across a muddy verge, his heart pounding inside his chest, as he realised the severity of the situation. The Beamer was long gone. It was only him out here. If he was caught for this, he'd be killed. Whoever it was following him would demand retribution for Jimmy.

Sweating now as he gripped the steering wheel tightly, Marlon forced his foot to the floor with force, putting some distance between them as he sped up once he reached Forge Road. Ahead he could see the old fort. That would be the obvious place to turn into, though, right now, Marlon couldn't afford to be obvious.

He skidded around the sharp bend, taking the narrow exit on the left instead. Opposite the fort, he veered the van up a narrow dark mud track, pulling in behind the hedgerow that lined an old abandoned dockers' pub that sat in complete darkness.

Killing the ignition, and switching off the headlights, Marlon sank down into his seat, his heart pounding so dramatically that he could hear the dull rhythmic thud inside his ears.

Glancing up into his rear-view mirror, he waited, praying that the car wouldn't pull in behind him as he saw another flash of bright white light. He winced. Closing his eyes, resigned to the fact that the game was up for him. Only to open them a second later to darkness.

The car had driven right past him.

Unable to believe his luck, Marlon wasn't taking any more chances. Leaving his headlights off, he started the engine and made his way back on himself, until he reached the muddy verge further back that he'd passed minutes before. Cutting across the grass, he entered the main industrial estate on the other side. Then hitting a couple of backroads and, minutes later, Marlon was back on the main road, switching his lights back on now as he followed the exit signs for the slip road that led to the motorway.

He kept his eyes on his rear-view mirror. Scanning the deserted road behind him, he felt a small fleeting sense of relief.

Though it was only fleeting.

Despite the fact that he'd managed to lose whoever it was that was following him, the night had gone horribly fucking wrong.

Jimmy Byrne was dead, and someone was onto them.

Marlon didn't have a clue what the fuck was going on right now, but what he did know was that if there was any chance of there being so much as a flicker of heat on them then he needed to do as he'd been told and lay low for a bit.

Wait for the next call.

The last place he intended to go tonight was home.

Speeding up, it looked as though Gina Jones would be getting that visit that she was harping on about after all.

CHAPTER THIRTY-EIGHT

Alex Costa had lost count of the amount of times that he had replayed the video on Gavin Hurst's laptop. Over and over again. Each time his eyes homing in on those piercing green eyes of Jimmy's. So blissfully unaware that he was being filmed.

Alex was taking it all in. Every word, every movement. He'd studied Jimmy's expressions, his body language, as he writhed around in the bed with the younger man.

He'd been right that Gavin had been young. This scrawny-looking prick of a kid, strutting about his flat completely naked as if he'd just walked in from shooting a Calvin Klein commercial. All buff, and toned. His mop of blond hair. Smiling and laughing playfully with Jimmy. At ease with the man. Gavin Hurst had been at least two decades Jimmy's junior. Barely twenty years old. Fuck! And to add insult to injury Jimmy looked smitten with the kid. This wasn't just a casual fling like Jimmy had made out. Alex could see how relaxed both men were in each other's company. The way that they fucked with the passion that only two men in love could. There was such intimacy between them both afterwards too, when Jimmy held the boy in his arms, as they'd both shared a cigarette in bed. The affinity between the two men disappearing quickly after that, as Gavin Hurst got up and sauntered across the room. Every part of him still exposed. Smiling into the camera as he passed it, his back to Jimmy. Though it hadn't taken long for Jimmy to cotton on to what the sly fucker had been up to.

Seconds later the kid was on the floor.

The wrath of Jimmy as the man lost the fucking plot. Punching the boy repeatedly, over and over again, until his body lay still on the floor. Completely motionless. Dead.

Alex watched then as Jimmy slumped down on the floor, staring at Gavin's body as he cried openly. This was the bit that cut Alex to the bone. The bit that made his heart physically ache inside his chest.

Jimmy hadn't just acted out of anger.

He'd acted out of love.

Hurting from being betrayed by someone he loved, Alex watched until the end. Seeing the shock as the man spotted the laptop filming him. Watching the anger on his face as he pulled the wires from the machine.

Alex slammed the laptop shut. He dragged the duvet from his body, throwing it across the back of the sofa that he'd spent the past two nights sleeping on, unable to face going to bed alone. That was the pathetic mess that he was now. He couldn't even bear to sleep, convinced he'd be hounded by nightmares. He chose to stay up and drink himself to oblivion instead.

Making his way across the lounge floor, still pissed, stumbling as he went, Alex had trashed the place. Books and magazines. A pile of paperwork that had sat on his dining table, all of it scattered across the carpet. An empty bottle of Scotch. Pizza boxes, full of food that he couldn't stomach finishing. The stale cheesy smell suddenly catching him off guard.

He only just made it to the toilet in time. Leaning over, his hands on the wall either side to steady him, Alex threw up. The memory of the video etched on his brain now, as he gagged violently until his stomach was empty, his throat raw. Wiping his mouth with the back of his sleeve, Alex moved over to the sink.

Staring at his reflection in the mirror, he barely recognised the wreck of a man that stared back at him. He looked like shit: dark, puffy bags under his eyes; the short designer stubble on his chin a full beard.

It had been three days since he'd heard the news that Jimmy was dead. Three days that somehow felt like no time at all and forever all at once. Alex hadn't left his apartment since he'd heard the news. He'd barely managed to leave his sofa. Consumed by such a complex web of emotions, his head was all over the place. He hated Jimmy for what he'd done to him and he was angry that the last time they'd seen each other they'd argued. Jimmy had only confessed about fucking the kid because he'd needed Alex's help. Alex would probably have never found out otherwise. Jimmy wouldn't have told him jack shit.

He'd been good at that – keeping secrets. He'd used him again. Right up to the very end.

About to play the video one more time, determined to inflict as much suffering on himself as he could so that he could numb all his feelings towards Jimmy, so that he could hate the man – then maybe it wouldn't hurt so much – he was interrupted as a call came in on his phone.

It was Jack Taylor: his friend who'd been discreetly looking into tracing whoever it was had blackmailed and murdered Jimmy.

'We didn't find anything, Alex,' Taylor said, regretfully.

Alex closed his eyes. The laptop and Jimmy's phone were the only leads they had. Alex was certain that they'd find something.

'Are you sure? Can't you check again?'

'I've personally checked both units a dozen times over, Alex; whoever it was behind Jimmy's demise was fucking clever. They made sure that there was no way of tracing anything back to them. I'm still waiting on a warrant so we can access the laptop's

IP address, but going on the findings so far, or lack of, I should say, I wouldn't hold your breath.'

There was silence, until Jack Taylor spoke again. 'I'm sorry I couldn't give you better news. I'll get onto the DI in charge of the case here and see if he's uncovered any other evidence from down at the dockyard. Maybe we'll have more luck with that?'

'Thanks, let's hope so,' Alex said, doubting that very much as he hung up the phone.

He was in limbo now. The last few days passing him by in a drunken haze while he'd waited for this phone call, and now it had been confirmed.

There were no clues, no fucking leads. Jack shit.

Unable to sit in this apartment on his own for the third day in a row, Alex decided to get dressed.

He needed to get out of here. Get some fresh air.

The four walls were closing in on him. Suffocating him.

Alex might have to live out the rest of his days broken hearted, knowing that deep down Jimmy never really loved him, not that way that Alex had loved Jimmy.

Jimmy Byrne was dead.

Nothing and no one could bring him back now and Alex's only consolation was that at least Jimmy couldn't hurt him anymore.

He couldn't have him, but no one else could either.

CHAPTER THIRTY-NINE

'Right that's it, you two little buggers are going to bed!'

Making a dive for his two sons Marlon dragged the boys apart just as Taye, the smaller of the twin boys, grabbed a fistful of Marlon Junior's hair. The boys were fighting over a toy that they both wanted to play with, screaming hysterically as they dragged each other across the patio.

'Are you just going to sit there and let them beat the living shit out of each other?' Marlon asked, staring over at Jordanna who was currently sprawled out on the sunlounger by the pool, dressed in her skimpy designer bikini and a pair of ridiculously high wedged sandals. She was blissfully enjoying the warm evening sun as if she was the Queen of bleeding Sheba.

Seemingly oblivious to the fact her children were near to killing each other, Jordanna took another sip of her white wine spritzer.

'Boys will be boys!' she pouted, as she did her usual of making allowances for her children's boisterous behaviour.

'Spoilt little shits more like!' Marlon spat. 'They don't do fuck all that you tell them.'

'They're two, Marlon!' Jordanna said in a huff, shooting Marlon a look as if he had two heads on his shoulders as she slammed down her half-finished spritzer on the patio table.

'I should have known that this last-minute romantic getaway of yours would be too good to be true,' she complained. 'How the hell is there supposed to be any romance when the kids are running me ragged?'

Jordanna was over the moon when Marlon told her they were going on a little holiday to Marbella. She'd always wanted to go there, and when they'd first rocked up at the luxury villa in the heart of Costa Del Sol, Jordanna had felt her dreams had come true. The whitewashed modern villa must have cost Marlon an absolute fortune, but he'd insisted that he had it all in hand.

Fuck knows how.

Still, Jordanna wasn't going to complain. As she stared out over the bustling marina of Puerto Banus, all she could think about was how far away she felt from her boring, monotonous life back home in their pokey flat in Vauxhall.

'Just sort them out, will you, Jord?' Marlon said, hoping she would get up off her fat lazy arse and actually do something today. Marlon was sick to death of listening to the boys screaming and crying. His head was already wrecked as it was. He just wanted a bit of peace and quiet so that he could think straight.

'I tell you what, crazy little notion here, I know, but seeing as you're their father, Marlon, how about you deal with them?' Jordanna said; the noise of her two boys playing behind her didn't bother her one bit. Of course they were going to fight from time to time, that's what boys did. She certainly wasn't going to stress herself out over every little spat that they had.

The truth was that Jordanna actually liked that her sons were both so strong-willed and had minds of their own. They might only be two, but already they were fearless and unrelenting and Jordanna didn't have any notions about taming them. Besides, constantly disciplining the two boys was too much like hard bloody work. Not that Marlon would know anything about that. Since the kids had come along, he'd been only too happy to leave her to the bulk of the children's care.

'Come on, Jordanna, my head is bloody killing me,' Marlon said, hoping his girlfriend would take pity on him, and take the kids off to bed, so that he could sit here and chill the fuck out in peace.

Only the boys had other ideas. Not picking up on his father's volatile mood, Taye started up again, trying to snatch another toy. Hitting out at Marlon Junior, he caught his brother on the cheek with his nails. Drawing blood. The sharp scratch sent his brother into a fit of rage.

Marlon lost his rag.

'Right, that's enough. ENOUGH!'

Getting up he slapped both boys hard across the legs.

'Marlon!' Jordanna screeched loudly, as both her boys immediately stopped fighting with each other, and instead started crying together in unison.

'What the fuck did you do that for?' Snatching her boys protectively away from Marlon, Jordanna hoisted them both on either side of her narrow hips. 'What's got into you, Marlon?'

'I already told you: I'm not in the mood for their shit,' Marlon said, sitting back down and rolling himself another joint. 'They are un-fucking-ruly, Jordanna.'

'And whose fault is that?' Jordanna was glaring at Marlon. 'You do know that in the two years that they've been alive you haven't bathed or fed them once? Not once. Yes, they're a handful. I'm well aware of that as it's me that has to keep an eye on them twenty-four-seven in case they touch something that they shouldn't or injure themselves. Me. On my tod. Because you never fucking help me!'

Jordanna was convinced he was hiding something from her. He'd been on edge all day. If she didn't know any better she'd guess that Marlon had been up to his old tricks once again. Maybe that's why they'd come here, so that Marlon could keep the heat off him for a bit. But even Marlon wouldn't be so stupid as to do that to her again. Not after she had warned him the last time what she'd do if she found out that he'd been cheating on her.

She'd meant it, too.

If her boyfriend even so much as thought about dipping his wick anywhere that he shouldn't, Jordanna would be dipping Marlon's bollocks into a blender while they were still attached, and then turning the fucker on.

'All you've done since we got here is drink whisky and smoke pot. Which, by the way, doesn't suit you, seeing as you're still acting like a miserable bastard. Considering the amount of gear you've smoked today, I'd have thought you would be at least chilled out.'

'Chilled out? With yous three? Fat chance.' Marlon rolled his eyes. His head was pounding. He was stressed as fuck. The last thing he needed right now was bloody Jordanna chirping in his ear. 'I'd need to smoke a whole fucking forest in that case!'

'Well something's not right. You've been acting as cagey as fuck since we got here, and I'm sick of you taking your bad mood out on me and the boys.' The holiday was ruined as far as she was concerned. 'Do you know what? I give up.' Though she was tempted to pick up her drink from the table and throw it into Marlon's face, she thought better of it. 'Me and the boys are calling it a night.'

Clutching the twins tightly to her she turned on her heel and stomped back into the villa.

'Fuck me, women are hard work,' Marlon mumbled to himself as he watched Jordanna march towards the house in a huff.

She had no idea how much shit he was in right now. She didn't have a fucking clue. Everyone would have heard about Jimmy being murdered by now. There would be people out looking for his killer. He was part of it. They'd be looking for him. And here he was living it up in the sunny Costa Del Sol.

Only he wasn't living it up at all. He was just doing as he'd been told. He had to sit this one out and wait for the heat to die down. Until then, he was stuck here putting up with all this fucking aggro. The twins might be a handful but the pair of them kicking off had nothing on what Jordanna alone was capable of. The woman was a walking, talking brain-ache and Marlon was glad she'd fucked off to bed.

Taking another long pull of the joint, Marlon breathed a thick plume of smoke down into his lungs, then out slowly, streaming it into the warm evening air. He didn't know what would be less stressful: going back to the UK and facing the music at what he'd been involved in, or doing as he was told, and sitting it out here in Marbella with that mad bitch.

CHAPTER FORTY

Looking down at the twins as they lay side by side in the bed, finally sleeping, Jordanna sat on the edge of the bed next to them, taking in the sight of their thick curly mops of hair, their tanned golden skin; their long wispy eyelashes resting on the tops of their cheeks, eyelashes that she herself had to pay good money to imitate.

Her boys were her world. Two miniature versions of their father. Though, her boys weren't going to grow up to be anything like him. Jordanna would make sure of that. Marlon was nothing more than a lying, cheating, no-good bastard!

Unable to hold back her tears any longer, Jordanna sunk down onto the floor on her knees. Burying her mouth against the mattress so that she didn't wake her children, she was unable to stop the sob escaping from the back of her throat. Why did he always have to ruin everything? They could have been happy together. But Marlon just couldn't help himself, could he? To think that she'd almost gone out there and tried to make it up with him. Looking for some paracetamol to help his pounding headache, the last thing she expected to find was this mobile phone stuffed down inside the side compartment of his wash bag.

As soon as she found it she knew: this was what the little holiday was really all about. This is why Marlon had brought her here to sunny Costa Del Sol. The bastard had been hiding something and now Jordanna knew what.

Her fingers fumbled with the small black buttons as she blinked through her tears, trying to read the text on the small grey screen; then, humiliated at what she read: the stream of messages that went back and forth between Marlon and her friend and so-called best mate, Gina Jones.

She'd been stupid to think that he'd ever change. Men like Marlon never did, they just got smarter at hiding their seedy little trials of deception. It came with the territory. Practice makes perfect and all that. Only Jordanna would always be ten steps ahead of Marlon. And to think that she'd loved the bones of that man. That she'd forgiven him time and time again for all that he'd put her through. All the hurt that he caused her.

Well she wouldn't be forgiving him again. They were done now. Jordanna was certain of that. What sort of life was that for her boys? Growing up watching their father constantly disrespecting their mother. Jordanna used to think that she was doing the right thing standing by Marlon. That if she broke up her family, her boys would suffer. The truth was her family was already broken. Marlon had seen to that.

Placing her hand over her mouth, Jordanna felt physically sick as she continued scrolling through, reading the other messages on the phone that left her blood running cold. She couldn't believe what she was reading.

Jimmy Byrne was dead? What the fuck?

Suddenly Marlon's irrational behaviour was starting to make sense. Marlon hadn't tried to whisk her away so that she wouldn't find out about Gina Jones, this had nothing to do with her friend. This was about something much more sinister.

Shaking her head as she realised the lengths that man would go to, to save his sorry arse, she switched off the phone and shoved it back inside Marlon's wash bag, so that he wouldn't know she'd seen it, while she worked out what she was going to do next.

It was about time that Marlon experienced first-hand what it felt like to be betrayed. For all the times that the man had almost broken her, without succession, Jordanna would break him. Without a doubt.

Despite what Marlon clearly believed, the truth always came out in the end.

CHAPTER FORTY-ONE

Marlon Jackson shook his head despairingly as Jordanna rushed around the villa like a whirlwind, picking up the handfuls of toys from where they'd been left abandoned on the floor of the villa's front room. Ever since they'd had the big row over the boys last night, she'd been acting really off with him.

In fairness though, he couldn't really blame her. She had every right to be pissed off with him. She was right. He'd been acting irrational, crazy. He could see that now. Worried sick about what was going on back home in England, his head had been all over the place, and it didn't help either that he'd downed half a bottle of whisky, and smoked copious joints which only made his paranoia go through the roof.

Jordanna was right. He needed to chill the fuck out. He was only going to draw attention to himself otherwise. What was the point in moping around, guilty? Yes, it was fucked up that Jimmy Byrne had lost his life, but Marlon didn't pull the trigger. He wasn't the one that killed Jimmy.

Reminding himself that Jimmy wasn't always an angel, he realised he needed to get it into perspective. The man may have made his vast fortune from the property he'd invested in over the years, but he had other lucrative incomes too. Not only did he run some of the seediest brothels in London, but Jimmy had a whole army of foot soldiers in the form of scrotes from all the run-down London estates doing his dirty work and selling all the coke and weed he imported. He dealt with some proper shady people. From well-known hardened criminals to wannabe plastic gangsters. Jimmy rarely did any dirty work himself. That's what Marlon and the rest of the lads on the firm had been employed to do.

Shit, there was even a rumour flying about that Jimmy had torched his own wife and mother-in-law out of their home years ago, so that he could buy the first real development he'd ever invested in. The one in Soho that had placed the man firmly on the map. It seemed everyone knew about it apart from the poor cow Jimmy was married to. That's how merciless he could be.

There were other rumours that Marlon had heard too. About Jimmy visiting rent boys in dives like King's Cross; Marlon had never believed any of those stories though. Jimmy had been straighter than a honeymoon dick. The man had been for ever surrounded by some of the best-looking pussy in London, there was no way that the bloke was a poofter.

Still, people talked.

Despite being a popular man, Jimmy had a fair few enemies too. But no one would even suspect one of Jimmy's own firm was involved; they'd never be able to pin any of this back onto Marlon.

He needed to calm the fuck down. A few days away, a week or so, out here in Spain with Jordanna and the boys was just what he needed. He'd be all right after that. He was certain.

Though so far, he couldn't even get that right. They'd only been here three days and already Jordanna was barely talking to him. Looking over towards the boys, both sprawled out on the sofa watching a DVD that Jordanna had put on for them, wearing only their nappies so that they could both cool down from the heat of the Spanish sun, even they were acting wary of him after the slap they'd both got from him last night. He knew he needed to pull himself together and he intended to, starting right now.

'Here, babe. Why don't you leave all that for now? I've got a surprise for you,' he said, knowing full well that once Jordanna got herself worked up in a strop, the chances were there would be no talking her down.

'A surprise?' Jordanna said, trying to keep a neutral face as she stared back at Marlon. She'd had enough surprises of Marlon Jackson to last her a lifetime. The last thing she wanted was another surprise from that self-conceited bastard. How she hadn't scratched the fucker's eyes out after what she'd found on the phone that Marlon had been hiding from her, she really didn't know, but she was all for playing the long game.

'Yeah, look babe, I know I've been a first-class prick lately, and I'm sorry. I just had some stuff on my mind. Some stuff to do with work,' he said truthfully, playing down his worries; Jordanna didn't have a fucking clue what he'd got himself into and that was just the way it would have to stay. 'Let me take you and the boys out tonight to make up for it, yeah? There's a place the other side of the marina. The best seafood in all of the Costa Del Sol.'

'I dunno,' Jordanna said. The last thing she wanted to do right now was go out. She'd already set the cogs of her revenge into motion and the nearer the time came to enacting Marlon's reprisal, the more she was starting to feel as nervous as hell about what she'd done.

Still, there was fuck all she could do about it now. It was out of her hands. All she could do was try and act normal as she hoped and prayed that it would all soon be over.

'Go on, love, let me make it up to you? The boys will love the restaurant. We can get them some calamari, and you can have those slippery black garlicy things that you love—'

'Moules-frites,' Jordanna corrected him, surprised that Marlon had even taken an interest in what she normally ordered.

'What do you say, eh?' he persisted. 'Let me make it up to you, babe, it's the least I can do.'

'Okay!' Jordanna said eventually, staring up at the clock. 'But I need to get ready. I want to sort out my make-up.'

Marlon grinned; she could hold a grudge for England if the mood took her. Still, as fiery as his Jordanna could be Marlon knew that she could never stay mad at him long. She just didn't have it in her.

'Well, I've already taken the liberty of ordering a cab, Jord – I know what you're like strutting around in those heels of yours – so you better get a move on.' Glad that Jordanna wasn't planning on stringing out this row of theirs, he was looking forward to tonight.

Marlon felt guilty then, other than the general nagging and earache he got from the girl, Jordanna was a good mother to the boys, and she'd been a loyal girlfriend to him, and Lord knows Marlon had tested her. He'd treated Jordanna appallingly over the years. Cheating on her, lying to her. He didn't even know why he did it half the time. He just got bored. Easily led astray. His mother used to say that he could resist everything except temptation, and the older he had got, the more he realised that was true. There was temptation everywhere.

He didn't even have to look for trouble, he was just one of those guys where trouble always found him. It didn't help that he was a good-looking fucker. Mixed race, milk chocolate skin. His eyes a piercing grey-blue. He had all the chat too. A regular jack-the-lad. The girls couldn't seem to get enough of him. What was a man to do?

'How about we kiss and make up before it gets here?' Marlon said, knowing that he was pushing his luck, and he laughed as Jordanna pushed him away, clearly letting him know that he wasn't forgiven just yet. Still, he couldn't help the heady, sexual pull of the girl as he tried to wrap his arms around her, hoping to cop a cheeky feel.

'All right, Casanova, there'll be plenty of time for all that later,' Jordanna said as she wriggled out of his hold, hoping that the hint of a promise was enough to placate her boyfriend for a bit longer. She couldn't even bear to look at Marlon right now. Couldn't stand the sight of him. Just the feel of his slimy hands on her skin, on her body, made her feel sick to her stomach, now she knew where they'd been. All over that skank, Gina Jones.

'Later, eh? I'm holding you to that.' Marlon laughed. Though knowing his Jordanna as well as he did, the girl would probably be hell-bent on making him work for it tonight.

'Right, I better get myself ready then. If the cab's on its way?'

'Do you want any help with the boys?' Marlon offered, not wanting a repeat performance of last night. He was determined to at least try and do his bit. Though, he did feel pleased when Jordanna shook her head.

'No, honestly it's fine. I'll be five minutes. Go and pour yourself a drink while you're waiting. I'll have one too.'

Doing as he was told, he went into the kitchen and poured them both a drink: a whisky for him, a gin and tonic for Jordanna. Large ones. They were celebrating. Tonight, Marlon decided was going to be a brand new start for them both. He'd been thinking about it all day. Jordanna and the boys. Jimmy. Life was too short. All this messing about and causing grief for himself, it wasn't fucking worth the aggro. It was time that he grew up. Manned up for the sake of his kids. As of tonight he'd made a vow to himself that from now on he was going to be faithful to Jordanna. He was going to put her and little Taye and Marlon Junior first for a change. He was keen to make a real start in turning all of their lives around. It was long overdue. That's what life was all about, he realised that now. When the chips were down, and everything was up against him, this was all he really had: his family. He didn't want to jeopardise that anymore.

Hearing the doorbell, Marlon shook his head. He'd barely had time to pour his drink.

'Fuck me, they don't hang around out here in Espagne, eh! The London cabbies back home could learn a thing or two by these lot,' he said, downing his whisky before he went to the door.

Only Jordanna had beat him to it.

Standing in the doorway, holding their boys in her arms, as the cab driver carried two large suitcases to the awaiting taxi.

'What the fuck are you doing, Jordanna?' Marlon said, laughing nervously as he wondered what the hell was going on. Jordanna was leaving? Taking the boys and their bags? 'I thought we were sorting everything out, babe?'

Jordanna shook her head. 'I know about you and Gina, Marlon.'

The half-smile slipped from his face. How? How did she know?

'Babe.' Marlon stepped closer, about to do his usual and spout off a load of lies in his defence, instead, he stopped. He'd promised himself a new start, no more bullshit. No more lies. He meant it too. 'Babe, please, listen, yeah?' Desperate to make her change her mind. 'I'm sorry, Jord, please. I'm going to change. I know you've heard me say it a thousand times before, but I really do mean it this time. You and the boys, you're all that matters to me. I was stupid babe, she meant nothing.'

'Nothing?' Jordanna said, shaking her head, disgusted. 'That's you all over, Marlon, isn't it? To you, she meant nothing. Just a quick shag, another conquest, but to me it meant everything. You've broken my heart, Marlon, and I'm not sticking around so that you can break me. I'm going home.' Even she was surprised by the emotion in her voice, the way that her words shook as they left her mouth. She'd imagined being so much stronger when she finally had her say to Marlon. Fuelled by her anger and fury at what Marlon had done to her with her best friend, she'd been prepared to read him the bloody riot act; only she didn't feel any of that now. All she felt was sadness. Sad that it had come to this. Sad that Marlon really didn't see how much she had always loved him.

'Me and the boys, we're going back to the flat. Without you.' Chucking down his passport onto the marble floor, Jordanna couldn't even bear to look Marlon in the eye as she spoke, and he knew with certainty that she really meant what she was saying this time.

This wasn't the usual dramatics, the normal screaming and fighting that Marlon had come to expect when Jordanna lost her temper with him. She meant every word she was saying. Cold. Withdrawn. She was really leaving him. Refusing to fall for Marlon's empty promises, his lies.

Jordanna clutched her boys to her hips as she carried them out the front door.

'I'm sorry!' Marlon called after her, knowing that it was hopeless. That Jordanna had made up her mind.

'So am I!' she shouted back.

Marlon watched until the cab disappeared out of sight, then going back in he slammed the door, leaned up against the frame. She'd really left him this time.

Only, making his way back in the kitchen to finish the rest of the whisky, Marlon realised that he wasn't alone.

CHAPTER FORTY-TWO

'Fuck!'

Turning around, the last person Marlon Jackson expected to see, sitting at the breakfast bar as he walked back into the villa's kitchen, was Jack Taylor.

'Jesus Christ, Jack, you scared the living shit out of me!' Marlon tried to keep the nerves out of his voice as he spoke, tried to look calm. He could feel the beads of sweat forming on his forehead, the sinking feeling deep in the pit of his stomach. 'What are you doing here?' he asked, but he already knew. Jack Taylor, Jimmy Byrne's bent copper, was here in Spain. Here at the villa. That could only mean one thing – Marlon was completely fucked now.

'Women, huh! It sounds like you've well and truly pissed her off this time though, mate,' Jack said, avoiding the question as he nodded over at the front door that Marlon had just slammed behind him.

'We had a row,' Marlon stuttered. His head was spinning, as he tried to piece together what the fuck was going on. How did Jordanna know about Gina? How? And why the fuck was Jack Taylor here?

He didn't have to wait long for the answers.

'These fuckers can land you in all sorts of trouble if you're not careful.' As if reading Marlon's mind, Jack Taylor waved the mobile phone that Jordanna had given him in the air towards the man, deliberately taunting him; unable to hide the smug grin on his face as he let Marlon know that he'd been caught red-handed.

The phone. Shit! Jordanna had found the phone.

'Not very smart, was it? Leaving shit like this lying about, especially given the content,' Jack said, his eyes not leaving Marlon's, drinking in the man's fear at being caught out.

Marlon didn't react. He didn't know how to. Standing there looking at Jack Taylor with a gormless expression on his face, his heart pounding in his chest, he looked as guilty as hell and he knew it.

'You know! I think Jordanna was more bothered about all those messages on here between you and this slapper,' Jack said, shaking his head as if Marlon needed reminding of how he'd brought this little visit on himself.

Then tapping the phone and scrolling through the messages, he shook his head disapprovingly.

'But, you know, as nice as these charming interactions between you both are, where you've been shoving your cock really doesn't interest me.' Glaring at Marlon. Waiting for the man to say something. To defend himself, to speak up, Jack Taylor continued: 'I have to hand it to your Mrs, she had balls calling me and telling me what she did.' He let the penny drop as to exactly why he was here. 'It's not nice, is it? Having someone fuck you over? I guess it's true what they say: Hell hath no fury like a woman scorned. Ain't that just the truth?'

He smirked then. 'Nice little gaff you're renting here. Jimmy must have been slipping you some money that none of the rest of us were aware of!' He glanced around the villa, knowing full well how Marlon had got the money. 'I have to admit it's impressive. All open-plan. Makes the place feel huge, doesn't it? All tiled in white too. Immaculate. Be a real shame to make a mess in here, wouldn't it?'

Reaching down to the waistband of his trousers, Jack pulled out the gun with a silencer on the end of it, and pointed it straight at Marlon's head.

'Whoa! What are you doing?' Marlon said, his words coming out in a nervous stutter as he held his hands up in protest.

Alone in the villa now. Alone and faced with a gun that Marlon had no doubt Jack Taylor would happily use, he glanced at the door, his eyes resting on the latch, wondering how much time it would take him to reach it, to get outside. Jack would be on him by then. He was certain of it.

'Don't even think about it,' Jack said, following Marlon's gaze. 'Now let's get down to business, shall we? We both know why I'm here, Marlon, don't we? Let's not play silly games. We're way beyond that now, don't you think? You've got some serious talking to do!' he sneered.

Jack Taylor had never personally been a fan of Marlon's. He'd always found the bloke far too cocky for his liking. The other men had all joked that Jimmy Byrne had a soft spot for Marlon. It had been a running joke because Jimmy had taken the lad on and given him a chance when most of them wouldn't have given the likes of Marlon so much as the time of day if they met him in the street. He was a regular wide boy. Too much chat, not enough action. Though, luckily for Marlon, he'd somehow managed to prove Jimmy right. He'd turned out to be a good little worker, doing whatever jobs that Jimmy had lined up for him without so much as a question; and because of how keen he was to always get the job done, Marlon had ended up working his way up the ladder.

He had become one of the firm.

He was trusted.

Only now he'd committed the ultimate crime: he'd conspired against his boss and double-crossed him.

'I didn't do it,' Marlon said. 'Please, I swear to God, Jack, I didn't shoot Jimmy.' Marlon was pleading for his life now.

He'd sworn that he wouldn't ever say a word. That he would take the secret he kept to his grave; only, faced with a gun pointed at his head, Marlon hoped he could see that promise through. He might be a lot of things, but one thing he wasn't was a grass.

'I swear on my boys' lives. Taye and Marlon Junior's lives. It wasn't me that shot him.' Marlon was crying now. Picturing it all in his mind, as if he was back there. 'If I'd known that Jimmy was going to get shot, I would never have got involved. I swear to you, Jack. It was only ever about the money for me. We were supposed to get it and get our arses out of there.'

'Who pulled the trigger?' Jack said, his finger hovering above the trigger of his gun.

Marlon was whimpering. He knew that he was damned if he did, damned if he didn't. Jack would kill him no matter what. The only way that Marlon might be able to get out of this was to try and distract the fucker.

Try and escape.

'Who was it?'

Marlon didn't speak. He wouldn't. His mouth had gone dry, his throat closing up. Losing his bottle, he felt like he was going to wet himself.

'I'm not saying shit,' he said, praying that he was doing the right thing trying to call Jack's bluff. He needed to try and buy some more time.

'Well you see now, that's a real shame,' Jack sneered. 'See, you are going to tell me who killed Jimmy even if it takes the very last breath in your tortured battered body.'

He walked towards Marlon, indicating to him to make his way to the front door. Jack kept the gun on Marlon. 'One false move, and I'm going to fucking shoot, do you understand?'

Marlon nodded. He could see by the look in his eyes that the man didn't need much encouragement.

For now all Marlon could do was try and stay alive.

'Good, now fucking well move. We've got a plane to catch. I know some people back in the UK that will be very interested to speak to you, Marlon.' Jack Taylor grinned. 'Very interested indeed.'

CHAPTER FORTY-THREE

His head pounding from the brute force of the kicking that Jack Taylor had given him, Marlon Jackson could barely lift his head. Back in England now, and sitting in what he recognised as one of Jimmy's many barns that the man had used to store his illegal shipments, every part of Marlon's body was screaming out in pain.

He could feel the hot sticky liquid dripping down the back of his neck. He was bleeding? Trying to raise his arms so that he could check, he realised he couldn't. They'd been tied tightly behind his back. Strapping him to the chair, the plastic cable ties were so tight that they were cutting in to his wrists.

Even trying to force his eyes open was a mission. Swollen shut, he could just about see out of the tiny gap in his left eye, focusing on a light that looked like a doorway, a shadowy figure standing nearby.

Marlon tried to scream, to shout for help. It was no use though. His lips were cracked and dry from where his mouth had been forced open, the material that had been shoved inside his mouth stopping him from calling out. He felt weak and exhausted from the beating that he'd received. He must have blacked out.

'Nice of you to finally join us again,' Jack Taylor spat, pulling the cloth from the man's mouth, glad that Marlon had regained consciousness.

He heard another noise then. The heavy footfall of a man nearing him. Getting faster as he approached; his footsteps speeding up. Then the full force of a punch to the side of his head.

Screaming out, crying, as his right ear exploded. An excruciating pain erupting inside his head, making him feel suddenly sick, dizzy, as if he was about to pass out again. His head lolled to one side.

'You fucking bastard!' this was Daniel Byrne now.

Marlon didn't even have time to pray for the attack to stop as another punch landed on the opposite side of his head, the dull thud radiating through him once more.

'That's enough.' A female voice.

Nancy? What the fuck was going on here?

'I'll say when it's enough!'

Carrying on with the attack, Daniel Byrne continued raining punches down on Marlon, lifting the man out of the chair by a few inches with the force of his blows, as the seat rocked violently from side to side.

Marlon could barely comprehend where he was, what was happening.

'I said that's ENOUGH!'

All he knew was that the female voice he'd heard had commanded the beating to stop. And then the punches had suddenly stopped. For that alone Marlon was grateful. As the ringing in his ears subsided, he concentrated on the clicking of heels as they crossed the cold concrete warehouse floor, the heady scent of sweet musky perfume filling the air around him.

It was Nancy Byrne, he was sure of it.

Trying to focus, to keep his head up, he could taste the familiar metallic bitter taste of blood in the back of his throat.

'He's no good to us dead,' Nancy said. In the four days since her father had been murdered, her world had been turned upside down.

Her father, as it turned out, had been living a lie.

'We know about the recording,' she said, barely able to digest what she'd heard had been on it. The sordid, disgusting recording didn't ring true in Nancy's world, but she knew that Jack Taylor had told her the truth. It hurt. The not knowing. Out of everyone, Nancy had always thought that she had been the one closest to her dad. That she'd known him the best.

Turns out she hadn't known him at all.

'We know about how you tried to blackmail our father.'

Daniel knew too, though he'd taken the news far worse than Nancy. Consumed with anger that he had no means of channelling, Daniel just wanted to lash out. To make Marlon pay for his part in their father's murder.

Nancy wanted that too, but first she wanted him to talk.

'Who pulled the trigger?'

Marlon shook his head. 'I don't know about any recording. I only went there to get the money.'

Bang!

Daniel administered another almighty punch to Marlon's head; this time perforating his eardrum with the blow.

'For fuck's sake, Daniel, do you want him to talk or pass out again?' Jack said, getting annoyed at how little progress they seemed to be making. He never liked Marlon, always found the bloke to be a cocky little prick; give the bloke his due though – he could take an almighty beating. He knew that he was fucked no matter what he said, and kudos for the man for not opening his mouth and blabbing like the snake Jack had had him down for. As much as he hated Marlon for being part of the plot to kill his friend, he also had a begrudging respect.

Many men would have given up ages ago.

'Tell us who did the job with you, Marlon,' Nancy intervened, trying to use a different tactic; her voice sounding soft, almost kind. 'We know it wasn't you, so if you tell us then you get to walk out of here. You're not who we want. You know that, don't you? Tell us who did the job, Marlon.'

Marlon didn't speak. He couldn't. Unable to even say his own name now, he was drifting in and out of consciousness. The pain in the side of his head was eating him up inside, so acute that he could barely tolerate it. Every now and again, he'd hear part of a sentence, a conversation. His name being spoken. The three people in the room talking.

'What do you want me to do?' Jack Taylor said, disappointed by the turn of events. He'd done what he thought was the right thing and served Marlon up to Nancy and Daniel so that Jimmy's kids could get the retribution for their father that they so needed.

Only Marlon wasn't even going to give them that. The sly little fucker was going to take what he knew to his grave.

'Alex will be here soon. If anyone will be able to get the truth out of him, Alex will,' Nancy said, the steeliness in her voice sounding just like her father's as she spoke with full certainty. Nancy was counting on it.

She just hoped Alex hurried up; they were getting nowhere fast without him. But Alex Costa would get Marlon talking.

'I want him dealt with.'

Marlon knew that they were just calling his bluff. Making out that they were going to kill him, so that he'd finally confess. Marlon knew how to play the game. They'd have to let him go eventually. He just needed to keep to his story and say jack shit. Though, that was getting harder and harder to do. He didn't think he could physically take much more.

Letting them all know that he would never talk, Marlon mumbled.

'Wait. He's saying something,' Nancy said.

'Say it again, Marlon, we didn't hear you.'

Spitting out a mouthful of blood, he half laughed, half cried as he mouthed: 'I said, fuck you.'

Daniel Byrne'd had enough now.

Grabbing Taylor's gun from the table, he pointed it straight at the man's head, as Taylor and Nancy flew at him to try and stop him.

'Don't do it, Daniel, he hasn't told us..."

"Told us what? Look at the fucking state of him, Nancy. He ain't going to tell us shit. He was there, Nance. He may not have pulled the trigger but he was part of it. This cunt is just as guilty."

Marlon lifted his head.

His vision blurred, he stared at Daniel Byrne. Standing over him, the gun pointed at his head.

His ears were ringing so loudly inside his skull. The pain so immense that he was barely conscious.

Opening his mouth to speak, to put an end to all this madness. Only now the words wouldn't come.

Daniel pulled the trigger.

'This is for my dad, you fucking obnoxious piece of shit!'

'Just wait—' Nancy's words came too late, abruptly stopping mid-sentence as she watched the bullet enter Marlon's head.

Marlon's last thoughts as his neck snapped back, as the bullet entered his temple, were how his accomplice had assured him that no matter what happened he wasn't to talk, no matter how convincing they sounded they wouldn't end his life.

He'd been played right to the end.

Covering for Jimmy's killer had cost him his life.

CHAPTER FORTY-FOUR

Watching helplessly as the six pallbearers lifted her father's coffin out from the back of the vintage hearse and onto their shoulders, carrying Jimmy Byrne to his final resting place, Nancy Byrne finally allowed herself to cry.

It was a welcome release.

For weeks now, since her father had passed, she'd been left numb, completely in shock.

Unable to comprehend that her father, so strong, so powerful, had really been murdered. His life snuffed out, just like that.

Nancy was so used to hiding her emotions from the rest of the world, from herself, that her father's death hadn't felt real.

Until today. Her father's funeral. The day that her beloved dad was being laid to rest.

There would be no escaping her grief now.

She switched off from the priest's recital, from the words that were thrown around. Empty, meaningless words.

Just another funeral. Another person laid in the earth, turning to dust. Nancy stared at the congregation. The sea of faces. So many Faces.

All of London's finest were here to pay their respects today. Her father's so-called friends. Crooks, criminals. Gangsters.

These people didn't care about her father, not really, not like Nancy did.

Her father was her hero. He was the one person that had made her feel as if she could one day rule the world, as if nothing was beneath her. The one person in her life that Nancy had adored and loved like no other.

Blinded by her tears, Nancy wiped them away and focused. Keeping her gaze fixed on the mahogany casket as it was lowered into the ground.

The casket that her grandmother Joanie had painstakingly designed, with a beautiful hand-crafted dark veneer, six shiny brass handles. Her nan had obsessed over it in fact, clung to every last detail, as if her son's coffin was of some great significance.

Which of course it wasn't. *It was just another distraction,* Nancy thought as she stared down into the gaping dark hole in the earth in front of her. The casket was nothing more than an overpriced wooden box; it's only purpose to sit in the ground and rot for all eternity.

Just as her father would.

Sobbing now as her sudden grief hit her with force, Nancy's body shook. She could feel the tightening inside her chest, her ribcage constricting her lungs as she struggled for breath.

She felt Daniel then, standing tall beside her. The warmth of her brother as he lovingly pulled her in close, wrapping his arms around her in a bid to offer her comfort.

Her brother, who was just like her in so many ways. Closed off to his emotions. Private. Today though, he had come into his own, offering her and her mother his unwavering support. Embracing his new role as the man of the family as he tried to hold them all together.

Nothing could fix this family now though, Nancy thought as she took a slow deep breath.

Determined to pull herself together, she tuned into the priest's final words, as she looked around at each family member standing at her father's graveside. Staring at each and every one of them.

Michael, Joanie, Colleen and Daniel. Jack and Alex too.

The Byrne family. In mourning… only a murderer was stood amongst them all.

Nancy's gaze stopped at her grandmother, dressed in her expensive fur shawl, her face plastered with a thick mask of make-up. Even in her seventies, even on the day of her one and only son's funeral, Joanie Byrne was always one for keeping up appearances.

The finery couldn't disguise the hurt she was feeling, though. The pain was written clearly across the older woman's face; etched into her skin with deep, burrowed lines. Jimmy's death had extinguished Joanie Byrne's fire, Nancy knew it. She recognised the feeling inside herself. Her grandmother was the only other person as truly grief-stricken as she was.

'Until we meet again, my beautiful Jimmy. Please God, until we meet again my boy.'

Holding his wife's hand tightly, Michael Byrne had been taking every detail of today's ceremony in.

Michael had never in all his days seen St John's so full, as Jimmy's friends and acquaintances lined the aisle and the back of the church, pouring out into the courtyard outside.

This was a gangster's funeral if ever he saw one. Every face in London was here today.

Another show – just how Jimmy would have wanted it. Even in his death, his son had to make a point of being better than everyone else.

Unlike his grieving wife and grandchildren, today was a very happy day for Michael.

He'd spent a lifetime loathing Jimmy, watching his every word and action in case he stepped out of line and upset Joanie, knowing that his son would retaliate on her behalf. Now suddenly, his tormenter was finally gone from this world forever. He could live out his last years in peace, without fear of being terrorised by his own flesh and blood.

I hope you rot in Hell, Jimmy, you bastard.

Nancy looked at her mother then, staring down at the ground with that same vacant look on her face as always. Though she could now see a subtle shift in Colleen, as if a weight had been lifted from the woman's shoulders. Her mother looked different somehow.

Colleen stared down into the grave. Two burials inside of one month.

First her dearly missed mother and now Jimmy, her husband. She hadn't even been able to look when her mother's coffin had been lowered down into the ground. Just the idea of it had given her a panic attack, only magnifying the gaping void inside her heart. Today though, Colleen wanted to remember everything.

Throwing a handful of earth on top of the casket along with the other mourners, a symbol of acknowledging that all bodies were returned to the ground, she bid her husband one final goodbye. To be certain that the man she'd been tied to for all these years, the man she'd loathed and hated and feared all at once was buried deep down under the dirt, where he belonged.

In Jimmy's death, Colleen was finally free.

She hadn't drunk for four weeks now. That was a record for Colleen and today, standing between her two children, Colleen knew that she wouldn't ever again.

She'd changed – and other people had noticed it too. She felt lighter, unburdened.

Unlike Joanie, who in the past few weeks had withered away with grief, Colleen had found her strength in Jimmy's death. It was as if her husband's murder had suddenly given her life.

The weirdest thing of all was that she and Joanie had somehow called a truce now that Jimmy had gone. Colleen wondered if perhaps Joanie no longer blamed Colleen for trying to take away her son, or maybe the woman was simply all out of fight.

Whatever's Joanie's reasons for thawing her hate towards her, Colleen was glad. She'd spent a lifetime fighting. With Joanie and Jimmy, and with herself. Battling with her conscience. Her mind.

All those years wasted. She'd lost herself, she knew that, but now that Jimmy was finally gone from her life, Colleen was determined to take control of her own destiny.

It was time to make a change for the better. To somehow try and build bridges with her children, Nancy and Daniel. She owed them both that much. And for the first time in her life, Colleen really believed that she could do it too.

She was going to get her family back.

I may have been a Byrne by name, Jimmy, but I will always be a Walsh by blood. I hate you, Jimmy, with every part of my being. I hope you rot.

Nancy stood and looked over to Jack Taylor and Alex Costa. The two men, though not related to her father, were probably closer to him than all of them.

Even her, she thought bitterly.

Jack had done all he could for her father since his death. He hadn't been able to uncover much regarding their father's killer, but he'd handed them Marlon Jackson on a platter so that she and Daniel could avenge their father's death.

Only, it wasn't Marlon who killed her father. His death was unnecessary.

Marlon had served his purpose. He'd covered up for someone and paid for the privilege with his life.

Nancy eyed Alex Costa then, catching the small, subtle nod of his head as he offered his condolences across the gravesite.

Her father's so-called best friend. Though Nancy knew now that Alex was so much more than that.

Jimmy's death had hit him the hardest. He'd lost weight. His skin looked grey, his eyes like slits, full of raw pain as he attended today's funeral. He was the shadow of the man he'd been just a few weeks ago.

Nancy knew that Alex was barely leaving his flat, instead spending his days drinking heavily, consumed with his grief.

Or his guilt?

Nancy knew all his secrets now.

How he and her father had conducted their sordid affair for the past twenty years. How Alex had been in love with her father and her father, it seemed, had reciprocated the feelings. Only her father had been too ashamed to admit that he was gay, choosing to live a lie all his life instead. He'd hidden behind his marriage and children as if his family were just some kind of mystical shield that would protect him, and everyone around him, from the truth.

The truth was out now though.

Nancy had learned more about her father in his death than she ever would have while he had been alive.

Shrewd, just like her father would have wanted her to be, she'd done her own digging.

She'd uncovered other secrets too. Like finding out about the boy in the video that Jack Taylor had told her all about. A rent boy from Kings Cross. Gavin Hurst. Just a kid by all accounts really, a little younger than her. The revelation of what her father had been doing had sickened Nancy to her core. He'd murdered him too.

When he realised that Gavin Hurst had set him up in order to blackmail him, the boy had unwittingly ended up filming his own murder.

Of course, Alex had helped her father to cover up the boy's death. What else would Alex do? After all, he loved her father, didn't he?

Poor, scorned Alex. Devastated by Jimmy's betrayal, Alex must have been fit to kill.

As the rain began to fall around them all, the other mourners moved away, pulling their jackets up around them to shelter themselves from the cold splatter of rain. Nancy stood and stared at her family.

It was true what her father used to say about loyalty and trust. That just because people were close to you, it didn't mean that they wouldn't stab you in the back. In fact, they were the most likely suspects.

He'd been right, too.

Nancy had used her own source to do some digging since her father had been killed. An old contact of her father's, from the Met's Cyber Crime Unit, who had owed Jimmy a few favours. She'd been waiting for days for this call. It was bitter irony that she'd received it just minutes after the church service had finished.

She'd been so convinced that Alex Costa had done it. Only it hadn't been him at all.

Her contact had apologised for the delay in getting back to her, explaining that he'd had trouble getting through all the red tape to finally get a warrant to access the data from Gavin Hurst's internet provider.

But now, Nancy's contact had struck gold. He'd said that the blackmailer had made one crucial error; they hadn't used an anonymizer to mask their internet activity. He'd managed to trace the IP address back to the ISP – which meant they had an address.

The trace had led straight back to the Byrnes' house.

There was a betrayer amongst them. A murderer.

Nancy stood watching, the priest's words still echoing in her ears.

Ashes to ashes, dust to dust.

She felt a hand slip into hers. 'Come on, Sis, let's get you home, yeah?' Her brother held her upright again as he guided her towards the awaiting car.

Nancy nodded, smiling back at her brother with a tight smile.

Her brother, who'd spent a lifetime living inside her shadow. Who had never quite measured up to her standards, nor their father's expectations.

Nancy couldn't even begin to imagine how that must have felt for Daniel. To see his sister placed on a pedestal, while Daniel never received so much as the time of day from their dad.

Nancy had always wondered if her dad sometimes picked at Daniel because he was so like their mother. That same vacant stare, the same sickly look.

She wondered if that's why Daniel had done it.

Why he'd blackmailed their father – so he could humiliate the man, just as Jimmy had humiliated him. So that he could publicly shame him. So that he could teach him a lesson.

If that was the reason why he'd pulled the trigger and murdered their father.

Her dad had been right all along. Daniel couldn't be trusted, and he certainly wasn't clever.

Even today of all days, making out that he was the person that could help put them all back together again – when the truth was, it was Daniel that had pulled them all apart.

Her brother. The dutiful son, the attentive brother.

A murderer and a coward.

While Nancy was truly Jimmy Byrne's daughter. She was her father's legacy.

As she slipped into the funeral car and sat alongside the rest of her family, Nancy Byrne stared out of the window, watching as the car made its way slowly out through the black wrought-iron gates.

She looked at the sea of headstones sweeping out across the cemetery either side, the rain lashing violently down on the windows.

Staring up at the darkening skies, she made herself a silent promise that she would personally avenge her father's death.

Daniel had committed the ultimate betrayal and for that, he was going to pay.

Nancy Byrne would make sure of that.

A LETTER FROM CASEY

Thank you for taking the time to read *The Betrayed*. If you fancy leaving me a review, I'd really appreciate it. Not only is it great to have your feedback, (I love reading each and every one of the reviews left) but adding a review can really help to gain the attention of new readers too. So, if you would kind enough to leave a short, honest review, it would be very much appreciated!

I really enjoyed writing *The Betrayed*. Jimmy Byrne was an interesting character to write. A family man, a business man but at the same time a ruthless face operating in London's murky criminal underworld. The story is ultimately about secrets and betrayal and how these elements effect the entire family unit. I have a feeling that we'll be seeing more of the Byrne family very soon!

I really hope you enjoyed Jimmy's story! I'm currently working on the next book so if you'd like to stay in touch and find out about the next release, or you just want to drop by and say 'Hello' I'd love to hear from you!

If you'd like to keep up to date with all of my latest releases, you can also sign up to my mailing list. We will never share your details with anyone else.

www.bookouture.com/casey-kelleher

Casey x

 OfficialCaseyKelleher/

CaseyKelleher

Website: www.caseykelleher.co.uk/

ACKNOWLEDGEMENTS

To all my fantastic readers, thank you so much for all your comments, messages, and interaction on social media. You are the very reason I write, without you, none of this would have been possible. I love receiving your feedback and messages, so please do keep them coming!

Massive thanks to my editor Keshini Naidoo – as always, for her amazing editorial skills and advice. I love that you get my style of writing and how your ideas and input always seem to help pull everything together. It's always such a pleasure working alongside you. Looking forward to our next project!

Thanks to the lovely Kim Nash – Bookouture's very own Media Star! – for all your hard work, support and encouragement. You really are a star!

Thank you to all my lovely author friends I've met along the way. To all the Bookouture gang and to all the other writers at the scene of the crime. Writing can feel like a very solitary career sometimes, and it's nice to know that i'm not encountering this sometimes insane journey on my own.

Special thanks to Lucy, Sean and Laura for always reading the very first copy of all my books and giving me your honest feedback. Extra special thanks to Lucy – my bestie – for all your #FreeAgent work, and most importantly for feeding me with gin at crime festivals, and to Tara for proof-listening to the audiobook – sorry about all the swearing!

As always I would like to thank my parents, family and friends for all their ongoing encouragement and support. None of it ever goes unnoticed.

Last but never least, to the most important people of all: Danny and my boys. My world.

Made in the USA
San Bernardino, CA
11 July 2017